THE CINDERELLA MOMENT

Living close to Cambridge, Gemma Fox adores shoes, her kids, cats, gardening and tall men, although not necessarily in that order. Constantly torn between being a born-again sex kitten – it's never too late – and cleaning out the litter tray, Gemma enjoys photography, long lazy suppers with friends and being old enough to be taken seriously in shops.

Visit AuthorTracker.co.uk for exclusive information on Gemma Fox and other HarperCollins authors.

D0774823

By the same author

Caught in the Act
Hot Pursuit

GEMMA FOX

The Cinderella Moment

HarperCollins*Publishers*

HarperCollins*Publishers*
77–85 Fulham Palace Road, Hammersmith, London W6 8JB

www.harpercollins.co.uk

A Paperback Original 2006

2

A catalogue record for this book
is available from the British Library

ISBN-13 978-0-00-717992-3
ISBN-10 0-00-717992-8

Set in Sabon by Palimpsest Book Production Limited,
Polmont, Stirlingshire

Printed and bound in Great Britain by
Clays Ltd, St Ives plc

For my family and friends, especially Sam, Ben, James and Joe, Suey Newey, Claire, Milly, Sarah, Tracy, Charlie, Peter, Maggie Phillips and Susan Opie, and the mutts, Beau and Molly. Between them they help make my life interesting, richer, fuller, happier, warmer and considerably more hairy than it would be if left to its own devices.

Prologue

'I need another couple of weeks.'

There was a long silence at the far end of the phone line and then the man said slowly, in an even voice, 'James, we both know you've had long enough. I want my money back, every last penny – or . . .' He paused. The quiet that filled James Devlin's office was darker, colder and more eloquent than any *or else*.

James Devlin nodded even though he knew that the caller couldn't see him. 'I just need a couple more weeks, that's all,' he said, making the effort to keep his voice steady, calm, confident.

'A week,' said the man. 'And if you don't pay up then –'

'I know,' said James Devlin, to the empty burring line. 'And what I don't know, I can guess.'

1

'So, would you like to tell us in your own words exactly why you'd like this job, Ms . . . Ms . . . ?' asked the woman, fishing around for a name. She had a face like a bullmastiff and a moustache to match. Had she never heard of waxing? Moustache fluttering in the breeze, the woman peered down at the application form in front of her. An application form with a ghost of pasta sauce smeared across the top right-hand corner.

'Mrs Hammond,' offered Cass helpfully. Not that anyone was listening.

'Ms Hammond?' the woman read. She smiled in Cass's general direction, although it didn't look as if she was experiencing any particular joy at the hand life had dealt her. 'So . . .' steepling her fingers, making determined eye contact, 'why *would* you like to work for Peck, Reckett and Gore?'

Good question. Cass hesitated. There had to be a reason – she'd filled in the application form,

3

posted it and everything. 'Because . . .' Cass took a deep breath, teetering, toes over the edge of the gaping crevasse that her mind had just become. 'Because . . .'

The woman leaned forward a little more in a gesture presumably meant to encourage her, and as she did the draught from an open window sent a ripple through the forest of hair on her chin that Cass had been struggling to ignore.

Damn. Cass grimaced, fighting to concentrate on the speech she'd concocted on the way there, while trying to hold back a honking great giggle.

She glanced at the rest of the interview panel; God they were ugly. The opening bars of the giggle slipped out.

She mumbled an apology, swallowing the giggle down with a cough. What would happen if she told them the truth? *Well, you've seen my CV; I'm not exactly spoilt for choice, am I? I need the money, my life is shit, my credit card bill would bankroll a small multinational, my son needs new shoes, and the man who swore he would love me until hell froze over and the seas ran dry has just buggered off with the girl who did our ironing, so not only am I heartbroken I'm also horribly creased.*

The Moustache tipped her head to one side and, glancing at her watch, tried out another smile.

Maybe the truth wasn't such a great idea after all.

'Take your time,' said one of the men on the

4

panel. The one who had spent most of the last fifteen minutes trying to get a really good look down the front of her blouse.

Cass painted on an expression that she hoped would suggest cheery enthusiasm, tempered with reliability and competence – a bit of a tall order with only the one face, but worth a shot.

Smile, relax . . . Taking a deep breath, Cass started to speak. It felt as if she was launching a heavy dinghy, pushing the answer away from the side: 'Well, I'm looking for a position that offers me a combination of interesting personal challenges, job satisfaction and a decent career structure – I think Feckett, Reckett and Snore can give me . . .'

Feckett, Reckett and Snore? Had she really said that? Cass felt a great breathless flash of heat and panic. Maybe her brain had just pretended, to keep her on her toes. Maybe they hadn't noticed. She looked anxiously from face to face. Across the table the panel were nodding, yawning and fiddling with their pens.

'. . . all those. This position seems ideal in . . . in, in lots of ways.'

It wasn't going well.

'. . . I'm a good team player with a mature approach to problem solving and good people skills. This project looks exciting and challenging and . . . and . . .'

Cass took another look, trying to work out how well she was doing. Did it all sound a bit too gushy? A bit too Miss World? A bit too, *I want to help old people, learn to play the guitar and promote world peace*? Maybe if she could master the pout, wiggle and flutter . . .

'. . . a jolly good thing to be part of . . .' Her voice faded. It had to be said that it wasn't the greatest finish of all time. Did any of them really believe this bullshit?

Cass tried out another smile. Blouse-man raised his eyebrows a couple of times and then winked conspiratorially while sucking something trouble-some out of his teeth. Cass held his gaze and the smile, wondering, when he'd said his role in the company's new project was very much hands-on, how literally she ought to take that.

'Well,' said the Moustache briskly, glancing left and right at her two male compatriots. 'Thank you. I think that just about covers everything. Thank you very much for coming in, Ms Er . . . er.'

'Mrs Hammond.'

'Miss Hammond. I think we've heard enough, don't you, gentlemen?'

There was an outbreak of synchronised nodding and paper shuffling. Cass looked from face to face. What exactly did *heard enough* mean? Did it mean heard enough to know she was exactly what they were looking for, or heard enough to know that they wouldn't employ her if she was the last crea-ture walking upright on earth? Cass realised she still had her mouth open and snapped it tight shut.

'It's been a real pleasure meeting you,' said the woman, without looking up.

Blouse-man got to his feet, signalling the interview was most definitely at an end.

'Thank you,' said Cass, scrabbling her things together and stuffing them into her handbag.

'Thank you for coming today, Ms Hammond. We'll be in touch over the next couple of days to let you know our decision,' he said, easing himself out from behind the desk and guiding her to the door by the elbow. His handshake had all the charm of a bag of warm haddock. At the threshold Cass looked back into the shabby conference room.

The woman with the moustache was already thumbing through the next application and the third member of the panel – a tall balding man with a very pronounced Adam's apple and a pigeon chest, who hadn't said a single word during the entire interview – was busy picking his nose.

Cass nodded to the man by the door. 'Thank you for your time. It's been a pleasure to meet you,' she lied.

He leered back at her, in a way Cass felt he hoped conveyed that lots of women felt exactly the same way.

Why would anyone ever want to commute?

The train journey home was hell. Worse than hell. It was hell with sweat and swaying and strange smells and people gibbering into mobile phones with earpieces so you couldn't tell the difference between those who were just plain barking mad and life's over-achievers, taking conference calls from Japan on the way home. And then there was the prospect of Danny waiting on the station platform with Jake – their next-door neighbour, who'd picked him up from school – asking her when David was coming home.

'Will Daddy be home tonight, Mummy?'

No, actually, the man whose arse you think the sun shines out of is currently tucked up in bed with a girl half Mummy's age who is thinking about how to spend the rest of her gap year, adultery not being that well paid.

There was no place for the truth there either.

'No, sweetie, not tonight. How about we go home and cook some chicken dinosaurs and chips? And there's ice cream.' Not that he was so easily distracted.

'When will Daddy be home? Will he still be coming on the school trip?'

'I don't know, sweetheart.'

'To the museum? He said he would. He promised. He said me and him could sit together on the bus. Can we ring him when we get back?' And those big, big brown eyes, David's eyes, looking up at her. Cass closed hers and tried very hard not to lean against the man who was wearing aftershave so potent it cast a shadow.

The train had emptied once they got to Cambridge. Cass finally sat down; the seat opposite was strewn with newspapers and coffee cartons. There was the *Evening Standard* and bits of *The Times* and *Guardian* that people always left behind, some sections folded back on themselves, some tented. Travel, sport and lifestyle, slim catalogues for expensive gadgets, stair lifts and garden awnings, a colourful clutter of them.

'Hi, sorry to disturb you – is that seat taken?'

'Sorry?'

'The seat? Is anyone sitting there?'

Standing opposite her in the aisle was a tall man with floppy dark blond hair, a tanned weather-beaten face and a rather nice, white button-down oxford shirt, broad shoulders and – and? And Cass stopped the thought dead in its tracks. What on earth was she doing? How was it her fancying radar was still up and running when she was feeling so miserable? Even if it was on standby, this was most certainly not the moment to start eyeing up strange men. She was supposed to be feeling heartbroken, angry, hurt and hard done by – and she did.

'No, you're fine,' Cass said casually. 'Help yourself.'

'Yours?'

'Sorry?'

He indicated the great scatter of debris. 'I wondered if they might be yours.' He spoke slowly, as if there was some chance she was deaf or foreign.

Cass held up her novel without smiling. Did she really look like the kind of woman who bought three newspapers, two takeaway coffees, something hot and greasy from the sandwich stand, then gutted them all over the carriage? God, some people could be annoying. He mimed contrition.

Cass flipped over the page and let her mind fix on the print. Now, where was she? Ah yes . . . Like a knitter finding a lost stitch, she picked up the end of the sentence she'd just read.

Across the small table that divided the seats, the man tidied and then settled down before picking up a review section. He had very long legs. It took him a while to get comfortable.

He smiled at her. It was a smile meant to placate and invite.

Cass sighed. She knew from experience that however grumpy or miserable she felt on the inside it didn't show itself on the outside, nor was it conveyed in her tone of voice. It was a curse. Since she'd been a child she'd always had to tell people she was angry and then they would look amazed and say things like, 'Really? I'm surprised. You always strike me as so easy-going and laid-back about life. I can't image you being angry.' This when she was livid. It seemed that, amongst a very rich repertoire of facial expressions God in his infinite wisdom had given her, he had left looks-bloody-furious off the drop-down menu.

The smile warmed up. Cass stared determinedly at her book.

'It's really good to sit down. I've been standing since King's Cross.'

She nodded just a fraction; she'd been standing too, but decided not to mention it in case it encouraged him.

'Long day,' he said.

Cass wasn't altogether certain whether that was a statement or a question, so didn't say anything.

'Me too,' he said, as if she had. It was meant as an opening, she was meant to say something. He stretched. 'It's been a good day, though.'

Depends on where you're standing, Cass thought grimly as she stared at the page; she had read the same line three times.

'This is such a beautiful part of the country, people really have no idea.'

Was that in general or just about the beauty of East Anglia in summer? growled her brain. Cass closed her eyes; if she wasn't careful, she was going to turn into a curmudgeonly old woman who talked to herself and who nobody loved.

What do you mean, *turn into*? snapped her inner bitch.

'It is breathtaking, isn't it?' the man said, staring longingly out of the carriage window at the great rolling expanse of the fens. The fens, flat as a newly brushed billiard table, stretched from horizon to horizon as far as the eye could see. Picked out on the pitch-black soil were row after row of celery heads and lollo rosso lettuces in startling greens and scarlets, and above them a cloudless cerulean blue sky that seemed to go on forever. It did have a peculiar, unforgiving beauty.

Cass looked across at him; he was still smiling at her. Maybe it was time to admit defeat. It was obvious that he was impervious to indifference and people who couldn't look grumpy however

11

hard they tried, and whatever had happened to him that day, it was obviously an ice age away from Feckett, Reckett and Snore.

'Yes,' she said. 'Yes. It is.'

'Good-oh.' He grinned as if her response was a personal triumph. 'There,' he said with delight. 'That wasn't so bad, now, was it?'

Cass laughed. 'What?'

He opened up the rucksack at his feet. 'Do you fancy a peach? I bought all sorts of fruit from this fantastic street market. Kind of celebration. I've had so much to sort out, lots of financial stuff – but I think I may have pulled it off. I think it's going to be OK after all.' He pulled out a selection of brown paper bags and set them down on the table. Some were damp at the corners where things inside had been squashed.

'Sorry, I'm sure you don't want to hear all my woes. Oh, how about cherries? Look at these, aren't they wonderful? Please feel free. Help yourself; there's loads.'

Cass stared at him over the growing pile of fruit. He had to be mad or, worse, he was a social worker or a psychiatric nurse; maybe he cared in the community and got people to make raffia lampshades and sing 'Kumbya' while he played the guitar. Whichever it was, he was obviously relentlessly cheerful.

He grinned, shaking a bag in her direction. 'It's all right, I'm not mad – it's just that I've had a really good day.'

12

Cass found it was particularly unnerving when people read minds, or told you they weren't mad. He held out a peach. 'Try one of these,' he said. 'They're absolutely amazing. Really.' He waved it at her again.

Cass took a bite. He was right.

'Sadly, blah blah blah, high number of exceptionally well-qualified applicants. Blah blah, on this occasion you lucked out, chuck.' Cass screwed the paper into a ball and slam-dunked it into the swing bin before taking a long pull on her coffee. 'Another one bites the dust.'

'Try and resist humming the tune, would you,' said Jake. 'From Messrs Moustache, Lecher and Nosepicker, I presume?'

'Uhuh – the very same. I could have done that job standing on my head while juggling puppies and playing the banjo.'

'Maybe you should have mentioned that in your CV.'

'This is driving me nuts, Jake. I've got to find a job. I needed this job. I've sent out dozens of applications, I haven't made the short list on half of them. What the bloody hell is wrong with me?'

'Nothing. If it's any consolation – and I can see that it probably isn't – in this particular case it sounds as if it was already a done deal. They'd got someone in the frame but they're still obligated to advertise.'

'Bastards. What the hell am I going to do? I have

13

to get a job. Maybe I should put a card in the post office window. Cleaning – or how about dog walking?' She sighed. It was just after nine in Cass's kitchen, the sun was shining and Cass was dressed in her interview suit. Well, most of it, the long-line flattering-for-the-pear-shaped-woman-jacket that she had bought on the recommendation of someone in the *Mail on Sunday* was hanging on the back of the kitchen door, well away from all the stray buttered toast, cat and dog hair.

'Maybe I've been setting my sights too high. Don't pull that face. I've got to find a way to earn some money, Jake. I've got a house, a dog, a cat and kid to look after, and you can't do that on nothing. Maybe I should take in washing?'

'What you need to do is go back and talk to your solicitor. David should be helping.'

'He did, remember? He helped himself to the hired help and buggered off.'

'Cass, if I made you a suggestion, would you promise not to slap me or go off on one?'

'Depends. If it's sex, then the answer is still no, Jake. I'm still way out there on the rebound.' She mimed a far distant horizon. 'And I draw the line at pensioners.'

He mimed deep hurt and then said, 'And if it's not?'

She smiled. 'Try me.'

'Well, I've got this friend –'

'Fitting me up with one of your peculiar mates is the same as having sex. You're my neighbour, we're good friends, we've been good friends for a long, long time, and I love you dearly, but I don't need you to procure men for me.'

'Wait, wait,' Jake said, holding up his hands in protest. 'I wasn't going to mention it, but please hear me out. I've got this friend who runs a little place in Brighton. Barney Roberts – you must have heard me talk about him. Anyway, he owns this great little gallery, deals in all sorts of art, there's some workshop space, a craft and gift shop. He's looking for someone to help him out for the summer.'

Cass glanced at her watch. 'Your point being . . . ?'

'Barney is an awkward old bastard. He's just had an operation on his back and needs a hand. Last time I spoke to him, he was like a bear with a boil on its arse.'

'Uhuh.' She took her jacket down off the hanger and slipped it on. 'Take my advice, Jake: don't ever go into advertising.'

'I know it's a long way away, but you can't keep going through all this. You need a change of scenery – a break. What do you think?'

'What do you mean, what do I think? I've just done a nine-year crash course in living with a miserable bastard. And, as you mentioned, it's in Brighton. Lest we forget, Jake, I live in Norfolk. And at the moment, as things are, I can barely afford to live here, let alone there. I read somewhere that it's more expensive to live in Brighton than London –'

'Yes, but that isn't the point. You need to change your luck, Cass, do something different. Underneath, Barney is basically a really good guy. OK, so maybe it's a long way underneath at times – but he's prepared to make nice and easy for the right person.'

'Meaning?'

'Well, for a start he's got a great big basement flat he's rolling around in, and he's lonely.'

'Oh, come off it, Jake – this sounds like procurement to me. I'm not a nurse. I'm sure Brighton is jam-packed full of people looking for jobs.'

'Yes, but he doesn't know any of them. He's not good with people – he can be funny – and besides, I've already told him about you.'

'Oh well, that was kind of you,' Cass said grimly. 'You told him about me? So I'm a charity case now, am I?'

'No, but please think about it, Cass. I don't want to see you go, but I do know that the offer is genuine. Barney is as straight as a die, and he really does need someone to help him out. I thought of you straight away.'

'Because?'

Jake sighed. 'Because you need to get away from here and stop mooning around. This way you could do some of your own stuff – paint, for God's sake – and still work. You look awful, Cass. You're not eating properly. When was the last time you picked up a pencil or a paint brush? Everyone is worried about you; you know that, don't you? David is stupid.'

16

'Everyone?' Cass said thickly. The sound of David's name still made something hurt deep inside her. How could she have been so blind? How was it she hadn't seen it coming?

'*Everyone*,' Jake murmured, leaning forward to stroke the hair off her face. Cass looked up at him; Jake was sixty-five if he was a day. He'd come round the day she moved into the cottage with a chicken-and-bean casserole and a bottle of red wine and had been part of her life ever since.

Cass smiled up at him; they were probably as close as two unrelated adults could get, without romance getting in the way. She loved him and he loved her, which had sustained them even when they didn't like each other very much. Like when Jake married Amanda (who had hated all his friends and especially Cass, although to be fair, eventually – so's no one would feel left out – Amanda had ended up hating Jake most of all), or when Cass caught vegetarianism and with all the zealous enthusiasm of a true convert had referred to his superb Beef Wellington as an act of evil, barbaric bloody murder, during a dinner party for one of his best clients. The memory could still make her cringe on dark and stormy nights.

'I'll keep an eye on this place. It would do you good to get away from here for a while,' he said gently.

Cass felt her eyes prickle with tears. 'Don't make me cry, I've got an interview to go to and

17

mascara doesn't grow on trees, you know. Took me bloody ages to do this eyeliner.' And then, after a moment's pause, 'I don't know what I'm going to do, Jake,' Cass whispered miserably. 'I loved David so much. Why did he leave me?'

'Because he's an amoeba,' Jake said, handing her a bit of kitchen roll. 'An amoeba and an idiot and a complete wanker. Anyway, all those people who love you thought you were far too nice and far too good to end up with a clown like David.'

'I married an amoeba?'

'You surely did.'

'My parents thought he was really lovely,' Cass sighed. 'I suppose that says it all, really. You'd think by the time we got to our age it would be easier, that we'd have it all sewn up and sorted.'

Jake nodded.

'And he hated you,' she sniffed.

'I know.'

'She's eighteen, Jake. *Eighteen*.'

He nodded. 'I know.'

'I thought I was doing her a favour. Some pocket money, baby-sitting, bit of housework. She told me she wanted to travel. It's so sordid.'

'I know.'

'David kept complaining about her, saying she wasn't doing things properly. Like he would know! How she annoyed him, how she was always getting in his way, and how we were paying her too much. I should have guessed, Jake. I should have known. That's what makes it so terrible. How come I

18

didn't see it coming? I love him, Jake – I've got the worst taste in men.'

'Your taste in men is legendary, Cass. Now just shut up and go, will you, or you're going to miss the train. When you get back, we could take Danny and the dog down to the beach, if you like, and then I'll cook supper.'

'You're such a nice man, Jake.'

'With instincts like that, it's no wonder you always pick total bastards.'

'And wankers,' said Cass, picking up her handbag. 'Let's not forget the wankers. You're OK to pick Danny up from school today?'

'I've already said yes, and I've laid in a stock of food shaped like extinct amphibians. Who is it today?'

Cass picked up a sheaf of papers in a manila folder from the kitchen table and read the letter-head on the inside page. 'Dumb, Bum and Stumpy, looking for someone to work in Human Resources.'

'You can do that?'

'I can try.'

'Cass, honey, this is ridiculous – you're an artist.'

'And a woman with a mortgage.' Cass looked at him and sighed. 'David said I needed to grow up and get a proper job. Now, hand me my brief-case.'

He picked it up and looked at it thoughtfully. 'Where the hell did you get that from?'

Cass licked a finger and scrubbed at a smear

of blue poster paint on the handle. 'The dressing-up box at Danny's school; they said I could borrow it till the end of term.'

Jake looked heavenwards. 'You don't have to do this.'

'I do. David told me that I see the world through rose-tinted spectacles and that my relentless optimism got him down. He said that I'd never be able to manage on my own in the real world without him. He said I was far too naïve.'

'Come off it, Cass. He was being cruel, that's all. You've got nothing to prove.'

'I have, Jake. I have to show him that I don't need him, that Danny and I can manage without him, thank you very much. And I need to do better than just manage – I need to do well. The worst thing I can do to David is be happy, solvent and successful.'

'Yes, but not like this. Why don't you at least think about Brighton?'

Cass nodded, even though she had no plans to give Brighton a second thought.

She checked herself in the mirror. 'What do you think? Will I do?' she asked, her attention on her reflection, doing a little half-turn so that she could check her back.

Jake looked her up and down. 'Just the job. You put me in mind of a young Margaret Thatcher.'

Cass growled at him and headed for the front door.

*   *   *

'So, what have you got to tell me, James?' said a male voice with a soft Scottish brogue.

James Devlin, queuing by the ticket machine, tucked the phone under his chin and looked round, trying to work out whether he was being followed or just being paranoid. 'Look, I can't talk right now, but don't worry, I've got the matter in hand. Everything will be sorted out by the end of the week.'

'Well, that's good news, I'm relieved to hear it. We'll be in touch.'

James retrieved his ticket, dropped the mobile into his jacket pocket, picked up his suitcase and headed off into the crowd, eyes moving back and forth across the faces.

The railway station was busy. The platform was already crowded with travellers. Outside the ticket office a winding crocodile of small children in school uniform with rucksacks and packed lunches were waiting, getting increasingly restless and noisy, shuffling to and fro.

Cass bought a takeaway tea and, finding a reasonably quiet spot, ran through her mental checklist for the interview: notes, mints, the printout she had downloaded about the company from their website. Lipstick, hairbrush. The plan was a morning spent being shown around the company's complex, a company film, a company buffet lunch and a series of informal company chats, followed by a company interview.

'Hi.'

'Hi?'

Cass swung round. The man with the peaches waved at her from across the ranks of mixed infants. This morning he was wearing a chambray cotton shirt in the palest blue that emphasised his tan and his big blue eyes, a cream linen jacket and darker chinos. He looked gorgeous. Cass rolled her tongue back in; this was not the moment. She really needed to get her fancying radar checked over.

'Yours?' he said, waving at the crocodile.

She laughed. 'No, not today, thank God.'

He glanced down at her briefcase. 'Another interview?'

Cass nodded and had another little go at the blue poster paint. 'Don't knock it. Apparently I'm extremely fortunate to have made the short list after a rigorous selection process. It says so in my letter.'

The man eased his way between the children until he was standing alongside her. 'Congratulations. What sort of job is it?'

Cass pulled a face. 'A proper one. You know, one with paper and deadlines and people on the phone wanting things.'

He nodded. 'Sounds serious.'

He smelt nice. There was one of those tight pauses when nobody can think of anything to say, and then he said, 'I'm going on a bit of an adventure today – a little trip – well, you know.'

22

Cass nodded; she had no idea what he was talking about, but was far too polite to say so.

Along the platform the crossing gates closed, the warning bell sounded, and a moment or two later the train pulled very slowly into the station.

The voice of the stationmaster echoed over the tannoy. 'The train now standing at platform one is for London King's Cross . . .' A few doors up from Cass the crocodile scrambled noisily aboard, whooping and giggling and pouring on to the train like happy, brightly coloured ants.

'Do you think perhaps we ought to get on?' the man said, picking up a small suitcase and extending an arm towards the open doorway of the carriage.

Cass looked up at him; what a novel idea. She had rather hoped that, as soon as the doors slid open, he would jump aboard and rush to find a seat, but apparently not. The age of chivalry, it seemed, was not dead. Damn, just when she was hoping to have half an hour with a book, the computer printout and her thoughts, and not having to make polite conversation with someone she barely knew. Although he was cute. Make that very cute.

'Why not?' Cass said, hoping that Jake had been joking about her looking like Margaret Thatcher, at any age. Stepping up into the carriage, she headed down to one of the double seats with a table between, well away from the school children. She sensed him following close behind.

'So, are you going through to London, then?' he asked, as he settled down opposite her.

'No. Just to Cambridge today.'

'Oh that's great – me too. Well, actually I'm going to Stansted. I'm off to Rome for a few days.'

'Wonderful.'

'Really?' He looked interested. 'Have you been?'

Bloody man. 'I went there on a school trip, on a whistle-stop tour of the Renaissance. It was wonderful. I loved it. One of those places I'd really like to go back to, if I got the chance, and spend more time exploring –'

'You're interested in history?'

'In art. In history – in both.'

He nodded.

'I'm an artist.'

'Oh right. But I thought –' he nodded towards the briefcase – 'interviews, people on the phone wanting things.'

'Needs must.' She reddened, not quite catching his eye, wishing she hadn't started this conversation. 'So is Rome your adventure?'

'Kind of. I've got to go and sort out a little business over there. You know.'

Cass nodded and then, taking a book out of her bag, she made a show of settling in, shutting him out.

'Good book?' he asked, as the train pulled out of the station. 'I love reading.'

Had the man no shame? She could feel him

watching, smiling, waiting for a reaction, and at the same time her colour rising.

'Did anyone ever tell you that you're a complete pain in the arse?' she said.

'Not recently. So tell me what you liked in Rome and I'll go visit it.'

'Seriously?'

He nodded. 'Absolutely.'

Cass considered for a moment. 'Well, I suppose the thing that surprised me most was that you can walk everywhere – all the famous things are a stone's throw from each other. The centre is wonderful but quite small, so you can walk from place to place, stop for coffee. The bad thing is every artist you've ever heard of has work there: da Vinci, Michelangelo, Caravaggio, Raphael – the list is endless. And that's without all the Classical Roman stuff . . . Do you know anything about art?'

He grinned. 'I know what I like.'

Cass laughed aloud. God, fate was cruel. How come she had met him now?

There was a dog on the line just outside Ely.

'Hi, this is Cassandra Hammond. I'm on my way to an interview this morning – yes, yes, that's me – well, I'm afraid I'm going to be a little late,' she said, her mobile pressed against one ear and a finger in the other. It could have been worse, at least there was a signal. 'The train's been delayed. No, nothing serious, fortunately. I am sorry about this, but I'll be there as soon as I can. Yes, thank you, see you later.'

As she hung up, Cass grimaced. 'Doesn't look very good if you're late for an interview, does it? They sounded OK about it, but it's not a great start. Maybe I should have driven.' It struck her that she was thinking aloud and she quickly shut up.

Not that the man seemed to mind. 'People understand. I'm sure it'll be fine.' He glanced out of the window; across a stretch of open farmland, two burly men had caught a Collie and were busy bundling it into the back of a Land Rover. 'At least you can ring in. I can't ask them to hold the plane for me.' He looked down at his watch. 'It's going to be cutting it fine if I'm going catch my connection.'

Cass groaned, feeling anxious on his behalf. 'I'm sorry. What time does it leave?'

'There's a ten-minute window. The trouble is I'm not sure what time the next train goes if I miss this one. Damn, damn –'

Cass took a long hard look at her watch; not that it helped. She had no idea what time they would get there, or what time his train would leave.

'We're moving now. Maybe it'll be OK. You never know, if your luck's in, the Stansted train will be running late as well.'

He laughed and offered her a mint humbug. 'So tell me where else I should go.'

At Cambridge he was up on his feet a long time before the train got into the station. 'Wish me luck,' he said, picking up his suitcase. And then, as an afterthought, added, 'I could send you a postcard, if you like.'

Cass laughed. 'What?'

'A postcard. As a thank you. You know, small square of cardboard, arrives back about a month after you do, badly tinted picture of the Coliseum on the front, *Weather lousy, wish you were here* on the back.'

'Are you serious?'

'Never more so,' he said with a grin. 'So how about it?'

'How about what?'

'Giving me your address. For the postcard – so I can let you know if I enjoyed your whistle-stop tour of Rome.' Cass hesitated long enough for the man to add, 'I promise you I'm not a stalker or an axe-wielding psychopath.'

'And if you were you'd tell me, obviously.'

He held up his hands in surrender. 'Obviously. Goes without saying.'

Cass considered for a second or two more, and then pulled the envelope containing the interview details out of her briefcase, emptied the contents and handed it to him.

He slipped it into his pocket and smiled. '*Grazie.*'

She giggled. It struck her as he hurried off down the train that she didn't even know his name.

'Have a great time in Rome,' she called after him.

He turned. 'I'm sure I will, and best of luck

with the interview. I'll keep my fingers crossed for you. *Ciao*,' he said, lifting a hand in salute, and then hurried down the aisle so that he was first at the doors. He was gone almost as soon as the open light flashed on.

Cass was far slower, gathering her thoughts and her things together. Notes, mints . . .

James Devlin, hurrying out towards the car park, felt pleased with himself. He'd set up a false trail, now he just needed to get into the city and pick up his car.

'Excuse me?' said a voice from behind Cass as she headed, embedded in the queue of travellers, down the aisle towards the doors.

'Excuse me?' said the voice again, more forcefully this time, followed by a hand tapping her sharply on the shoulder. Cass looked round in surprise.

'Is this your phone?' said a small plump woman. She held out a mobile towards her, so close it was almost in her face.

Cass squinted, trying to focus. 'No, I'm afraid not – I –'

The woman waved it in the direction of the seat Cass had so recently left. 'Only it was on the floor where you and your husband were sitting,' the woman said.

'My husband?

The woman nodded. 'Yes. It was under the seat. It must've fallen out of his bag or his pocket.'

'Oh – oh thank you.' Cass looked out on to the platform, trying to spot her travelling companion, but there was no sign of him. Nothing, zilch. He appeared to have vanished into thin air. Maybe he had managed to catch the Stansted train after all.

The woman was still holding the phone out towards her and, without really thinking, Cass took it, thanked her again and dropped it into her handbag. She would ring him later, tell him that he'd lost it but that it was safe. Maybe it was fate; he was very cute. Cass reddened as the thought took hold and caught light. It felt so much better than the dull David-shaped hurt she'd had in her heart.

Outside the station, with one eye on the time, Cass grabbed a taxi and headed out towards the science park instead of taking a bus as planned. In the back of the cab she ran through the menu on the man's phone.

She moseyed on down through names, numbers and text. In the phone book section she scrolled down until she found 'HOME' and pressed call. After three rings a BT callminder answering service cut in.

'Hi,' said Cass. 'I just wanted to let you know that you left your phone on the train this morning. It must have dropped out of your bag or something. But don't worry, I've got it and it's safe, and –' she laughed nervously – 'it was nice to have your company. I hope your trip goes well . . .'

Cass hesitated. 'I'm not normally so snappy. Things are a bit rough for me at the moment.'

What the hell was she saying?

'So, anyway, I hope you managed to catch your connection, and have a great time . . .' Cass paused. He was nice; he had been kind and funny and – OK, so maybe she had fancied him just a little even if it wasn't the right time and didn't make any sense at all. 'If you'd like to give me a ring when you get back, we can arrange for you to pick your phone up.' Cass laughed again. 'Who knows, maybe I can return the compliment and we can have an impromptu picnic on the train or something. Anyway, you know your phone number, although I'm a bit worried that the batteries on your mobile might go, so I'll give you my home number and my mobile . . .'

When she was done, Cass dropped the phone into her bag, paid the taxi driver and headed up the very impressive canopied shiny steel walkway into the huge glazed atrium of Caraway Industries, which appeared to be planted with a miniature rain forest.

'Hi, and welcome to Caraway. So glad that you could make it,' said an American guy coming out from behind the front desk to greet her. 'You must be Cas-san-dra,' he said, lingering lovingly over every syllable.

Before she could reply, he continued, 'If you'd like to follow me, I'll take you down to meet Artie and the rest of the guys. My name is Nathaniel

T. Coleridge. I'm vice co-ordinator on our Human Resources initiative.' With this he offered her his hand – as cool and limp as a dead eel – before clasping hers in a presidential handshake, all the while dazzling her with a smile honed to a sharp social point in California. Cass winced, indiscriminate gushing was so much worse than the Moustache woman's barely veiled indifference.

Nathaniel, making deep meaningful conversation about planetary issues, global warming and the ozone layer in response to her casual remark about how much she liked the trees, led Cass down a huge spiral stone staircase – a homage to the nautilus shell and the genius of Fibonacci, apparently – to an impressive conference room with one glass wall overlooking a Japanese rock garden. The twenty or so other applicants for the various positions Caraway had on offer were arranged in a horseshoe of chairs around their host, who was standing behind an onyx-and-steel lectern, his great hands holding tight to the sides as if he was delivering a eulogy.

'How-dee and welcome, Cas-san-dra,' said Artie, waving her in. No quietly slipping in at the back with this lot. 'Why don't you come on down and take a seat with the rest of the guys. We were all just getting acquainted.' A big bluff Scandinavian-looking man, Artie looked as if he would be more at home at a barn-raising in Minnesota than in Fenland's answer to Silicone Valley.

Rather self-consciously, Cass took up her seat, arranged the little flip-up flip-over desk thing on the side of her chair, opened the complimentary Caraway introduction and orientation pack, all the while watched by her fellow job seekers. When she was finally settled, Artie began to speak. 'Okey-dokey, now, as I was saying . . .'

Artie's voice was low, soft and even, with barely a flicker in pitch or tone or inflection. The sun shone in through the wall of glass, warming the room to a cocoon-like heat. After fifteen minutes or so, despite eating the complimentary mints and doodling on the complimentary notepad with a zippy Caraway complimentary roller ball, it was taking a colossal act of will on Cass's part not to slip down in the chair and fall asleep.

Alongside her, a plump blonde woman in a trouser suit the colour of ripe plums had given up the struggle. A thin glistening guy-rope of drool clung to her bottom lip and tethered her head to her lapel.

Cass winced; it could so easily be her. She could feel herself starting to nod, just as the woman alongside her began to snore softly. It was like a siren call. She needed this job; she couldn't afford to drop off. Cass snapped her attention back to Artie, who was now in full, albeit soporific, swing, giving an almost evangelical presentation on the benefits of working for Caraway – not merely a company but a caring family – when somewhere close by a phone started to ring. There was a little flurry of activity as everyone nervously tapped their pockets and bags and looked round to try and track it down. It rang and it rang and then it stopped for a few seconds and then it rang again, and then again. People started to move. The woman in the purple suit woke up with a start.

From the lectern Artie leaned forward. Breaking off mid-flow, he said, 'Guys, would you like to check your cellphones?'

Cass looked round. Smugly. And still the phone kept on ringing and ringing, and then an icy finger of doubt tracked down her spine. Bugger. It couldn't be, could it? Very slowly she opened her handbag. The ringing got louder. Not from her phone but from Mr Humbug-and-Peaches-Gone-to-Rome's mobile. Home was phoning.

All eyes slowly turned and fixed on her.

Cass reddened and smiled sheepishly, mouthing apologies to the other applicants and Artie, whose perfect fixed smile made it look as if rigor mortis might well have set in.

'Err, sorry, I – I think I really ought to take this,' she said, making a break for the door. 'Emergency. Family stuff,' she lied. 'I told them it would be OK to ring – I didn't think they would – well, you know, obviously –' Art lifted a hand and managed to widen the smile another notch.

'Whatever it takes,' he said, sounding as if he meant it.

Bloody Americans. Cass scurried across what felt like a mile and a half of shiny blonde wood floor to the nearest exit; she could feel the attention of the whole room following her. God, there was no way she could work for a company like Caraway, the people were far far too nice and way too squeaky clean.

'Hello,' Cass said, taking the call the minute she was through the door.

'Who is this?' a cultured female voice demanded furiously.

Female voice?

Cass hesitated.

'And can you tell me exactly why you have got my husband's phone?' the woman growled.

'I –' Cass began.

'There's nothing you can say, is there? I told James that if this ever happened again it was over. Do you hear me? Do you understand? Do you? Over – no more chances. No more second chances. What did he tell you about me? Did he say that I'm cold? Difficult? That I don't care? Did he? Did he? The bastard.'

'Well,' Cass began, 'actually . . .'

'Did he tell you that he's got a family? I bet he didn't. We've got two children – two beautiful children. I bet he didn't tell you that, did he? Did he tell you about Snoops?'

'Sorry?' Cass spluttered.

'Snoops adores him. We've had him since he was a tiny puppy. Just a baby. The bastard, how could he do this to us? How could he do this to Snoops?' The woman began to sob. 'I'll hunt you

34

down, you heartless evil bitch. How could you do this?'

Cass stared at the handset, not sure what to do next; she had left her home number, for God's sake. If the woman had rung there first she also had Cass's name and her mobile number, because they were on her answer-machine message.

'Just tell me one thing,' the woman bawled. 'Have you slept with him? Have you? Please tell me that you haven't slept with him.'

'I haven't slept with him,' Cass said firmly in as even a tone as she could manage.

'Oh God, I don't believe you,' the woman wailed. 'How could he do this to me? How could he? After all that I've gone through.'

'No, no really,' said Cass, more emphatically this time, trying to calm her down. 'I haven't slept with him, cross my heart. I barely know him. We met on the train.' This was crazy.

'You cow, you cow – how could you?' screamed the woman. 'How could you sleep with another woman's husband? You home wrecker.'

That did it. Cass had had enough; she snapped.

'Whoa now, hang on a minute there, lady. I don't know who you are, but I'm bloody sure I haven't slept with your fucking husband, all right?' she roared at the top of her voice.

Which might well have been an end to the matter if at that very moment Artie hadn't opened the double doors to the conference room and said, 'Are we OK out there?'

'He's with you now, isn't he?' wailed the woman.

Cass looked heavenwards. Artie's smile didn't falter. 'Perhaps you should take a few moments.'

The train ride home was very uneventful.

There were five messages on the answer machine when Cass got in. The first was from the madwoman with a dog called Snoops, then one from David, one from the girl who did their ironing and one from the parents of the girl who did their ironing, and the last one – with the number withheld – was something that consisted mostly of sobbing and screaming, interspersed with snarling and possibly some swearing, but it was difficult to pick out because there was a dog barking frantically in the background.

Cass had just got to the end of them when Jake appeared through the front door, pulling on a sweater. 'Danny's ready, I've put the dog in the Land Rover, and a curry in the oven for when we get back from the b—' He looked at her. 'What?'

Cass pressed play, skipped the loony and went straight for David.

'Hi, Cassandra, it's David.' As if she didn't know. 'Just a quick call. I think we need to talk. I appreciate that you may feel a little aggrieved at the moment, but, after all, marriage is a game of two halves.' He laughed at what passed for a joke in his neck of the woods. Jake shook his head as the message continued. 'So, I wondered if I might pop round one evening . . . Probably once Danny is

36

in bed would be better, don't you think? Wednesday would be good for me. After squash.'

'Amoeba,' spat Jake, pressing the skip button.

'Hello, Cass, it's Abby,' said an uneven, rather thin, weepy little girl voice. 'I just wanted to explain . . . you know, about everything and stuff.'

Jake groaned. 'Do we have to listen to this?'

'I don't want you to be angry or anything,' Abby interrupted. 'It just happened, you know. I don't think that either of us, we – you know, me or David – meant it to. Not really. It was just, you know, like, one of those things, and that, you know.'

'Fuck, these things should be banned.' Jake pressed skip again.

'Er, hello there. This is Abigail's dad here. We wondered if we could pop round for a bit of a chat one night,' said a gruff no-nonsense voice. 'We were hoping for some kind of explanation, really. I mean, me and her mum feel that Abby was in your care, technically. And we didn't think –'

Jake pressed the button again. 'Maybe you should arrange it so that they come round the same night as David?' he said, skipping to the last one, the wailing and the barking. 'What the hell's that?'

Cass sat down on the bottom stair. 'Snoops, possibly. What did you say your friend in Brighton's name was again?'

*   *   *

37

Hidden away in his motel room, James Devlin slipped off his jacket, very carefully hung it up in the wardrobe, settled down on the bed with his hands behind his neck, and considered his next move.

2

A few days later, a Thameslink train slowed to a crawl and pulled into Brighton Station. Cass collected her things together and peered out of the grimy carriage window; she wasn't sure what she'd been expecting, but this wasn't it. Brighton didn't look at all like a seaside town, more like King's Cross on a bad day, maybe even grimier. There were the sounds of seagulls, but Cass wouldn't have been surprised if they were a recording being played over the tannoy.

Pulling up the handle on her suitcase, Cass made her way along the platform towards the exit, looking at the sea of faces as she did. Barney, Barney – what the hell did a bad-tempered artist called Barney look like?

Oh, there, that just had to be him: leaning against a pillar was a small plump man with grey skin, bloodshot eyes, a beard like a bird's nest, and a lot of hair growing out of his ears. He was smoking a roll-up and wearing a nasty oversized well-stained sweater that would have passed muster on any self-respecting artist from eighteen to eighty.

She was about to walk over to him when a cultured voice said, 'Cassandra?' She swung round to be greeted by an elderly man who was leaning heavily on a walking stick. His thick silver-grey hair was slicked back and tucked behind his ears, and he was wearing an expensive, beautifully tailored grey suit and a paisley waistcoat. He looked like a well-heeled country squire.

'Barney?'

The man extended a hand and smiled. 'Absolutely. Delighted to meet you, my dear. Bartholomew Anthony Hesquith-Morgan-Roberts. Jake sent me a photo of you; it does you no justice at all.'

His deep, dark brown voice came straight out of one of the better public schools, pure top-drawer, clipped and nipped and terribly posh, and Cass – although she smiled and shook his hand – could feel the chip on her shoulder weighing heavy. David was an ex-public schoolboy too and the most terrible snob, and thought some of what he referred to as 'her funny little habits' anything but funny.

'But do feel free to call me Barney,' the man was saying. 'Everyone else does, despite my best efforts to stop them. Still, it's rather nice to give the whole moniker an airing once in a while. So, what did Jake tell you about me?'

Cass looked him up and down. Barney was tall

and nicely made with broad shoulders, a generous mouth and a big hawkish nose that dominated his large suntanned face. She had no doubt that, in his day, Barney had been a total rogue – and most probably still was when he got the chance. He had bright blue eyes, and when he smiled his whole face concertinaed into pleats like Roman blinds and promised all manner of things.

'That you're a miserable old bastard,' she suggested.

He nodded thoughtfully. 'You know, it's such a cliché, but sadly it's absolutely true. I used to be a miserable young bastard, but it doesn't have quite the same ring to it, does it? For years people – mostly women, it has to be said – have been convinced that I'm complex and deep, a wounded soul who needed saving from a cruel and uncomprehending world, but to be perfectly honest I've mostly just been in a foul mood for the last sixty-odd years. I was a dour and grumpy child, spent almost all of my twenties being annoyed about something or somebody, my thirties were worse, and I was absolutely unspeakable in my forties. It was such a relief to get into my fifties; people take it for granted that you're grumpy then. My sixties have been an absolute dream.' He paused. 'I think it would be best if we took a cab. Getting a car in and out of here and then finding somewhere to park would very possibly have given me heart failure. Besides, it makes me swear dreadfully at people – who can, it has to be said, be bloody infuriating.' He tucked the cane under his arm, grabbed hold of the handle of her suitcase and marched off towards the taxi rank at top speed, Cass having to run to keep up.

'I thought you'd got a bad back?' she said, scuttling after him.

'I have,' he grumbled. 'I hate the fact it slows me down. Although my mood's improved tremendously since the pain eased up. I'm bloody awful at being old. Jake told me that you have a son?'

'Danny.'

Barney nodded gravely. 'I hate children.'

Cass tried to work out if he was joking.

'Is he quiet?'

'Of course he's not quiet. He's six.'

Barney looked thoughtful. 'Right. I see. And you're expecting me to let you live in my flat with your noisy son, are you?'

Cass ground to a halt and glared at him. 'Whoa. Hang on a minute there. Is this some kind of trial by ordeal? Because if it is, I'm not interested. Right now my life is about as messy as I ever want it to be. If you expect me to help you out and work in your gallery, that's fine. But I don't need to jump through hoops of fire to prove anything – all right? Is that clear? And being rude and then telling me you've always been like that doesn't cut it as an excuse. *Capiche*?'

Barney stared at her and then nodded appreciatively. 'I think we're going to get along just fine,' he said. 'You remind me of my mother.'

Cass carried on glaring at him. 'How do you really feel about children?'

Barney mulled it over for a few moments. 'I hate them,' he said cheerfully.

'I'm sure, given time, Danny will hate you right back.'

Barney nodded. 'Sounds like a very equitable arrangement. And you've got a cat called Bob and a dog –'

'Called Milo.'

Barney smiled. It lit up his face like a flare. 'Oh, that's wonderful. I adore animals. Now, let's find a cab. I thought we'd go to the flat first, leave your luggage there, and then we'll come back into town once you've got your bearings.'

'And look at the shop?'

He nodded. 'Yes. It's in the Lanes.'

'Sorry?' Nothing that Cass had seen of Brighton so far suggested there were anything approaching lanes within miles.

'Have you never heard of it? It's a magical little area, very arty – better than the rest of Brighton put together, in my opinion. You'll love it. It's between North Street and the seafront. It predates the Regency rush to Brighton; gives you an idea how the whole place must have looked when it was a fishing village.'

'And your shop is there?'

'Oh God, yes. It's wonderful, whole place is like a North European souk – bohemian, busy, bubbling, vibrant. There are designer shops and hippie shops and gem shops and juice bars, all sorts of amazing little treasures nestled together. And, well, you'll see – my place has an eye on the commercial; beautiful things designed for broader tastes.' He paused. 'We've got all sorts of wonderful old tut in there.'

Cass looked along the busy concourse. It certainly didn't seem the kind of place you'd have problems getting staff. 'And you want me to work there *because* . . . ?'

Barney considered for a few moments. 'Because I trust Jake's judgement, and mine is bloody awful. Good help is still hard to come by, however old the cliché. I need someone who is versatile, enthusiastic and talented, and who won't keep moaning about what a pain in the arse I am.'

Cass laughed. 'Is that what Jake said about me?'

Barney nodded as they stepped up to take the next taxi in the rank. 'That and the fact that you've got the most terrible taste in men.'

Barney's enormous basement flat looked as if it could easily have belonged to the man on the station, the one with the hairy ears and the well-stained sweater. As Barney guided Cass in through the little outer lobby and then the galley kitchen that ran parallel to an enormous sunlit sitting room, he looked decidedly apologetic. 'I need someone to take care of me,' he said miserably.

Cass looked round. He was right. It was the most beautiful room – or at least it once had been – with large windows at street level, giving ample light even though they were below ground. By the enormous open fireplace stood a scarlet linen sofa and two huge armchairs draped with ornate embroidered throws. There was a gilt mirror on the wall opposite the windows, another above the fire catching every last glimmer of sunlight, and waist-height bookcases running all the way round the room, full of everything from first editions through empty milk bottles, cans of paint, cats' skulls, odd shoes and umbrellas, to piles of what looked like striped pyjamas and a checked dressing gown. On one shelf stood a row of old clocks in various states of disrepair, while below them, on the broad bottom shelf, half on and half off the well-worn, well-chewed wood, lay a grizzled black and white greyhound, sound asleep amongst a nest of old magazines and newspapers, and an enormous ginger cat curled up against the dog's belly. The cat watched their progress through one rheumy, world-weary eye.

Barney waved towards them. 'The dog is called Kipper, because that is what he does best, and the ginger menace is called Radolpho. In the world of the brainless dog the one-eyed cat is king, and needs to be saved from himself, prevented from stealing from shopping bags, eating dog food and anything he can prise from the fridge, your plate or the bin. He likes to pee in the sink and the dog likes to have sex with stuffed toys . . . In fact, they both have very sordid tastes in general.'

The cat closed his eye, stretched and then settled down.

'I really need someone to help me get the place under control,' Barney said reflectively, flicking a long tail of cigarette ash into the bowl of a dead pot plant.

'I can see that, but I'm not a cleaner or a house-keeper, Barney,' said Cass, setting her suitcase down amongst the debris.

He looked aghast. 'Good Lord, no – of course you're not. I wasn't suggesting for one moment that you were. But you could find one for me. I can't do any of that kind of thing. I'm completely useless. I get myself into the most terrible muddles, get taken in and hire people who use my credit cards to buy sports cars and then steal my shoes. It's dreadful.'

Cass looked at him. 'Barney, you don't need me, what you really need is a wife.'

He shook his head. 'No, no, I don't,' he said emphatically. 'No, I've had several of those and, trust me, while it sounds all very well and good in principle, it always ends in tears. Besides, my mother invariably hates them.'

'Your mother?'

Barney nodded. 'Extraordinary woman. She's upstairs now, so I don't have to worry about her quite so much, knowing where she is.' As he spoke, he looked heavenwards. 'It's been a weight off my mind.'

Cass hesitated, wondering if 'upstairs' was a euphemism for dead as a stuffed skunk, but apparently not.

'She used to be such a worry when she lived up in town. She pretends she is as deaf as a post, drinks like a sailor, is built like a wren, and has the constitution of a Chieftain tank. She terrifies me. I keep thinking the only way I'm ever going to get rid of the old bat is to shoot her.'

At which point Cass's mobile rang.

'I hate those things,' grumbled Barney.

'Is there anything you *do* like?' Cass said in a voice barely above a whisper while pulling the phone out of her bag.

Barney considered for a second or two, apparently taking the question seriously. 'Quite a few things, actually. Strip clubs, blue paint, those nice little cups they serve espresso in. Seasonal vegetables. Oh – that woman on breakfast TV with the fabulous . . .' He mimed those parts that he was particularly fond of.

Cass decided to ignore him and looked at the phone to see who was calling.

'Hi, Jake, how are you?' she said, pressing the phone to her ear. He didn't answer at once, which was ominous. 'Is everything all right?'

'Well, it depends really,' he said.

Something about his tone made Cass's heart sink, although surely it couldn't be anything too awful; she had taken Danny to her mum and dad's to stay overnight. If anything had happened to him, then they would have rung her, wouldn't they? What about the dog? The cat? In the split seconds before Jake began speaking, Cass's mind was running down a mental checklist that included fire, flood, pestilence and sudden pet death.

'The police have been round.'

'What?' The police featured nowhere on Cass's checklist. Although hot on the heels of that thought it occurred to her maybe something had happened to David, something nasty and well deserved . . .

'You know that phone you found on the train?'

'Yes.'

'Well, apparently the man it belonged to has disappeared.'

Cass laughed. 'Of course he's disappeared – he was going to Rome.'

'Unfortunately that isn't what his wife said. Apparently he was meant to be going to some sort of shareholders' meeting in London, and then going home. He hadn't got his passport with him, and no one has seen or heard from him since.'

'You can't be serious. That was last week – what, four or five days ago?'

'His wife has reported him as missing.'

'The one who rung me? God, if I was married to her I think I'd go missing. She was a complete cow. He told me he was going to Rome.'

'Whatever, they would like to talk to you. I've told them you'll be back tomorrow.'

'OK, I'll sort it out when I get there. There's not much I can tell them. How's Milo?'

'Fine – farting and scratching, and sound asleep on my sofa at the moment.' Jake laughed. 'He knows we're talking about him; his tail has started to wag.'

'And Bob?'

'Sunning himself on the window sill in your kitchen about half an hour ago when I went round with a can of Felix. How's Barney?'

Cass laughed. 'Farting and scratching and –'

'I'd worry if his tail starts to wag. He's a good man. Bear with it.'

'He's barking mad.'

Jake was quiet for a few seconds as if considering the possibility. 'Yes, but in a good way. Have you seen his shop yet?'

'No, we're going there next. We're at the flat at the moment.'

Jake laughed. 'Wait, it gets better. You'll love it.'

'I'm sorry. No comment,' said Margaret Devlin weakly, raising a hand to fend off any questions, while pressing a large white lace-trimmed handkerchief to her exquisitely made-up face with the other. She sniffed, struggling to hold back a great flood of tears. 'I'll be issuing a statement through my solicitor later today, but in the meantime I would just like to say that this has been the most terrible time for our whole family. James's death is a tragedy. I'd like to thank everyone for their tremendous support and help over the last few days. James was so very special, so very precious to us and everyone who knew him. I always saw him as a bright flame in an otherwise dark and uncaring world. Thank you.'

Margaret's voice broke as she tried out a brave little smile on her reflection in the sitting-room mirror. Not bad at all. Although, if she was going to wear black, she would need a lot more lipstick and maybe some bigger earrings.

She leaned forward and adjusted the brim of her hat so that it framed her face a bit more and emphasised her eyes. Black was so chic, so flattering. She turned to gauge the effect. Perhaps she ought to buy a couple of new suits; after all, she wouldn't want people thinking that she had let herself go now that she was a widow – and she would be able to afford it, once the insurance paid out. If James Devlin was dead, then Margaret would be a very wealthy woman indeed. Both of their houses paid for, the large endowment policy that had blighted their lives for so long would cough up, and she would finally be able to get her hands on all his assets: the boat, the villa in Spain, the flat in Paris, the plane, the stocks and shares, the Monopoly hand of properties he had bought to let. At last it would all be hers and she would be free of him – the tight, philandering, double-dealing, double-crossing, arrogant bastard.

James Devlin, dashing entrepreneur and man about town, always appeared so warm and affable to everyone else, but Margaret knew the truth; she knew how selfish and cruel and self-centred he could be. But if he was dead, that was a different matter altogether. She would get his pension, his savings, his classic car collection, and lots and lots and lots of sympathy. Death somehow wiped the slate clean and tidied away so many of life's little misdemeanours.

And Margaret would have no problem at all mourning James once he was gone. Oh no, she would smile bravely and, in stronger moments, joke about what a card he had been. What a lad, what a character, but Margaret of course had always loved him, and James had always come home to her despite the other women and the gambling and the drinking and the string of questionable business deals.

She tipped her head to one side, trying to look philosophical and understanding. James Devlin was a man's man in a world where such men were rarities. Margaret took another long hard look at her reflection framed in the mirror and made a mental note to practise looking up coyly under her eyelashes.

A flicker of movement caught Margaret's eye; she swung round. 'Get that fucking dog off the furniture. *Now!*' she shrieked at the au pair, who had just appeared through the sitting-room doors.

'How many times do I have to tell you that the bloody thing's not allowed in here? *Not in here,* do you understand? Not – in – here. Put it outside in the run.'

'But Mr Devlin, he loves Snoops,' said the girl defensively, stepping between the dog – a wildly over-enthusiastic springer spaniel – and Margaret, to protect him from her icy glare.

'Don't you dare tell me what that miserable lying bastard loves. Put the dog out *now*. Look at the state of that sofa! Sodding animal, hair everywhere, and it keeps cocking its leg up the standard lamps and making the place stink.'

The girl scooped up the dog in her great big arms. It wasn't just her arms that were big. She was heavyset and clumsy, with a face as flat and round as a full moon, hands like coal shovels, and a body like a pile of wet sacks. Margaret Devlin had gone to the agency and had personally chosen her from all the girls on file, just in case there was a repeat of the blonde Swede incident or the curvaceous Italian accident, which had resulted in Margaret having to whip a hysterical 23-year-old rabid Catholic off to a private clinic and pay her a year's wages as hush money before sending her on a pilgrimage to Lourdes. Oh yes, James would be so much easier to deal with if he was dead.

'And then you can go and collect Alison and Christopher from school.'

'Yes, Mrs Devlin.'

Margaret checked her appearance again; the police had said they'd pop by to let her know how things were going, and she wanted to make sure she looked the part. Maybe black was a bit premature. She hurried upstairs to change into something navy or chocolate brown and put on a touch more lipstick . . .

'Devious little bastard has done a runner. I should have bloody guessed. No backbone, no balls. I don't like it when people take the piss,' Gordie Mann said reflectively, almost to himself. He spoke with a soft Scottish accent. He was a businessman and banker of sorts – the sort that don't offer internet access or radio alarm clocks when you open an account, but do come round and break your legs if you miss a payment.

He leaned across the table and looked vacantly into the middle distance for a few seconds before his attention snapped back to the small man in a beige mack seated opposite him.

'The thing is, Mr Marshall, in a perfect world I'd like to find him and fix him and get my money back. But the problem is I've got to find him first – and that's where you come in. There's way too much police interest in this one already. He's not just shafted me but all his bloody shareholders as well. If I go around shaking anybody's tree, the Old Bill are going to be down on me like a ton of bricks. That bastard owes me. Him and his fucking "sure bets". I should have known better. I should have sussed him out. Greedy wee git.'

Mr Marshall nodded. Not that he really understood dotcoms or futures or any of that crap, but he did understand revenge and frustration and a decent fee – unlike Gordie, who, he sensed, was more fluent in pain and fear. 'So how would you like to start, Mr Mann?'

Gordie thought about it for a moment or two. 'I thought you'd know.'

Mr Marshall nodded. 'To some extent it was a rhetorical question. It's usual in cases like this to start close to home.' He took out a notebook. 'You say that you know Mrs Devlin?'

Gordie reddened slightly. 'Aye, I've known Margaret a good few years. Fine woman, is Margaret,' he added, in a way that Mr Marshall suspected was meant to sound casual.

Mr Marshall tucked a stray thought away so that it didn't show on his face. 'In that case, I think we should start by paying Mrs Devlin a visit.'

Jake was right: Barney's shop had to be seen to be believed. The main doorway was so low that you almost had to stoop to get through it and then immediately step down on to a broad flagstone floor. The windows were unmanageably small with deep sills, and Cass assumed that it would be dark and cosy inside. She was wrong.

Inside, the shop opened up like an Aladdin's cave in a cavernous space. Part of the upper floor had been cut away, adding to the feeling of openness and light. A spiral staircase, made from what looked like a wisp of twisted silver and steel, led up into the room above, while modern prints hung on the chalky white walls, with long mirrors artfully catching every ounce of usable light. Nothing inside was dark or heavy – instead, jewellery was arranged in elegant discreetly illuminated glass cases set with salt-whitened driftwood and plaits of sea-tangled rope. Across the ceiling and down the walls thin curling bronze lighting tracks lit magical corners and hidden recesses. One was full of sea birds; waders and spoonbills made from seed pods and wire and other found objects, picking their way through a landscape of seashells and creamy white pebbles. In another alcove was a selection of silk flowers, so realistic that when she first walked by, Cass thought she could smell them. In a third was a flutter of butterflies made from crinkled handmade white paper, silver filaments and azure blue beads.

Cass stared; it was amazing and beautiful and impossible to know where to look next.

Behind the cash desk a tall languid blonde wearing manically tight jeans, an off-the-shoulder leopard-skin print top and a creamy fur stole uncurled herself slowly and smiled lazily in their direction. Barney extended a hand to introduce her.

'Cass, I would like you to meet Daisy. She is a little cow. Between them, she and her bitch of a mother are bleeding me dry. She hates me, but other than that she is quite a nice girl. Although her taste in clothes leaves something to be desired.' He glared at Daisy with what Cass took to be censure; not that the girl noticed. 'It's some sort of gift she has. She always manages to look like a cross between a streetwalker and circus performer,' he said wearily.

Daisy pulled a face at Barney, although in amongst it all her smile broadened and instantly Cass could see the family resemblance.

'Actually, we both hate him,' said Daisy, warming to the subject. 'He plied my mother with drink and drugs, seduced her, and then left her for a younger woman. It totally ruined her life and broke her heart, you know. She's never really got over him.'

Barney's jaw dropped and he stared at Daisy aghast. 'Is that what she told you?' he spluttered.

Daisy shook her head. 'Good God, no. But since she can't talk about you without swearing and throwing things, I've had to read between the lines and make it up. Is it all right if I shut up shop now?'

Barney took a moment or two to regain his composure and then said, 'Another half hour.'

Daisy's bottom lip jutted out grumpily. 'Oh, go on. It's been really quiet today.'

Barney was unmoved. 'There may be a last-minute rush.' Daisy was still not impressed, so Barney continued, 'You see the opening times on the door, on that little sign? Well, when it says on there that we're open, funnily enough, we're supposed to be. Bit quirky, I know, but it's an idea you can get used to over time.'

Daisy sniffed and carried on looking hard done by.

'If you've got Daisy . . .' Cass began.

'Oh, but that's just it – I haven't got Daisy,' Barney said. 'Not only is she unreliable, but she's off soon on her travels, on this gap-year thing that everyone does these days – and she is expecting me to help fund it. I told her she would have to work her passage.'

'And believe me, I am,' growled the teenager.

Hate had never looked so affectionate.

Barney turned his attention back to Cass. 'So what do you think of my emporium, then?'

Cass shook her head. 'I don't know what to say. It's amazing.'

'I knew you'd like it. Wait,' said Barney, holding a finger to his lips. 'There's more.' Like a mad pied piper he indicated she should follow him upstairs.

'Daisy, do the lights, will you?' he said over his shoulder.

The gallery proper was painted white, the uneven walls with their odd-shaped bricks covered in crumbly flat whitewash, which brought out the beauty of the pale sanded wood floors. The ceiling opened up into a pitched roof space set with skylights and tiny twinkling halogen spots. The current exhibition was of abstract seascapes in the most wonderful soft blues, greens and golds. Cass was enchanted. Even more so when she looked at the current catalogue and realised the work was all Barney's.

She stared at him. 'For someone so horrible, you paint like an angel.'

He nodded sagely. 'I know, it's a complete bastard, isn't it? I think we would all prefer to believe that talent is visited on the worthy, the humble and the genuinely deserving.'

Cass raised an eyebrow.

'But you don't have to worry,' said Barney. 'I'm none of those things. Now, how about I show you the studio, and then we can go and have an early supper? I'm starving. There is this wonderful little Italian place down the road. The staff fight all the time and swear at each other – I feel so at home. We'll take Daisy so's she doesn't have to go home to her poor demented mother on an empty stomach. After you . . .' He indicated a small door to one side of the gallery, set back in what should have been an outside wall or maybe the wall of the adjoining property. Barney grunted when Cass mentioned it.

'The arse ache that's caused me over the years. It's a flying freehold. To be honest, I'm seriously thinking about renting somewhere else to work. I've got a room in my mother's place, but I can't work there – she never shuts up,' he continued as Cass headed up a set of stairs that twisted round so sharply they were almost a spiral, while behind her Barney struggled and swore, puffing and blowing like a train. 'Nag, nag nag; the woman is a complete menace. I'm sure my father only died to get some bloody peace.'

The room Cass stepped into had to be above someone else's shop or storeroom. The roof had skylights and, in contrast to Barney's domestic life, was almost clinically clean and tidy, practically spartan. Painted white, one wall was shelved from floor to ceiling, each shelf neatly stacked with sketchbooks arranged according to the dates running down their spines; albums, magazines and books arranged alphabetically; labelled boxes, jars of brushes, bottles of linseed oil and turps. There was a set of Perspex drawers filled with tubes of paint; neatly stacked tins of charcoal and pastels; a jam jar full of pencils which sat alongside another full of feathers and a third and fourth with brushes and palette knives. One shelf held a row of pebbles that ran unbroken from one end to the other. Against the wall adjoining the shelves, boards stacked in a metal frame, canvas stretched and ready in another. But all these things were so tidily and methodically arranged that the studio felt uncluttered. An easel dominated the centre of the room, the bare floorboards below it covered with a delicate filigree of spilt gold, blue and red paint.

'Those bloody stairs play havoc with my back,' grumbled Barney. 'I keep thinking it would make a decent storeroom, but I'd only fill it up with crap. If you like it, you could use it – if you want to, that is,' he added grudgingly. 'There's a kitchen-ette thing through there and a toilet.' He waved towards another door in the far wall and then pulled a cloth off something fixed on a cantilevered arm to the wall opposite the easel. Underneath was a small television monitor, currently switched off.

'It's the shop,' said Barney in answer to Cass's unspoken question. 'In theory, you could work up here and mind the fort, although in practice it is a perfect fucking nuisance. You just get into something and you're interrupted by some bloody moron wanting to know if you sell T-shirts. And if you don't go down, they get annoyed. Assuming you're that quick. People are in and out before you can get down the stairs – nicking the stock, stealing money out of the till . . . Although I suppose the bonus is that at least you've got their faces on video for when you take the thieving bastards to court.' He looked up at her. 'So, when can you start? You are going to take the job?'

Cass shrugged. 'Maybe,' she said, trying hard to sound noncommittal, while knowing that she planned to say yes.

Once they had closed the shop, Barney, Daisy and Cass walked down to the restaurant, Barney and Daisy bickering all the way. Cass smiled to herself. Jake was right: a summer in Brighton was exactly what she needed.

Margaret Devlin looked at the man on the doorstep and said with genuine surprise, 'Gordie, how are you?' He was the last person she had expected to see.

He smiled. 'More to the point, how are you, Margaret?'

Gordie Mann had a bluff rugby player's face, broad cheekbones, the skin around his eyes cut and shaped by great swathes of scar tissue, and a nose broken and badly set more than once.

'Bloody awful,' she said grimly. He towered above her like a badly constructed crane.

'I would have been round sooner, but I thought what with the law here and everything, you wouldn't want any more visitors. I'm so very sorry to hear about James.' He handed her a bunch of flowers.

Margaret Devlin looked coyly up at him. 'You know that I'm always pleased to see you, Gordie. Why don't you come in and have a drink.'

He nodded. 'Don't mind if I do, Margaret – only I've got someone with me.' Gordie stepped aside to reveal a small, weaselly-looking man with thinning reddish-grey hair, wearing a mack and dark horn-rimmed glasses. 'This is Mr Marshall,' he said.

Margaret Devlin peered at him. 'Mr Marshall?' she said, both as a muted welcome and a question. She would have much preferred it if Gordie had been on his own. It wouldn't be the first time that she had cried on his big broad shoulders.

Gordie nodded. 'He's working for me. He's a private detective. We're looking for James.'

Margaret Devlin stared at him. 'But why? I'm not with you.'

Gordie smiled and, sliding a bottle of Gordon's gin out of the pocket of his Crombie, said in an undertone: 'How about I come inside and explain it to you?'

Margaret blushed and then stood aside to let him pass. Gordie Mann and Margaret Devlin went back a long way.

'So, Ms . . .'

'Mrs.'

The policewoman nodded. 'Mrs Hammond, you said that you'd never met Mr Devlin before.'

'No. What I said was that we'd met on the train before.'

'Several times?'

Cass glanced at the WPC, wondering why the hell she should be feeling guilty, and at the same time annoyed that the policewoman was asking her the same questions over and over again in different ways, quite obviously and very heavy-handedly trying to catch Cass out.

'Once. I met him once before. He gave me fruit.'

The woman nodded and looked down at her notes. 'Peaches?'

'Yes.'

'Right. And are you normally in the habit of taking fruit from strangers, Ms Hammond?'

This was ridiculous. Cass stared at the small, dour policewoman trying very hard not to lose her patience, laugh or swear. 'Well, it's not something

I do every day, no – but then again, on the whole most strangers don't offer me fruit.'

The policewoman's expression tightened. 'Please, Ms Hammond,' she said between gritted teeth, 'this is a very serious matter.'

Cass nodded. 'I don't doubt it, but I've already told you everything I know. I had met this man once before. The second time we met he told me he was going on an adventure to Rome. He got off at Cambridge, told me he was going to catch the Stansted train, and that was the last I saw of him.'

The woman nodded and then said softly, 'And the phone?'

Cass sighed. 'What about the phone?'

'You were handed it by a woman who –'

'Who found it under the man's seat, or on it – I'm not sure now. So, I rang his home number and left him a message to let him know he'd lost it, but that it was safe.'

'And to arrange to meet him and give it back?'

'Yes, that's right.'

'And other than calling his home number, you haven't done anything else to the phone, subsequently? Edited the phone book or deleted any information regarding incoming or outgoing calls, texts or anything?'

A small sleek silver mobile phone lay on the coffee table between them, all neatly sealed up in an evidence bag. As Cass's eye moved over it, the policewoman smiled without warmth.

'No,' said Cass, wishing the bloody woman would just leave.

'Mrs Devlin said that your manner on the phone was –' the WPC read from her notebook – '"flirtatious and over familiar".'

Cass reddened furiously. 'I'm not sure that's exactly how I'd put it. OK, he had been very friendly, chatty – very chatty. I didn't know he was married. I certainly didn't think I was leaving a message that would be picked up by his wife.'

The policewoman's expression didn't change. 'So, you were attracted to Mr Devlin?' She didn't wait for Cass to answer. Instead she added, 'You know, it wouldn't be the first time that a woman was taken in by an attractive and plausible man, Ms Hammond.'

Cass stared at her, wondering if the WPC had met David.

The policewoman leaned forward, as if to imply that this was really just a cosy girl-to-girl-chat, and continued in a low conspiratorial voice. 'And James Devlin is quite a charmer, apparently.'

Cass felt a growing sense of indignation; the insinuation made her skin prickle. 'Meaning what, exactly?' she growled.

The woman aped empathy. 'Oh, come on, Ms Hammond. Meaning that James Devlin has a knack of getting women to do what he wants. He's got quite a reputation, you know – bit of a ladies' man, bit of a lad.'

Cass considered the possibility. All that grinning and bumbling boyish enthusiasm for life, she could see how that might work. 'Uhuh. Your point being . . . ?'

This was obviously not the answer the WPC was expecting. 'What I'm trying to say,' she snapped, 'is that you wouldn't be the first woman to be taken in by him.'

Cass was fed up of feeling put on, patronised and annoyed. 'Look, let's get one thing straight, shall we? I wasn't taken in by him. He gave me fruit and a mint humbug.'

The policewoman glanced down at her notes. 'A mint humbug? You didn't mention –' she began, the implication being presumably that if Cass had overlooked a boiled sweet, it was quite reasonable to assume that she might have overlooked a secret assignation, an extra-marital affair, or a plan to run away to Rome together.

'Officer,' said Cass, as politely as she could manage, which wasn't very, 'I think this has gone on quite long enough. I've got things to do, I've got to collect my son from school. I've answered your questions and told you everything I can remember. And I don't think going over and over and over is going to help.'

The woman nodded and she and the young policeman she had brought with her got to their feet.

'One more thing,' the WPC said, while still almost bent double. 'Your neighbour mentioned the fact that you are thinking about moving to Brighton.'

Trust Jake.

'Yes, that's right,' said Cass, well aware of how defensive she sounded. 'Just for the summer.'

The policewoman's eyes narrowed thoughtfully. 'Right. Any particular reason? I mean, why you're thinking about moving there now?'

'Why not now?' said Cass.

'You said that your husband is no longer living here with you and your son?'

'No, what I said was that he had left me for the girl who did our cleaning. And no, I haven't got any plans to set up a secret seaside love nest, if that's what you are implying. I just wanted to take a break, think things through – the last few months have been tough.'

The policewoman stared blankly at her. Cass wondered if she was protesting too much, an emotion only equalled by her growing sense of frustration and fury. She made an effort to smile. 'I don't really see how this is relevant, but, OK, yes, I am moving to Bright –'

'To meet Mr Devlin?' the WPC asked quickly, as if Cass might not notice that she had slipped the question in.

'No, not to meet Mr Bloody Devlin. I've been offered a summer job there,' snapped Cass.

The policewoman nodded and scribbled something in her notebook. For all Cass knew, it might have been a note to pick up a frozen pizza on the way home. Whatever it was, she had had enough.

'What sort of job?' the WPC pressed.

Cass was already halfway across the sitting room, guiding the two of them towards the door. 'In a gallery,' she said briskly as she opened the front door.

The policewoman's eyes lit up. 'Oh yes,' she said gleefully. 'You're an artist, aren't you?' She managed to make it sound like it was a career choice that was up there somewhere between mass murder and self-employed puppy-strangling.

'Yes, I am,' said Cass grimly.

'Um, well, we'll be in touch,' said the policewoman. 'And if you remember anything else in the meantime, or Mr Devlin makes contact, please don't hesitate to ring.' She handed Cass a card. Cass slipped it into her pocket; there was really no point in protesting.

Margaret Devlin had the most terrible hangover when she got up, although it could easily have been down to mixing gin with the sleeping pills that the doctor had given her. She hadn't had that much. Gordie had had quite a lot, although the private detective, Mr Marshall, had had only one – a very small one at that, which probably said it all – explaining that he was driving and wanted to take notes during their little chat. Margaret narrowed her eyes, trying to reconstruct their conversation from the fragments she could remember.

It appeared that James had been involved with Gordie in some sort of business investments and Gordie wasn't convinced that the police were working as diligently as they might to track James down. And over another G & T, Gordie explained that he had other ways and means at his disposal – things and methods not always available to the law, more direct methods. And then Mr Marshall explained that he was working for Gordie – but Margaret couldn't remember the exact details now.

She had told them everything she thought might help. Mr Marshall had written down the phone numbers and name of the woman who had rung and left a message for James.

'And you think that your husband and this Mrs Hammond were having an affair?'

'Well, she said she had picked up the phone on the train. I mean, what sort of story is that?'

Mr Marshall didn't say a word. Margaret sniffed; she could tell he didn't believe her. And then they had all traipsed up to James's office. At the door, Gordie and Mr Marshall pulled on surgical gloves, then searched the place from floor to ceiling and photocopied James's diary and address books.

'You can take them if it will help,' she had suggested.

Gordie smiled and patted her hand. 'Thank you, Margaret.' And then he looked at his companion. Mr Marshall tapped the side of his nose and very carefully slid the books into a plastic carrier.

Now, stone-cold sober, sitting in her bedroom, Margaret cursed her naivety. She ought to have gone through the diaries and the address books and seen for herself if Cass Hammond's name was in there. Men weren't any good at that kind of thing. Margaret had a nose for codes and little hints and subtle marks in the margin. She had always caught James out before; she knew the signs. Bastard.

She dropped two soluble aspirin into a glass. The plink, plink fizz made her wince, and she wished for the hundredth time that she'd saved the woman's answer machine message – all that bloody giggling and flirting. If they'd heard that, the police and Mr Marshall would have understood why she was so sure and so bloody angry.

Cass closed the front door behind the policewoman, laid her forehead against the wood, and closed her eyes. So far it wasn't proving the easiest of weeks.

The only good thing was that the madwoman hadn't rung her again, although Cass wasn't convinced she'd heard the last from the hysterical, dog-loving, Mrs James Devlin.

By contrast, David had been bleakly sane when he showed up, a couple of hours or so after she arrived home from meeting Barney, which was quite a feat for someone red-faced, sweaty, with wet hair slicked slyly over his bald patch, wearing a bright turquoise tracksuit and carrying a squash racquet in a fluorescent green-and-yellow case. Seeing him made her heart lurch miserably.

'The thing is, Cass, I need a little time and space to think about the future – our future,' David said, sitting on the sofa, wringing his hands. 'Well, all right, my future.'

'Really,' Cass said flatly. When they had been together she had never realised just how self-centred and conniving he sounded. Pain and the sense of loss made her see him so differently. Was it clearer and truer, or was it that betrayal coloured her vision?

'There's no need to be so negative, Cass. You see,' he said, seizing on the word like a terrier grabbing a trouser leg, 'to be perfectly honest with you, I think that's the problem really, isn't it?'

'Sorry? I'm not with you,' said Cass in surprise.

'Well, you're always so negative about everything, and so petty. For example, I've been here, what? Nearly ten minutes?' He pulled back the sleeve of his tracksuit and peered at his watch to emphasise the point. 'And you know that I've just walked up here from the sports centre, but you didn't ask me to sit down and you haven't offered me so much as a glass of water, let alone a cup of tea. It's all a bit petty and vindictive, isn't it?'

Cass stared at him; he was incredible. 'David, the last time we spoke, you said my relentless optimism was the real problem, that my being so cheerful was driving you mad. Always looking on the bright side, no sense of reality, never taking things seriously – that's what you said.'

'I've had time to reconsider, since the . . . get some sense of perspective.' He glanced round the room. 'I'm parched. Harry Fellowes and I had a really cracking game. He sends his regards, by the way. Now, about that cup of tea –'

Cass looked at David as if seeing him for the first time; he really was a piece of work. How was it she had never noticed that before?

'I thought as you said you didn't want to see Danny, you weren't staying for long,' Cass snapped.

What on earth had she ever seen in him? And why, if he *was* so bloody horrible, did it still hurt so much? Cass watched him as he tried hard to hold his pot belly in, and sighed. Being a woman could be such a pain in the arse at times.

He was still talking. 'I thought that you'd understand. It seems obvious to me – we really have to look at it from Danny's point of view, Cass. I think that it's better if he doesn't know I'm here. I really don't want to upset him.'

Cass nearly choked. 'Upset him? For Christ's sake, David, you've already upset him. You walked out and left us, remember? There isn't a day goes by when he doesn't ask where you are, or when you're coming home. He misses you like crazy. He wants to see you. I'm running out of excuses as to why you don't want to see him. He adores you, David. You're his daddy –'

'You see, there you go again – everything a huge drama. You're so demanding and difficult, there's never any room for manoeuvre with you, is there, Cass? You always see the worst in people,' David growled.

This was not the way Cass saw herself at all. She struggled to keep the sound of tears and hurt and anger out of her voice. 'Why can't you come round and see Danny? Tuck him in and read him a story, take him out for the day. You could go to the zoo or the beach – or just take the dog for a walk.'

David avoided meeting her eye. 'Cass, you have to understand that things are a little difficult for me at the moment.'

Oh, Cass understood, all right. Having a six-year-old around calling you Daddy probably didn't go hand in glove with David's new teenage sex-god ethos.

'I am very concerned about the way you've inter-preted things, the way you look at life,' David continued.

'You don't think,' said Cass conversationally, 'while we're on the subject of personality traits, that the main problem here is not my doom-laden, overly pessimistic nature, but the fact that you ran off with Abby, by any chance, do you?'

David looked shocked, or at least made a good fist of trying to look shocked, and then shook his head. 'Is that what you've told Danny?'

'No, of course that's not what I've told Danny.

I told him that Mummy and Daddy loved him very much, but that we couldn't live with each other any more because Daddy had got a new friend.'

'Oh, Cass, there you go again – you have to be in the right, don't you? You have to be the good one. And you always jump to the wrong conclusion.' He managed to make it sound like the summing up in the case for the defence, not to mention everything being entirely her fault. 'Let's face it, Cass, this thing with Abby – surely you have to understand it's a symptom of the problem between us, not the cause?'

'And what do you think the cause is?' she prompted.

David looked almost apologetic. 'Well, we've already talked about your attitude –'

Cass felt his words stoking up the murderous rage that had been growing in her belly for the last fifteen minutes. 'Have we? And what do you think about my attitude?'

'Well, it's hard to know where to begin, really. I'm very conscious of not wanting to hurt you – but, let's face it, you've always had a very naïve take on life. I suppose it's all your creative brainpower –' He laughed in an unpleasantly patronising way. Thinking about it now, he sounded a lot like the policewoman.

'Unworldly.' His expression suggested he was being generous in his description. 'You know, sometimes I felt that being with you was too big a responsibility, Cass.'

She stared at him, noting the past tense and wondering who the hell he had been living with for the last nine years? 'And are you saying that Abby isn't a big responsibility? Please don't tell me she's very mature for her age,' Cass snarled. She saw he was about to speak and held up a hand to silence him. 'What the fuck are you talking about, David? You're making this up as you go along. It's complete and utter rubbish. This is my house. When we first got together you couldn't get a sofa on tick because your credit rating was so bad. I've always paid my way and sometimes yours. Even when Danny was a baby, I worked; I've sold stuff, I've taught . . . I don't know how you dare accuse me of being unworldly. We've always got by.'

David nodded and rested his fingertips together as if passing sentence. 'You see, that's just it, isn't it? Scraped through, managed, got by.' He smiled indulgently, as if these were the worst words in the world. 'The thing is, Cass, I don't want to scrape by any more. It's time to move on, but I don't want you to feel bitter or unhappy about the past, pet. We've had a great time.'

'Pet? A great time?' she yelled. 'We're talking about a marriage here, David, not a day trip to a bloody theme park. Would you like to tell me what you came round for – aside from letting me know that everything is my fault – if you don't want to see Danny?'

'There's no need to talk to me like that.' David

looked hurt. 'And I'd be grateful if you kept your voice down. We don't want to wake him up, do we? I've been to see my solicitor today.'

Cass's eyes narrowed; she could sense a trap.

'The thing is –' he said quickly, before she could interrupt the flow – 'I've got a lot of responsibilities and outgoings with the new business. I mean, we're doing well – but . . .' David hesitated. 'It's not been an easy year for the firm, one way and another, and I was wondering . . . well, you've got this house . . .' He looked around thoughtfully, while Cass tried to work out exactly where the conversation was leading.

'Your point being?' she said.

'Well, for one thing, I've come to discuss the idea of maintenance for Danny. I was thinking that maybe we could settle with a one-off payment rather than all this monthly malarkey. I was thinking something in the region of . . . what shall we say?'

Cass waited with bated breath.

'I mean, presumably you will remarry at some time.'

'David, you've been gone three months.'

'Exactly. That's what I'm saying – things move on, times change. How would you feel about, say, five thousand pounds?' he said cheerily.

Cass stared at him, not quite able to believe what she was hearing. 'What?'

'Well, it seems fair. I mean, if we want to go with the letter of the law, legally I'd probably be entitled to half your house if I wanted to push it. But that would be mean, wouldn't it?'

Mean? Cass didn't know what to say, or where to begin, or at least she didn't trust herself to open her mouth. What a complete and utter bastard.

'So what do you think?' he pressed.

'I think that you ought to leave.'

He smiled. 'So you'll consider my offer then?'

'I had Abby's parents round over the weekend,' countered Cass, her tone icy cold.

David paled. 'Ah, right. And how are they?'

'What do you mean, *How are they*? How do you think they are, David? They're looking for someone to blame for why you ran off with their precious little girl.'

Cass paused, waiting for David to suggest that that, too, was her fault, but fortunately he just nodded. 'You know, it's sad really. They simply can't see that the way they've treated her is at least half the problem. She is so, so complex – so fragile. It's not easy. They're not easy people to get on with, apparently. Abby has been telling me how they –'

'David,' Cass snapped, 'they are perfectly reasonable people who are worried to death about their eighteen-year-old daughter running off with a man old enough to be her father.'

David flinched as if she had punched him. 'Hardly old enough to be her father, Cass. Come on now, you have to admit that that's a bit of an exaggeration.' He ran a hand back over his thinning blond hair – which, it struck Cass, was several shades lighter than when he had left.

'David. You're forty-four –'

'Forty-three, actually.'

'All right forty-three, but you'll be forty-four next month and, whichever way you add it up, surely to God you can see that Abby's parents are worried sick about what's happened – and they have every reason to be. As far as they were concerned, come October their precious little girl was off to De Monteford to do something meaningful in social sciences, and now here she is shacked up with some ageing Lothario in a love nest above the laundrette.'

David glared at her, his face fire-engine red. 'You can be so bloody cruel at times.'

'You mean when I'm not being pessimistic or a terrible burden?'

'This is no joke, Cass,' he snapped.

She got to her feet. 'I wasn't being funny. I think you should leave now.'

Reluctantly, David got to his feet. 'So what do you think of my offer?' he asked again.

'I took it in the spirit in which it was made, David,' she said, guiding him towards the front door.

'Meaning what, exactly?' he asked.

'That I think you're taking the piss. I'm going to see my solicitor and, in the meantime, I am seriously considering accepting a managerial position I've just been offered in Brighton.'

David's jaw dropped. 'What?'

'You heard me.' If she was going to be accused of being a cow, Cass decided, she might as well enjoy a few of the perks. She also didn't bother pointing out that she was only going for the summer, nor that she would be managing Barney.

It totally wrong-footed David. 'I hadn't thought – I'm not sure how I feel about that. I mean, where does that leave us?'

'Us?' Cass said incredulously. 'What the hell do you mean, *us*?'

'What about Danny?' he blustered.

It was all Cass could do not to punch him. 'Don't talk to me about Danny. You're the one who planned your visit so that he was asleep when you got here.'

And then there had been Abby's parents, who had been another complete nightmare. They couldn't see beyond the fact that it had been Cass who had offered Abby the job after she had replied to an ad in the corner-shop window. Everything that had happened from then on, it seemed, had been everybody else's fault except Abby's.

'She's very naïve and young for her age. We thought it would be safe, letting her work here, didn't we, Moira? We're very upset about how things have turned out,' said Abby's father. It didn't seem to occur to either of them that Cass might be hurt or upset too, or that their daughter might have had any part in seducing, flirting with, or encouraging David. Oh no, that it seemed was absolutely impossible.

'We thought of her as our little girl,' said her mum, tearfully. 'You know, she hasn't rung or been round or anything since . . . well, you know.' They were talking about Abby in variations of the past tense, as if running off with David was the same as dying.

'She was just a baby, really,' agreed her father.

Cass nodded. Their little girl, their baby, who turned up to clean house in a pink lycra crop top with *Sex Kitten* in silver sequins across the front, no bra, breasts so pert they would have taken an eye out of the unwary, and a denim micro skirt that, combined with the top, was every dirty old lecher's dream ticket. Abby may well have been young, but Cass had a horrible feeling that she had known exactly what she was doing when she sashayed across the sitting-room floor pushing the Hoover and plumping cushions. Certainly she had been just what David's mid-life crisis needed.

3

Cass, holding her breath, standing up on tip-toe
and reaching as far as she was able, struggled to
tease a big holiday-sized suitcase down from the
top of the wardrobe with the very, very tips of her
fingers, watched by a wide-eyed and increasingly
anxious Danny.

'Are we going on holiday?' Danny asked in a
nervous little voice.

'No.'

'Is it for my school trip?'

'Nope.'

Cass was trying to avoid going downstairs for
a chair or to get the stepladder. She'd already sorted
out a couple of portfolios, her art box and two
small cases for Danny and . . . and . . . Cass took
a deep breath, straining to stretch up that last half
an inch. She was so close, so-very-very-close.

'Am I going to stay at Granny's for a very long
time?' Danny whispered.

'No, sweetheart. God – bloody thing,' Cass

groaned, blowing hard. One more big stretch and
. . . and she still couldn't reach.

'Are you going to take all my toys away and
give them to poor children because I've been so
naughty?'

Very slowly Cass turned to look at him and
resolved to have a strong word with her mother.
Danny was sitting on the end of the bed. He was
dressed in a navy blue T-shirt, oatmeal-coloured
shorts, blue socks and sandals, his big brown eyes
watching her every move – he looked so cute that
Cass could have scooped him up and eaten him.

'No, sweetheart, no. I'm not going to do that
and neither is anyone else, and I can't imagine
you're ever going to be that naughty, ever. Take
it from me, Granny Annie can be pretty bad herself,
and no one ever threatened to take her toys away.'

Danny nodded solemnly.

'The thing is,' said Cass, reaching up again for
the case, trying to fool herself that the first couple
of attempts were just a warm-up and this time she
would get it, no sweat. 'You know that Mummy's
been looking for a job? Well, she's got one and
it's going to be really good fun. We're going to go
and live by the seaside. Just you and me – and
God, I really wish I was two inches taller.'

Danny considered the implications for a few
seconds. 'The seaside?'

Cass nodded. 'Uhuh.'

'With a beach and stuff?'

She nodded again. 'With a beach and funfair

and a swimming pool and ice cream and lots of places to go, and stuff –'

'Are you still going to paint?'

Cass nodded.

'And do books and cards and things?'

Cass wasn't sure how much more nodding she could manage. 'Yes, just like now, but I'm going to work in a gallery too, and do all sorts of other stuff.'

'Are you still going to work at my school?'

'Yes. We're only going for the summer, for the holidays.'

Danny put his head on one side for a few seconds, and then said, 'What about Daddy? Is Daddy coming too? How will he know where we live? He won't be able to find us. And what about Milo and Bob?' The words tumbled out in a breathless rush.

Cass gave up on the suitcase and turned her attention to Danny. 'It's all right. We're only going for a little while. Jake is going to look after Bob and we'll take Milo with us. And we'll tell Daddy exactly where we are. OK? We're going to live in a flat in Brighton and Mummy's going to work for a man called Barney, and he's got a cat and a dog too . . .' Cass hesitated, it was probably best not to suggest that Barney was a nice man.

Danny's eyes widened in horror. 'Oh no. Barney's not your new boyfriend, is he?'

Six, and he should be working for the local police force. 'No, honey, he's not my boyfriend.

He's an old friend of Jake's.' Cass paused; child-care was going to be a nightmare. Danny, swinging his legs, studied her thoughtfully.

The job, as explained by Barney over a lot of frothy coffee, a glass too much of house red and a crash course in Italian profanity, was a complex, fast-moving combination of PA, nanny, shopkeeper and head wrangler for Barney's various family, art and business interests. These would include his pets, mother and various ex-wives, children, step-children, girlfriends, ex-girlfriends, creditors, artists, and such domestic help as he could lay his hands on, explained Barney conversationally, topping up Cass's glass with the brandy that the waiter had left on their table.

To be fair, although Barney swore blind he didn't like children, he seemed more than willing to accommodate Danny. And Cass, over dessert, had finally agreed to take the job for the summer holidays. Although on reflection maybe it was the booze talking.

'Daisy's going to be here for most of the summer and I thought we could hire an au pair – or at least you can. I'll pay her, you just have to pick someone who won't steal the teaspoons and hide bread in the airing cupboard,' Barney had said, dipping a little crispy almond biscuit into his coffee so that the froth crept up it like a rising tide. 'She can clean house and mind Danny and feed the animals. Actually, I'm not sure why I didn't think of it earlier. It'll be perfect. I can teach her to play backgammon and she will think I'm wounded and complex, and moon around after me with her hairy armpits, wearing strange clothes in peculiar foreign ways. They like a father figure, in my experience. I will try to be strong for both of us. It will be absolutely wonderful,' added Barney gleefully. 'When did you say you can start?'

'As soon as the school holidays begin, although maybe we need to talk about living arrangements. For a start, I barely know you. You're grumpy, rude and untidy – not to mention an alcoholic.'

'You just said you didn't know me.' Barney looked wounded. 'Jake never told me how rude you were.' He paused. 'Presumably you're worried about your virtue?'

Cass didn't think that deserved an answer.

Barney sighed. 'You've seen for yourself how big the flat is. There are two decent-sized rooms and a little bathroom at the back – all yours, own key, everything. You'll have to share the rest, but I'm sure Jake will give me a reference. And don't worry, you're not my type at all – my woman of choice is a neurotic bunny boiler who is stalking her therapist.' He looked sadly down at the remains of his dessert. 'God, I miss that woman.'

'Own rooms? Own key?'

Barney nodded and extended his hand across the wreckage of supper. 'So, it's a deal then?' he said, closing his great paw over hers and shaking it firmly before waving the waiter over. 'Let's have some more booze, shall we? How's your tiramisu?'

Now, back at home in the spare bedroom, Cass stared down at her son; she must have been nuts to agree. But then again, maybe it was just the kind of thing that they both needed, a summer by the sea.

Easy. Or at least that was how it had seemed when Barney explained it to her.

She looked up at the wardrobe. It was no good, she would have to go and get a chair.

'Cass?' Jake's voice made her jump. 'Are you there?'

'We're upstairs,' she called back. 'Packing.' Or at least they would be if she ever got the bloody case down. Jake was tall. 'Come on up,' she continued cheerily. 'We're in the spare room.'

Danny still looked anxious. She stroked sunshine yellow baby-boy hair back off his face. 'It's OK,' she said softly. 'Daddy will know exactly where we are going. And you can ring him every day if you want to. Maybe we can arrange for you to stay with him for part of the summer holidays. It's going to be all right. Promise. Cross my heart –' Was that for Danny's benefit or hers?

Danny's solemn expression didn't alter. 'Yes, but what about Jake?' he whispered as their neighbour lumbered noisily up the stairs. 'Who's going to look after Jake if we're not here?'

Good question. More to the point, who was going to look after Cass if Jake wasn't there to make tea, pick up the pieces and say it would be all right even if it quite obviously wasn't true? He was like a father, big brother and fairy godmother all mixed into one.

Before she could think of a good answer, Jake sprung across the threshold, clutching a folded newspaper. 'Have you seen this?' he said, thrusting it under her nose. The headline read, 'Local businessman sought for questioning in multimillion-pound accounting scam.'

Cass looked up at Barney. 'Don' t tell me.'

He nodded. ''Fraid so – Mr Peaches,' and then began to read: '"Local businessman, James Devlin, forty-one, is wanted for questioning in connection with the disappearance of company funds believed to be worth in excess of two million pounds from Devlin Holdings Ltd of Little Lamport, near Ely. Mr Devlin, a prominent and popular local figure, vanished last week after an emergency meeting was convened to discuss cash-flow problems and discrepancies in the accounts revealed during a routine audit. A company spokesman told our reporter yesterday that company representatives were keen to speak to Mr Devlin as soon as possible."'

Jake looked up to see if Cass was still listening. 'There's a dreadful photo. Looks as if it was taken when he was at school,' he said, before reading on: '"At their home, Mrs Margaret Devlin was unavailable for comment, but in a statement made through her family solicitor said she was anxious for her husband's safety and mental well-being. He has been under a lot of pressure over the last few months, Mrs Devlin added, and said she had no doubt her husband would be happy to cast some light on the company's present financial position as soon as he returned, and on a personal note added that she hoped that he would be home soon as his family missed him dreadfully."'

Cass held up her hands in surrender. 'Don't look at me like that, Jake. It's got nothing to do with me.'

'I just thought you might be interested, that's all. I mean, you were one of the last people to see him alive.'

Cass stared at him. 'What do you mean, see him *alive*? As far as I'm concerned, he is still alive; he was off to have an adventure in Rome. He gave me a mint humbug, for God's sake, not his last will and testament.'

'Well, this comment by his wife suggests . . . you know . . .' After checking that Danny wasn't looking, Jake drew a finger ominously across his throat. He waved the paper at her again. 'Anyway, I thought you might be interested. Here –'

Cass peered at it. Jake was right about the photograph. It looked like it had been blown up from some kind of eighties team photo and, other than the mop of blond hair, it looked nothing like the man she had met on the train.

'Well, like I said, I'm not interested. When I saw him he was very chirpy, no hint of . . . you know.' She expertly mimicked Jake's tone and gesture as she returned the paper to him.

'Have you talked to anyone about seeing him,

besides the police?' asked Jake. 'The press or anything?'

'No. Why on earth should I?'

'I just wondered. Only there's a car been sitting at the end of the lane for most of the day. I noticed it parking up when you came home. I wouldn't swear to it, but I think the guy inside has got some sort of camera or maybe binoculars. I wondered if it was a reporter, the paparazzi.'

Cass laughed. 'Oh, stop it. You're being paranoid.'

Jake shrugged. 'Maybe, but I was just thinking, what would happen if the national press got hold of your connection with the case?'

'Got hold of what connection? I haven't *got* a connection. I saw him on the train – it's hardly headline news, is it? "Woman sees man on train."'

'Maybe you're right. But you don't know what his wife might have said about you.'

Cass groaned. 'Please, Jake, stop, will you,' and then added casually, 'Is there any chance you could get that case down for me?'

Jake looked heavenwards. 'Work, work, work, what on earth are you going to do without me?'

At which point Danny, still sitting on the end of the bed, sniffed miserably.

At the end of the lane where Cass and Jake lived, Mr Marshall had logged Jake's arrival and taken a couple of photos with the long lens on his new digital camera.

*   *   *

A few miles away in Little Lamport a stream of police officers, as industrious and diligent as worker ants, were busy carrying box after box of James Devlin's papers and personal effects out from the office he had had built above the double garage and stacking them neatly under the carport. Alongside the papers and folders were computers, screens, boxes of CDS, DVDs, files, folders, and God knows what else, all neatly sealed in evidence bags which were being carefully logged and double-checked before being packed into an unmarked navy blue Transit van.

Margaret Devlin watched their progress from the sitting-room window and bit her lip, holding back a great torrent of fury.

Detective Inspector Turner, the officer in charge of the investigation, who was sitting opposite her drinking tea and eating his way through a packet of Garibaldis, took it for grief, which was most probably a good thing. Margaret glanced at him. He was a large affable man with wavy grey hair and a rather natty moustache that made him look distinguished and added a slightly military air.

'We really appreciate your co-operation, Mrs Devlin. My men and I will try and ensure there is as little disruption to your day-to-day routine as possible. I realise that life can't be very easy for you at the moment.'

He could say that again; her solicitor had just rung to tell Margaret that an application had been made by the shareholders to freeze all James's assets. Why couldn't the bastard have had the decency to die quietly in his bed and leave her in peace? She really hoped Gordie Mann's weaselly friend tracked James down. Life would be so much simpler if James was dead – a heart attack or something quick and terminal – but obviously only if he hadn't been using the company funds as his own personal current account. Bastard. Outside in the run, Snoops, pressed tight up against the wire, threw back his head and howled miserably.

'I'm afraid I need to ask you a few more questions.' DI Turner's voice focused her attention.

'I'm so sorry,' she said. 'I was miles away.' If only.

He waved her apology away. 'It's perfectly understandable. Would you prefer to wait until your solicitor is present?'

Margaret shook her head. 'No, of course not, Inspector. I've got nothing to hide. Ask away.' She smiled at the WPC who was perched on the edge of the sofa, taking notes. The girl really didn't make the best of herself, a bit of eye makeup and a decent bra really wouldn't go amiss; what did they teach them at police training college?

The Detective Inspector took a deep breath as if he was about to launch into a big speech, but at that moment the au pair appeared at the sitting-room door, anxiously wringing her paws as she looked from one face to the other, finally settling on Margaret with those big brown watery eyes of hers.

'Missis Devlin?' The au pair smiled wanly at her. Margaret glared right back. This, after being told on numerous occasions that she wasn't to interrupt when Margaret had guests, even if the guests were in this case the police.

'Yes?' said Margaret, feigning interest; she still wasn't altogether sure what the girl's name was, despite her having been with them six months. It was something Eastern European, maybe Romania, which sounded like a cross between a sneeze and a hacking cough, and refused point-blank to stay in her head, even after she had written it down phonetically on a whole pile of post-it notes and stuck them at various key points around the house.

'What is it, dear?' she added, mostly for DI Turner's benefit. 'Only, as I'm sure you can see, I am a little busy at the moment.'

The girl smiled nervously. 'Sorry to disturb you, but this eeeez important.'

Margaret sniffed; that remained to be seen. Probably another defrosting, how-many-minutes-to-let-it-stand-between-microwaving emergency. She was tempted to suggest whatever-her-name-was went back into the kitchen and read the bloody packet, but held fire. The girl took this to be a green light.

'This won't take long, I just want to tell you that I have to leave now.' Margaret had to pick her way through the words, the girl's accent was as thick as a hand-knitted vest.

Margaret smiled indulgently at DI Turner and

then back at what's-her-name. 'No, dear, not yet. It's barely three o'clock,' she began, her eyes narrowing. 'It's not time for you to finish work yet. You finish later.' She tapped her watch for added emphasis. 'Later. Six o'clock.'

But the girl was insistent. 'No,' she said emphatically, shaking her head. 'No, I hef to go now.'

'No, you don't. You leave off at six, after you've cooked the children's supper. Then it will be time for you to go to your language class.' Margaret talked slowly, her smile stretched as tight as a drumskin as she enunciated every last word. God, the girl was such a bloody moron. 'I'll tell you what, why don't we talk about this later. I'm rather busy at the –'

But the girl would not be stopped. 'No, no, no, you not make of me any understanding. I have to go. Really. I do.' She mimed walking away, using two pale, podgy fingers to represent those dumpy-lard white legs of hers. 'Now.'

'Oh, I understand perfectly, dear,' said Margaret, keeping her tone as even as she could manage, while pulling a jolly 'sorry, what-can-you-do-face' for DI Turner. 'But you don't leave off until six. *Six*.' She held up six fingers. 'Six o'clock.'

The girl frowned. 'No, not six, I know six. I have to go to my mother's.'

'Your mother's?' snapped Margaret incredulously. 'What on earth do you mean, *your mother's*? Your mother lives in, in . . .' Margaret fished around for the exact location and, coming up empty, settled for, 'abroad.'

The girl's eyes lit up. 'Yes,' she said. 'Yes, that is it. Abroad, yes.'

'Yes?' said Margaret grimly, her awareness of DI Turner slipping away as her patience finally began to fail her. 'What the hell do you mean, yes? Yes what?'

'Yes, please, I am having to going to my mother's abroad.'

Margaret's eyes narrowed. 'When?'

The girl smiled beatifically 'Soon. But I have to leave here tonight. Now.'

'Excuse me for one moment,' said Margaret brightly to DI Turner as she got to her feet. 'I'm not sure precisely what is going on here.' And then to the girl, in a cooler tone: 'Perhaps we should discuss this later, my dear, or at least go into the kitchen to finish our conversation. The Detective Inspector really doesn't want to hear all our domestic –'

But the girl shook her head. 'No, no. I have not got to talk. I have no time. I have to go now. I have to pack.' It sounded like i-heftogonow-I heftopec.'

'No, you don't,' Margaret growled. 'We need to talk about this.'

The girl pulled herself upright, mouth narrowing down to an angry little slit. 'It is in my contract.'

Margaret stiffened. 'I'm sorry? What did you say?'

The girl pulled a great, dog-eared many-folded wedge of paper out from her overall pocket. 'Page four, it is in my contract, it says my mother's health it is not good. She is a sick woman.'

She waved the paper under Margaret's nose and then, for good measure, under DI Turner's. 'It says here that I am able go to assist her any time if she ring me.'

'And she rang you?' asked Margaret icily.

The girl nodded. 'Oh, yes. She ring me.'

'When?' snapped Margaret. 'When did she ring you?'

'A little while ago, maybe a few minutes, on my mobile. She say I have to go home. Excuse me, I have to go and pack now. I'm sorry.'

You will be, thought Margaret murderously.

The girl turned on her heel and made for the door at around the same time that DI Turner continued, 'As I was about to say, Mrs Devlin, I would appreciate if you could answer one or two small points. Although I can see that this may not be the moment. Perhaps you would like me to come back at a mutually convenient time?'

Margaret painted on a smile and waved the words away. 'No, not at all. It's fine, Inspector. I'm sure I can sort er . . .' the girl's name refused to come '. . . sort things out when you've gone. She has always been a little volatile, and her command of English, well, you know.' Margaret held up her hands to encompass all manner of craziness and misunderstanding. The Inspector smiled and nodded encouragingly, so Margaret carried on. 'James drew up her contract of employment. I really had no idea about the sick mother clause,' she said with false heartiness. 'Laughable, really. But it's so like him. Ah well. Now, what did you want to know?'

The Inspector seemed delighted that she had brought James up voluntarily. 'Did your husband always deal with your domestic arrangements? You know, the hiring and firing of staff and that sort of thing?'

'Yes, as a matter of fact, he did,' agreed Margaret; why not blame James for her dilemma? She had completely forgotten about the stupid girl's sick bloody mother. Fancy bringing it up now, at a time like this when it was quite obvious Margaret needed all the help she could get. Selfish little cow. Margaret felt a great wave of self-pity settling over her. What on earth was she going to do now? Who was going to clean and cook for the children? Good Lord, it was dreadful, unthinkable. Mrs Hill, her daily, would never be able to manage it all on her own.

Inspector Turner leaned forward. 'Are you all right, Mrs Devlin? Can I get you something? A glass of water?'

She pulled out a lacy hankie and sniffed back the tears. 'No, thank you. It's very kind, but I'll be fine, Inspector. James usually interviewed the girls we employed. In fact this is the first au pair I have ever actually chosen myself. James never really asked the right questions, if you follow me; he didn't seem to realise how important it was that they could cook or clean or look after the children adequately.' She left the implication hanging in the air between them.

DI Turner smoothed his moustache and then looked her up and down; it was a most provocative glance. Margaret felt herself blushing.

'So what do you think he chose them for, if not for their domestic skills?' the Inspector asked in a low voice.

Coyly Margaret looked down at the Oriental rug and noticed rather sourly that there were still biscuit crumbs on it from yesterday. 'I'm sure you can imagine that life with James hasn't always been easy. You must be aware of my husband's reputation, Inspector,' she said in a low voice.

DI Turner nodded. 'I am. But, to be honest, having met you, Mrs Devlin, I'm surprised.'

'Surprised?'

'Absolutely. I'm surprised that he bothered, not with a good-looking woman like you waiting at home.'

At least the WPC had the good grace to look away. Margaret's colour deepened to a warm, flattering pink.

Outside, the worker ants continued to empty James's office, and from upstairs somewhere came the throbbing bass beat of a pop song. Margaret couldn't work out whether it was coming from one of the children's rooms or the au pair's. Whoever it was, she would make sure somebody paid for it later.

By the time DI Turner finally got to the end of his questions, Margaret had some idea of exactly how bad things were. James had managed to head off into the sunset with around two million pounds, give or take a bob or two; not to mention various assets – property, shares, God knows what – which he had liquidated. DI Turner didn't mention Gordie Mann's investment, or the whereabouts of James's diary or address books. Perhaps they didn't know about them.

It seemed that even their house had been mort-gaged more times than was credible. In a nutshell, Margaret Devlin had nothing. In fact, given the state of the mortgage situation, probably consid-erably less than nothing.

Once he had finished speaking, Margaret stared at DI Turner for a very long time. Finally he looked down at his notes.

'And you say you have no current photos of your husband?'

Margaret shook her head. 'I'm afraid not. James liked to take photos, but he was practically phobic about being in them.'

DI Turner nodded thoughtfully. 'It's amazing. It appears that your husband has vanished, which, in an age of CCTV and modern technology, is close to a miracle. And have you any idea as to the whereabouts of his diary?' Margaret shook her head. It was true; she had no idea where it was now – the weaselly Mr Marshall could have taken it anywhere; same with James's address books.

DI Turner paused, looking out into the middle distance. 'I have to ask you, Mrs Devlin, if you have any idea where your husband might have gone?' he said, after what seemed like an eternity.

Margaret shook her head. After the revelations about the state of her finances, she didn't know how to speak, couldn't find the words to say exactly what it was she felt. But one thing was certain: any ideas she might have about James Devlin's whereabouts weren't going to be shared with the police – at least not until she had had her five-penn'orth. Maybe she would ring Gordie and see if he and his man had come up with anything.

If she could find him, James Devlin would rue the day he'd done this to her. She would make him pay in ways he had never ever dreamed of; he would be glad to give himself up to the police and possibly even Gordie by the time she had done with him.

'I'm afraid not, Inspector,' Margaret said, letting the words catch in her throat to emphasise her regret. 'Would you like some more tea, or would you prefer something a little stronger? To be perfectly honest, I think I could use a drop of brandy myself.'

DI Turner barely hesitated. 'I don't mind if I do,' he said, ignoring the look from the WPC on the sofa.

* * *

'Your husband, Mr David Hammond, has agreed, under the terms of his credit agreement with our company, to surrender the car in lieu of any further payments.' The repo man, who had been reading his little speech from a laminated prompt card, paused and tried out a smile. Cass wondered if perhaps it was suggested in the script. 'Do you understand?' he said. He had a nasty nasal twang.

Cass nodded. What was there not to understand?

'And then, obviously, once we've gone through all the formalities I'll write you out a receipt.'

'Oh well, that will really help,' said Cass grimly. The formalities presumably meant taking her car keys away.

He smiled at her again. 'You know, there's absolutely no need to be upset. You really don't have to worry. I mean, people do get upset, but this kind of thing happens all the time.'

'Not to me, it doesn't,' said Cass through gritted teeth. First thing she'd heard about her car going was a cheery note from the finance company arranging a date and a time.

'So let's see, where have we got to? Oh yes, here we are,' he said, running a finger down the laminated card. 'Do you have the documentation, or know where it can be located?' he read. The guy was a real genius. 'The log book –'

The car in question, a bright shiny black Vauxhall Corsa that Cass adored, had been a birthday present from David. *A present*, a nasty little voice in her head reminded her, not something to be surrendered in lieu of bloody payments.

Cass remembered it quite clearly, her birthday last year – David had stood by the back gate and handed her the keys, all smiles, all puffed up and magnanimous, doing his Winston Churchill impression, with matching inspirational speech.

'I know that it's been a real struggle and I know how much you've put up with, and how much you have supported me over the years, Cass – so now that my business is finally taking off, you deserve a proper thank you present. Happy Birthday, sweetheart.'

The business hadn't been the only thing that had taken off.

Cass handed the man the car keys, turned on her heel and walked back towards the cottage. There was still a car parked out in the lane. She couldn't see who was in it or whether he had a set of binoculars or, come to that, a bloody telephoto lens. And she didn't care.

'What about your receipt?' the man from the finance company called after her.

'Post it,' Cass snapped, without turning round.

'You know, I could help,' said Jake, as she reached the front door.

'This is true. I've got a bottle of Rioja in the kitchen that I can't get the cork out of, and you're a big strong lad.'

He looked at her and raised his eyebrows.

'Oh, all right, I know what you're saying and

I'm grateful, but I can't start over owing money.'

Undeterred, Jake followed her inside. 'But you wouldn't,' he said. 'We're friends. I've got bugger all to do with my money other than book Saga holidays and go on coach trips with the other old farts. I pre-date David by several years, I'm a better vintage. And anyway, I'm sure we could work something out –'

Cass handed him the bottle of wine and the corkscrew. 'Jake, that's disgusting.'

Jake shrugged. 'Worth a shot, though.'

'Stop pretending to be an old lecher.'

'Who's pretending?' he said. The cork popped out of the bottle with a reassuring tock. Cass took two glasses off the draining board.

'Should you be drinking during the day?' he asked.

'Well, I won't be driving, will I?' Cass said grimly.

'Oh, by the way, I asked that man what he was doing out in the lane,' continued Jake, pouring the wine. 'The one with the camera.'

'Really? And?'

'And he's some kind of traffic survey, apparently.'

'You wouldn't have thought there was much call for it out here. I wonder how much they pay per hour,' said Cass. 'I've just about enough money to put a deposit down on something –'

'Something?'

'OK, a clunker, something made from scrap with

six months' MOT and no brakes, the kind of thing that they warn you about on TV. Then again, I suppose I could always hire a car to get me and Danny down to Brighton.'

'Why don't you let me take you?'

'I'm a charity case, aren't I?'

Jake shrugged. 'No.'

Cass watched him over the rim of her wine glass.

'Oh, OK then, yes,' he conceded. 'But I don't mind, it's perfectly all right. I've always fancied myself as the kind of man who saves fallen women. Besides, it would be good to see Barney again.'

Cass nodded. 'When was the last time you saw him?'

Jake narrowed his eyes thoughtfully. 'God only knows. We were so pissed I can't even remember where we met, let alone where we went. The only thing I do remember quite clearly is one of his ex-wives coming into a station buffet and beating him over the head with a rolled-up umbrella.'

Cass frowned. 'What? Was he leaving her?'

'No, no – at least, I don't think so. Wherever we were, I seem to remember that the station buffet was the only place in town that you could get a drink at that time of the day.'

'Which was?'

Jake's face concertinaed in concentration. 'About half past eight, maybe nine o'clock in the morning, I think. Although, to be honest, I'm not a hundred per cent sure.'

Cass laughed. 'Those were the days, eh –'

'Sorry?'

'Well, you know, drinking all night, being young and stuff.'

Jake took a long pull on his wine and then said thoughtfully, 'I think it was last Christmas, actually.'

Margaret Devlin – in full makeup and suit – backed her black Audi with its personalised number plate out of the garage and, having navigated her way between a growing posse of reporters, headed into Ely. The petrol gauge was almost on the red and she wondered if they still had an account at the service station and, if not, whether her credit cards were good – and if not, what the hell she would do then.

Maybe Gordie could help her with that, too? Maybe she should suggest they meet for lunch, then cry on his shoulder. Having decided that he was her best bet, Margaret had already rung and given Gordie the name and address of a massage parlour she'd found a matchbook for in one of James's tracksuit pockets, together with the name of a hotel in Rhyll that she'd found a receipt for, a couple of months earlier, tucked inside a magazine in his briefcase – it had taken her hours to pick the lock and even longer to super glue it back in place when her patience failed her.

Margaret had known for years that Gordie's idea of retribution was considerably more biblical than anything the police could come up with, and that suited her just fine. Mind you, there *was* someone else who might know exactly where James was hiding, and Margaret planned to drive over there and find out.

Over the years Margaret had hunted and tracked and traced and found all manner of skeletons in James's closet – trouble was, of course, that the cleverer and more perceptive she had got over time, the more devious and cunning James had become. The bastard. Oh, on the surface he might well appear handsome and laid-back and oh so bloody charming, but she knew that it was all a front. Sometimes Margaret thought that theirs was less a marriage, more a game of espionage, duplicity and double-dealing.

'Oh wow, look, Miss – Miss Hammond, look – fossilised dinosaur pooh. Can I buy some?' said a small curly-headed boy; he was holding up a lump of greyish brown rock. 'Please?'

'Eeeeeeeuyyuuuh, no, put it down, you'll get it all over your hands,' said the small girl standing next to him, her nose wrinkled up, her expression one of total disgust. 'What does it smell like?'

Cass, who was still very slightly hung-over, said, 'It's all right, it's so old it's turned to stone, like the other fossils we saw.' She peered at the label and, squinting, read the text. 'The proper name for them is coprolites and they are between sixty-five and one hundred and forty-four million years old.' Around about the same age as she felt today.

The little girl was not impressed. The boy sniffed the lump speculatively, watched by a couple of the other children, just in case there was some lingering whiff of dinosaur's bum.

Cass was one of the fielders and catchers on Danny's school trip, making sure that nobody made a break for it while they were shepherded round the Natural History Museum. Despite his promise to Danny, David hadn't shown up.

It was a long day, longer after a bottle of Rioja, and several post-repossession glasses of Archers and orange the night before.

'How much is ten pounds, Mrs Hammond?'

'Ten pounds is seven pounds more than you've got,' Cass said to a chubby little girl clutching a large fluffy turtle. 'Now go and put it back.'

They had been in the museum shop for maybe ten minutes; long enough for a line of children clutching pencils and postcards and key rings to form at the tills, but not so long that fist fights and biting had broken out.

'Cass?' She turned at the sound of her name. Danny's class teacher grinned and tapped her watch. 'Can we hurry it along?'

She nodded, very carefully in case her hangover broke loose again. 'Shouldn't be long now. They're more or less all done. Just the paying.'

'Only the coach is here, and you know what the driver's like.'

The checkout lines were moving fast and, aided

and abetted by the rest of the helpers, Cass guided her posse back into the main pack.

Her head ached, her feet ached – actually, there wasn't much that didn't ache. It was barely half an hour past lunchtime. Across a sea of faces, Danny waved and triumphantly held aloft a diplodocus to add to his dinosaur collection.

Cass looked around at the rest of the group, helpers and children – soon they would be saying goodbye to everyone for the summer. Unexpectedly, Cass felt a lump in her throat. What if going to Brighton was all a big mistake, what if David was right, what if it really was all her fault, after all?

Cass sighed and looked away, blinking furiously. Sometimes life felt much too complicated. It wasn't that there was anything she couldn't cope with, but just not all at once. She tried to sniff back a nasty tidal wave of self-pity and tears. Maybe before she ran away to Brighton she ought to wait and see how things turned out. Maybe . . . But before Cass could form the rest of the thought, a voice called out, 'This way, everybody, the coach is here.' The head teacher waved her arms enthusiastically.

Cass swallowed hard. What the hell was she supposed to do? Anxious that no one should see how close she was to tears, Cass looked across the road – and immediately froze.

There, large as life, standing on the edge of the kerb hailing a taxi, stood Mr Peaches, James Devlin. Cass looked again in case her eyes were playing tricks and to her amazement he looked up, caught her eye, grinned and waved with what looked like genuine delight at seeing her. In the same moment a cab pulled up and he climbed inside.

Cass had stopped mid-stride; she felt hot and strange – her stomach doing that odd nippy thing that's all about desire and attraction and in this case bringing a queue of shopaholic mixed infants to an abrupt and potentially catastrophic halt.

'Are you all right?' asked Danny's class teacher, who was riding point towards the back of the crocodile.

Slightly bemused, Cass looked around, trying to regain her composure. Meanwhile James Devlin sailed past them in a taxi, grinning and waving.

Cass was completely dumbstruck. If he was on the run with two million quid of other people's money surely he ought to be in hiding in an isolated cottage somewhere, not hailing taxis bold as you like in broad daylight. What the hell was he playing at?

With her eyes still firmly fixed on the cab, Cass moved aside so the children could clamber aboard the coach.

'Are you OK?' said Danny's teacher anxiously. 'You look as if you've seen a ghost.'

Cass shook her head. 'It's OK. I'm a bit tired, that's all.'

'God, tell me about it,' said the woman. 'Everyone is going to be dead on their feet by the time we get back tonight.' She paused. 'I just wanted to say that I was really sorry to hear about you and David. If you ever want to talk . . .' She left the sentence and the invitation hanging between them.

Cass tacked a smile on over the dark, sad feeling that, thank God, was receding and also surfacing less and less as the weeks went on. 'Thanks, that's really kind, but I don't know what I want to say.'

'I understand. It must be hard for you.' The woman nodded. 'I don't know how I'd cope, to be honest. I taught Abby, you know,' she added conversationally. 'It must have been awful, being left for someone so young and so pretty . . .'

It was well after nine when Cass finally pushed open the back door of the cottage. The walk up from school had nearly finished them both off. Cass cursed David for taking the car, dropped her and Danny's bags on the kitchen table, and sighed. It felt so good to be home and finally get her shoes off – if they could, her feet would have broken into a round of spontaneous applause as she padded across the cold floor and plugged the kettle in.

Meanwhile the cat oozed in from the garden and started a long melodious whinge that included veiled threats regarding supper and the horrendous lack of attention, along with various accusations of abject neglect and cruel, cruel apathy.

Danny trailed in well behind the cat, dragging his fleece jacket behind him, hollow-eyed and pale as skimmed milk, still clutching his new dinosaur to his chest like a holy relic.

Cass smiled and snuggled him up against her. 'OK, honey-bun, we're home now. Upstairs, clothes off and into your pyjamas. I'll get you a glass of milk and then it's teeth, toilet and straight into bed – 'K?'

Danny started to say something, but Cass gently shushed him. 'And before you ask, no – it's way too late for a story tonight. Off you go. I'll be up in a while to tuck you in.'

Cass had barely got around to dangling a teabag in a mug when there was a knock at the door. Punch drunk from too many hours awake and one too many mixed infants, Cass didn't bother with the security chain and opened up, expecting to find Jake and Milo standing on the doorstep. Instead, framed in the doorway, was a small angry whippet of a woman, dressed in red high heels and a sharp navy suit. She had an expensive haircut, and her exquisitely made-up face was screwed into a mask of fury.

'So, at last we meet,' she snapped. It sounded ridiculous and melodramatic, like something out of a black-and-white Sunday afternoon movie.

Cass stared at her. 'What?'

The woman laughed maniacally.

Maybe Hammer House of Horror, Cass thought. All she needed was a cape to swing dramatically over one shoulder. 'I'm sorry? Do I know you?' Cass asked.

'Oh, don't you come over all innocent with me,' the woman growled. 'I've been waiting for you for bloody hours. You've been with him, haven't you? In some little love nest somewhere, shagging away like rabbits. You don't fool me for a second, Mrs Hammond.'

The penny dropped; it was the barking mad woman and possibly her dog too.

'Look, I'm very sorry,' said Cass, as calmly as she could manage, 'but you're mistaken. I've just got back home from a school trip to London with my son. This is crazy. I don't even know your husband. I met him twice on the train and that is all. Honestly. I'm really sorry, but I can't be any more help than that. Do you understand?'

The woman hadn't moved an inch, so Cass continued, 'I'm not having an affair with him. I barely know him. Now, I would be most grateful if you would please leave, go home, go away, or I'll have to call the police.'

Margaret Devlin stared at her, and then her face went purple. '*You'll* call the police? That's bloody rich. They want him for embezzlement, you know. Two million quid apparently. The bastard. Did he tell you he'd share the money with you? Keep you in the lap of luxury? Take you away from all this? Did he? Did he?' She gazed around the kitchen as if it was a swamp. 'Is that what he told you? Where is he? Is he here?'

110

'Please,' said Cass, trying to fend her off. 'This is ridiculous. Just go, please.'

'Don't you tell me what to do, you bitch. I have a right to know where he is. He's still my husband, whatever he's done. I have a right to –'

'Oh, for God's sake!' This was the last thing Cass needed. 'Are you deaf?' Cass snapped, rapidly losing her temper. 'I've told you once – you're talking to the wrong person, Mrs Devlin. I have absolutely no idea where he –' But the last few words stuck in her throat as in her imagination she saw James Devlin climbing into a taxi in Kensington. Damn. She did have an idea. Not that Margaret Devlin noticed.

'Whatever you say, I don't believe you,' Margaret yelled. 'I heard that message on the answer machine, remember? You might fool the bloody police, but you don't fool me for an instant. Oh no, not for one single solitary moment –' And with this Margaret Devlin stepped forward, chubby little hands raised, fists clenched.

Cass gasped in amazement and horror, unable to move, but before Mrs Devlin had a chance to land a punch or whatever it was she had in mind, Jake appeared behind her with Milo.

'What the hell is going on here?' Jake growled – unlike Milo, who hung back, looking on with mild amusement, all the while wagging his tail enthusiastically; some guard dog.

Margaret Devlin swung round mid strop. 'Who the fuck are you?' she snarled. Cass shook her head. God, sometimes it was so useful to be tall and muscley and male.

'More to the point, who the fuck are you?' countered Jake, not giving an inch.

Pulling herself to her full height, Margaret Devlin pointed an accusing finger at Cass. 'This woman is having an affair with my husband. The pair of them have taken two million pounds of other people's money, not to mention the bonds, the stocks – everything. That miserable bastard has left me bankrupt and begging, and I plan to have his balls in a basket – and hers too. Someone has got to pay for this and it's not going to be me.' She glared at Cass, who was still rooted to the spot. 'Do you hear me?' she screamed.

'I should think half Norfolk heard you,' said Jake. And with this Margaret Devlin burst into tears and threw herself against him, sobbing hysterically, her tiny fists hammering against his chest in a fury of frustration.

Jake held up his hands in a big, no-touch, hands-off gesture. He stepped back, making no effort to comfort her or even to hold her away from him, so after a few moments the woman rather self-consciously withdrew and pulled herself together, at least enough to teeter back down the path in her impossibly high heels.

As she got to the gate, Margaret turned and said, 'You haven't heard the last of me. I'm going to get you, you bitch, if it's the last thing I do.'

And with that she strutted away down the lane.

Jake, shaking his head, watched her go. 'How in God's name do you women drive in those things?' he said.

Cass shrugged. 'I don't know, I've never tried.'

'I suppose she came round dolled up to the nines hoping that lover boy would still be here and she could show him exactly what it was he was missing.'

'She did that, all right,' said Cass in disbelief, and as she spoke her voice fractured and broke, and shock rippled through her like little earth tremors. Cass began to shake, and then she shook some more and then she began to cry and then she realised to her horror that she couldn't stop.

'W-what-what a bloody cow. I can't handle this, Jake,' Cass sobbed. 'I don't know what to do. What the hell am I going to do? She said she was going to get me. I haven't done anything. She's nuts –'

Gently, Jake put his arm round her and guided Cass back into the kitchen, Milo trotting close behind.

'Mummy?' Danny called from the top of the stairs, sounding anxious. 'What's happening? Are you all right?'

Cass didn't know what to say, and even when she opened her mouth to try no words came.

'It's all right, Dan, your mum's just tired – she needs a cup of tea,' said Jake brightly. 'Tell you what, why don't you get into bed and put on a story tape and Mummy will be up to see you in a little while.'

Danny considered for a few seconds. 'Can Milo come up?'

'Yep, I think that will be just fine. Call him,' said Jake.

Danny, dressed in his pyjamas, bobbed down on the landing and called, and obediently the dog padded upstairs, followed by the cat, who was afraid he might miss something and hated to see a woman cry.

In the kitchen Cass was shaking so hard she couldn't hold the mug Jake handed her.

'It's all right,' he said gently.

Cass looked up at him. 'No, it's not all right. It's all crap. I bet I look like I've done ten rounds with a welterweight, and I can't hold a bloody teacup. No, it's not all right at all. I'm falling apart, Jake.'

'It's hardly surprising, is it?' he said, pouring them both a stiff gin and tonic, as tea quite obviously hadn't done the trick. 'You're suffering from delayed shock: David, Abby, the job thing, this bloody woman. You haven't really let yourself cry about David yet, have you?'

Cass stared at him. 'You've been listening to *Woman's Hour* again, haven't you?'

Jake's expression didn't change. He dropped a slice of lemon into the gin and handed it to her, as Cass continued:

'Of course I've cried about David. I've cried so

114

much I thought my head would explode, but I'm trying hard to stop. I mean, what good is it going to do to keep on crying? And besides, how would you know?'

'Oh, for fuck's sake, Cass, I've known you for years, I can tell. You're full up to the brim but afraid to let go in case, once you do, you'll lose control. You're terrified of chaos – you're –' He looked at her watching him and frowned. 'What?'

Cass peered at him over the rim of her glass and laughed. 'Was it *Woman's Hour* or *Cosmo*?'

'I'm right, though, aren't I?'

'Probably, but I've got to keep it together for Danny.'

'I know you have, and you are, but that doesn't mean to say you can't cry or be angry or sad. You're not a fucking saint, Cass, and nobody is going to think any the worse of you if the buses don't always run on time.'

Cass looked out of the window; the sky was darkening slowly. 'What if she comes back? You know, Mrs Bunny-Boiler?'

Jake hesitated. 'I don't think she will.' And then more robustly, 'No, she's had her say now. I'm sure it'll be fine. She'll probably go home and calm down.'

Cass laughed. 'God, Jake, you are such a terrible liar. Of course she won't calm down. She'll be back. I'm the only clue she's got. She wants to try and catch me out; she's convinced that I'm seeing her husband.'

'But you're not. I think you ought to ring the police. They'll have a word with her, you know, warn her off. Tell her to keep away.'

Cass looked at him, not sure if she was able to say the words aloud. 'She frightened me, Jake.'

His expression softened. 'I know. How about if you and Danny come round and stay at my place for the night? I really don't mind.' He made cow eyes at her.

Cass laughed. 'It's not going to work. You're not my type.'

He aped a broken heart. 'You mean I'm not a bastard.'

'Besides,' said Cass, deciding to ignore him, 'I've got to front it out otherwise they win, don't they? David, the madwoman – up until now this cottage has always been my refuge, the place I've escaped from the rest of the world.' She looked around at the homely little kitchen, warm and inviting and lit by soft lamplight.

'It still is,' said Jake gently.

She stared at Jake and sighed. 'It doesn't feel like it at the moment.'

'It'll be OK,' he said. 'It will, really. I promise.'

Cass wasn't convinced. She jiggled the ice around in her glass and then looked up at Jake. 'I saw him today.'

Jake frowned. 'Who? Not David again?'

Cass shook her head. 'No. James Devlin.'

Jake's mouth dropped open. 'Really? Where? You're not really screwing him, are you?'

116

'No, of course I'm not. For God's sake, Jake. No, he was getting into a cab in Kensington. And you know what, it didn't look like he'd got a care in the world.'

'Bloody hell. What are you going to do about it? You should ring the police.'

'I know. But there's part of me thinks bloody good luck to him. Fancy being married to her. And then . . .' She looked away. 'Oh, I don't know. Maybe I was wrong, maybe it wasn't him.'

'So what *are* you going to do?'

Cass smiled. 'I'm going to finish packing and go to Brighton for the summer. And then – well, who knows.' She lifted her glass in a toast. 'Here's to a fresh start and mad old artists.'

Jake laughed. 'I'll drink to that.'

Sitting at the end of the lane, Mr Marshall handed over to his replacement, thanking his lucky stars that neither Margaret Devlin nor Cass Hammond had spotted him still sitting in the car. He'd have to have a word with Gordie Mann and get him to explain to Mrs Devlin that hounding their main lead was not a very bright idea. He'd been talking to Cass's neighbour that morning – friendly sort of chap. He'd told him all about her and the boy going on a school trip for the day and moving down to the South Coast.

While her neighbour went down to Tesco's, Mr Marshall had slipped into Mrs Hammond's house for an hour or so and had a good look round. He had found all kinds of interesting things, including her new address in Brighton and some rather nice paintings, and while he was there he tapped her phone, because although there was nothing there that directly linked Cassandra Hammond to James Devlin, he had a gut feeling that he was on the right track.

4

Later, in his office, Gordie Mann looked across his desk at Marshall's report and sighed. 'So tell me again, exactly what am I getting for my money?'

Mr Marshall smiled. 'Patience. James Devlin is clever, rich and resourceful, and I told you when we first started that jobs like this are never short haul. But I do believe we're closing in – call it a gut instinct, call it a hunch – call it a professional nose for a hot lead.'

Patience was not Gordie's strong point. He looked up at Mr Marshall from the file containing his interim report. It said all the right things, but then again, so did Marshall. 'Well, let's hope your nose is accurate, because you've got fuck all else to go on.'

Mr Marshall winced. 'I am having to make best use of our resources.'

'Meaning?'

'I've got operatives watching Mrs Devlin and others engaged in surveillance on Mrs Hammond.

I've put out all manner of feelers, interviewed close contacts, business associates, friends, employees – people at the railway station, people at Mr Devlin's offices. All we can do is wait. Mr Devlin's bound to make a mistake sooner or later, get too cocky. Given a little time, he'll probably try to make contact.'

'With?'

'Mrs Hammond.'

'Look, I don't mean to piss on your fireworks, Mr Marshall, you come highly recommended, but you've got no proof there is any kind of link between this woman and James.'

Mr Marshall sighed. 'In my line of business, you have to trust your instincts.'

'All right, so who else is in the frame?'

'His dog.'

Gordie stared at him. 'What?'

'His dog. I was talking to the family gardener and he said that James Devlin loved his dog more than anything else on earth. Including his children.'

Gordie snorted. 'Right, and I'm paying you my hard-earned money for this rubbish, am I? All the hours I've been billed for, and you've come up with nothing concrete. You know, I'm tempted to ditch the softly-softly approach and send the heavy mob in, crack a few heads. Some bastard must know something.'

Mr Marshall looked at him and in a low, even voice said, 'And who exactly are you going to beat up, Mr Mann?'

Gordie hesitated for a few moments and sighed. There was no obvious candidate; although, at the moment, Mr Smart-Arse Marshall came pretty high up on his list.

'So then, as he came towards me, I grabbed him by the balls and, as he pitched forward, I pulled him down and kneed him in the face – Buuuff – just like that. And his glass eye popped out and rolled across the floor like a big green-and-white marble.'

Cass caught the tail end of the conversation as she came in from one of the spare bedrooms in Barney's mother's flat which Barney was currently using as a storeroom cum studio. Cass had been working there for most of the afternoon, stock-taking, while Danny crayoned and played with his toys and watched TV on a portable Barney had loaned her.

When Cass had stopped to make some tea, Mrs Hesquith-Morgan-Roberts had said, 'You know, Daniel could come in here and watch television with me, if you like. I really don't mind. To be perfectly honest, it would be nice to have the company. Seems a shame to shut him away in there.'

It was around four o'clock, when Mrs HMR liked to have a cup of Earl Grey with a slice of lemon, and Cass suspected she probably added a slug of gin when no one was looking.

'And I've got chocolate biscuits and some sort

of pink bottled milkshake affair in the fridge that Barney seems to think will do me good,' she added. 'A boy doesn't want to be cooped up in there all afternoon. We could play cards. I could teach him how to play poker. I don't suppose you know how to play five-card stud, do you?' she had asked Danny conversationally as he trotted across the room and wriggled himself up on to the sofa.

When Cass had checked a few minutes later, the pair of them were engrossed in children's TV, each sucking a strawberry milkshake through a straw.

An hour or so later Cass folded the final box top down. Enough was enough. Over the last few days, since arriving in Brighton she had cleaned the flat, worked in the shop, met his mother, and taken a complete inventory of all Barney's stock – God, the man was a hoarder.

She sorted through all manner of things at his mum's: the great piles of boxes, crates and cartons in his flat downstairs, things stacked precariously in the little back room at the shop, and of course the things on the shelves in the shop. Armed with Barney's digital camera, she now not only had numbers, sizes and descriptions, but photos, all neatly taped, along with their location, in a bound file. It had been like trying to do a stocktake in Aladdin's cave.

Jake had driven them down in his Vauxhall. Barney had welcomed them at the door with fish and chips, mushy peas and champagne cocktails.

Things had gone very sharply downhill from there. Cass had had the good sense to stop after two glasses; the others had managed two bottles before getting bored fiddling about with champagne, bitters and sugar cubes and decided, after some debate, to concentrate instead on the brandy. It had taken Barney two days to recover.

'Danny, I hope you're being a good boy for Mrs Hesquith-Morgan-Roberts,' Cass said, pulling the bedroom door to, and looking across at the demure old lady sitting in a large armchair by the window. The name was twice the size she was, as was the large red silk hat she was currently wearing. Everything else, she had assured Cass when they first met, was Chanel or Norman Hartnell.

Perched on the sofa opposite, Danny, eyes wide, mouth open, was totally engrossed in the tale of how Barney's mum had thwarted some dastardly villain years before. She did all the actions, too, just in case Danny might miss the point.

'How's work going?' Mrs Hesquith-Morgan-Roberts asked conversationally, pouring herself a generous measure of gin, followed by a whisper of tonic from the drinks tray conveniently set on a table alongside her.

'Oh, OK, not bad. I've got everything more or less sorted out now, I think.'

The old lady shook her head. 'Not Barney's bloody boxes – your art, your painting, *your passion*.'

Cass smiled. 'It's been a while since I did any

real work. It takes time to settle into a new place, but I'm getting there. It's been a tricky few months in lots of ways.'

Mrs Hesquith-Morgan-Roberts nodded. 'So I hear. Daniel tells me that you illustrate children's books.'

'That's right, although I do other things too. I exhibit, do some occasional magazine work, design cards, teach a bit, run a few courses . . .' Cass paused. Said out loud, it sounded quite good; but David was right, she usually just scraped by. Still, it meant that she could do the thing she loved best. It would be good to get back into work again. Not being able to paint wasn't just about moving house or starting a new job. It was about finding her voice again. But it was coming back.

Cass was beginning to see things in terms of illustration, always a sure sign she was on the mend. Mrs HMR in her hat, perched like a small angular bird on the huge chair and framed by white nets against a sunlit window, made Cass's mouth water. Danny, sipping from his glass, looking up at the older woman, caught in profile. Maybe tonight or tomorrow she could make a start sketching, maybe some pen and ink, maybe a little gouache . . . The thought of it made her smile.

On the far side of the room Mrs HMR, oblivious to Cass's thoughts, was still talking. 'How wonderful. And real pictures, Daniel said, not like those bloody daubs Bartholomew knocks off. I'm always saying to him, "Bartholomew, I have no idea what they are supposed to be. Why don't you paint something real, something that people recognise? People want proper pictures, not a cryptic crossword." Why can't he paint real things – fruit or something, or a nice dog? I asked Daniel to bring some of your work up for me to look at, some of the books – you don't mind, do you?' asked Mrs Hesquith-Morgan-Roberts, smiling beatifically at Cass.

'No, not at all.'

The old lady nodded to Danny. 'See, I told you she wouldn't mind.' And then to Cass, 'Would you care for a G & T? I did offer Daniel one, but he said he didn't think he was allowed. We were just talking about the good old days, Daniel and I. It's so very nice to have someone to talk to. Bartholomew is always busy running around, getting married, buying things, and painting peculiar pictures. He never has any time for me these days. His father was exactly the same, you know. I remember once we were in New York – 1952, September – we'd been to Macy's and I said to Gerald – that was his father's name – I said . . .'

Cass leapt into the torrent. 'I'm terribly sorry, but I'm afraid we really have to go. I promised Danny that we'd go for a walk with Milo and then it'll be suppertime. Thank you for letting him sit with you.'

'My pleasure. It was lovely to have him here,' said Barney's mother brightly. 'He can always come back; maybe when you're at work? I appreciate that you might be a little nervous leaving him here with a frail old biddy, but when the carers are here . . .' She let the suggestion hang in mid air and then added, 'I pay them, they won't mind. Besides, I've promised Daniel that I'll teach him how to play cards. I also said that one day when they take me out for an airing he could come too – just along the front. We could have ice cream.'

'That's very kind. We'll see. We've got to be going now, though,' said Cass, and then to Danny, 'Say thank you to Mrs Hesquith-Morgan-Roberts.'

Danny pulled a face; the one that was meant to imply he was perfectly happy where he was, thank you very much. Cass pulled one right back.

'Now,' she growled, adding a little steel to the tone, just in case he thought she might be joking.

'He can stay longer if he likes, dear. I really don't mind,' said Mrs HMR, all innocence.

Cass looked at the pair of them and smelt a conspiracy.

'We have to be going,' she said to Mrs HMR in exactly the same tone she had used on Danny.

'Why don't you call me Mrs H? Everyone else does. Actually, I'm rather peckish too. I've asked Charlie to bring me an Indian when he comes on duty,' she said. Charlie was one of her carers, a gorgeous Caribbean guy, who Barney referred to as his mother's keeper.

'Well, I hope you enjoy it,' said Cass, fixing a bead on Danny and beckoning him towards her.

Very reluctantly, the boy clambered down off the sofa and, heavy footed, followed Cass out.

'She was going to show me her tattoo,' grumbled Danny as they got out on to the landing.

'Well, you're not to let her.' Cass shook her head; she'd thought her own mother was bad enough. She wiped a smear of strawberry milk-shake off Danny's chin.

'Hermione was telling me about these guys who –'

'Hermione?'

Danny nodded. 'Uhuh, Mrs H. She said it was all right for me to call her Hermione. As you're living in sin with her only son, she said that it almost made us family. Anyway, there were these men in a place she went to in Paris.' He screwed up his face thoughtfully as if trying to work out how best to describe it. 'She went there with her lover Amelio – it sounded a bit like a shop or a hotel or something, somewhere where they play music on a piano and drink a lot, and the ladies don't wear very many clothes.'

Cass stared at him. Fortunately, before he could finish, Charlie came into the hall, saw them on the stairs, high-fived Danny, grinned at Cass, and then jogged on up carrying his holdall and a bag of takeaway Indian.

'How is Mrs H today?' Charlie called back over his shoulder. Before Cass could answer, Danny said, 'She's cool.'

127

Cass looked down at her son. They had been in Brighton under a week and already he'd gone cosmopolitan.

It had taken Margaret Devlin almost the same amount of time to realise that Snoops the dog had gone missing. When she first noticed that the run in the driveway near the back door was empty, she had organised Mrs Hill, her daily, to check under the beds and in the obvious places like the shed, the children's bedrooms and in James's old office, just in case the police had accidentally shut the stupid thing in while they had been clearing the place out. After all, when James was working from home, it liked to lie under his desk. But no, no dog.

Over coffee, Margaret tried to work out exactly when it was she last remembered seeing the damn thing.

She asked the children, she asked Mrs Hill, and rang Bob the man who cut their grass and tidied the garden, and they all came to the same conclusion: Snoops had vanished at around the same time as What's-her-name had packed up and left.

Bloody typical. Margaret did consider ringing the police and reporting that the dog was missing. After all, Snoops was a pedigree, he'd cost a bloody fortune, and dog-napping surely had to be an offence. But in the end Margaret decided against it; she had enough on her plate and hated the bloody animal anyway. It was one less thing to worry about, though God alone knew what the girl thought she was going to do with it. It wasn't as if she could take it to . . . Margaret struggled for the name of wherever it was her mother lived.

She wondered briefly if the dog might turn up. After all, it was chipped and wearing its collar with some sort of highly expensive tag welded to it. But by the end of the week, when there was no sign, Margaret forgot all about Snoops and What's-her-name.

A Mrs Caroline-Anne Lancaster of Epping, on holiday with her husband Robert and their three children, found James Devlin's clothes on a Cornish beach while she was out walking the family dog. At first Mrs Lancaster thought they might belong to someone who had gone off for a swim, but when she came back over an hour and a half later and they were still there, she raised the alarm.

The small cairn of possessions apparently marking James Devlin's last few minutes on earth was an orderly little arrangement. The white hand-made shirt neatly folded, the red silk tie and discreet gold cuff links tucked into the pocket of James's favourite Armani suit, all rolled up into a tight bundle, his monogrammed socks tucked carefully inside his handmade black leather brogues. His cream silk boxer shorts were notable by their absence, but then again who wanted to be found naked, however good your body or snappy your tan?

The wind was fierce that day and flurries of sand had banked up around James's clothes, making it look in the photos as if they were emerging from below the beach, making their way to the surface, revealing James's secrets.

In the inside jacket pockets were various credit cards, a brown calfskin wallet, the keys to his silver BMW – which was parked up on the clifftop – and keys and a receipt for a holiday chalet James had been renting while he was in hiding, a few minutes' drive back down the coast. All that and a suicide note.

The note, handwritten with a fountain pen on thick watermarked hand-made paper read:

I'm so sorry, but I really can't go on like this. Those people who know me best know that I feel as if I have been living a lie for the past few years. I'm afraid that the money has all gone. I've taken some gambles that have paid off and rather more that haven't. I'm sure some people will see the former as brave, inspirational decisions and the latter as stupid, foolhardy mistakes. I realise now that I should have said something earlier, asked for advice or help – but I didn't. I was arrogant enough to believe that I could make things come right if I only tried hard enough and stuck to my guns. I'm truly sorry for the pain I've caused everyone. I know I have been terribly foolish and I feel genuinely

*sorry for those people who believed and
trusted in me to see them through the dark
times and share their joy in the good. I leave
everything that can be salvaged from this
chaos to my dearest darling wife Margaret,
who has had to put up with so much over
the years.*

*Goodbye
James*

Dearest darling wife? Margaret Devlin, watched
by DI Turner, read the note twice. Tears filled her
eyes and spilled unchecked down her discreetly
made-up cheeks. Fortunately, the note was sealed
into a polythene bag to retain any fingerprints and
forensic evidence, so it wasn't affected.

'Oh my God,' Margaret whispered thickly,
wringing the life out of the hankie DI Turner had
handed her. 'Oh my God, I don't know what to
say.'

DI Turner patted her thigh gently. 'It's all right,
Mrs Devlin . . . Margaret,' he murmured. 'I quite
understand. You don't have to say anything. It's
all right.'

It most certainly was all right – if it was true.
Margaret struggled not to laugh. James really was
dead, thank God. She sighed with relief. Her tears
were of pure undiluted joy. Finally, after all these years,
the bastard had done the decent thing. Better still, he
had paid a huge extra premium on his insurance each

year to cover him in case of suicide. James was dead and she was rich. It was all she could do not to hug DI Turner and skip round the living room. God, she was so excited. Trying hard to retain control, Margaret took a deep breath and let the tears fall, all the while suppressing a huge grin.

Margaret would be comfortably off. James's business was a limited company, so the shareholders had no lien on his personal assets. Besides, what sort of bastards would steal the bread out of the mouths of a grieving widow and her two darling, fatherless children? The life insurance would presumably pay out on the house too, and she could always downsize and free up some of the equity. Ummm, it felt like a plan and the first really good news Margaret had had in days. Maybe the bank would extend her overdraft till the insurance paid out. She would need that little black suit now. Fantastic.

Artfully, Margaret dabbed at her eyes with DI Turner's hankie, very careful not to smudge her eye makeup. She would assume the role of grieving widow at the children's school too, see if she couldn't get the fees paid out of their hardship fund; maybe get them boarding places. After all, James had been the one who had always wanted children; she'd never been keen. It was a bit like getting the dog, really – all very well and good in theory, but in practice all the hands-on stuff, the mess and the fuss and the clearing up, fell squarely on her shoulders.

Oh yes, boarding places would be such a good idea. She would try to persuade the school that the pair of them needed a stabilising influence. Yes, it all made perfect sense. And if the children went then Margaret wouldn't need such a large house. Obvious, really. She wouldn't need to pay an au pair, wouldn't need a house with a nanny annex or a playroom. She could buy something new, something off-plan on the new luxury estate out at Heathmore that James said was a tasteless nouveau riche abomination. Maybe one of the executive townhouses with all that creamy Italian marble and light wood. Ummmm. Oh yes, that was a wonderful idea.

James liked places with character, which roughly translated meant uneven floors and mice, whereas Margaret preferred life to be more wipe clean and draught-free. God, she was so glad he was dead. Better late than never.

Sitting alongside her on the couch, DI Turner patted her thigh again. 'Would you like me to arrange for a pot of tea or something? Or maybe phone someone, a friend or a neighbour? One way and another, you've had a rough few weeks, haven't you?'

Margaret nodded, still not quite trusting herself to speak. For the first time she noticed that DI Turner had nice eyes.

'Well, hopefully it's all over now,' he said. 'Let me be the first to offer you my most sincere condolences.'

She smiled and caught hold of his hand. 'Thank you, Inspector, you've been so very kind.'

He coloured slightly and then said, 'Only doing my job, Mrs Devlin. Obviously, there are a few formalities that will still have to be dealt with.'

Margaret sniffed bravely. He'd got quite a nice way with him for a policeman; good jaw, strong hands. She wondered fleetingly how much a detective inspector made a year.

'We are hoping,' DI Turner continued, 'that our colleagues in Cornwall will come up with a body over the next few days, in which case things will be relatively straight forward.'

Margaret felt an icy finger track down her spine. She stared at him. 'What?'

'A body – James's body.' He was watching her face intently. 'Now don't go upsetting yourself,' he began.

'I don't understand,' she said.

DI Turner's face contorted into a grimace. Margaret sensed that something was about to go horribly wrong.

'What happens if they don't find a body?' she whispered, hardly daring to contemplate what the consequences might be.

'Well, things get a bit complicated then, I'm afraid. You see, no one actually saw your husband arrive at the beach, or go into the sea. No one saw him swim out. To be perfectly honest, there aren't any signs of him being there at all.'

'But his car was parked close by, and then there were his clothes,' Margaret protested.

'Yes, but unfortunately that doesn't prove anything. Anyone could have driven it there, anyone could have parked it.' He spoke slowly, as if she was a child or hard of hearing.

'But what about his clothes? His wallet, *his credit cards*?'

DI Turner looked at her. 'Please, don't upset yourself, Margaret. You have to understand that we're just doing our job.'

'What exactly are you saying, Inspector?' snapped Margaret icily.

'Well, your husband could have very easily put those things there and simply walked away – or got an accomplice to do it for him. He left a note, so must have been assuming his things would be found. Now, I'm not saying that that is what happened, I'm just suggesting that it is a possibility. We need to find a body to declare your husband dead. If we don't find one . . . in cases such as these it is usual, after a period of time, to apply to the courts to have a person declared dead. Once that's done, the legal side can be sorted out – you know, the financial stuff: wills, bequests, insurance claims . . .'

Insurance claims? Margaret's eyes narrowed. 'A period of time? What does that mean?'

'It's normally a minimum of seven years, although in cases like your husband's, where there are valid reasons for believing he may have falsified his death to escape prosecution, it may well be longer. A lot longer. And I'm afraid that, unless there is a body, no death certificate can be issued. I think you would be best talking to your solicitor.' He paused and squeezed her hand. 'I know it's no comfort to you, Margaret, and I understand that it will probably be distressing, but I think the best we can hope for is that a body turns up quickly.'

'A body,' she whispered thickly.

He nodded.

'Quickly?'

He nodded again, and then said gently, 'I'll get the WPC to put the kettle on, shall I?'

There were two bodies hauled out of the sea off the Cornish coast over the next few days. Sadly, neither of them was James.

Meanwhile in Brighton, Cass's new life was beginning to take shape. First thing in the morning she would walk the dogs with Danny, come back, feed him and the animals, peel Barney's cat, Radolpho, off the dog food or out of the bin or the milk jug, and then go through the post.

Barney had a very strict postal policy: he refused to look at anything that wasn't a cheque or the promise of one.

The shop opened at ten o'clock, so on days she was working there Cass took Danny with her – although Mrs HMR and Charlie said that if he was bored he could always stay with them – the rest of the shop hours being covered by Daisy or Barney. On days she didn't go to the shop, Cass was theoretically supposed to be working on her own projects, but was still not quite able to settle. It was coming, though; she could feel it, like the promise of a storm in the air. Looking at the dogs curled up on the hearth made her want to sketch them. Maybe it was going to be all right, after all.

Meanwhile she'd spent a lot of time trying to make sense of Barney's rather avant garde accounting system, sorting out and paying invoices or going through the stock. She put an ad in the local paper for a cleaner, tidied the flat and, oddly enough, began to feel as if life was getting better. Living so close to the sea it almost felt as if they were on an extended holiday.

There was no pressure, no David, no Abby and family, no Snoops, no Margaret Devlin, and a town full of music, cafés, restaurants, galleries, and lots and lots of life. It was so different from living at the cottage.

As a rule Barney spent very little time at home, giving Cass the run of the flat plus the two rooms of their own that Barney had promised: one small bedroom for Danny and a huge room for Cass that she used as a bed-sitting room, with a TV, comfy sofa, table and chairs. Cass had brought cushions and throws from home, and added a few plants and pictures that set off the whitewashed walls. It almost felt like she was a student again.

Women rang, one or two for the cleaning job, but mostly to talk to Barney – wives and girlfriends ancient and modern. Some conversations began suspiciously – 'Who are you?' – while others started more stoically – 'Oh, you must be the latest one. Just let me tell you . . .' But before they could hit their stride, Cass would quickly cut in, saying, 'Actually, I'm working for Barney as his PA. I'd be very happy to take a message if you'd like to leave one.' PA was the best title that either of them could come up with, other than 'Fixer', which sounded a bit dodgy, and 'Girl Friday', which sounded even worse.

Periodically Daisy popped by to have cheques signed, bum cash, fags or food, and generally moan about Barney.

'I'm afraid your dad's not here at the moment,' said Cass, letting her in at eight o'clock one morning. Cass had just got back in from a walk with Danny, Milo and Kipper. Daisy looked as if she had probably not been home yet.

'Can you close the door?'

Daisy, who had ambled in behind her, seemed confused and then, looking back, mumbled, 'Yeah, sure,' in a way that suggested door closing really wasn't her thing.

She didn't seem to mind about Barney's absence. If anything, she seemed to prefer it. While Cass made the tea, Daisy opened the fridge and, having browsed the contents for a few seconds, pulled out a bowl of strawberries and a big carton of

Greek yoghurt. 'So, have you seen him this morning?'

Cass shook her head. 'No, I saw him last night. Have you tried upstairs? He sometimes stays at his mum's if he is very late, so as not to disturb the dogs.'

'That's what he tells you. I bet he's got himself a new bird. You can always tell,' Daisy said, rootling through the drawers for a spoon. 'He wears gallons of aftershave and sings a lot when he's all loved up. It's disgusting. All that body hair and wrinkles – yuk.' She pulled a face, shuddered and then, recovering quickly, asked, 'Is that tea in the pot?'

Taking out a pint of semi-skimmed, Cass nodded, while sliding the cryptic note that Barney had left, presumably the night before, out from under a magnet shaped like a luminous green whelk on the fridge door.

'Here we are: "Gone out."' She scanned the rest of it: *Some artist coming round at noon. If you like his work, book him. If not, come up with a decent excuse that doesn't include me. I've left half a dozen signed cheques in the back of the book. Don't give Daisy more than fifty quid, and don't give her any of the cheques – her and that bitch of a mother have every intention of bleeding me dry. Love, B xxx*

Surreptitiously, Cass pocketed the note. 'You're in the shop this morning?'

Daisy, eating Frosties out of the box by the

handful, nodded. 'Uhuh. I was wondering if I could have a shower here. You know, save time and stuff.'

Danny, outraged, grabbed the cereal away from her. 'They're mine,' he growled.

'Says who, short stuff?' said Daisy, snatching them straight back.

'I do. Mum, tell her,' he whined, grabbing hold of Daisy's arm and pulling hard. Daisy and Danny had quickly forged a working relationship: big sister, little brother. As they struggled, the dogs barked, the cat leapt on to the table and made a grab for the butter, and it looked like there was a good chance that the Frosties were going to end up all over the floor.

'Stop,' Cass shrieked, banging the table with her hand, making everyone and everything jump except the cat. Remarkably, Daisy and Danny were instantly silent and still. Cass handed Daisy a bowl. 'Now sit down and behave yourselves, the pair of you. Daisy, your dad left you fifty quid. Apparently some artist is coming round at noon? Do you know anything about that?'

Daisy settled herself at the table alongside Danny, who watched her every move.

'Yeh, it'll be for the gallery. He makes them come round here and grovel for exhibition space. You need to check in the diary to see when Barney's offered him a slot and the commission rate. Around Christmas time we have lots of extra small stuff in, so you need to know whether he's a one-man big gallery hero or a small-time in-with-the-rest-of-the-riff-raff kinda guy.'

'Uhuh. And how will I know that, and what should I do?'

Daisy pulled a face and lifted her hand in a gesture of resignation. 'You're asking me? What do I know? I'm just a kid.'

Cass glared at her. Daisy was wearing a black rubber micro skirt, a pink-and-gold satin crop top, matching hooped tights and black leather thigh boots all wrapped around with a faux-fur leopard-skin coat. 'Really?' said Cass wryly.

'OK. Ask to see his letter – Barney is very big on letters – that will give you the slot this guy has been offered. Then just make your mind up whether you like his stuff or not. S'easy.'

Cass stared at her.

Exasperated, Daisy continued: 'Surely you've realised by now that Barney is total crap at taking responsibility and decisions? He wants you to see if this guy's work is any good. You'll take the fall if he doesn't sell a bean and, trust me, he'll take every last drop of the glory if the exhibition sells out. Come on, didn't you see the note?'

'And how am I supposed to decide?'

Daisy shrugged. 'God alone knows. Go with your gut instincts. Barney is really good at delegating responsibility. The only problem with that is he hasn't got the sense to give it to people who can cope.'

Cass lifted an eyebrow.

'Sorry. Present company excluded, obviously,' said Daisy quickly, holding out a hand to fend Cass off. Then, pouring herself a cup of tea, she added, 'You haven't got a fag, by any chance, have you?'

Cass shook her head. 'I don't smoke.'

Danny, who was busy pouring milk over his cereal, looked up. 'Hermione does. I'm sure she wouldn't mind you having one of hers. You should go up and ask her. She says that you never go to see her these days.'

Daisy sniffed. 'He's got his feet under the table upstairs, hasn't he? She's my grandmother and she doesn't even let me call her Hermione.'

'That's because we're friends,' Danny continued solemnly. 'She likes to talk about the good old days. You should go and ask her. It's special tobacco to help her old bones. It smells funny. Charlie gets it for her. You have to roll it up in little papers.'

Daisy and Cass looked at each other across the table.

At which point the post clattered in through the letter box. Cass got to her feet and hurried over to get it, skimming through the bundle, sorting the letters into piles: Barney personal, Barney bills, circulars and, right at the bottom, a big envelope with Jake's round bold handwriting across the front, containing Cass's post from home.

It felt like a Red Cross food parcel. Jake's note was bright and cheery, full of tales about the cat, the state of the garden, and trying to run David over outside Tesco's. Cass decided to leave his letter till later, to be savoured at a more leisurely pace, and moved on to the rest of her mail.

Apparently Caraway Industries were unfortunately unable to offer her a position in Human Resources at this juncture. However, they would like to keep her name on file. Should they ever want a tardy loon with a mouth like a drunken navvy, then she would be first on the list, Cass thought, as she consigned the letter to the bin and moved on to the rest of the mail. Across the table, Daisy and Danny bickered over who was going to have the free plastic toy from the cereal packet.

Her electricity bill was red, as was the gas bill, the council tax, and David's credit card bills, there was a circular for double glazing, and there, tucked away in amongst the final demands and offers for loans at very reasonable rates of interest, was a postcard.

Cass stared at the front of the card. It was a badly tinted photo of the Coliseum. In Rome. For a moment she felt hot and dizzy. Daisy and Danny's voices faded into the background. Handling the card as if it were an unexploded mine, Cass turned it over. It read:

Hi, Hope you're well. Rome is wonderful, although I find it hard to believe these are the same people who conquered half the known world. Went to see the Sistine Chapel today. This is what happens when Italians run out of magnolia. Weather is wonderful. I hope you got the job, if that's what you wanted. Wish you were here to show me around, the tour would be better with decent company. The fruit's fab. I know I said I wasn't a stalker, but maybe we could meet up some time when I get back? Best wishes, J. x

Best wishes, J. x? Cass struggled to breathe. The postmark was an undecipherable blot, no more than a squiggle of smudged ink.

She looked across at Daisy and Danny.

J – James bloody Devlin.

What was she supposed to do now? Ring the police? Call his wife? Cass considered her options. How the hell had he got hold of her address? And then she remembered: she had given him an envelope on the train, just as he was leaving to catch the connection to Stansted. Her heart tightened. How would that look? And how did he plan to meet up, if he didn't intend getting in touch again? Cass could hear the pulse banging out a tango rhythm in her ears. Bugger. Double bugger.

'Are you OK?' asked Daisy. 'You look as if you've seen a ghost.'

'Hermione sees ghosts,' said Danny through a mouthful of Frosties. 'Charlie says it's because she smokes too much of her special tobacco.'

Cass felt as if she was losing control. A great

144

wave of panic threatened to engulf her. 'I've got to go home,' she muttered.

Daisy looked at her. 'What? Don't be daft. You can't, you've got an artist to see at twelve.'

Cass stared blankly at her and then picked up the mobile and dialled Jake's number. He answered after the fourth ring.

'Did you see the postcard?' she said. He had barely had time to pick the phone up, let alone say hello.

'Uh?'

'The postcard, the one from Rome in the bundle of mail that you sent me.'

She heard Jake take a deep breath. 'Rome?'

'Uhuh, Rome. You know, Rome – Mr Peaches.'

'Oh bugger. You must think I'm a real thicko. I saw there was a postcard, and it never registered, it just never occurred to me. It's from him, isn't it?'

'It certainly is.'

'Bloody hell,' said Jake. 'Another thing – your phone has been ringing off the hook for the last couple of days. I was about to go and check to see if you'd got any messages.'

'It's all right, I can pick them up remotely. The problem is, Jake, I don't know what to do about this card.'

'If I were you, I'd call the feds in and tell them everything you know.'

'But I've already done that. I'd just forgotten that I'd given the bloody man my address.'

'So tell them that – now. People make mistakes.'

Cass thought for a few moments. 'They'll think I've been lying to them.'

'And have you?'

'No, of course not.'

'Well, in that case, you've got nothing to worry about. Now, other than that, how are you?'

Cass laughed. 'What do you mean, other than that?'

'Well, you know: other than that.'

'Other than that, I had been thinking how well it was going down here – always fatal.'

'Don't be such a cynic.'

'How's the cat?'

'Just fine.'

She paused and walked into the bedroom so that Danny and Daisy couldn't overhear her. 'I'm really worried, Jake.'

He sighed. 'I know, but you haven't done anything. What's the worst that can happen?'

Cass considered for a few moments. 'That's a stupid thing to say – I've got no idea.'

'No, me neither, actually. Just ring the WPC you spoke to before and let her sort it out. It's better that way.'

'Right. I didn't tell them about seeing him in London, either, though.'

'But you weren't sure it was him, were you?' said Jake.

'No,' Cass lied, hoping that Jake wouldn't

notice. 'You sound grumpy this morning. Are you hung over?'

She would have staked her life that it was James Devlin; it was just that some part of her wanted him to be free, for all the wrong reasons, not least of which was that she couldn't bear the idea that a nice man like him was tied to a screaming harridan like Margaret Devlin. Although there was a part of her that wondered which had come first. What if the way he behaved had made Margaret Devlin the way she was? It was possible, but a thought too horrible to contemplate.

On the other end of the line, Jake was still talking. 'There's another thing that you should know, Cass. Are you sitting down?'

Cass wasn't sure whether he was joking. 'Why?'

'There's no easy way to tell you this. I read in the paper that they think James Devlin may have topped himself.'

It felt as if Jake had punched her in the stomach. 'What?' she whispered.

'Cass, I wasn't sure whether to tell you or not. But I was worried that maybe you'd have read it in the nationals before we'd had a chance to speak. I've saved the newspaper cutting for you. I was going to put it in with your post, and then thought . . . well, you know.'

Cass did know, she could feel it. There was an odd, cold dead spot right in the middle of her chest. 'I haven't had time to read the papers,' she mumbled. It was hard to breathe. How could James possibly be dead when he had been so alive? He didn't feel dead in her head. Or her heart.

'Do you want me to read you the report?' Jake said.

'I don't know. No . . . I . . . if he really is dead then none of this matters anyway, does it? It's over.' She said it quickly, although it wasn't what she meant at all. She just wanted Jake to stop talking.

'Shall I send it to you?'

'OK.'

'Are you all right?'

'Jake, please stop asking stupid questions. I have really got no idea. Tell you what, I'll ring you back later. I need a few minutes to think.'

Cass put the phone down and sat on the bed, turning the postcard over in her fingers. How could fate be so cruel? His handwriting was big and bold, and she felt sick and sad and numb and angry.

'Cass?' Daisy called from the kitchen.

'I'll be out in a minute,' she said quickly, sniffing back the emotion that threatened to drown her. She grabbed the mobile and dialled her home number, put the code in and picked up the messages from her answer machine. David was first: 'Cass, I really need to talk to you. I seem to have lost your mobile number. My new number is – Oh, hang on a minute – I'll call you back in a –' The line burred like a bad-tempered bee.

Beep.

'I hope you're satisfied, you cold, heartless bitch, driving a good man to kill himself.' Cass winced. 'Well, I just want you to know that all the money has gone – that's what he said in his note. So you'll get nothing from this, do you hear me? Nothing. And what's left he's willed to me. Everything. Every last thing.' Margaret Devlin, psycho and aggrieved widow.

Cass stared down at the postcard she still had in her hand. The cold spot throbbed. Was he really dead? It didn't seem possible, and it didn't feel right at all. The phone moved on to the next message but her mind didn't.

'Hi,' said a vaguely familiar voice. 'Hi, how are you? Remember me? We met on the train going to Cambridge, just before I went off to Rome?' He sounded as if he was smiling. The voice caught her off guard. Cass felt the breath catch in her throat. This certainly didn't sound like a man about to commit suicide.

'I hope you got my postcard. I looked you up in the phone book. I know I said I wasn't a stalker, but I lied,' he laughed. 'I was going to put my mobile number on the card, but it seemed a bit presumptuous . . .' He paused nervously, as if expecting to be rebuffed. Cass froze.

'I was thinking that maybe we could get together for lunch some time. Or something. My number is . . .'

Cass wrote it down and then stared at it before replaying the preamble from BT, so that she also got the time and the date of the call. James Devlin had rung her yesterday. So, whatever the newspapers said, he most certainly wasn't dead, and he hadn't killed himself.

Cass swallowed hard. What was she going to do now? This was a man being hunted nationally – probably internationally – by the police. He was also presumed dead. Had he faked suicide? And, if so, why was he ringing her? Was he totally stark staring mad? She really ought to call the police . . . Or should she talk to him, maybe persuade him that, if he gave himself up, things would be all right?

Cass took a deep breath, trying to work out what to do for the best. James Devlin was a criminal, a philanderer, a cheat and a liar – that's what the policewoman and his wife had said. But that wasn't at all how he had seemed when they met. He'd seemed so very nice. Mind you, that was probably because he was good at what he did. What were her instincts up to? Surely she should be able to sense he was a bad lot. How could she be so gullible? Still with her mind on James, she skipped to the next call, almost without thinking.

It was David again, more anxious this time. 'Perhaps you could ring me. Did you get my number? I can't use my old mobile at the moment.' He laughed uneasily. 'Got broken during a little fracas. Accident, really – you know how it is. Right, OK, well, I'll catch you later.' He sounded unnaturally jovial. 'OK. Oh, and I'd rather you didn't ring me on the landline. Things here are a bit, well . . . you know. It's not easy for any of us at the moment. So, if you could ring me on my mobile. My new number is 077 –'

Cass dutifully wrote it down under James Devlin's number.

Finally, calls all over, Cass folded the piece of paper and, slipping it into her pocket, she headed back towards the kitchen, only to discover that Barney had materialised from somewhere and was sitting between Danny and Daisy, eating Frosties with strawberries and drinking tea.

'I've been thinking about this whole nanny/au pair idea,' he said conversationally, as if they were already mid sentence. Cass looked him up and down, resisting the temptation to ask him where the hell he'd been. He looked considerably more bedraggled than Daisy, but just as perky.

'What nanny/au pair idea?'

'You know, the au pair – blonde, leggy, capable, with really good –' His hands started a very graphic mime which Danny watched with considerable interest.

'I thought you said we'd start by looking for a cleaner?' Cass reminded him, before he could complete the sentence or the gesture.

'All right, all right, I was, we did. But I've been thinking that maybe we need someone with a broader range – someone reliable, good with children,' said Barney, looking first at Daisy and then

Danny, who smiled up at him with an expression close to adoration.

'Not to mention grumpy old men,' Cass added.

'There is that,' Barney conceded with a shrug. 'So I meant to tell you, I've already put an advert in *The Lady* and the *Guardian* – and the *Telegraph*. Should be out today.'

Cass looked at him. 'What? But I thought you told me that you couldn't do this kind of stuff?'

Barney looked hurt. 'I didn't say that at all. I just said I wasn't any good at it.'

He pulled a piece of paper out of his pocket, unfolded it and then patted himself down and located his reading glasses. '"Wanted for eccentric, artistic, bohemian household: reliable, flexible au pair, own room, excellent remuneration, must like children and animals."'

'You forgot grumpy old men,' added Danny helpfully.

'My mother told me "bohemian" actually means unwashed, unfaithful and untidy,' said Daisy. 'And I think "flexible" sounds dead dodgy. Are we talking physically or mentally, here?'

Barney didn't bother to reply. 'Right,' he said, picking up Danny's milk and drinking it. 'Ever upwards and onwards. Oh, and by the way, I wondered if you might like to have an exhibition at the shop. Shame to work for me and not take mean advantage of a poor old man's natural generosity. Everyone else does. We've got a slot; someone had a fire, or maybe it was a nervous breakdown – I can't remember the exact details now. My mother says you're really talented and very saleable.'

Cass frowned. 'But she hasn't seen any of my work.'

'Apparently she has. She and Charlie were on the internet all last night Googling you down over a chicken korma and a peshwari naan. Seems that you paint proper pictures, with people, fruit and flowers and dogs. I think she has ordered every book you've ever illustrated. And Jake says you've got a lot of work in Norfolk in your spare bedroom that needs dusting off, framing, and getting up on a wall somewhere.'

Cass stared at him. It felt as if she was in the middle of a benign conspiracy. 'When did you talk to Jake?'

'Oh, I dunno, about half an hour ago. I thought maybe he could bring it all down in his car. I've got a guy who can do the framing, and it seems such a long time since I've seen Jake.'

Cass looked at him and lifted an eyebrow. 'It was the beginning of last week.'

'Oh really?' Barney frowned. 'I miss him. We're good friends. We were at college together. We're soul mates.'

Cass laughed. 'You're booze hounds. It took the pair of you days to sleep it off after he brought me down here.'

Barney nodded and, sounding philosophical, said, 'I know. Isn't it terrible? When we were younger, we used to be over it by the next day, up and at 'em. God, I hate getting old. So, when shall we get Jake to come down? How about the end of the week?'

In his office above a dental technician's on the outskirts of Cambridge, Mr Marshall turned his attention to the taped conversations from Cass's home phone and smiled to himself.

He'd stopped the postman and intercepted the postcard, read it, and made a note of the salient points.

His hunch was bang on. James Devlin wasn't dead after all, and he *did* have the hots for Mrs Hammond. Two out of two wasn't bad. Mr Marshall turned up the volume and fiddled with the bass so he could pick out what they were saying more clearly. The quality of the tape wasn't quite as good as he would have liked, but any distortion was more than made up for by content. Mr Marshall smiled. If Gordie Mann wanted to listen to them himself, he would need to arrange to get the sound quality cleaned up a bit. Shame the mobile phone numbers weren't crystal clear, but they weren't bad.

Mr Marshall pressed a button on the desk. Seconds later he handed the tape to his secretary. 'Type this up ASAP, will you? And I'd be most grateful if you would get me Mr Mann on line one.'

The girl looked at him; they only had one line.

She sniffed and turned the tape over in her hand, leaning closer to stub her cigarette out in the saucer on his desk. 'All right, Dad,' she said. 'And then is it all right if I go and get an egg-and-bacon butty from Mick on the corner, only I'm starving?'

He nodded and, satisfied, she headed back into the small outer office.

James Devlin stared at the mobile and wondered if he dare phone her again. It had been a day or so since he had left the last message on her answerphone. He had very mixed feelings about leaving a message, but he was also lonely.

There were lots of things to consider. What if she shopped him? What if the next phone call he got was from the police? Or from her, agreeing to meet up? What if she was followed, what if he turned the corner and there sat a squad car with his name on it? James bit his lip, thoughts bubbling through his head like surf over pebbles. He daren't leave his mobile on for long because Gordie Mann had once told him that the Old Bill – as Gordie always called them – could track a mobile down to within ten metres. But then again, hopefully he would soon be gone. He just wasn't sure where to.

If only she would ring him, let him know that it was OK, talk to him. James felt that if he heard her voice, he would know instinctively if she had betrayed him or not. Most of all, he needed someone to talk to who didn't know all about his past, or his peccadilloes, or his sexual proclivities. Someone who thought he was worth saving, someone who still believed in him.

Cass sat for a long time with her mobile on her lap, looking at James Devlin's phone number, wondering exactly what she should do. Once she got over the shock of hearing his voice, the first thing Cass felt was pure undiluted relief. Should she ring him, or did it make more sense to call the police? Or would it be better to ignore the call and pretend that she hadn't picked it up? It would be easy to phone home and delete the message from Call Minder. If she closed her eyes, she could see his face – he wasn't dead, he was grinning. It didn't help.

Daisy had gone to work, Barney had buggered off to God knows where, and she was upstairs in Mrs HMR's flat sorting through a box of dumpy blown-glass birds which Barney thought would make a great window display. He was right; they were all different, about the size of tangerines, and a nice mixture of cute and arty.

'Cass?' She looked up from her thoughts.

Charlie was smiling down at her. 'There's someone to see you downstairs.'

She pulled a face. 'Sorry?'

'Barney just rang. There's some artist who has got a twelve o'clock appointment?'

Cass snorted. So Barney was there, but was still going to leave the decision up to her. She put the box of birds down on a side table along with her phone, notepad and pen, tucked David and James Devlin's phone numbers in the back pocket of her jeans, and headed downstairs. Danny was busy watching videos in the sitting room with Mrs HMR and was happy to leave her to it.

Downstairs, sitting at the table in Barney's kitchen, was a tall angular man with skin the colour of double cream, tiny rectangular glasses, spiky black, heavily gelled hair, and an Adam's apple that looked as if a finger was sticking out under the turkey skin in his throat. He was sipping a glass of water, and had a portfolio and slides set out neatly on the table alongside him. Other than that the flat appeared to be totally deserted.

As Cass introduced herself and settled down at the table opposite him, in what she hoped was a businesslike manner, she saw a familiar pair of legs heading past the window: Barney, who had to have been hiding somewhere, and was now on his way upstairs to his mother's.

'So,' Cass said warmly, extending a hand and resolving to ignore her lunatic boss, 'let's get started, shall we?'

The man simpered in her direction. 'I just wanted to say how very grateful I am for your time, Ms Hammond,' he said. 'The gentleman who showed me in, he told me he was your assistant. Charming. He said that you were very, very influential in the local arts scene – major exhibition coming up, very talented. I am truly honoured.'

Cass flicked on the lightbox and smiled wryly, wondering if the big build-up was Barney's idea of an olive branch.

'I hope you don't mind, but I helped myself to a glass of water,' he said, indicating the galley kitchen with one long thin finger. 'I always worry about dehydration. I usually bring filtered, but, well, any port in a storm.'

He didn't look like someone who would fare well in any kind of storm.

'Would you prefer some tea or maybe coffee?'

He shook his head. 'No thanks, I'm mid de-tox at the moment. It always makes me feel good, full of energy. Four pints of water a day and as many lentils as I can eat.'

Picking up the box of slides, Cass smiled and made a mental note not to stand downwind of him.

5

'So, where do we go from here?' said Gordie Mann, as he skimmed through the transcripts of Cass's most recent telephone conversations.

Mr Marshall, dressed à la Clouseau in a trench coat and trilby with wispy tufts of ginger hair peeking out under the brim, smiled wolfishly. 'You know, I thought you might ask me that. This new information makes our lives much simpler.' He pulled out a flow chart, smoothing out the paper with his small hands as he set it down on the desk. 'For a start, it narrows the search down to one relatively small area, so we can make best use of our resources. We'll take the bulk of our operatives off everything else we've been covering and concentrate our efforts on tracking Mrs Hammond.'

Gordie glanced at the row of interconnecting coloured dots on Marshall's chart, while Marshall continued: 'The plan is that we watch her, we follow her, we get a tap on her phone in Brighton. Basically, although we don't know the whereabouts of James Devlin, we do know that he is talking to Mrs Hammond. There are no other leads that have really gone anywhere, so I suggest we wait and use her as bait. I've already arranged to set up a scanner to listen on her mobile.' He glanced down at his watch. 'They should be setting that up even as we speak. My feeling is that it won't be long now before we have our man. Not long at all.' He smiled and folded the flow chart with a kind of triumphant finality.

Gordie, who was seated behind a large oak desk in an office well away from the noise of the construction company that provided a front for all manner of nefarious schemes, dodges and scams, picked up the pile of transcripts and banged them, edge on, into a neat stack. He didn't look wildly impressed.

'And?'

Mr Marshall looked puzzled. 'And nothing. As I said, all we have to do is sit and wait. Don't worry, Mr Mann. James Devlin is close, I can feel it in my bones. This is the most realistic opportunity we have of flushing him out. We just need to bide our time and wait, and let Mrs Hammond reel him in for us. What we need now is patience.'

Gordie's expression suggested that that might well prove to be the most difficult part of Mr Marshall's plan.

'We've already had the talk about bloody patience. What I need now, Mr Marshall, is results.' After a second or two Gordie sniffed and steepled his fingers in front of his lips, eyes hard as flint as he held Mr Marshall's gaze. 'Tell you what, I've got a better idea. Why don't we just grab this bloody woman Hammond, ring Devlin, tell the bastard that we've got her and unless he gives himself up, we'll . . .' He paused, watching Marshall's face closely. 'Well, I'm sure you can fill in the gaps for yourself,' Gordie growled, his eyes narrowing to dark angry slits. 'Or do I have to lay it on the line for you?'

Mr Marshall paled visibly. 'No, no, not at all. Obviously that is an approach that may very well work, Mr Mann – except that we have no idea how close James Devlin is to Mrs Hammond. My information suggests that their relationship is still extremely new . . .' Mr Marshall struggled to come up with a plausible reason. There surely had to be at least one. He hated violence.

'If you ring him, Devlin may run and we'll have lost the advantage. What if he calls your bluff?' Mr Marshall managed. 'If that happens, you've lost everything. It seems to me that James Devlin is the kind of man who – when the chips are down – will save his own neck, regardless of the effect it might have on other people. Let's try it my way first. If it doesn't pan out then you've lost nothing. And this way is less risky, less messy . . .' His voice dried up as he contemplated Gordie Mann's impassive face. He doubted that Gordie had any problem with mess.

'We'll try it your way for a wee while longer,' said Gordie. 'And then . . .' He let the possibility hang between them in the air.

Mr Marshall swallowed hard. He wasn't a man who condoned violence, particularly against women, and wished now he had followed his instincts when Gordie Mann had shown up at his office and told him that he was busy. God alone knows who had recommended him. It had occurred to Mr Marshall over the last few days that the recommendation was more an act of spite than any kind of favour.

'Right then,' said Gordie briskly. 'Was there anything else?'

Mr Marshall nodded. 'Well, yes. With the greatest of respect, I wonder if you could have another word with Mrs Devlin? I'm a little worried that her threats might make Mrs Hammond go underground. It would be disastrous at this stage if we lost contact with her.'

'What do you mean, "threats"?'

Mr Marshall shifted his weight. 'She went round to Mrs Hammond's house, and I have her on tape, badgering her.'

'What you really mean is that without Cassandra Hammond you've got bugger all.'

Grudgingly Mr Marshall agreed.

Gordie shrugged. 'I can try, but I can't promise anything. I'd planned to nip round this evening and see how Margaret's getting on, so I'll have a quiet word with her then. It's understandable, though. You have to see it from her point of view, man. She's very upset. That bastard Devlin left her penniless; screwed around for years with God knows how many other women, rubbed her nose in it every which way.' He paused and smiled wistfully. 'She's a very sensitive woman, is Margaret.'

Mr Marshall nodded, not daring to add that he had seen more sensitive rattlesnakes.

'I'm looking for a present.'

Cass smiled. 'Well, you've certainly come to the right place. Had you anything specific in mind?' It was later the same afternoon. Danny was in the storeroom, eating a snack supper in front of the TV, and in between games of snap and Lego, Cass was doing a two-till-six in the shop. It had been busy all afternoon, so time was passing quickly.

The American woman's eyes moved avariciously around the display cases. 'I was hoping to buy a couple of things. Something for my parents' wedding anniversary, and a move-of-house present for a friend of mine. Some of this stuff is just so cute. Can you handle the shipping?'

Cass glanced up at Barney, who had arrived looking all excited and windswept and terribly pleased with himself about two minutes earlier – just long enough to say hello and steal a packet of Danny's cheesy Wotsits – and who was now hovering around in the background. The American's arrival had stopped him launching into any kind of convoluted explanation.

From the other side of the shop he was nodding furiously.

'Certainly,' said Cass with a smile. 'Shipping is no problem at all, although there will be a surcharge.'

Across the shop, Barney's smile broadened and the nodding became even more vigorous; apparently that was exactly the right thing to say. Barney liked surcharges.

The woman nodded. 'Sure, no problem. How much?'

How much indeed. Cass's smile held. 'Depending on what you choose we can either wrap it for posting here and you post it yourself, or alternatively –'

'Alternatively,' Barney stepped forward, his smile as wide and inviting as a slice of newly cut watermelon. 'I could make you a pot of tea and have my assistant here nip down to the post office and sort it all out for you.'

Artfully, Cass took out a booklet from under the cash desk. 'Alternatively, I could just wrap it and weigh it and save myself the trouble.'

Barney pulled a face, but he needn't have worried, the woman was totally and utterly enchanted. 'You know, I think whichever I do, I may go for the tea option anyway. I've walked miles today,' she purred as Barney moved in for the kill. Behind the American woman's back, as he directed her towards a display case of jewellery, Barney mimed chalking one up.

Cass laughed, shaking her head in a mixture of disbelief and amusement, and then went back to rearranging the window with a flurry of glass birds and sand-scoured driftwood. Ten minutes later Barney was guiding the American woman upstairs to the main exhibition. It was a masterly performance. In well under an hour, Barney persuaded her to buy two pairs of earrings, two small sculptures, a silk butterfly and one of his paintings.

And while Cass wrapped and weighed the smaller items and then made a phone call to check the cost of shipping the painting, Barney had made the woman a pot of Earl Grey, opened up a packet of Belgian apple and cinnamon thins, and asked her out to dinner.

It was by far the best and most entertaining sale of the day.

As the shop door finally closed on their well-preserved caramel blonde Colonial cousin, Barney swung round with an enormous grin on his face and rubbed his hands together.

'Fan-tas-tic, bloody marvellous – real live money, dinner, the promise of a lot of heavy-duty flirtation, followed by potential seduction. Fan-tas-tic, and there was me thinking that maybe I'd lost it.' He paused mid-stride. 'Now, what was it I came for? Oh, yes, I remember – I've found an au pair and, and . . . There was something else, but I can't remember what it was now.' He pulled a face as if trying very hard to drag the memory back from some distant corner of his brain. 'You know, when I was a young man,' he said cheerily. 'I used to blame my terrible memory on drugs and booze. The ravages of old age is so much more respectable an excuse.' He practically skipped towards the door.

Cass handed him a parcel. 'Whoa, cowboy, while you're on a roll, how about you nip down to the post office with this?'

He grimaced. 'Don't be ridiculous – I'll get Daisy to do it first thing tomorrow. I've got to go home and get scrubbed up. I thought I might take Ms Middle America dancing. They've got a great blues band at the Buena Vista tonight.' He rolled his shoulders and shimmied across the floor, grinning like a loon.

'Wait, wait before you go –' said Cass hastily, elbowing her way through a bow wave of exuberant lust. 'What do you mean you've found an au pair?'

'Oh yes,' said Barney. 'Good point. She's foreign, obviously. Sounded really capable. Likes kids and cooking and keeping house – oh, and dogs. I think she may have one. Actually, I'm sure that's what she said. Anyway, she had some kind of falling out with her last employer. The woman hated the dog apparently. She said that she could come down tomorrow. I've told her that she could start straight away. She can help with the house, Danny, the ironing . . .' He was jubilant.

'But what if we don't like her?' said Cass in astonishment. 'What if she's a raving loony, or drinks? Or steals things?'

Barney stopped dead in his tracks as if the thought hadn't occurred to him.

'You can't just give a job to someone over the phone like that,' Cass continued incredulously. 'What about taking up references, going through reputable agencies and things like that?'

Barney looked puzzled and then all hangdog and hard done by. 'Oh, bugger. You see, that's why you should handle this sort of stuff, not me. I'm absolutely useless. That's why I put your mobile number on the ad.'

Cass stared at him. 'What?'

'I put your –'

'I heard what you said, and I really think you might have mentioned it to me before doing anything. Asking would have been a good start. But I don't understand – if you put my number in the ad, why – how did she phone you?'

Barney thought for a moment and then smiled. 'Oh yes, I remember now. That was the other thing I was going to tell you. You left your phone at my mother's this morning. The ringing was driving her mad. She thought she'd started hallucinating.' He sniffed. 'Again.'

'Where's my phone now?'

Barney pulled it out of his jacket pocket. 'There we are. I thought you'd be pleased.' He sounded hurt. 'She was the first one who rang. And she sounded perfect.' He set the phone down on the counter. 'I brought it with me. I didn't want you to miss anything else important. Oh, I know, there was another thing . . .'

Cass waited.

'I rang Jake and suggested that he come down for a visit.'

'And . . .'

'And he said he could come the day after tomorrow, but he had no idea which illustrations and stuff you would want him to bring, so . . .' Barney rootled in his other pocket and produced a set of car keys. 'So, I've had the car insured for you. You can drive home tomorrow and bring Jake back down on Friday. He can get the train home. Probably safer that way, given the amount he drinks.'

Cass sighed and held out her hand. Barney dropped the keys into her upturned palm.

'I didn't know you'd got a car.'

He shrugged. 'I try and keep it quiet in case anyone asks me for a lift. I hardly drive at all these days; mostly because when I go out I'm inevitably too pissed to find the bloody thing and am terrified that, if I do find it, I might be tempted to drive home in it. I've got a mate in Hove who keeps it in his garage for me. I've asked him to bring it round first thing tomorrow morning – about eight, OK? Right, ever onwards. I need to go home and find my dancing pumps. Do you think, given our Colonial cousin's taste in trousers, that maybe I should wear something in plaid?'

Trying to ignore him, Cass glanced down at the mobile. It was switched off. She turned it on and it rang almost instantly.

'See, there we are,' said Barney. 'You haven't missed anything at all.'

Cass glared at him as the voicemail service number came up on the screen. She answered it and hung up and then it rang again and it rang and it rang and it rang. There were eleven messages from all manner of home helps, foreign nationals, unemployed nannies and mother's helps. Cass reached for a notepad and started to make notes, just in case Barney's first-come first-served approach didn't work. When she looked up after replaying the first message, Barney had already left.

The twelfth message was from David. 'Cass, hi, how are you? Just a quick call. The thing is, well, I need to see you.'

He sounded dreadful; although he was trying to disguise it under a veneer of forced good humour, she knew him too well.

Sitting in a parked car not more than a couple of hundred yards away from Barney's emporium – with an official-looking *Traffic Survey* sign in the windscreen to allow him to park illegally – a man in a T-shirt and shorts smiled as his recorder buzzed yet again and then whirred into life. He pushed the earpiece in a little further so he could hear better; lulled into a stupor by girls gabbling on about work, references and how good they were at sewing and playing with small children, the sound of a male voice woke him with a start. Finally, he thought. This was more like it.

Cass added David's new mobile number to the phone book on her mobile and then rang him. He answered on the fifth ring, his voice barely above a whisper. 'Cass, is that you?' he hissed.

'Yes, of course it's me. What on earth is the matter? Why are you whispering?'

'No reason. Well, nothing really . . . err, it's just that I can't talk right now. Things are a bit difficult here at the moment. Do you think we can meet for a chat?'

'I'm at work.'

'Please, Cass,' David's voice dropped down even lower so that she could barely hear him. 'I need to see you. We need to talk.'

'Look, I haven't got time for this. I'm in Brighton, I can't just drop everything and pop round for a cosy little tête-à-tête.'

'Please, Cass, I need to talk to you.'

God, he could be so bloody infuriating at times. 'So you keep saying.' She couldn't work out whether to sound angry or sympathetic. What was the best tone for a whining manipulative selfish shit of a husband?

'I've made the most terrible mistake. Nothing's

gone right since I left. I keep thinking that maybe it would be better if I came back,' he wailed, sounding close to tears.

Cass stared at the phone in horror. Bloody hell. The breath caught in her throat as she tried hard to gather her thoughts. Wasn't this exactly what she had dreamed of? David on his hands and knees, begging to come home? A shiver rippled down her spine as a nasty realisation dawned, a realisation which grew and grew until she could barely contain the thought.

The truth was that, all these months on, *she didn't want David back*. What's more, the idea of clambering back into a miserable marriage with him made her feel physically sick.

And as the thought formed, for an instant she saw James Devlin in her mind's eye, all smiles, enthusiasm and floppy blond hair. She could see him sitting opposite her in the train, blue eyes twinkling, making her laugh in spite of herself, offering her full, ripe peaches. Cass frowned, wondering why her subconscious was offering him, of all people, as a cheery little morsel – except of course that she knew why.

However crazy it sounded, however much Cass tried to deny it, however out-and-out mad it seemed, even if she did nothing about it, there was a part of her that wanted to be with James Devlin, not David Hammond. And how mad was that? How in heaven's name could she fancy a known criminal, a man she barely knew? *Have you not got the sense you were born with?* said a nagging voice in her head that sounded remarkably like her mother.

'I'm being followed,' said David.

It was all Cass could do not to laugh. 'Oh, for God's sake,' she said.

'Cass, I'm serious, I'm in big trouble,' he said.

'I don't understand,' she said. 'What sort of trouble?'

'I need to see you.'

Cass paused; this was crazy.

'Please, Cass,' said David anxiously, still waiting for her answer.

Cass thought for a moment or two and then said, 'OK, I've got to come up and collect some of my work for an exhibition. I could see you then.' She realised that she made it sound like a favour.

'When?' said David. He was obviously desperate.

'I'm driving up tomorrow. How about if we say two o'clock at the cottage?' Cass said, wondering how long it would take her in whatever it was that Barney owned. If she started out early enough, it should be OK. 'I've got to go, I'm at work,' she said and hung up.

In his parked car the man grinned and picked up his mobile. He tapped in Mr Marshall's number. 'We've got them,' he said.

*   *   *

Mr Marshall grinned. 'Well done, my lad. Let me have the details.' In his tiny neat handwriting he made a note of the time and the place, and then smiled to himself.

Marshall didn't like to say anything to Gordie Mann in case it made him look a fool, but he hadn't been able to work out which of the two male callers on Cass's answerphone had been James Devlin. To be perfectly honest, it could even have been the same person ringing twice; one of the mobile numbers had been almost totally obscured by a blast of white noise, so the caller might have rung back to make sure Cass had definitely got his number. Or perhaps he had two numbers and was giving her both – quite reasonable, given James Devlin's circumstances.

Something else he hadn't mentioned to Gordie Mann was that the pick-up on Cass's phone was a bit dodgy and had a lot of interference on it. He looked at the notes he'd made about Cassandra Hammond's latest conversation: 'It's all very odd up here. I realise now that I've made the most terrible mistake. Nothing's gone right since I left. I keep thinking that maybe it would be better if I came back,' and the clincher: 'I know I'm in big trouble.'

Mr Marshall sucked his teeth. Surely that had to be James Devlin? In which case he knew exactly where James Devlin was going to be at two o'clock the next day. He smiled to himself. Time to spring the trap.

*   *   *

When Cass got back with Danny from the shop, she opened the door into the basement flat and, looking around Barney's untidy wonderful magical life, realised that she wasn't ready to go home and play unhappy families with David. It was too late. And if she was honest, it had been too late the moment he told her that he was leaving and setting up home with Abby. God knows what had gone wrong in his little love nest, but as far as Cass was concerned he had shot his bolt; there *was* no going back. The thought, and the strength of her resolve, genuinely surprised her.

She glanced at the pile of post. In amongst it was James Devlin's postcard. Feeling in her pocket, she pulled out the piece of paper with his phone number on it. She dialled the number from her mobile.

'Hello,' said a dark humorous voice on the far end of the line.

'Hi,' said Cass. 'It's me.'

He laughed. 'Hello you. Great to hear from you. How's it going? I didn't think you'd ring. I was afraid that you might think I was a stalker. So, did you get the job in Cambridge?'

'No,' said Cass. 'Did you have an adventure?'

'Yes and no – depends how you look at it. Apart from seeing the sights, I was looking at a property out there, a little hideaway in a beautiful old palazzo.' There was a funny pause and then he said, 'I was wondering if maybe we could get together some time. Maybe have lunch?'

'That would be good,' Cass said, wondering how she was going to broach the subject of his running off with two million quid, not to mention him already having a wife and being wanted by the police and faking his own suicide. Maybe over the phone was not the right way.

There was something else that Cass hadn't expected but knew she wasn't imagining. It was that hot shivery feeling she'd had when she imagined his face as she was talking to David, and she would have laid money on it being mutual.

'I'm coming up to Norfolk tomorrow,' she said.

'Coming up?' He sounded surprised. 'But I thought you lived here?'

'I do normally, but I'm working in Brighton at the moment. For the summer. I'm coming to collect some work.'

'OK, in that case, if you've got the time,' he said, 'how about I take you out for supper while you're home? I've just moved into my new place, or I'd offer to cook.' He laughed. 'Maybe I should do that anyway.'

Surely he was meant to be in hiding, not out on the town wining and dining strange women?

'It sounds like a nice idea. I'll have to sort out a baby-sitter for my son.'

There was a pause. It suddenly occurred to Cass that he had no idea about Danny, and then she smiled. Compared to the size of James Devlin's secrets, one small boy was hardly big news. But before she could say anything, he said, 'Oh, OK, why don't you bring him? How about we dump the posh supper idea, go for a walk on the beach and then grab a chip supper? Do you know Wells-next-the-Sea? They've got the most fantastic chip shop on the front there. How about we meet in the car park down by the pinewoods – at the bottom end, down near the boating lake? About four o'clock?'

Cass laughed. 'You really know how to impress a girl, don't you? If we're going to do that then I'll bring my dog along. But maybe not my son this time.' *This time*, what the hell was she saying?

The man laughed. 'OK, good idea. I really miss mine. My ex-wife kept the dog.'

Cass reddened. She didn't like to tell him that she knew all about his dog.

The man listening in the car looked down at his notes, rang Mr Marshall and read back the salient points. Mr Marshall pondered for a few moments: Caller One, Caller Two? Everything pointed to Caller One being their mark, right down to what his man described as his subdued nervous tone: 'sounded like he was on the lam, hiding – bit paranoid.' Playing the hunch, Mr Marshall picked up the phone and called Gordie Mann.

Unfortunately, DI Turner had very little to tell Margaret Devlin. Still pursuing various lines of enquiry was how he put it as he slipped off his coat and she went over to a side table to pour him a glass of brandy and soda.

'Been a long day?' Margaret asked, in a tone meant to infer that she cared.

The policeman nodded and settled himself in one of the big leather armchairs that flanked the inglenook fireplace in Margaret Devlin's sitting room. It was getting to be something of a habit, his dropping by on his way home from work.

'I truly wish that I'd got something more positive to tell you, Margaret, but so far we've come up empty. None of the leads we've been following have panned out so far. James must have had help. We've had lots of calls and possible sightings and, trust me, every last one of them is being followed up. If we find anything, you'll be amongst the first to know. Don't you worry, we'll get to the bottom of this.' He sighed. 'I keep hoping Cornwall will come up with a body.' He coloured furiously as he realised what he'd said. 'I'm so sorry, that wasn't very tactful of me.'

Margaret waved his apology away. 'It's all right, Inspector. I understand. To be perfectly honest, I just want it sorted out one way or the other.' She let her voice crack a little in case he thought her callous. 'Obviously I don't wish James dead, but I'm sure you can understand that it would be a huge relief to have a sense of closure.'

DI Turner nodded. 'You didn't mind me popping by, did you? Only I was in the area.'

'Not at all,' Margaret said graciously, catching

sight of herself in the mirror. They both knew it was a lie. He's already told her he lived near Swaffham; Little Lamport was nowhere near Swaffham, and this was the third time this week he had been 'in the area'.

'It's always nice when you look in. I'm really pleased to see you.' A little grief and anxiety had done wonders for her figure; she'd lost about half a stone, dropped a dress size, and the pallor and smudges of shadow under her eyes made her look more fragile and vulnerable than ever.

And DI Turner was most definitely looking. A lot.

'There we are, Inspector,' she said, smiling just a fraction as she handed him a glass of brandy. 'Would you like some more ice in there?'

'No, I'm fine, thank you,' he said. He looked up at her and, with the tiniest of moves, Margaret engineered it so that their fingertips touched. He reddened again. Desire crackled between them like static electricity.

Margaret smiled. 'Enjoy,' she purred.

'Why don't you call me Henry?' he said thickly.

As their eyes met again, she feigned a coy look of surprise and added, 'Well, thank you, *Henry*,' in a lispy breathy voice that sounded at least twenty years younger than she was. Margaret was standing so close to DI Turner that she could see the hint of five-o'clock shadow on his strong square jaw, a tiny nick that hadn't healed up close by his ear. And as she looked she drank him in.

Their gaze locked and for a moment she wondered if he might lean forward and kiss her. But, as if afraid he was overstepping the mark, DI Turner hastily composed himself and pulled them both back from the brink. 'And how are the children coping with it all?' he asked briskly.

Bugger.

With the moment having passed, Margaret sniffed and settled herself down in the other armchair. She wasn't about to tell him that it was hard to work out how the children were, because she had packed them off to her mother's for the duration. Instead, Margaret painted on a brave face.

'It's not easy for them,' she said, adding a splash of soda to her own glass. 'It's not easy for any of us.' It would be a lot easier for everybody when they started as weekly boarders next term, she thought, taking a sip from her drink. Whining, miserable little buggers. They missed James, they missed the bloody dog – God, they even missed What's-her-bloody-name.

It seemed, though, that DI Turner hadn't totally turned his attention to the social niceties. He leaned forward, glass cradled between his fingers. 'I was just wondering . . .' he began, reddening. Now it came to it, he was all hesitancy and apprehension. Margaret preened and waited patiently, looking up at him, trying hard to pretend that she had no idea what he was going to say, all cow-eyed and adoring.

'Well, I was just wondering whether you might like to come out to dinner with me one evening. No pressure, obviously.'

Margaret made as if to reply, but Henry Turner held a hand up to silence her. 'The thing is, you're a fine woman, Mrs Devlin – and I don't want to offend you. If I've misread the signals, then please forgive me. I appreciate that, given the circumstances, you may well think that the question is inappropriate and now may not be the time, but . . .' It sounded as if it was a speech he had been working on for a while.

Margaret smiled. 'Not at all,' she purred. 'And I'm very flattered, Inspector. Dinner sounds lovely. The last few weeks have been very grim. It would be so nice to have something to look forward to.'

That part at least was true. The bank had said they wouldn't extend the overdraft, the garage had refused her credit cards, and Mrs Hill, Margaret's cleaner, had said that, while she quite understood things were tight and she didn't want to see Margaret in a fix, come the end of the month unless things changed she would be looking elsewhere for employment. Margaret closed her eyes and tried not to think about it. She didn't even know where Mrs Hill kept the Dyson.

Teetering on the edge of ruin was not something Margaret found particularly easy to contemplate, particularly when it wasn't her fault. The thought of doing her own ironing made her feel positively nauseous. The indignity of it. The doctor had given her sleeping tablets and some sort of white happy pills that he assured her would help. Nights were the worst; sleeping was close to impossible because every time she closed her eyes, Margaret imagined she was standing on the edge of a very tall building looking down into the steaming, screaming lanes of traffic below. Sometimes she could swear that James was there too, watching, gloating, willing her to jump. It was all she could do to hang on.

Margaret gritted her teeth; she had to keep it together. She would find James, she would win. As the days passed, the more she thought about it the less she was convinced that James had topped himself. It would be convenient, but he was far too selfish for that. In which case the bastard might very well still have two million quid squirrelled away somewhere and she was going to get a slice of it if it was the last thing she did.

'I was thinking that maybe we could go to the –' But before DI Turner could finish the sentence, the doorbell rang. Damn. Margaret looked lovingly across at him and tried to ignore it. Perhaps if she wished hard enough, whoever it was would go away.

Henry looked at her; she smiled. 'Do you think you ought to get that?' he said.

The bell rang again. 'It's probably nothing important,' she said, trying to wave the sound away. Margaret pulled a face; there was a very faint chance it might be journalists, although since the announcement of James's suicide – once they had been given another statement and some rather nice photos of her in her new black suit – they'd gone away. Old news. And DI Turner had ensured that there had been a discreet police presence ever since the news had broken. She had even agreed to a phone tap, in case James rang – fat chance of that. God knows what would happen when the bill came in for her mobile; she'd had to keep it for all those calls she needed to make that she had no wish for the police to hear.

There were just too many things to worry about. Despite the pills, if she started to think about it, it felt as if her head was filling up with thick prickly sand.

The doorbell rang again. Whoever it was wasn't going to go away. Margaret reluctantly got to her feet and went out into the hall. Damn, and just when Henry had been warming up nicely.

Preoccupied with thoughts of where DI Turner might take her for supper, whether he would try anything else, whether she could cope with a man with a moustache, and how much he would be prepared to help her, Margaret opened the door without thinking about who it might be.

Out on the doorstep in the early evening sunshine stood a familiar figure. 'Gordie,' she hissed in astonishment, glancing back nervously towards the sitting room.

'Maggie, hen.' He stepped inside and wiped his feet. He was carrying a bottle of gin and a bunch of blood-red roses, their colour accentuated by a sprinkling of snow-white gypsophila.

'What are you doing here?' she said in an undertone.

'How are you doing, m'dear?' he said, kissing her warmly on each cheek. 'Nice to see you. You smell wonderful and look even better. I got your message. I came as soon as I could.'

Margaret looked up at him, feeling increasingly uncomfortable. 'My message?'

But even as she said it, she knew which message. The one she'd left on his answer machine after a lot of booze, a couple of sleeping pills and a long slow decline into self-pity. The one that began, 'Gordie, I wish to God I had left James and gone off with you when you asked me. I don't know what I'm going to do. Everything is so awful, so terrible. What am I going to do, Gordie?' The one where she had sobbed and cried and begged and – and, it was all coming back to her now in glorious shame-red Technicolor.

'I'm so sorry,' she began, 'what on earth must you think of me?'

He smiled sympathetically. 'You needn't worry, lass, I'd never see you in a muddle, you know that. Besides, I thought you'd like to know that J—' Before he could finish the sentence, DI Turner stepped out of the sitting room still holding his glass of brandy.

'Is there a problem, Margaret?' he asked briskly. He sounded almost proprietorial.

The two men looked each other up and down, eyes locked. Margaret shivered, feeling a frisson of delight as the two of them drew back and puffed up like bucks fighting over a doe. She would have fluttered her eyelashes if she could have managed it on the tablets.

DI Turner sniffed. 'Gordon,' he said icily, inclining his head in greeting without giving an inch.

'Henry,' said Gordie, doing the same.

'I had no idea that you knew Mrs Devlin,' said Henry Turner coldly.

'Aye, well, it's a small world,' said Gordie, not moving and then, to Margaret, 'I'm sorry, m'dear, it's obvious I picked a bad moment. I'll drop by another time. I just came by to offer my condolences.' He suddenly sounded terribly formal and distant, although Margaret suspected – hoped – that it was to protect her from Henry asking too many difficult questions once he'd gone. Turning back towards the door, Gordie handed her the bunch of roses. 'I'm so sorry to hear about your tragic loss.'

Margaret looked up at him beseechingly. 'Let me walk you to your car,' she said.

Gordie shook his head. 'No need, hen.' Margaret noticed that he had surreptitiously slipped the gin inside his Crombie. 'Your husband will be sadly missed, Margaret. If I can help in any way . . .'

Margaret looked up at him, eyes full of pleading.

'Have you had any news of James?' he asked

briskly, talking over her shoulder to Henry Turner.

DI Turner shook his head. 'Not a whisper. Family friend, are you, Gordon?'

Gordie nodded. 'Aye, we go back a long way, Margaret and me.'

She could feel her colour rising. Turning back towards Henry, she said quickly, 'Gordie was my first boss when I left school. I used to work in the office, with his wife.'

Gordie smiled beatifically which was hard when you had a face like a sackful of blunt chisels. 'Aye, those were the days, eh, lass? Those were the days.'

If Henry Turner had a problem with Margaret's answer, it didn't show.

Cass dreamed all night long. She dreamed about job interviews and au pairs and rich American widows in red tartan slacks and Daisy. She dreamt of her Corsa and the cottage in Norfolk, of painting and Mrs HMR sitting upstairs smoking a giant spliff with Charlie. She woke up in the middle of the night and thought for one horrible moment that David had tracked her down and was trying to clamber into bed with her – but fortunately it turned out to be Milo, the dog, trying to do something repulsive with one of Barney's socks.

Relieved beyond belief, Cass rolled over and slipped back into unconsciousness, dreaming of walking along Wells beach with James Devlin, while behind them, skipping hand in hand along the sand with David was Margaret Devlin and a huge crazed hound that foamed at the mouth while whining pathetically, and who Cass assumed had to be Snoops.

DI Turner stayed just long enough to finish his drink, then made his apologies and left. He said he had to be on his way, that he'd got things to do, although there had been no sign of that earlier. Nor had he mentioned where he might like to take her for dinner. Oddly enough, Margaret felt rather sad to see him go. She realised that she wanted him – against all the odds – to think well of her.

Henry Turner was a good man, something that Gordie Mann most definitely was not. Which was why she would never really have left James for Gordie – although once upon a time, when things between her and James had been at rock bottom and she needed a shoulder to cry on, it had been important to make him think that she might. Respectability mattered to Margaret. But more than that, *much* more than that, she thought, sitting there at her dressing table, gazing into the mirror, sliding off the day's face with cotton wool and the last of the Clarin's cleanser, Gordie Mann was not good with things that he thought he possessed.

She had known instinctively, even when she was a teenager, that the best way to keep Gordie Mann interested was to play hard to get. *Very hard to get*. To keep him hooked, it was far, far better if she appeared elusive, vulnerable and tender, and impossible to pin down.

Margaret massaged a smear of night cream into her face and stared at her reflection, wondering what had happened to all those years and what had become of that supreme confidence that had let her play Gordie like a fish when she was seventeen? Her mobile rang. She looked at the screen and smiled. Well, talk of the devil.

Gordie Mann. Whoever would have thought that he knew James Devlin? There was a stitch someone had missed along the way. DI Turner poured himself another drink and picked up the phone. He needed to make sure that it wasn't overlooked again.

When the alarm went at 7 a.m. and Cass opened one bleary eye she was exhausted, having spent all night avoiding being mashed, attacked or savaged.

'Barney, there is no way I can drive a bloody Bentley –' It was just after eight o'clock the following morning outside Barney's flat in Sussex Square.

Barney looked at Cass. 'Don't be so ridiculous – of course you can. It's wonderful to drive. Once you've driven this, you'll never want to drive anything else. Get in, give it a go. It'll be so useful;

you can run Mother down to the bookies when Charlie's on his day off. That other tight-lipped bitch who comes in to look after her thinks gambling and drink are the devil's work. I'm convinced Mother only keeps her on to torment her.'

Cass looked at the huge and very beautiful black car now double parked outside Barney's front door.

'Why don't you drive it round the block? It'll give you a chance to get a feel for it before you trek back to the sticks. Off you pop. I'll go inside and keep an eye on what's-his-name till you get back.'

'Danny,' she said crossly, as if he didn't know already.

'Right. Oh, and did you want that other slice of toast that you left on your plate?'

Cass glowered at him. 'I can't put the dog in the back of this.'

'Of course you can. They slip about for a while on the leather, but they get the hang of it eventually. And the claw marks hardly show – I usually whip over them with some Cherry Blossom shoe polish. Or they settle down in the footwell. I used to have a lovely brown whippet called Tally – I'd brake like buggery and she'd come flying over the back of the seat like a big hairy bird. She adored it. Now, go on, we haven't got all day and the toast is getting cold.'

'I can do this,' Cass whispered to herself, slipping inside. Checking that she was in neutral, she turned the key. An instant later the engine purred into life, a purr so soft as to be almost inaudible.

'There – what did I tell you? Piece of cake. Jake and I used to have to beat the pussy off with a stick when we went out in this,' said Barney, eyes bright with nostalgia.

'Go inside and eat your toast,' said Cass.

Less than an hour later, Cass and Danny were on their way home to Norfolk. Driving the Bentley was a wonderful and strange experience. Quite a few people stopped on the side of the road to stare at her, with Milo and Danny in the back seat. Some gave way as if there was a possibility that she might be a minor member of the royal family or maybe a diplomat, and others sneered and flicked the V's. One thing was for certain, Cass had never driven any car that had attracted so much attention.

Jake applauded her as she pulled into the cottage driveway.

'I don't know what you're looking so pleased about,' she said, jumping out to embrace him. 'You're going to have to reverse it out.'

At the end of the lane a small balding man, working under cover of a striped workman's tent, tipped the radio mike up towards his mouth and said triumphantly, 'The Eagle has landed.'

* * *

The blonde woman looked James Devlin up and down from under her roots and fringe, not quite meeting his eye. 'Right. S'Mr Smith, isn't it? I've been expecting you. If you'd like to follow me up to the flat. Dustbin day is Wednesday – bins are in the alley, they're all numbered,' she said, wiping her hands on the arms of her sweatshirt. 'It's quiet here. Everyone keeps themselves to themselves, know what I mean? And that's how we like it. Quiet.'

The stairwell smelt of Jeyes Fluid and gave dingy a bad name; the stairs were pre-cast concrete with a grey metal handrail, each flight and landing lit by a grimy bulkhead light.

'You're up on the second floor, number 5. New to the area, are you?'

James Smith nodded. He was new to this kind of place too.

'Now, you understand about the rent, don't you? In cash, first of the month. There's no credit for arrears, so don't insult me by asking. Working down here, are you?' The words all ran together. She slid the key into the lock of flat 5 and eased the door open as if she might disturb something inside.

'Your security deposit don't cover damage to the windows, doors, or any of the bathroom fittings,' she added, while stubbing her cigarette out in an ashtray on the window sill. 'No subletting, no open fires or gas welding.'

James nodded.

'So here we are, then. Nice size bedroom, lounge, kitchenette. Bathroom's through there,' she said, with a grand sweep of her arm. 'Shouldn't go out on the balcony, if I was you. Not sure about the handrail.'

James's heart sank. There was anonymous and then there was oblivion. The tiny flat was entirely furnished in various shades of brown: brown carpet, dark brown Formica table with two matching chairs upholstered in tan vinyl, brown floral curtains, a brown teak-effect cabinet with smeared glass doors, and a light brown rug in front of the brown-and-cream gas fire.

'Meter for the gas, and the electric's in the kitchen cupboard – they run on cards. Five quid each. If you want to come down once you've settled in, I'll get you a couple. There's an immersion in the bathroom. Now, is there anything else you want to know?' She paused to draw breath, crossing her arms over her ample chest, waiting for him to speak, but there was nothing James wanted to know.

'Anything you want, just pop down and see me.' She smiled flirtatiously, which was disturbing. 'My Jas' can get you a telly, DVD – anything you like. Very reasonable prices, too. You're lucky, these flats don't come up very often.'

Lucky didn't cover any of the sentiments James was feeling.

In an ideal world he would have much preferred to have rented the flat a few months in advance or moved into one of the places he already owned. In fact, that had been James's plan, working well in advance and slowly, so as not to arouse any suspicion. It wasn't that he didn't have a place of his own – far from it, he had several. But things had come to a head quicker than he'd anticipated and the last thing James Smith needed at this moment was any hint of a paper trail that might lead anyone to his door.

The flat had been found for him, close to a port with regular routes bound for the Continent. Somewhere large enough for him not to stand out. He knew he was meant to be grateful.

The woman's smile faded. 'There we are,' she said, handing him a key. The flat number was printed in red Biro on a crumpled luggage label.

As soon as she was gone, James Devlin checked his watch. It wouldn't be long now before he saw her again, but the hours were dragging so slowly. He wondered how she would be, whether she would bring the police with her. He walked across to the window and looked out at the grey-blue morning sky. It was so good that she was going to bring the dog.

It felt like Cass had never been away, or rather that she had stepped back into the things she liked and missed most about the cottage. Danny was out playing in the garden in the sunshine whilst Cass sorted through her work in the studio. Jake had helped her convert it from the old washhouse not long after she moved in. It was a lovely space with casement windows, red-brick walls outside, and warm creamy-white lime-wash inside, all snuggled up under a faded red Norfolk pantile roof. The front windows, framed by hollyhocks and lupins, overlooked the lane, while the back door opened up straight into the garden where, by the doorstep, a languid blousy yellow rose crept up towards the sunlight.

It was the most beautiful place to work. Not that she had managed to get a lot done over the previous few months, Cass thought regretfully. The studio felt neglected, the air stale and heavy with dust. A spider had set up home amongst her paintbrushes, weaving them together under a shroud of tight webbing. She tucked a stray tendril of hair behind her ear, and looked carefully at the pile of paintings arranged on the table in the centre of the room. It had taken her an hour or so to get them sorted this far.

It seemed so long since she had done any serious work that it was as if some of the paintings had been done by other people. Aside from some framed landscapes and seascapes, most of her work had been stored in a large free-standing plan chest. There were various drafts and rough sketches for books that she had illustrated over the years: one with a wise owl sitting in a church tower, another with a small boy flying a kite, another with a child setting sail in a tiny cockleshell boat, sailing into a night sea of dreams.

Cass turned towards the light to get a better look at a nightscape painted in gouache, the little boy sailing through a stylised urban landscape in the tiny boat, trailing stars behind him like foam. She smiled. He looked remarkably like Danny as a toddler. Cass sighed and set it down amongst the others.

Maybe in some ways David was right: she was naïve, child-like. The children's books were the things she liked doing best, both for the colours and the content. A retreat from real life into a simpler, richer, altogether less painful place.

Cass glanced round the studio, considering which pieces she might take down to Brighton for an exhibition. There was certainly enough material. She pulled a portfolio up on to one of the benches and began to choose a group of illustrations that worked well together. It felt quite strange to go through so many of them, one after the other, ideas and images taking her back to other places, other times, each one evoking an emotional response.

Cass moved closer to the window and smiled. This one she had painted just before Danny was born, when all the women were as plump as butter. This one soon after they had got Milo as a puppy and in almost every picture, in the background, a hairy puppy with enormous feet leapt and tugged and tumbled or slept curled up into a tight ball.

Cass thumbed through the last few years, over-come alternately by nostalgia and a sense of loss. Tears pressed.

'Knock, knock,' said a familiar voice.

'Daddy, Daddy,' whooped Danny from the bottom of the garden.

Cass turned and was stunned as David stepped into the studio and pulled a face. 'I didn't know you were going to be bringing Danny up with you,' he said uncomfortably.

She shook her head in disbelief. 'Oh, David. What was I supposed to do, leave him behind? Don't be ridiculous. How can you be so bloody cruel?' Although it struck her that perhaps it wasn't so much cruelty as guilt.

Before David could reply, Danny hurtled up to him. There was a fraction of a second when Danny hesitated, but then David smiled and Danny leapt towards him, clambering up him as if he were a tree, cuddling and hugging and snuggling in tight as he went. Cass's heart ached.

'Hi, son,' said David stiffly. 'How's Brighton going?'

Danny started to tell him, the words all jumbled, bits about the dogs, the shop, Mrs HMR upstairs, learning to play cards, walking on the beach.

'Why don't we go into the house?' said Cass. 'I can sort everything out in here in a little while.'

'And Danny can go and play in the garden while Mummy and Daddy talk,' said David. 'Can't you, Danny?' It was obvious from his

195

expression that that was the very last thing Danny wanted.

Cass went inside, trying very hard not to catch David's eye.

In the stripy workman's tent down the lane the bald man grinned and, pulling the head mike closer, said, 'Wagons roll, the other Eagle has landed too.'

It wasn't the most eloquent call to arms, but even so Mr Marshall, who planned to co-ordinate the snatch operation from a converted bread van that was even now making its way into position, smiled to himself. With a bit of luck they would have James Devlin in their clutches by suppertime. He rubbed his hands together with delight; he only hoped that Mr Devlin had the good sense to tell him exactly where the money was stashed before Gordie Mann got involved.

Mr Marshall's plan was to appeal to Devlin's better nature, mention Gordie's involvement – which surely ought to soften Devlin up a bit – and then he would question him. Once he had found out how to retrieve the money, Mr Marshall would deposit Mr Devlin somewhere nice and safe, bound and gagged, ready for the police to collect him. The old anonymous tip-off trick should have them there in no time – hopefully well before Gordie Mann showed up with his heavies.

Mr Marshall parked the van up under cover of a high hawthorn hedge and waited. He could see Cassandra Hammond's cottage a little way up the road. His man was outside it, crouching in his stripy tent, all set and ready for action. James Devlin's car was parked in the lane outside the cottage, the drive having been taken by a Bentley.

Plan A was to wait until Mr Devlin left Mrs Hammond's. A hundred yards beyond Cass's cottage the lane came to a dead end, so Mr Marshall would pull out in the bread van, blocking the road, and his men – four great lumps dressed in camo gear who were currently waiting in a Land Rover not far behind, with what looked like fishing tackle strapped to the roof rack – would leap out and grab Devlin, subdue him, load him into the bread van and then away. It was far less messy than bursting in and snatching him from the cottage. Things always got broken and, besides, the fewer people who saw the snatch the better.

The only houses in the lane were Mrs Hammond's and her next-door neighbour's, so hopefully the operation would go unnoticed. The idea was to create a sandwich so that Mr Devlin's car would be trapped between the two vehicles, which would also hopefully help to mask their activity.

Mr Marshall looked down at his watch. Devlin had barely been there five minutes. Waiting was always the worst part.

Danny didn't want to go out into the garden to play. He wanted to stay with David, he wanted David to play with him and talk to him and read a book or maybe watch a video. Or if he was going to go outside, he wanted David to come with him and play in the sandpit, which Cass thought was very reasonable but David found increasingly frustrating.

'The thing is I really need to talk to you,' David hissed between clenched teeth as Danny went off to find his Lego dragons for them to play with. 'Alone.'

Cass could sense a storm brewing and went upstairs after him. 'Danny?'

He looked up from his toy box.

'Mummy and Daddy want to talk for a little while. If you don't want to go into the garden, you could always go round to Jake's. I promise we won't be long.'

Danny looked at her with big sad eyes. 'Are you going to shout at each other?'

Cass felt something horribly painful well up in her chest, and realised she didn't know the answer. 'I hope not,' she said gently.

Danny thought for a moment. 'Can I take my dragons round Jake's?'

Cass nodded. 'Uhuh, good idea. Let me just ring him.' She went out on to the landing and covered the receiver so that neither David nor Danny could hear. 'Jake?'

'Uhuh?'

'Would you mind if Danny came round for a while?'

'Christ, don't tell me you're having a conjugal visit with laughing boy,' he said grimly.

'Don't be ridiculous.'

'So what does he want? We both know that he's trouble, that man.'

'I know. I've no idea what he wants, but he's being horrible to Danny. Can I bring him round?'

'Of course. I've missed being in loco grandparentis.'

Cass waved to Danny, who stood up, dragons in hand, and they went back downstairs. Cass saw David look at them and smile as she guided Danny out of the door. She hoped Danny hadn't seen the triumphant expression on David's face. How bloody awful to be so pleased that your son was leaving.

As Cass left, Danny and Jake were breaking out the chocolate-chip ice cream. Back in the cottage, David had settled himself down in his favourite armchair in the sitting room.

'So,' said Cass coolly. 'What exactly did you want to talk to me about?'

David glanced over his shoulder, as if there was some possibility that they might be overheard and then suddenly his eyes filled up with tears.

'It's Abby,' he said, his voice thick with emotion. 'God,' he sniffed. 'Sorry.' He pulled out a tissue and blew his nose.

'What about Abby?' asked Cass cautiously.

'Well, I'm not sure how much you know, but, let's be frank, it's not been easy over the last few months for any of us,' he said. 'And then a couple of weeks ago, Carl turned up. He's been backpacking in Thailand with Chris and Boogie.'

'Carl, Chris and Boogie?'

'Uhuh.' David blew his nose again. 'That's right. They went to school together. Carl's Abby's old boyfriend. And then, when I was out, Stephanie said that she saw them –'

'Whoa, whoa,' said Cass quickly. 'This is turning into an episode of *Hollyoaks*. We're grown-ups, David. Can we just cut to the chase?'

'She's left me. For Carl. He's twenty, with a tattoo and a nose ring.' His lip started to tremble. 'Twenty. God this is so awful.' And with that he burst into tears.

Cass stared at him wondering whether to laugh or cry or be angry, and instead handed him a box of tissues. David looked up at her, snorting and sniffing, and mumbled his thanks.

'She said that I – I was dull and boring and she wanted to go out more, she didn't want to stay at home playing happy families and cooking and doing the garden,' he said after a few moments. 'I tried to explain that eating burgers all the time gives me heartburn, and that they were full of rubbish, but anyway we went to this club. I thought it went OK, but she was worried about what her friends might think, in case they thought I was her dad. And she hates my music and my clothes. I understood that – we all get set in our ways so I went out and bought a few new things. She said I looked ridiculous. She said she didn't feel she could bring her friends back to the flat if I was there. So I gave her some space, you know, to sort things out. She may seem mature, but I would be a fool not to acknowledge that there is an age gap. Anyway, I'd come home from work and they'd all be there, watching TV, eating junk and drinking . . .' David paused. 'I felt left out, but if I told them to leave it made me sound even more like her dad. I suppose Carl must have come round then, or maybe when she was there all day on her own.'

'But you said something about being followed.'

He nodded, great big tears rolling down his rapidly reddening face. 'Uhuh, Carl's friends came round to the office and threatened to beat me up if I tried to get back with Abby and kept ringing her and stuff.'

'Right,' said Cass slowly. 'What do you want me to do about it?'

'Well, I thought I could move back in here. I mean, we all make mistakes.' He tried to make it sound low-key, matter-of-fact, as if it was the most obvious thing in the world. 'No point in keeping the flat on really, is there? And this place is empty at the moment. We're both adults, I'm sure we can find a way to sort it all out.'

Cass stared at him.

'What?' he said blankly. 'What have I said?'

'David, you are unbelievable,' she said.

He stared at her. 'I'm not with you. What have I said?'

Cass got up, not trusting herself to be within

striking distance, and glad that there was nothing sharp within easy reach.

'David,' she said very slowly, struggling to stay calm, 'you can't move back in here.' He opened his mouth as if to speak, but she was ahead of him. 'I don't want you back. Not now, not ever. Do you understand?'

'What do you mean, you don't want me back?' His eyes widened. 'For God's sake, Cass – after all we've been through. I mean, I can understand that you're hurt –'

'Hurt doesn't anywhere near cover it,' said Cass, holding the same low, even voice, terrified of what might happen if she let go. Why couldn't he see how livid she was, how bloody furious?

'But –' he began.

'But nothing,' she said. 'Now, is there anything else you want to say before you leave?'

'You're being very unreasonable. I intend to go and see my solicitor,' he said, full of surprise, outrage and indignation.

Cass could feel her control crumbling. 'Good idea. I hope he has the sense to tell you what a complete and utter bastard you are, because if he doesn't, mine will. Now get out of my house before I stop trying to be civil.'

'What about Danny?' he said. 'I thought –'

Cass fixed him with angry hurt eyes. 'I'll tell him that you're sorry but you couldn't stay.'

'But I can,' said David. 'I can – I've just told you –'

She shook her head, rage building like a head of steam. 'Oh no you can't,' she yelled. 'No, you can't! Now get out of here, you miserable little bastard!'

6

Once the door was shut behind him, Cass, blind with raging fury, swept her arm across the top of the worktop and cleared it. Mugs, bread, a pile of magazines and letters, the teapot and God knows what else flew across the kitchen and crashed down on to the flagstone floor like a wave of mortar bombs. Jars and bottles exploded as they landed, while Cass sobbed furiously, 'Bloody man. Bloody-bloody-sodding man, bloody-bastard-sodding-bloody man,' into the empty house.

As the sobs subsided, Cass could hear a noise. Her mobile was peeping in her handbag. It was a text. Who the hell was texting her? If it was David, making some patronising, lovey-dovey stupid manipulative comment, she would hunt him down like a dog and, and . . .

She dragged the back of her hand across her face to wipe the tears away, took a deep calming breath, and pulled the phone out of her bag. The text read:

Looking forward to seeing you later. Give me a ring if there are any problems. J. x

J. x? Cass sniffed and stared bleary-eyed at the screen. Exactly how many problems did a girl need? She blew her nose and tried to get a grip, while looking around miserably at the trail of devastation in the kitchen. A jar of strawberry jam had smashed against the door, its contents oozing lazily down the stripped pine panels in a great bright red gout of gore. It looked like someone had been shot.

Cass sighed and swore softly under her breath. Having a temper tantrum was all very well, but the clearing up was a real pain in the arse. The floor was littered with lids and goo and shards of broken crockery and glass, which crunched unpleasantly underfoot like bits of broken tooth.

Cass got out the brush and dustpan and then glanced at the clock. If she was to be on time for her liaison with Mr Peaches she needed to get a move on. Chaos or no chaos, eyes this puffy needed some serious seeing to.

As Cass was tidying the last of the mess away, Jake reappeared with Danny and the Lego dragons in tow.

'I thought I'd give you a minute or two,' Jake said ruefully. 'I heard the crash.' He sniffed. 'And the screaming. I won't ask how it went.'

'Oh, it's all sorted out now. I just dropped a tray,' Cass said briskly for Danny's benefit. 'Bit clumsy really. I'm going to nip upstairs and get in the shower and then – oh, damn.'

Jake looked at her questioningly. 'Anything I need to know about?'

Cass reddened. 'No,' she snapped, turning her attention back to Danny, who had pulled up a chair and was busy making the dragons wrestle across the kitchen table. 'I was going to ask if you would take care of Danny while I nipped out – I didn't think the David thing was going to be a problem.'

'He'll be fine. Besides, I've still got half a bag of deep-frozen pterodactyls to get through,' said Jake, picking up a stray shard of willow pattern from the flagstones.

'Thank you,' said Cass. Even though he had suggested it, taking Danny on a date with a master criminal wasn't such a bright idea. Maybe going along at all wasn't a bright idea. 'Are you sure you don't mind?'

Jake shook his head. 'No. I've missed him, although I think he was hoping to have a word or two with David before he left.'

Cass stroked Danny's hair. 'I know. Daddy couldn't stay, sweetie. But you can ring him later, if you like,' she said as lightly as she could manage.

Without looking up, Danny said, 'If he ever gets home.'

Cass and Jake both stared at him, and then at each other. Cass wondering where a comment like that had come from. Maybe the break-up and seeing David today was unsettling Danny more than she thought.

'What do you mean, love, "if he gets home"?' she said, trying hard not to sound worried.

Danny looked up and continued conversationally, 'He probably won't get home. He was kidnapped by action men. I saw them when I was at Jake's. Like on the cartoons – they jumped out of a Land Rover, ka-boom, and grabbed him – whumpf – and then they stuffed him into a big white van. Boooooom. He's probably tied up in a dungeon somewhere right now.'

Cass stared at her son, envisaging a life that revolved around weekly trips to see the child psychologist, long-term medication and lots of group therapy, while trying to work out what all that really meant. Danny had always had an active imagination, but he had never deliberately lied to her before. Meanwhile he was busy re-enacting the supposed kidnap with the dinosaurs. The small one was being heartily leapt on by a couple of bigger, muscular ones.

'They just stopped and grabbed him – ker-pow,' he said, one dragon whipping another off his feet. 'Daddy didn't say anything. Do you think they were just playing or doing it for a joke?'

Playing? Cass wasn't altogether sure what to say, so she just nodded and then looked at Jake, who shrugged.

'OK, sweets. Tell you what, Mummy's going to go and have a shower now. Do you want to come up and have one too? I've got bubble stuff.' After all, what else was there to say? Maybe if they didn't say anything or make too much fuss, it would go away.

'Uhuh, OK,' Danny said, although he carried on playing.

Jake puffed out his cheeks thoughtfully. 'While you do that, I'll go and take a look around outside,' he said. 'You know, just in case any of the action men are still lurking around.'

'You won't see anything, they've all gone now. They all went off in the Land Rover,' said Danny brightly, as the little dinosaur's head pinged off and flew across the kitchen table.

Fifteen minutes later, with her hair still damp from the shower, Cass stood in front of the wardrobe and peered inside. Out on the landing, Danny was scuttling about wrapped in a towel, pretending to be a dinosaur.

What exactly do you wear for a date with a good-looking, adulterous embezzler? Trinny and Susannah had never had to deal with that as a makeover brief. And *why* exactly was she going? Cass ignored the voice of reason in her head while thumbing her way along the hangers, looking at various stalwarts, and considering the possibilities.

Perhaps something with concealed pockets so he couldn't run off with her purse and credit cards? Low heels so she could make a break for it when the law showed up? Something neutral and unremarkable so there was nothing to put on the photofit or point out in the line up? Cass sighed. This was probably not a very constructive line of thought. So why was she going? He was a thief, a liar – and very nice-looking, said her brain all in the same sentence.

Finally Cass settled on jeans and a white cotton vest top, a cornflower blue cardigan and canvas deck shoes. A lick of makeup and a bit of lippy. She looked in the mirror – not bad, she thought, adding earrings and a few silver bangles. The wind on Wells beach would take care of any ideas she might harbour about looking smart, sexy and sophisticated.

After a bit of shouting and a little cajoling, Danny went and got dressed. He looked cute, too, in shorts and a sweatshirt, with a T-shirt and various bits and bobs packed away in a little rucksack to cover all eventualities. Milo the dog, who had been sound asleep on Danny's bed since they got home, didn't have to make any kind of effort; cute was his middle name.

As Cass was putting the finishing touches to her face, Jake, hands in pockets, meandered over from his cottage. 'All set then?'

Cass nodded. 'Uhuh. Did you see any sign of Danny's Daddy-stealing action men?'

'Nothing – not a sausage, zilch. David's car is gone. It's probably just an overactive imagination. But it was such a peculiar thing to say – not like him at all. There's a set of skid marks on the road, but they could have happened any time. Weird, though.'

'Do you think we should do anything about it?'

'You could try ringing him.'

'Jake, if I never saw him again it would be too soon.'

'OK, well in that case give me his number and I'll ring him.'

Cass agreed. 'Right, I'd better get going. And you're all set for the trip down to Brighton tomorrow?'

He nodded and began to count things off on his fingers. 'Oh yes, I've packed me cossie, pink flip-flops, a white knotted hankie, and a big bottle of suntan lotion. You're not thinking of going early, are you?'

Cass laughed. 'No, why?'

'Thank God for that. You know that I'm never at my best first thing. And what about this date?'

Cass stared at him. 'What date?'

Jake peered at her from under furrowed eyebrows. 'Cass, don't do that – I've known you too long. Last time we went to Wells you went in khaki boy-scout shorts, flip-flops and a sweatshirt.' Jake retrieved the headless dinosaur, dropped it into Danny's back pack and then said, 'Whatever you're up to, just be careful.'

Cass reddened.

In Brighton, Barney was busy showing the new au pair around.

'And this will be your room,' he said brightly to Antashinia, pushing open a door and waving an arm to encompass the tiny bedroom that overlooked the light well. He waited with a slight sense of apprehension; it wasn't exactly the Ritz. But he needn't have worried. The girl beamed at him.

'No, it's good,' she said, dropping her suitcase on to the narrow single bed wedged tight up under the window. 'Very good. I am very much liking it – yes, very much.'

'We can always get it sorted out more to your liking,' he said. 'Brighten it up with a few pictures, get a table and things. You know, once you've settled in.' Given the size of the room, any more furniture and they wouldn't be able to open the door, but Barney was working on the premise that it was the thought that counted, and the girl seemed to agree.

She nodded. 'No, it's nice,' she said, in a dense East European accent. 'I really am liking it very much. It's not right, the words, is it?' she giggled, then embarrassed and self-conscious, held her hand in front of her mouth. 'I put them in all ways, the words? My English is very bent.'

Barney beamed. 'No, no, it's absolutely fine,' he said. 'Charming. And we'll all help you get it right, don't worry.'

She giggled again and Barney felt his heart melt. OK, so Antashinia wasn't quite what he had in mind. She wasn't lithe and leggy and blonde as barley, but Barney had liked her as soon as he had opened the front door. She reminded him of a nanny he'd once had when he was a boy; a big capable, hairy, broad-shouldered woman with hands like a catcher's mitt, for whom nothing was a problem, nothing too much trouble, and who had sheltered him in the folds of her capacious bosom from all manner of evils – big spiders, thunder, the dark, and moths in his lampshade.

Oh yes, Antashinia would do very nicely, very nicely indeed.

'How about I leave you to unpack your things. Then we'll have a nice cup of tea and I'll show you the rest of the flat and take you up to meet my mother,' he said cheerily.

The girl smiled at him and pushed up her sleeves. 'Oh no, I can very soon come back and unpack later. Anyway, I haven't got so many stuffs. There are a few more boxes, but not much. If you show me where everything is, then I will make the tea – and perhaps a sandwich. Are you hungry? Do you like cakes? I love to bake cakes. I get this recipe book. By Delia? Do you know her? Lemon drizzle cake, madeleines and Bakewell tart?' The words rolled around her mouth sensually, longingly. 'Apple crumble? You know Delia, she is a fantastic cook and a very good footballer – you like her?'

Barney nodded, awash with delight. God, Antashinia was absolutely perfect. 'Well, actually, yes I do. And now you come to mention it, I am rather peckish,' he said. 'Why don't you follow me? I'll show you where the oven is.'

Behind them, as if glued to Antashinia's heel, trotted a stocky black-and-white springer spaniel, all big brown eyes and enthusiastic slobbery obedience. Maybe he liked cake, too. Barney stooped and patted the dog's head. The dog craned up and licked Barney's fingers. 'Lovely animal. What did you say his name was again?'

Antashinia smiled and scratched the dog lovingly behind the ears. 'Snoopy,' she said warmly. 'Like in the cartoon?' The dog looked up at her adoringly and began to wag its tail. 'But everyone, they call him Snoops,' she said, pulling a crisp white apron out of her handbag.

Cass parked Barney's Bentley opposite the café in the car park next to Wells beach, working on the assumption that it would be less likely to be broken into if she left it close to civilisation. In the back, Milo, nose wedged through the open window, was keen to get out, his body wagging from the neck down.

'Come on then,' said Cass.

The wind, sun-warmed and playful, whipped across the coarse grass, tugging at her clothes and muzzing her hair up. A connoisseur of wind and fine smells, Milo sipped and sniffed appreciatively while Cass went off to buy a parking ticket.

Behind the car on the seaward side was Wells lifeboat station and, running along from that was a huge sandbank topped with pine trees, that ran for miles back towards Holkham; a great protective arm curled around the low-lying land to defend it against the bullying, insistent waters of the North Sea.

This late on in the day, the car park was barely half full. Cass looked around as she stuck the ticket on to the windscreen, wondering where James Devlin was and what he would look like since his disappearance – had he dyed his hair? Grown a beard? Was he hiding somewhere? Maybe lurking in the shadows by the café, wearing a mack, shades and a wig.

'Hi. Great car,' said a familiar voice.

Cass felt her stomach tighten and looked round. James Devlin was standing no more than ten yards away, all smiles and looking exactly the same as he had when she'd last seen him on the train. No false moustache, or glue-on beard, nothing. He was dressed in a rugby shirt and jeans and was carrying a backpack slung casually over one shoulder. No doubt it was filled with fruit – unless he was carrying the missing two million quid around with him. Worse still, he looked gorgeous and fit and good enough to eat.

Damn. Cass, aware that she had her mouth open, snapped it shut and smiled. She realised with a start that she'd been really looking forward to seeing him, a feeling that was totally unexpected.

'I wondered if you'd show up. I thought you

might chicken out – you know, think maybe I was a mad axeman or something,' he said, grinning at her as he wandered over to the car.

Cass looked at him. Oh, he was something, all right. Milo wagged his tail, which Cass thought ruefully just goes to show that all that crap about dogs being good judges of character was complete rubbish, except that if she had a tail she would have wagged it too.

James smiled as if he knew what she was thinking. 'This yours?' He nodded towards the car.

'Unfortunately not. It's my new boss's.'

'Wow, some company car. Those are the kind of perks I'm after. So you obviously got the job then?'

Cass was about to say something ambiguous, wondering if now was the moment to bring up his various jobs – embezzler, serial philanderer and conman – when James Devlin said, 'Sorry, I realised on the way down here that you don't even know my name. I'm Joe – Joe Bennett.' And he extended his hand.

Cass stared at him. Presumably Joe Bennett was a pseudonym, a *nom de guerre* – or was he just a natural-born liar? Whichever it was, Cass sighed, wishing her brain was less willing to offer so many explanations and excuses for him.

'Joe?' she repeated.

He nodded. 'Yup, Joe Bennett. Sorry about that. I felt a bit bad – I've got all your personal details, your name and address, and you've got none of mine. So,' he said, 'pleased to meet you.' Then he smiled some more and shook her hand.

Cass wondered what on earth she should say now. Liar, liar, pants on fire? And why the hell did touching his hand make her shiver? Should she say, *Look, I know who you are, there's no need to pretend. You're James Devlin, thief, married man and – and God knows what else.* Wasn't now exactly the moment to call him out?

Taut as piano wire, Cass looked up at him, opened her mouth to speak – and nothing happened, not so much as a squeak, not a whisper. She just couldn't find the words. And then she had the most terrible, ridiculous thought: she wanted him to kiss her.

She also realised that he was still talking. 'So, do you want to head down to the woods and the beach straight away, or do you want a cup of tea and a bun first?' he asked.

'I'd just like to pop to the loo,' said Cass, struggling to regain her composure.

Joe nodded. 'Fair enough. I'll hold the dog if you like. What's his name?' Milo was looking up at him, full of undiluted adoration, tongue out, tail wagging wildly.

She was tempted to give Milo an alias, but grudgingly settled on the truth. God, this was ridiculous. She had to say something. The man was wanted by the police; they could be here now, waiting to pick him up. Cass looked around casually while Milo – now in Joe/James's hands, skipped and whined and whimpered with delight. Maybe they had got the car park staked out, maybe there were police marksmen watching their every move? Maybe they were about to be pounced on any second.

Cass put her head down and went into the ladies. Maybe they'd arrest him while she was inside. Hopefully, they would leave the dog.

When she re-emerged a few minutes later, East Anglia's Most Wanted was sitting on one of the rail-and-post fences that divided up the parking spaces, swinging his legs. Milo, the shameless tart, was happily rolling around on his back having his belly tickled and wagging wildly. So much for holding up under pressure.

'So tell me all about this new job of yours,' said Joe/James as they headed down the path towards the trees, while Milo scampered off ahead.

He loped alongside her, hands in his pockets. 'Are you happy? What's it like? How come you've ended up in Brighton? It seems a long way away. Or have you got family down there? Tell me all about it.'

As they got to the gate that led into the pinewoods, he opened it for her and Cass looked across at him. 'Hang on, which do you want me to answer first?'

The sun had lightened his hair a shade or two. He was tanned and nice looking, with kind gentle eyes, and Cass sighed, thinking about just how bloody cruel was fate.

'Oh, all of them,' he said, grinning, completely unaware of her thoughts.

This was most certainly not the right moment to meet someone she could fall for, and surely this was *not* the right man. There was a long warm soft silence as he held her gaze. And she felt her stomach do that funny fluttery back-flippy thing that happens when you fancy someone. Damn, damn, damn. Her mother had always warned her that she would come to a sticky end. Mind you, this was the same woman who thought David was a lovely man.

Cass realised she didn't know what to say and she'd forgotten what he'd asked her. Worse, he was so close that she could smell him, all warm and outdoorsy – fresh air, sun and sandalwood – and she thought, as he leaned towards her, for one glorious crazy unlikely moment that he was probably going to kiss her – and then he did.

Cass gasped in amazement. Although it was difficult to work out who was the more surprised, her or him. Even so, as he pulled away he said, 'I've been thinking about doing that since we first met on the train. You don't mind, do you?'

She looked up at him and realised that she didn't, not at all.

'Now, look, it would be an awful lot easier if you just came clean and told us exactly where the money is hidden,' said Mr Marshall, his tone more sad than angry. 'If you tell us now, then all this can stop.' He lifted his hands to encompass some great threatening chaos. 'Let's be honest, none of us want any more trouble than we can help and none of us want to involve Mr Mann, now, do we? We all know what he's like.'

'Well, no, actually, we don't,' snapped the man, currently tied hand and foot to a rather battered kitchen chair. He was quite obviously furious. 'And I suggest, if you've got any sense at all, that you let me go now. Do you understand? I presume you realise that kidnapping is against the law? Do you? Did Abby's dad send you? Or was it that arsehole she's going out with? Carl – the little bastard! That's who it is, isn't it? How much did he give you? There will be trouble, you know that – I'm warning you. I'm starting to lose my temper. If you let me go now, we'll say no more about it.' He started to jiggle and jiffle about in the chair. The muscles in his neck were as tight as hawsers, and his face and neck were turning a dangerous shade of puce.

Mr Marshall grimaced, not that the man could see his face. He wished he would just sit still, tell them what Gordie Mann needed to know and stop messing about. This was not how Mr Marshall had expected the interrogation to go at all. The snatch had gone like a dream. James Devlin, bundled into a van with a sack over his head, trussed up like a turkey in the twinkling of an eye. Seamless. Textbook stuff.

But given that Devlin was a businessman and

not a thug, and was certainly not known as a hard man, Mr Marshall had assumed that, having been dragged from his car, bound and gagged, roughed up a little on the way to the interrogation, and then left tied with nothing but his thoughts for company, he would be singing like a canary by now. Mr Marshall knew he would be.

'You want me to take over, boss?' grunted Eddy, cracking his knuckles theatrically. Eddy was an ex-soldier, six foot three in his lovat green army-surplus socks, with a neck like a car tyre, although rumour had it he had been a bandsman. It was Eddy who had insisted that they all wore bala-clavas or ski masks, which had seemed a bit excessive to Mr Marshall, not to mention terribly hot and itchy.

What was far more of a problem for Mr Marshall was that, rather than being terrified or in the slightest bit cowed, the man in the chair, once he had recovered from the actual abduction, was getting increasingly indignant.

'Look,' said the man, in a tone that suggested he was barely able to control his displeasure. They were in an abandoned Portakabin on a strip of waste ground alongside the main King's Lynn to London railway line, miles from anywhere. No one would hear him scream if Mr Marshall did unleash Eddy, but his captive didn't seem to give a tin shit how vulnerable he was.

'I don't know what all this is about. If you wanted to have a bit of fun and maybe teach me some sort of lesson, fine. But you're too late. Abby and I aren't seeing each other any more. *Capiche?* We've split up. And come on, she's eighteen – and if you know her, then you know she's very mature for her age, she knows her own mind. As far as I know, she's gone back with what's-his-face. Fucking Carl. And this rope is rubbing my wrists red raw. I've got a squash match on Wednesday evening. Veterans' inter-regional semi-finals. We're the defending champions. How the hell do you think I'm going to hold the racket?'

Mr Marshall stared at him. What was he going on about?

'My client doesn't care what you did with Abby. And he doesn't care about your bloody squash match. He just wants his money. So where's that two million quid that you've got stashed away?'

'Two million quid?' the man roared incredulously and then laughed. 'You really are a complete shambles. I've already told you, I don't know what the fuck you're on about. How many more times do you want me to say it? *You've got the wrong bloody man.* I was on my way home from seeing Cass when you grabbed me.'

'Ahah,' said Mr Marshall, hoping he had finally found a way in. 'So you admit that you know Cass Hammond, then, do you?'

'Of course I bloody know Cass Hammond – she's my wife,' bawled the man, his face now contorted with rage.

At which point the door to the office burst open

and in stepped Gordie Mann and assorted henchmen, all wound up and ready to go, wearing masks that made them look like something out of the *Phantom of the Opera* – although they were a lot better than balaclavas, thought Mr Marshall wistfully.

'So where is he then?' growled Gordie, squaring his shoulders and looking around the room expectantly.

Mr Marshall nodded towards the man in the chair. For God's sake, how many kidnappings did Gordie think he had on the go at any one time? Gordie's eyes registered non-comprehension, then bemusement and then surprise and finally anger. 'Who the fuck is that, then?' he snapped.

'James Devlin?' suggested Mr Marshall.

'No, it's not,' said Gordie.

'I told you so,' said the man in the chair. 'What is this, fright night? What have they come as?'

Mr Marshall, sweating hard under the balaclava, wished the man would shut up. 'But it must be him – the meeting was all set up. You read the transcripts –' And then, swinging round to the man in the chair: 'You hadn't got any papers on you – no wallet, nothing. Clean as a whistle,' he spluttered, finally running out of steam and admitting defeat.

'That's because I live half a mile down the bloody road, you moron. Anyway, what's that got to do with anything?' shouted the man, livid now. He was wriggling ever harder in the chair, rocking it back and forth in a furious effort to escape.

'Stop it, stop it,' said Mr Marshall, 'you'll tip yourself over. You were on the tape – I heard it myself.'

The man looked up at him as if he was speaking total gibberish. 'Tape, what fucking tape?' he snapped.

Gordie Mann nodded towards Eddy, who had finished cracking his knuckles and started on his wrists and elbows. 'I think we've all heard quite enough of this crap. Blindfold him, untie him, and take him back to his motor.' And then, to the bound man, 'You all right with that?'

'Well, I suppose I'll have to be, won't I?' said the man grumpily, finally settling back into stillness.

'Whereabouts is his motor?' asked Gordie.

'Tesco's car park.'

'Get him gone, then,' he said. 'Now.' Then, turning to Mr Marshall: 'I think it's about time you and I had a wee word.'

Mr Marshall swallowed hard; he could feel the sweat trickling down the inside of his balaclava, gluing the wool to his skin.

Meanwhile, in Wells-next-the-Sea, the sun was warm, the wind wafted the smell of pine resin, sand and sea salt through the late afternoon like a subtle invitation. Cass stared up at Joe/James. She had to say something and she had to say it soon, before he kissed her again. Which, she suspected, if they stood looking at each other for much longer, all cow eyes and beating hearts, would probably be sooner rather than later.

A hundred yards ahead along the path Milo yapped frantically as if calling them. Saved by the bark.

Joe grinned. 'Come on you heard what he said,' he called, and jogged off towards the dog, who was now springing from side to side with enthusiasm. Cass followed along behind, while her mind tried out various opening lines.

So, James, how are your wife and the kids? Or how about, *Embezzling: discuss?* Or maybe, *What in God's name are you doing here flirting with me when every policeman in the country is out looking for you? Are you completely and utterly mad?*

Maybe that wasn't the question to ask.

A few yards ahead of her, Joe/James threw a stick for Milo, who obliged by bringing it back in case it was something important.

'So you were going to tell me about this new job,' said Joe/James over his shoulder. Cass thought about all the things she needed to ask him, all a million times more important than anything she had to say about her job, took a deep breath and then said, 'Well, actually, it's great. I'm working for an artist; he's got a gallery and a shop – I'm kind of a Jill-of-all-trades . . .' And then she laughed, while kicking herself for having chickened out.

'Sounds interesting. Much better for you than an office job,' he said.

Cass looked across at him. 'It is, and I'm hoping to be able to get on with some of my own work.' Maybe Joe/James would bring the embezzling and stuff up once he felt more relaxed and at ease with her. Maybe he would just drop it into the conversation. In passing.

Cass took another look. Who the hell was she kidding? He was ambling along, all smiles, hands in his pockets, quite obviously happy to be there. Any more at ease and laid-back and he would be horizontal.

Over in Brighton, Antashinia was just bringing the first of a perfectly matched pair of Victoria sponges out of the oven. She had found all manner of bowls and tins, cutters and tools and an ancient sugar dredger in the back of one of the kitchen cupboards, and was planning a great snowstorm of icing sugar over the top of the cake when the two halves were cool and glued together with a fluffy pile of butter icing and strawberry jam. Barney had taken her by taxi down to Asda to lay in a mammoth supply of cooking ingredients and he seemed very pleased with the results so far. Two batches of currant buns and some jam tarts were already cooling on a wire rack on the table, while Snoops lay sound asleep under it, with Kipper and Radolpho for company.

When her mobile pinged to announce an

incoming text, Antashinia smiled and with floury fingers pulled the phone out of her apron pocket and opened up the mailbox.

Good to see you and Snoops today, read the message. *I love you both very much*. Antashinia flushed scarlet with sheer delight, the grin splitting her great moon-shaped face in two, like a jolly watermelon.

Barney, who had been sitting on the far side of the kitchen table, watching her bake and helping by eating the remains of the raw cake mixture straight out of the bowl, was desperate for something, anything, to be cool enough to eat. Optimistically he set down his side plate, with the remains of his second ham salad sandwich on the table. 'Good news?' he asked cheerfully.

Antashinia nodded. 'Oh yes, a friend of mine he has just moved in near here. He is wishing me luck, much luck and a hello. I see him today before I come to here. Would you mind very much if I baked him a cake too? He very much likes my cakes.'

Barney nodded. 'Of course you can bake him a cake, that would be fine. And I think it's good for you to have some local contacts. Are those ready yet?'

He pointed towards the buns.

She hesitated for a moment or two, struggling to find the right words. 'Maybe they still, still . . .' she huffed and puffed and mimed burnt fingers. It would be a shame to damage such a nice man.

This was a lucky break, finding Mr Barney. 'A few more minutes maybe?'

'Oh, I'm sure they will be fine.' Barney smiled and, prepared to take the risk it seemed, leaned over and whacked two buns on to his plate, followed by a jam tart. 'I'm sure that you won't be lonely here, but it's always nice to know other people, so you can talk – escape for a while. Moan a little. Got a boyfriend, have you?'

Antashinia blushed furiously. How on earth did Barney know that she moaned?

'Sorry,' Barney said, holding up his hands in surrender. 'I didn't mean to pry.'

'. . . And he's offered me an exhibition of my work, and help with getting it framed, which is why I'm home today. I've come to pick up some of my stuff – some illustrations and calligraphy that I've done,' said Cass, looking out across the wide expanse of almost coral-white sand. Framed by Scots pine with a sky as blue as Wedgwood china, it looked more like Sweden or a tropical island than North Norfolk.

They had walked along the beach towards Holkham, past the dunes, away from the holiday-makers, and were now making their way back, clambering up the walkways near the tea hut, between the row of brightly coloured beach huts, which were strung along the woodland edge like carnival bunting. Across the sand a child threw a kite up into the teasing, nipping wind and pulled

227

the string tight as it spun away up into the rising thermals.

'Great.' Joe/James looked impressed. 'Sounds perfect.' And as he spoke, he caught hold of her hand and for an instant pressed it to his lips. Cass didn't resist. It *was* perfect, but she wasn't thinking about the exhibition and he kept kissing her – this had to be at least the sixth time – and each time he lingered a little longer and the kick in the bottom of her heart, the one that drove lust, desire and longing, got louder and louder and louder. It was amazing she could hear herself think, really.

'I'm so glad you came,' he said, his voice barely audible above the roar.

Cass looked away, pulling a stray tendril of hair back off her face, and sighed. Why did he have to keep doing that? It was ruining her concentration.

Her plan to ask Joe/James about his career as a master criminal was not going very well. They had been walking and talking for the best part of an hour, and yes, there had been lots of opportunities for her to broach the subject, but no, she still couldn't quite find the right words despite having tried out lots in her head. Besides, she wasn't planning on repeating the experiment, was she? *Was she?*

He grinned across at her. 'I haven't been to Brighton in years,' he said. 'Maybe I could come down and see you, wander round your exhibition?'

Damn.

At which point Cass's mobile rang.

It was Barney, who sounded as if he was talking through a handful of dusters. 'Hi. Are you all right?' Barney didn't wait for her to answer. 'I just wanted to tell you that the au pair's arrived and she's perfect. Bloody, buggering perfect.'

Cass put her finger in her ear. 'I'm sorry, I can hardly hear you.'

'My fault, I'm eating a cheese straw – fresh out of the oven. God, they are wonderful. She cooks, she cleans – she's been here hardly any time at all and the place looks better already, she's doing something to the oven with a cloth and some stuff right now.' He sounded jubilant. 'I've already taken her up to meet Mother.'

'And?'

'And she has promised to make her a Pavlova with summer fruit. When I left, Mother had Charlie looking up a recipe for bombe surprise on Google that she and my father had when they were in Singapore. Oh, and one of those things with meringue on the outside and ice cream in the middle. What do they call them? They were all the rage at pretentious dinner parties a few years ago, in the seventies? It's on the tip of my tongue.'

'What about her references?'

'What?'

'Mary Poppins' references? Did you ask to see them?'

There was a heavyweight pause, and then Barney snapped, 'You know, you are such a stick-in-the-mud, Cass. She can make pastry and she was talking about cleaning the windows – on the inside, for God's sake – and washing the paint-work down. She's going to start properly tomorrow. What on earth is that pudding called?'

'Barney,' said Cass slowly, in a firm but no nonsense let's-put-the-gun-down-shall-we voice. 'I thought one of the main reasons you employed me was to help save you from yourself. To stop you from employing strange people who steal your stuff and do weird things with your shoes? Remember?'

He sniffed. 'Yes, yes, yes, I know, but this is different. She is lovely. So's the dog. They have matching moustaches. Oh, I know – Baked Alaska, that's it. And she said she can make ice cream. I thought I might nip down to Argos and get one of those machines, and maybe some more baking tins and a set of scales – can you think of anything else? Maybe I should ask her.'

Cass wondered if the noises she could hear were him skipping round the kitchen. And then from somewhere close by she heard a police siren and froze, although no one else did.

'Now, are you going to be all right to drive home?' asked Eddy solicitously as he and David pulled into Tesco's car park. 'I'd nip inside and get your-self a cup of coffee and some Savlon for them rope burns, if I was you.'

David, trussed up on the back seat like a joint of pork, and for the most part covered up with a

Black Watch tartan travelling rug, growled angrily. 'Just hurry up, get it over with and let me go, will you?' he snapped.

'That is the plan,' said Eddy calmly, pulling away from the main ebb and flow of shoppers into a quiet corner under the trees. 'Now, what I'm going to do is drive up alongside your motor. I'll get out and unlock it. You stay nice and still and quiet in the back there till I'm done, and then I'll help you out and put you in your jam jar. No sweat, no fuss – OK?'

'OK? What do you mean *OK*? Tied up and with this stupid mask on? You must be mad.'

'That,' said Eddy, even more slowly, in case David missed the point, 'is so's you can't see my face. And then, when you're in your car, I'll loosen the rope, so's you can get yourself free as soon as I'm gone.'

'I'd know you anywhere, monkey boy,' spat David. 'It's a bloody stupid idea. Do you hear me?'

Eddy sighed. 'Look, let's try and keep calm, shall we? Just keep your head down and don't draw attention to yourself. And it's not stupid. It's a pair of goggles with gaffer tape underneath.'

'Oh well, that's all right then. That's really going to be inconspicuous, isn't it?' sneered David.

Eddy was fast losing patience. His passenger had moaned all the way there, every last yard, from being manhandled into the Land Rover back at the Portakabin to the supermarket car park, and so far there was no sign of any let-up.

'Look,' said Eddy again, trying to remain calm, 'we can do this the easy way, or we can do it the hard way. It's entirely up to you, matey.'

From under his blanket, David snorted. 'Jumped-up little oik, don't you "matey" me. Who the hell do you think you are? What do you mean, the hard way? *The hard way?* You think you're so bloody tough, don't you, Rambo? Well, just let me tell you –'

Eddy, his patience finally exhausted, swung round and gave his passenger a hearty crack on the back of the head with a small cosh he always carried with him in case of such an emergency. David Hammond crumpled like tissue and an instant later was blessedly quiet.

In the blissful silence that followed, Eddy unlocked his passenger's car and with the minimum of fuss, manhandled a bemused and befuddled David into the back seat, where Eddy arranged him into something as close to the recovery position as he could manage, peeled off the ski goggles and left David to his own devices.

'You bastard, I'll get you,' mumbled David, as Eddy shut the door behind him. Eddy clambered back into the Land Rover. There was just no pleasing some people.

Over by the trolley shelter, a boy tipped him a snappy salute as he drove away. Eddy beamed; now that was more like it.

*   *   *

Cass hastily said her goodbyes to Barney and looked up anxiously at Joe/James who was walking through the trees, happily heading back towards the car park. In the distance, as they rounded the corner, Cass could see blue lights flashing on the far side of the open field. She slowed the pace down to a crawl.

Obviously he was completely mad. Was this some sort of gung-ho gesture, a last fling before he gave himself up after one final afternoon of joy?

'The police –' she began. But if Cass expected him to stop, to turn back or run away, she was wrong.

He didn't seem to have heard her or noticed, and then he said, 'Oh yes, so it is. Look, they're round your car.'

Cass looked again and realised he was right. 'Oh my God, so they are,' she gasped. They must have seen her arrive, must have seen her with him. 'Oh my God,' she hissed again, and stopped dead in her tracks. 'What are we going to do?'

'Come on,' said Joe/James, heading towards them.

'What?'

'Let's get over there. See what they want.'

'What?'

Joe/James stared back at her. 'Well, they're not there for their health. It'll be fine, come on. Always assuming you didn't steal it.'

Cass stared at him. 'Are you mad?' The look he gave her suggested that he thought she might be asking the wrong person.

And then he stopped mid-stride. 'Oh my God, I thought it was too good to be true. You didn't steal it, did you?' He sounded serious and concerned. 'You know, the car?' He nodded towards where she was parked.

She shook her head. 'No, of course not.'

'Then what on earth is the matter?' he asked in a low voice, trying not to draw attention to the pair of them.

Cass didn't know how to answer or where to begin. 'You can't go over there,' she spluttered. 'What if they arrest you?'

He looked even more puzzled now. 'I'm sorry, but I don't know what you're on about. Why would they want to arrest me?'

Cass stared even harder at him, hoping that finally he might 'fess up. 'The money,' she hissed furiously. 'All that money. You know, *the money –*'

He stared at her and shook his head. 'Look, I don't know what's going on here . . . I'm not with you.' There wasn't any kind of comprehension on his face. God, he was good. 'Money? What money?' was all he managed.

'You know,' said Cass furiously, struggling to keep her voice down to a whisper. 'The two million pounds that you took.'

'What?'

'From your company – the money you

embezzled. It's all over the papers. You must have seen it,' she hissed.

'*What*?' His face contorted with incomprehension.

'And then you went on the run . . .' Her voice faded towards the end of the sentence, as it became increasingly obvious from his expression that he had absolutely no idea what she was talking about.

'You didn't do any of those things, did you?' she said in a tiny voice.

Joe/James shook his head. 'No. Look, are you sure you're feeling all right? Are you saying you think I stole . . . What? Money? And then came here to meet you?'

Cass nodded.

He stared at her as if she might go off bang at any minute. 'Are you on some kind of medication? Tablets or something?'

Cass felt her face flush crimson. 'No, but maybe I should be,' was all she could manage, although he looked more confused than cross.

'I really think we ought to go over and see what's happening.'

Trailing behind him, Cass nodded. 'So you really are called Joe, then?'

'Uhuh. Yes.'

'Not James?'

'No, that's right – not James. Look, let's talk about this after we've worked out what the hell the law are doing to your car? Or is there someone you would like me to call?'

'What?'

'A carer or social worker or something?'

'Are you serious?' she snapped.

'I don't know – I feel like I've missed something.' And with that he began to hurry across the shrubby grass towards the Bentley. Milo was almost there, it was only Cass who lagged behind now, feeling at a total loss.

What on earth was going on? And if he wasn't James Devlin, who was? And if he wasn't James, then who was he? And if he wasn't James Devlin, why was his wife ringing Cass up and turning up on the doorstep and scaring her? And where was Snoops in all this? Her head hurt.

'Is this your car, madam?' said the police officer standing beside the Bentley.

Cass took a deep breath. 'Yes. Well, no – actually it's not. It belongs to my boss. He lent it to me for a couple of days.'

'Oh, he did, did he, madam?' said the man, quite obviously not believing a single word she was saying. 'And this employer of yours, what might his name be?'

Cass hesitated, her mind a void. 'Barney.'

The officer nodded again. 'Barney?'

She heard Joe groan.

Cass nodded. 'Yes.'

'I think we may need a little more than that, madam. May I see your driving licence?'

Fiddling in her bag under pressure, Cass could no more think of Barney's convoluted multi-barrelled name than fly. 'Um . . .' She knew she was pulling a face, knew that they thought she was lying, knew that any minute now they would arrest her and drag her off in handcuffs, leaving Milo with what's-his-name, the mystery man, who already thought she was totally insane. Just out of the policeman's field of vision, she could see the ex-embezzler willing her on, trying to look encouraging, as if a benign expression and lots of smiling might help jog her memory.

'I tell you what,' Cass said after a second or two more. 'How about I give you his telephone number and then you can ring him.'

The policeman looked very dubious. 'So are you saying you don't remember your employer's name?' he began.

'It's quite a complicated name,' hedged Cass.

'Complicated?' echoed the policeman.

'That's right,' Cass said, and nodded. 'With hyphens.'

A small crowd had gathered around the Bentley. There were people licking ice creams, a woman in a pink sundress clutching a digital camera and a fat red-faced man in tracksuit bottoms and a muscle vest, who was videoing the whole thing, presumably hoping he'd have some action-packed footage to sell to *Look East*.

The policeman peered down at Cass, who closed her eyes and tried to chase Barney's name to ground. It felt like she stood there forever. 'Bartholomew, Bar . . .' she repeated, and then in a flash she saw his mother, Mrs HMR, sitting with Danny. And it was there – 'Bartholomew Anthony Hesquith-Morgan-Roberts,' she said triumphantly. 'I'm sure that he would be very happy to explain about the car.' And with that she handed the officer her mobile. 'His number's on there. Under Barney.'

The officer sniffed. 'I see. If you'll just bear with me for a few moments, madam.' And, clutching her phone, he headed off while his oppo, a thickset man with a couple of very impressive chins and a well-combed moustache, watched Cass like a hawk.

'Nice car,' he said after a moment or two, nodding towards the Bentley.

'Yes, it is nice. Great to drive,' she said.

He nodded again. 'Nice dog.'

Cass forced a smile. Almost out of earshot, the other officer was busy talking into his car radio. She couldn't catch quite what he was saying, although she could have sworn that he said 'Baked Alaska' at least twice. A moment or two later he made his way back to the car.

'Seems as if that is all in order, Miss . . .'

'Mrs Hammond.'

'Righty-oh. We had a tip-off from someone who was passing – you know, strange car parked in a peculiar place. Lot of money, these things. Could have been used in the perpetration of a crime, or stolen and then abandoned. We were in the area and thought we'd check it out.'

Cass smiled. 'Thank you, officer.'

The policeman handed her phone back. 'Nice car,' he said.

Cass nodded.

He looked at Milo and scratched him behind the ears. 'Nice dog.'

'Now, just so's I make myself perfectly clear, Mr Marshall,' said Gordie Mann, shooting his cuffs and straightening his tie as he spoke, 'I can't afford any more cock-ups. No more mistakes, no more duff intelligence or second-rate surveillance gear. You do understand, don't you? We're going to go in, get this bloody woman and her dog and kid and her fucking budgie, if that's what it takes, and then we make her talk. You understand me? Simple, direct and to the point.'

Mr Marshall nodded. 'Absolutely. You do realise that violence is not my forte, Mr Mann. I'm more au fait with covert security operations – the mechanics, the electronics, fine tuning. Not strong-arm stuff.'

Gordie sniffed. 'I have noticed, and I don't go in for violence against women myself. I don't want to get any dirtier than is absolutely necessary on this one. Don't want people looking too closely at my involvement or my investment. But this bloody woman is an artist – how tough can she be? And I can't see that she owes James Devlin anything. Shake her up a bit, and I bet you ten bob to a tenner that she'll tell you exactly where he is.'

Catching sight of his reflection in the window, he straightened his lapels; a man who took his appearance very seriously was Gordie Mann.

Mr Marshall nodded and then cracked his knuckles, aping Eddy and hoping Gordie Mann was convinced that he meant business.

Apparently it worked. Gordie slapped him on the back. 'Good man,' he said, and then added, 'Oh, and you can take that balaclava off now, I know what you look like.'

'You look like you could use a cup of tea,' said Joe Bennett as the police pulled away. Cass nodded.

'And I think we need to talk,' he said. 'Do you want to go to the café? Or we could go to my place in town – it's only five minutes away.'

Cass stared at him. 'I know what you're thinking, but I'm not mad. Really.'

'Uhuh,' said Joe. He didn't look altogether convinced.

'I just thought that you were someone else.'

'Uhuh. Someone who embezzled two million pounds.'

'Well, I know it sounds crazy *now*,' she protested.

There was a funny little pause and then Cass said, 'So, whereabouts do you live?'

They drove up from the beach in Barney's Bentley in a peculiar, rather tense silence, which made Milo, who was crouching in the footwell, fret and whine miserably.

Joe owned the most stunning apartment right slap bang in the centre of waterside Wells, in a converted grainstore overlooking the tiny harbour. 'You can park round the back,' he said, indicating a small, gated courtyard behind the old granary. 'I haven't lived here very long, so it's still a bit unfinished in places.' Cass noticed that there were two other cars parked in front of the garages, a black BMW and a silver Merc; no need to worry about the Bentley standing out there.

'After you,' said Joe, guiding her into a cool tiled service lobby with muted lighting and rattan furniture. He sounded formal and distant and wary of her, but who could blame him? He seemed a long way away from the warm, laid-back guy who had kissed her on the beach and caught hold of her hand as they walked along in the pinewoods. Cass felt uncomfortable and also a little sad.

They didn't take the lift. Two flights up were a set of double doors that opened on to a large glazed landing, set out with pots and lush green plants and interesting found objects, and beyond that was Joe's apartment.

'Here we are,' he said, rather unnecessarily, opening the doors for them.

'Oh my God,' said Cass in amazement, quite unable to help herself. 'What a beautiful place, and what a view —'

The main living area was huge, dominated by a great circular window set into the end wall that gave an interrupted view out over the protective sandbars and banks in Wells harbour and the watercolour mix of boats and yachts moored and beached on the water's edge. Pleasure boats and dinghies rubbed shoulders with rusted fishing boats, leaning at odd angles as they waited for the tide to flow in and right them.

'Would you like a glass of wine?' Joe asked. 'Are you allowed to drink?'

Cass sighed and then nodded, deciding it was probably better to make lots of approving noises rather than try to start the conversation that was looming over them like thunder clouds; not that it was that hard. The apartment was truly breathtaking.

The light was wonderful; mellow afternoon sunshine flooded through the windows, warming the wooden floors to the colour of ripe grain. Although the furniture was modern – square blocks of rich red leather – a rough open fireplace with a cast-iron stove set into the delicate red-gold bricks of one unplastered wall made the room look inviting rather than stark. The rest of the walls were painted cream, with beamed ceilings and lots of plants and prints and driftwood and beautiful things, and warm rugs making it look like a home, not a show house.

The kitchen was all wood, with brushed stainless steel and granite work surfaces. In the centre, dividing it from a sunlit dining area, was an island unit with a hob, set around with stools.

While she and Milo explored, Joe opened a bottle of white wine for them.

'So,' said Joe, handing her a glass of wine. 'Do you want to tell me about James Devlin and the two million quid he nicked – or, more precisely the two million quid you think *I* nicked.'

Cass looked up at him. 'First of all I want to say that I'm not mad and I am sorry. I don't know where to begin – I feel stupid now.'

'Really?' he said. 'How stupid?' He lifted an eyebrow and waited.

Cass considered for a few seconds, wriggling uncomfortably under his unflinching gaze. 'Do I have to?' she asked miserably.

He nodded. 'I think you do. Or do I have to get the police up here?'

Cass looked up at him in astonishment. 'What? What on earth for? There's no reason to get the police – I haven't done anything wrong. It's just that I thought . . .' She paused. 'I thought you had.'

'Right. And what? You were going to set me up? Get me arrested? Were you planning on acting as bait while they jumped me and slapped me in handcuffs?'

Cass reddened. 'Good God, no – no, of course I wasn't,' she protested. 'I'm not sure what I was going to do really.' She looked at him, trying to work out whether all this subtle indignation was just another clever lie, bending her away from the truth. It certainly didn't feel like it. Maybe this was the naïve optimism David was so angry about. Was she believing what she wanted to believe?

Maybe he was James Devlin after all.

He looked at her and sighed. 'I should have guessed you were trouble the first time I saw you.'

But then again, maybe he wasn't.

'I said I'm sorry,' she said.

'Not good enough,' he said.

'So what do you want to know?'

'Everything.'

'Everything?'

He nodded. 'And while you're telling me, I'll cook us something. I don't know about you, but after that walk I'm ravenous. How about some pasta and salad and garlic bread?' He paused for a few seconds and then said, 'Well . . . ?'

'Pasta will be great. I love pasta.'

That wasn't the question and it most certainly wasn't the answer and they both knew it.

'What I don't understand,' said Joe, as he rummaged in the fridge, 'is why you met me at all, if you thought I was a villain.' He diced a red pepper and a huge Spanish onion into a big copper-bottomed pan with olive oil and garlic and lots and lots of black pepper, then pulled a pot of fresh basil towards him and tore off a few leaves, ripping them into bits as he spoke. The smell from the pan filled the kitchen like a promise.

Cass stared at him. There was nothing for it now but to tell him the truth. 'Because . . . because I wanted to . . . I really wanted to see you again,' she said. It sounded ridiculous said aloud.

'You really wanted to see me? Even if I was a crook?' he said, shaking the pan.

'What can I tell you?' said Cass miserably. 'I've got the most terrible taste in men.'

7

Mr Marshall settled himself down at his desk with a mug of tea, a packet of plain chocolate Hobnobs and the Hammond tape transcripts, and re-read them to try and see where he had gone wrong. It had all seemed so perfectly clear earlier. Now it was about as clear as cold cocoa. He thumbed through the dog-eared pages again, a single stubby finger moving slowly under the words, lips moving in time. Did this mean that Mrs Hammond was currently having a day out with James Devlin in Wells-next-the Sea? And if that was the case, why hadn't he been able to work that out before?

Mr Marshall paused thoughtfully. He didn't like Gordie Mann's plan one iota. Snatching women and scaring them was not something that he saw as acceptable operating procedure. He imagined how the ex-Mrs Marshall would respond in that situation. She'd probably punch his lights out. No, no, surely there had to be a better way to find out what he wanted, if only he could find it. No point sending anyone to Wells now. Best to stake out the cottage again. Mr Marshall picked up the phone and called the team that had snatched David Hammond.

'Get the kettle on, lads,' he said in an undertone when the phone was picked up. 'We have a situation developing here.'

'Righty-oh,' said Eddy. He sounded cheerful. 'Same money?'

'Same money. I want you back in position in fifteen minutes. And get Bob back in the tent by the phone box.'

'Wilco, over and out, guv,' said Eddy, and then added as an afterthought: 'Might be a while – Bob's popped out to pick up some stair rods and a can of Duraglit. Who's the package for this time?'

'Mrs Hammond.'

'Oh, what, the little dark-haired bird lives in the end cottage? The one in the Bentley?'

'The very same.'

'Right you are, guv. Are we playing it the same way?'

Mr Marshall thought for a moment. 'I think we should handle this one a little more softly-softly. But we'll liaise once we're in position.'

'Roger that.'

Mr Marshall took his jacket down from the coat stand. He only hoped Mrs Hammond had more sense than the misguided, misbegotten son-of-a-bitch she was married to.

*   *   *

In Little Lamport, Margaret Devlin reached across to the chair beside her bed, picked up a white lace negligee and slipped it on, before turning and smiling coyly at DI Henry Turner. He was leaning back amongst the great nest of pillows, master of all he surveyed. He had a very hairy chest for a man so otherwise pale and pink. Fortunately, the children were still staying with her mother, despite the latter having rung twice to suggest that Margaret might like to come and take them home.

Warm golden sunlight picked out the bone china figurines arranged along the window sill; the shepherd and shepherdess entwined in a chaste embrace, watched by a few of their flock, a buxom milkmaid looking up under fluttering lashes at the burly, bewhiskered farmer. It crossed Margaret's mind as DI Turner ran a proprietorial hand over her knee, that they were probably worth a bob or two. Gordie would know someone who could shift antiques. Although she didn't so much need a fence as an antique dealer, there was probably a lot of stuff around the place she could flog if only she could find the right buyer.

'Penny for them?' said DI Turner softly. 'What are you thinking?'

Margaret considered the possibility of telling the truth for an instant, then, shaking her head, she said, 'Whatever must you think of me?' and, blushing demurely, pulled the flimsy garment up over her narrow shoulders and tied the ribbons tightly across her chest.

DI Turner, a man positively incandescent with afterglow, stroked an unruly tendril of hair back off Margaret's face. 'What do I think of you? I think you're marvellous, I think you're wonderful. Absolutely perfect,' he purred, his eyes moving slowly over her. 'You've got a fabulous body, a wonderful mind, and a kind, kind heart, Margaret Devlin. How could that man have treated you so badly? I've no idea. No idea at all. The man must be mad.'

Margaret practically purred with delight. 'Oh, Henry,' she said, winding the pale pink ties of the negligee around her fingers. 'You say the sweetest things.'

'No, no, I mean it,' said DI Turner more forcefully. 'My life has been so lonely, so very empty since Doreen . . . Well, you know.'

'Died?' Margaret suggested in a whisper.

'God no, she didn't die. To be honest, it might have been easier if she had. No, she ran off with our local churchwarden. You know, all the years I knew her, I never truly trusted that woman.'

'Oh, that's awful,' said Margaret. 'I know how that feels, living with someone you feel you just can't trust.'

Henry shook his head. 'Oh, I never lived with her. I only used to see her once a week for a couple of hours on a Sunday.'

'Sorry?' said Margaret, now even more confused.

'The churchwarden – I used to see her at St

Edwin's. I always thought there was something very dodgy about her.'

Margaret blushed as the penny dropped. 'You mean . . . ?' she began. 'Your wife and . . . Oh, my goodness, how awful.'

'Exactly,' said Henry with some feeling. 'Like a lamb to the slaughter was Doreen. They went away on the Ladies Fellowship long-weekend coach trip to the Lakes, and she came back a changed woman. They live in Cambridge now. Doreen's taken to wearing dungarees and calling herself Dodie. I see her occasionally. Looks like a plumber.'

Margaret patted him gently on the arm. 'Oh, Henry. I'm so very sorry.'

He smiled. 'It's all right. It took me a while, but I'm over it now. Of course, you can imagine the ribbing I got from the lads down at the station.' Pausing to stroke his moustache, he looked at Margaret. 'I'm sorry, I shouldn't be talking about me. You've got enough on your plate without listening to my troubles. The thing is, meeting you has given me such a lift, Margaret. I only wish there was something I could do to help, some way that I could make things easier for you.'

Margaret looked at the shepherdess and wondered if he knew any antique dealers.

Meanwhile David Hammond sat in the café at Tesco's, at a small table close to the window. He was sipping a cappuccino, eating a jam doughnut, rubbing calendula cream into his rope burns and trying very hard to collect his thoughts. The lady refilling the shelves in the pharmaceuticals, beauty and hair-care aisle had said calendula was very good for minor cuts and grazes, it was all natural and besides that it was on special. He'd bought a large tube and a bottle of Paracetemol.

He stirred his coffee, trying to fathom out what the hell had happened. It wasn't every day you were bundled into a van with a sack over your head. He was still seeing stars and couldn't work out what it was all about – not the stars, the kidnapping.

David carefully scraped the froth from the side of his cup and spooned it into his mouth. Should he go to the police? And if he did, what could he tell them that made sense? And would they listen? Last time he'd reported a robbery at the factory unit he rented no one came, although they had sent him a leaflet offering victim support and a help line number to ring. He had another spoonful of froth. And besides, if he told the police, he'd have to tell them about Abby and Carl, and how stupid would that make him look?

On the far side of the café the girl behind the counter smiled at him, her interest breaking into his thoughts. It had been quite obvious when she'd served him that she thought he was drunk, or worse, but David didn't give a shit, not after the afternoon he'd just had. She'd been peering at him out of the corner of her eye since he'd sat down,

251

surreptitiously glancing his way when she thought he wasn't looking, all the while he'd been drinking his coffee.

And now, just when David was about to glare right back at her, she was all smiles. As he turned his full attention to her, she ran her fingers back over her disposable paper hair snood and giggled. It was such a provocative gesture that David reddened furiously and felt an interesting stirring in his groin. Well, what a little minx – maybe she didn't think he was drunk after all. Or maybe he was just the kind of guy that attracted younger women.

David preened, which involved squaring his shoulders and running his hand back through his hair – an action he instantly regretted. There was a bump on his head the size of a golfball and he had a thumping headache which the Paracetemol hadn't yet touched.

He winced as his fingers touched the lump through the thin patch of hair that he was very careful to comb over and gel down first thing in the morning. Cass had never noticed, but then he thought she had let herself go since having Danny. After all, appearance was important. Abby had helped him pick out some new clothes and pointed out the odd grey hair – in a jokey way, obviously – telling him he looked distinguished and then adding casually that he hadn't got anywhere near as many as her dad.

David shifted in his seat and straightened his

jacket. There weren't that many grey hairs actually. OK, so maybe one or two – that was what the girl at the hairdressers had told him. Not many for a man his age, was what she'd said as she'd slipped him into a robe and laid him back over the basin.

He tried to catch a glimpse of his reflection in the window. It wasn't vanity, getting a few highlights put in; no one would think twice about it if he were a woman. Oh no, it was just about keeping up appearances, something very important for a man in his position, CEO of a vital young business. Women weren't the only ones with a duty not to let themselves go. Instinctively David sucked his gut in and lifted his chin.

The girl working the café till smiled again and started to tidy the sauces into pots. She wasn't bad looking in a plump, homely sort of way, thought David, looking her up and down, while smiling right back. And then, holding his gaze, she did the fingers through the hair thing again. And he copied her. And this time as his fingertips went towards the back of his head, carefully circumnavigating the bump, David touched something. Something sticky, something large, something glued firmly to his head. Bugger.

It took him a second or two to realise what it was. There was a strip of gaffer tape stuck to his hair. He winced miserably, wishing the earth would open up and swallow him. Christ, what must he look like? It occurred to him a split second later that it wasn't desire on the girl's face so much as pity. David closed his eyes. All that snood-rubbing had been a hint, a bloody clue, not a come on after all.

He ripped the tape off, pulling away a great strip of hair with it, probably off the thin spot. Fuck. Looking down at the table, angry and struggling to regain his composure, David gritted his teeth. When he looked up briefly the girl was still smiling and nodding encouragingly. To his horror, as their eyes met she picked up a J cloth and made her way over to his table.

'All right, are you?' she asked, sounding genuinely concerned.

'Yes, I'm fine. Thank you very much,' he said briskly, trying to avoid meeting her eye.

'Right,' she said, dabbing the cloth ineffectually around on the table next to him. 'Only, you look a bit pasty. You've got to move on, you know, get over her and stop mooning about.' She spoke while chewing down hard on a wad of gum. Up close, David could see the blue tape stuck over the ring in her nose. 'I know that it's not easy. I was just the same over Kieran who works in the deli, but life goes on.'

David had to sift through the words to make sense of them, because as well as chewing gum she spoke in an odd mixture of broad Norfolk overlaid with even thicker Estuary English.

'Sorry?'

The girl started to tidy a pile of dirty crockery

on to a tray. 'I'm mates with Abby – or I was when we was at school. She ain't worth it, you know. Do you want me to take that?'

She held out her hand and obediently David dropped the strip of screwed-up, hairy gaffer tape into her outstretched palm.

'So, let me get this straight,' said Joe Bennett to Cass, chasing a prawn round his plate, using it to mop up the last of the rich creamy sauce. 'You thought that I was this man, James Devlin?'

Cass, who was doing much the same with a piece of bread, nodded. 'Uhuh.'

The seafood pasta was superb.

'And despite the fact that he is married –'

'– to a fruit loop,' Cass interrupted.

'OK, OK, to a fruit loop, that's as maybe, but the main thing is that, despite everything you thought you knew about me, you still drove over here to meet me?'

Cass nodded again. This was getting embarrassing. Said aloud, it sounded even madder than when it was just rolling around inside her head.

'Because?' he prompted.

Cass squirmed uncomfortably under his unwavering gaze. 'Because,' she began, wrinkling up her nose and trying very hard to come up with something that didn't sound pathetic and didn't go, *Well, I know this sounds crazy but I really fancy you. No, honestly, that is the reason.* But so far, sadly, she had come up empty. 'Umm, because,

because . . .' This was worse than any job interview.

'Well?'

'Well, for a start don't bully me.'

He held up his hands in surrender. 'Sorry, you think I'm a villain and then you worry about being bullied? OK, look I'm just curious – intrigued, actually. I mean, I know they say women go for bad boys but –'

'OK, stop speculating, will you? I know this sounds crazy, but I . . . I thought you were, were . . .' she stammered, the words sliding out all over each other in an effort to escape. 'I mean, OK, I thought you were – attractive . . .'

'Attractive?'

'OK, so I fancied you. All right? Happy now?'

Joe speared the prawn in one go and laughed. 'Right,' he said, shaking his head. 'Well, that explains everything.'

Cass stared at him. He obviously thought it was a joke. She wasn't sure whether she was relieved or offended.

'I mean it,' she said angrily. 'I'm serious.' This was ridiculous. 'I fancied you. I know it sounds crazy, but honestly, it's true.' It came out sounding like a barely veiled threat.

'OK, I believe you. So what happens now?' he asked.

Cass pointed at the big dish of pasta in the middle of the table with her fork. 'Second helpings?' she suggested.

'That isn't what I meant, and you know it.'

'Dessert?'

'I'd really like to see you again,' he said. 'Assuming you're not horribly disappointed that I'm not a thief, a liar, or married. Oh, and that I haven't got two million quid stashed away somewhere.'

Cass waved the words aside. 'I'm tolerant, me – easy come, easy go.' And then she looked up and realised for the first time since they got back from the beach he was smiling at her.

'Actually, you've got no idea how relieved I am,' she said softly. 'I'm not usually a bad judge of character and I didn't have you down as any of those things, whatever everyone else said.' And as she spoke, Joe leaned forward and, stroking her hair back off her face, he very gently kissed her. 'Unless of course you're lying,' she whispered as he pulled back a fraction.

'There is that,' he said. 'But I can prove who I am – certificates, photos – a whole lifetime's worth of paper and printer's ink.'

Cass looked at him and this time didn't fight the ripple of desire that shimmied through her body like bubbles in a champagne glass.

'Umm, that was really nice,' she purred.

'The promise of some written proof?'

'No, silly – the kiss.'

So he did it again.

'Just one thing,' Joe said when he finally pulled away. 'If I'm not James Devlin, then you don't know him. And if you don't know him, then you never met him – and you really need to make sure that his wife knows that . . .' he paused. 'And anyone else who is after him.'

'Sorry?'

'Well, if I were you, I'd ring the police and explain the situation.' As he spoke, Joe pulled out his wallet and handed her his business card. 'Get them to ring me. I'll explain that we met on the train and that your picking up Devlin's phone was an unfortunate coincidence. As I said, I can prove that I'm not James Devlin.'

Cass nodded. The card read *Joe Bennett, architect*. And under his name and phone number was his home address. Cass slipped it into her bag. 'OK. I'll do that as soon as I get back. And I'll give you my address and stuff in Brighton, if you like. Have you got a pen handy?'

As Joe walked across to pick up a pad of paper, Cass watched him and sighed. Great bum. What a strange thing to have happened now. He was really nice, warm, gentle, funny – perfect. Against all the odds, it looked like it was going to be all right, after all, and it felt so much better now that he was Joe and not James. This way, there was a possibility things might be OK. He came back and handed her a notepad.

'I'm really glad you're not a criminal,' she said brightly.

'Oh, I didn't say that I wasn't a criminal, I said that I wasn't James Devlin.' And then, when he saw her expression, Joe laughed. 'Relax, it's all right. I haven't got so much as a parking fine, let alone a criminal record. Here, tell me where you live and I'll come and see you in Brighton.'

Dessert was delicious: ice cream and strawberries sprinkled with broken ginger snaps and grated dark chocolate.

Setting her spoon down, resisting the temptation to lick the plate clean, Cass said, 'That was wonderful. I hate to eat and run, but I ought to be getting home. I've still got quite a lot of things to do before tomorrow.'

Joe looked crestfallen. 'I was hoping you could maybe stay a while.'

'Do you want a hand to clear up?'

'No, not at all – I'm going to whack it all in the dishwasher once you've gone. I was just hoping to spend some more time with you. I hope you're not too disappointed that I'm not a master criminal.'

Reddening, Cass shook her head, got up and began collecting her things together – her jacket and bag and her composure. 'No, I've really enjoyed myself, but I do need to go.'

'We could go for a drink later, if you wanted.'

Cass smiled, maybe he was a bit slow on the uptake. 'It would've been nice, but I've got to get back, I really have got things to do – and Danny needs to go to bed early.'

'I could drive over later if you like,' said Joe casually.

'To mine? Really? Are you serious?'

'Why not? As long as you don't think I'm stalking you. You're leaving tomorrow and I can't see me getting down to Brighton for a while – and, and . . .' He laughed and reddened furiously, which was kind of cute. 'And I fancied you too.'

Cass glowed. 'You don't say? Really? OK – well, if I leave now, I should be all done by nine or so. I'm sure my friend Jake would be OK to baby-sit. There's a pub in our village – it's the only pub in the place, just off the main road – you can't miss it. It's not that picturesque, but it's not bad.'

'OK. Nine, then.'

Cass nodded. 'Let's be on the safe side – half past.'

'OK.'

There was a funny little pause and then Cass said, 'I'm so glad you're not a two-timing embezzling master criminal.'

'You say the nicest things,' said Joe and kissed her again.

Cass sang all the way home, let herself in, picked up the phone and rang Jake to let him know what was going on.

Bob had managed to get the tap and trace back on in no time. 'She's going out about quarter past nine, meeting some bloke called Joe at the local pub, on the green,' Bob said confidently to Mr

Marshall. 'She's just rung her neighbour to arrange for him to baby-sit.'

Mr Marshall smiled; if he was quick, he could get everything they needed to know before Gordie Mann got wind of what was going on. Mrs Hammond could be home safe and sound before midnight. And this way there would be no problem with her kid either. It was perfect.

'You hear that, lads?' said Mr Marshall to Eddy and his mob in the Land Rover.

'Certainly did,' Eddy grunted. 'Roger that.'

In Cass's kitchen Jake watched with interest as she slid the last of a pile of illustrations into a large clear plastic pocket and then snapped it into the portfolio. 'There we are,' she said, rubbing her hands together gleefully. 'All done and dusted. I need to go and get ready. What do you think I ought to wear?'

'Wait, let me get this straight,' Jake said, his face a picture of concentration as he lit up a cigarette. 'The man on the train who you met – that wasn't James Devlin?'

'No, his name is Joe and he really did go to Rome, and the phone belonged to someone else. Isn't that wonderful?'

'Apparently,' said Jake. 'I haven't seen you this perky in ages.'

'Dress or trousers – what do you think?' She paused and looked into the mirror by the back door. 'I've got that nice cream pair I bought from

Cambridge, the ones that make my legs look long.'

'But the phone really did belong to James Devlin?'

'Yes, but Joe isn't James. Isn't that wonderful?' she said with a grin. 'What about that pale blue column dress, the one that makes my eyes look incredibly blue? Damn, I wonder if I took my pashmina down to Brighton.'

Jake pulled a face. 'I have a feeling this would be easier with subtitles.'

Cass peered around the kitchen. 'Have I got everything I need for tomorrow?' she asked distractedly. 'Have you got everything you need for tomorrow?'

'And you're going for a drink with him?' Jake pressed.

'At nine thirty.' Cass glanced at her watch. 'God, I better go and get ready. I said I'd meet him down there.'

'At the Chequers?'

'Of course at the Chequers.'

'I just wanted to make sure, things seem very topsy-turvy at the moment.'

Cass laughed, took a cold bottle of beer out of the fridge for Jake and stood it on the countertop. 'Come on, Jake, we could both use a bit of romance and things going right for a change.'

He sniffed and nodded his thanks. 'Fine for you to say. I'm on the sidelines; so far, all I get to do is mind the fort and watch the kid. It's not exactly James Bond, is it? And I'd wear the blue dress with those kitten-heel mules, if I were you – show off your tan.'

'Jake, you're an angel and I never had you down as a cross-dresser. I don't know what I'd do without you. Do you want me to bring you anything back? A pie or something?'

He grimaced. 'You're all heart, woman. If you're serious, I'll have a jar of cockles, a packet of cheese-and-onion crisps and a pickled egg.'

Cass pulled a face. 'That is disgusting.'

'You did ask. You could get me the phone number of that new barmaid as well, if you like – in which case don't bother with the pickled egg.' Jake took a pull on the beer. 'So, did you ring that policewoman and put them right about Joe Bennett and the phone thing?'

Cass grimaced. 'No. Damn! Oh, never mind. I'll ring tomorrow. I can't see what difference a few more hours will make, and besides, she's probably off duty now, and I want to talk to someone who knows what's going on, not have to explain it all over again. Right, you know where everything is?'

Jake raised an eyebrow. 'Uhuh, mostly because I put it there, built it or bought it for you' he said grumpily. 'And where's Milo?'

'Sound asleep on my bed. He was totally bushed after the walk on the beach.'

'And Danny?'

'Much the same. Washed, cuddled and all tucked in. When I looked in, he was sound asleep. He's exhausted, bless him.'

'OK, and what time do you think you'll be home?'

Cass pulled a face.

Jake matched it. 'Don't give me that look,' he said. 'I'm not checking up on you, it's just that if you're going to be coming in late, I'll be camped out in the spare room, snoring, when you get back.'

Cass laughed. 'Don't count on it. Closing time plus him walking me home, probably – so half eleven at the latest, I reckon.'

Jake nodded. 'OK, in that case I'll take my beer and go watch some rubbish on TV.'

Cass put the portfolios on the kitchen table and then went upstairs to get ready. She looked out into the garden. It was the most beautiful evening; it would be a really nice walk. The pub wasn't that far, and she could take the footpath at the bottom of the lane and cut across the playing field as long as she didn't wear high heels.

Heels! Cass opened her wardrobe and took out the blue sundress, which was hanging on the same hanger as the pashmina, and from the rail underneath a pair of pretty kitten-heeled sandals she'd bought in Morocco. *Fantastic*. Cass grinned, sometimes things just came together like magic. She had a quick shower and got changed, then smudged on a little kohl and twisted her hair up in a clip. She couldn't help but smile at the transformation: her eyes were alight, the walk on the beach had lifted her colour, and she looked like a woman who fancied someone rotten and had just discovered that they fancied her back.

Just as Cass was about to leave the phone rang. Barney. No preamble, no hellos. 'What time will you be back tomorrow?'

'I don't know, soon as I can. Why?'

'Just so's I know. Have you sorted everything out? You know – work, canvases, illustrations, all that sort of thing.'

Cass nodded. 'Yup, all done.' She was looking out of the front window. Down the lane was a bread van parked in the lay-by, which seemed very odd, as did the BT tent near the phone box. They were working late. 'All packed. Jake's here, do you want to talk to him? I'm just on my way out.'

'In a second. Can you hear that noise?' said Barney triumphantly. 'That's Hoovering. She Hoovers.'

Cass laughed. 'Wonderful. Is that Kipper barking?'

'Good God, no, he's far too idle to worry about anything so mundane. No, it's Antashinia's dog. He's lovely, but a bit highly strung. Quite young, I think.'

'Amazing name.'

'Amazing woman,' Barney purred appreciatively. Cass smiled. Oddly enough the dog's manic yapping sounded familiar. She dismissed the idea as fanciful. 'Jake doesn't want to make too early a start but hopefully we'll be there before closing time.'

'Bloody well better be,' snapped Barney. 'See you tomorrow,' he said. 'I thought I'd take Antashinia out to supper, celebrate. Although last time I mentioned it, she said she would prefer to cook, so I thought we might take another drive down to the supermarket. We've been twice already, once for cake things, once for cleaning stuff. The woman is a bloody marvel. You'll adore her, and the dog. He's a real bundle of energy.'

Cass skipped down the stairs and handed the phone to Jake. 'It's Barney. See you later,' she mouthed, picking up her bag from the back of the chair.

Jake lifted a hand in salute. 'You look fab. Don't forget the pickled egg,' he said with his palm over the handset.

'The Eagle is out and about,' said a voice on the radio.

'What? Where?' said another voice. 'She can't be, I'm watching the front door.'

'She's in the lane,' said Bob in the BT tent. 'I just saw her going down her path. There's a shortcut at the bottom of her garden that takes you right into the village.'

Mr Marshall in the control bread van slapped his forehead. 'Bugger. How come nobody else knew about that, then? And why wasn't it covered? Come on, guys, let's move it. Move it.'

Bob, who had a map with him, said, 'You won't get ahead of her on foot, but if you drive along the main lane, turn left at the bottom and skirt round the edge of the playing field, you can cut her off at the first entrance.'

'Roger that,' said Eddy from the other vehicle. 'Masks on, everyone: time to rock and roll.'

Mr Marshall winced. He'd still got a nasty itchy rash from when they grabbed David Hammond. This was the last thing he needed. Why the hell couldn't she just walk down the bloody road like everyone else? Mr Marshall made a managerial decision and leapt out of the van, still clutching his radio.

'Eddy?' he barked.

'Uhuh?'

'You drive round to the end of the shortcut with the rest of the guys, and I'll try and catch her on foot. I don't want any rough stuff if we can possibly avoid it.'

'You already said that.'

'Well, I'm saying it again. No heavy-handed stuff, all right? And try not to frighten her. When we grab her, be efficient not rough – understand?'

'Sure thing, guv.' Eddy sounded hurt, as if Mr Marshall's comments were some terrible slur on his professionalism.

Meanwhile Mr Marshall was trying to catch up with Cass Hammond. The entrance to the shortcut was through a hedge by Cass's back garden gate. Breaking into a brisk trot, Mr Marshall hurried towards the gap, his pulse drumming in his ears. As he stepped into the narrow green lane, Cass

Hammond vanished around the first corner. Bugger. He quickened his pace. God, she walked fast.

When she was about twenty feet ahead and maybe fifty yards from the end of the lane, Mr Marshall realised that, barring a miracle, there was no way he was going to catch her, so he called, 'Mrs Hammond?'

She swung round. And screamed. Mr Marshall was about to call again and ask what was the matter, when he realised he was wearing the balaclava. When Eddy had said 'masks on', he had instinctively done as he was told. To his horror, Cass began to run.

'No, no, wait, come back,' he called. 'Come back. I don't want to hurt you.' Struggling to pull off his mask as he ran, he shouted, 'Stop, I only want to talk.' But it was too late, she was up on her toes and away. As Mr Marshall looked he saw Eddy and one of the others appear at the entrance to the lane. Eddy looked like everyone's worst nightmare: built like a brick shithouse, dressed in camo gear, and wearing a ski mask with white-rimmed eye holes. Mr Marshall groaned; this was not how he wanted it to go at all. Bugger, bugger, bugger.

Cass Hammond spotted Eddy and his sidekicks in the gateway and this time, instead of screaming, she swerved right and ran straight through another gap in the hedge on to the village playing field. This was going from bad to worse. Without thinking, Mr Marshall followed and immediately wished he hadn't. On the far side of the hedge were half a dozen youths lying around on the grass, drinking beer and smoking, surrounded by their motorbikes, under a sign that read *Motorbikes are forbidden on this playing field by order of the Parish Council.*

The gang of boys took a split second to appraise the situation. Mr Marshall was too slow to turn. He could already see Eddy and the rest of the gang making their way along the pavement outside the hedge towards the main gate, obviously hoping to cut Cass off when she got there. As she ran, she looked back at him. Mr Marshall winced. Cass Hammond didn't need to say anything, her face said it all.

Before he could call again or try to explain, the largest of the lads, who was already up and on his feet, said, 'What the fuck do you think you're up to?'

Well, at least that was what Mr Marshall guessed he was planning to say, but he never found out because the boy got bored halfway through and laid Mr Marshall out. The last thing he saw before the world went black was Eddy vaulting over the fence to come to his rescue. Cass Hammond, meanwhile, was running full tilt towards the main road.

In Brighton, Barney pushed his dish away and puffed out his cheeks. Splendid, better than splendid, probably even superb was an inadequate superlative to describe how he felt about the supper they had just eaten. He was replete, stuffed, totally satiated.

Daisy, his mother, and Charlie – who he had invited down from upstairs – had polished off an obscene quantity of ham, eggs and homemade chips, served up with great doorsteps of bread and butter, copious quantities of tea, followed by freshly baked apple pie and proper custard. Perfect.

The menu had been democratically decided by drawing lots, although no one actually felt they'd lost as the rest of the menus had been left in the bowls they'd been drawn from – one for main courses and another for desserts. Antashinia had promised that they could pick another one out tomorrow morning, and the next day and the next. And, yes, if they really wanted to they could put the old suggestions back in, as long as they didn't blame her if they had the same thing four nights in a row. And, yes, of course they could add extra dishes, if they really wanted to.

His mother and Charlie had already gone into a huddle in the corner to try and come up with some more exciting suggestions, tonight's impromptu dinner-draw having taken everyone by surprise. Antashinia had made the suggestion after a fistfight had broken out after tea. She'd given them paper and felt-tips and told them each to come up with three ideas for supper, and no conferring. It was a stroke of genius.

Barney belched discreetly into his napkin. Surely to God even Cass couldn't fail to be impressed; cooking, cleaning, crisis management, one small boy and running the flat would be a doddle if the girl could manage rabid hungry adults with such aplomb.

Barney dropped his napkin on to the table. 'Antashinia, you are wonderful.'

The girl, who was busy clearing the table looked up and glowed beetroot red.

'You know, if I weren't married, I'd snap you up for myself,' he said, toasting her with the last of the cabernet sauvignon.

Daisy swung round and glared at him. 'You never told me you'd got married again, you bastard. Who is it this time and how old is she? Do I know her? I was at school with the last one.'

'Don't exaggerate,' he said.

'I'm not.' Daisy pulled a pouty, miserable face and Barney instantly regretted spoiling the mood.

'I'm sorry. It was just a turn of phrase, I didn't mean –'

But Antashinia was on hand to save the day. 'Don't worry, Daisy. I wouldn't marry a grumpy man like him, anyway – good to work for, but I don't like hairy ears. Also I am already loving someone else. And I am thinking that he loves me too. It was very hard for us not to be together. He escaped before me, but now I am gone too and soon we will be together.'

Daisy looked at the au pair in admiration.

'Escaped?' she hissed. 'What, like from a tyrannical regime?'

Antashinia nodded. 'It was terrible,' she said.

Margaret Devlin waved Henry off from the bedroom window. He'd insisted that she didn't come down. He wanted to remember her just the way she was. She smiled till her face ached and then, when he was out of sight, picked up her mobile. Gordie was bound to know someone who could shift antiques.

Outside the Chequers, Joe Bennett looked down at his watch for what must have been the hundredth time and then looked around the pub garden. It was nearly quarter to ten and there was still no sign of Cass. He took another walk around the garden, out past the benches and tables and people sitting around on the grass and low wall, looking inside for the umpteenth time in case he had missed her. And as he did, Joe wondered whether Cass was being fashionably late, or just running late. Had she forgotten? Was he being stood up? What if she had changed her mind? What if she didn't fancy him after all? What if she'd decided she really wanted a gangster in her life?

Waiting was unsettling. He'd already rung Cass's mobile and got her voice mail. After another circuit, he finally rang her house. A man answered, which threw him a bit.

'Sorry, I think I must have the wrong number,' Joe said hastily.

'Why – who do you want?' asked a cultured voice.

'Cass Hammond.'

There was a pause and then the man said, 'Well, you've got the right number, but I'm afraid she's not here at the moment. I'm Jake – her next-door neighbour. I'm babysitting. I could take a message if you like.'

'Oh, OK, right. I'm Joe – the thing is, I'm supposed to be meeting her at the Chequers.'

'Joe Bennett – the guy who isn't James Devlin?'

'That's right. Has she left yet?'

'Yes,' said the man, sounding perplexed. 'Actually, she went out about . . . I don't know, twenty minutes, maybe half an hour ago. She was walking.'

'How long does it take to walk to the pub?'

'Five, ten minutes at the most. Bugger,' said the man at the end of the phone.

'And she was definitely walking?' asked Joe, feeling a ripple of anxiety.

'Yes, I saw her go. She was going to cut through the playing field. And you're saying she's not there?'

'Well, I can't see her. I'm worried. Her mobile is switched off.'

'She ought to be there by now. Listen, I can't leave Danny here on his own. I'll call David to come and keep an eye on him.'

'David?'

'Cass's husband.'

'She's married?' Joe said in astonishment. It hadn't crossed his mind that he was seeing a married woman.

'Well, yes and no. They're separated. David ran off with their cleaner, but I think from what I can gather it's not going well. I'm sure she'll explain. Give me five minutes and I'll ring you back. In the meantime, if she turns up, can you let me know?'

Five minutes. Joe looked at the phone. Five minutes was five minutes too long. Where the hell was Cass. Given the whole James Devlin scenario, was she in danger?

'Excuse me, can you tell me how to get to the playing field,' Joe asked a couple sitting outside on the terrace. 'Is there some sort of footpath round here?'

The guy nodded and pointed across the village green towards a row of poplars. 'Yeah, you see the lane down there by the bus shelter?'

With the instructions firmly in his head, Joe hurried across the grass, and as he did his mobile rang.

It was Jake. 'I think we ought to ring the police,' he said.

Joe froze. 'Why, what's happened?'

'I just talked to David. Apparently he was grabbed today by some men who thought that he was James Devlin. Danny said something about it earlier, but we thought he was making it up. David didn't ring anyone because he didn't think it was that important. To be perfectly honest, I reckon he was too embarrassed to mention it.'

'Embarrassed? What do you mean *embarrassed*? What sort of person thinks that being abducted isn't important?' said Joe in amazement.

Jake sighed. 'It seems he wasn't sure what was going on. He assumed that it was his ex-girlfriend's new boyfriend trying to frighten him off. He's on his way over here now. Anyway, one thing he did say was that they weren't very professional.'

Joe stared across the wide-open spaces of the playing field; what was that supposed to mean? And, worse still, did unprofessional mean that Cass was in more danger rather than less?

'I'm on the playing field now,' said Joe.

'OK, I'll meet you there in about ten minutes,' said the man. 'Or you could come here if you like. Head for the end of the field where the church is and you'll see a break in the hedge. Do you think I should ring the police?'

'Yes, I think you should,' said Joe.

As Jake gave Joe directions he walked across the field through the gathering gloom, trying to get some sense that Cass had been there. In the grass by one of the gates was a sandal. Seeing it made Joe's heart lurch. He bent down to pick it up, realising as he did that, if it was Cass's, he had just messed with the evidence and that this whole thing might end up being far more serious than any of them thought.

'Looking for something, are you?'

The sound of a human voice made Joe jump. Where the hedge fell back around the gate a thin gangly boy sat hunched on the grass, busy smoking a roll up. He was dressed in greasy jeans, a faded tour T-shirt, and had acne so fierce that it was almost luminescent in the half-light.

'Yes, a friend of mine – a woman – I think she might be in some sort of trouble,' Joe said, looking around the field. 'She was walking down to the pub to meet me.'

The boy nodded. ''Bout five foot five, slim with dark hair, nice looking – lives over the back there?' He nodded in the general direction of the cottage that Jake had described.

'Yes, have you seen her?'

The boy nodded again. 'Yup. She was here, I dunno, maybe half an hour ago. Some blokes grabbed her.'

Joe stared. 'What?'

The boy seemed unruffled, and Joe wondered exactly what it was he was smoking.

'Billy and the rest of my mates followed them. They hadn't got another skid lid or I'd have gone as well.'

'Where did they go?'

The boy shrugged. 'I dunno. They'd got a Land Rover, the blokes who took her – It was bloody weird. She came running through the hedge there –' He pointed. 'And there was this was bloke behind her in a ski-mask thing. He pulled it off when he saw us lot. Enough to frighten the living shit out of anybody. Anyway, Billy grabbed the geezer and punched him, and then this other bloke turned up and, while that was happening . . .' he paused, as if trying to get it straight in his head. 'To be honest, I'm not sure what happened then, but I think she must have run through here –' He indicated the gate. 'And they grabbed her and stuck her in the Land Rover.' He looked at Joe to see how he was doing. 'I could ring them on me mobile, see if they caught up with them.'

Joe tried hard to keep the sense of panic out of his voice. 'Great. That would be a good idea.'

Across the playing field an elderly man appeared. Joe waved him over.

'Hello, I'm Jake,' said the man, extending a hand. 'I rang the police, but they said it might take a while for someone to get over here. I had to ring Norwich.'

Joe looked at him. 'Why?'

'Some sort of central dispatch system. They said I was to stay calm and they would send somebody round as soon as they could.' He looked at Joe. 'I'm worried that they thought I'd been drinking.'

'Did you tell them about the link with James Devlin, and about Cass's husband being grabbed earlier?'

'Well, I tried,' said Jake, 'but it's not easy to explain. I'm not sure they were convinced.' As he spoke, Jake looked down at the sandal in Joe's hand and winced. 'Oh my God,' he whispered.

'I found it over there on the grass,' said Joe.

'Oh my God,' said Jake again. 'It's one of Cass's. You know, I really think that we ought to go back to the house and wait for the police to arrive.'

In the lee of the hedge, the boy, his finger wedged firmly in his ear, was talking into the phone. 'You're breaking up, Rabbit. Yeah . . . OK, and they're where? . . . Oh, right, I know where you mean. I'll tell 'im.' He looked across at Joe and gave him the thumbs up. 'I know where they've taken her. Have you got a car?'

At which point Jake's phone rang. 'Hello?' He squinted down at the screen, and then, staring into the middle distance, turned away to take the call.

'Right, well, the thing is, there's this chap here who knows where Cass is. I think it sounds like the same . . . Yes, that's right. OK, OK . . .' And as the conversation continued, Jake walked away, chasing the signal.

Joe watched him, trying to work out who Jake was talking to, and realising it annoyed him that they were discussing Cass and not including him in the conversation, when Jake turned to him.

'It's David,' he mouthed. Joe felt a peculiar sinking sensation in the pit of his stomach, as Jake continued into the phone: 'Right, give us about five minutes. Yeah, we're on our way back.'

Jake snapped the phone shut. 'He wants me to go home and look after Danny while he goes to get Cass. He said if anyone was going to rescue her, it ought to be him. After all, she is his wife.'

'I thought you said he'd left her?'

Jake nodded. 'He did. Best thing that ever happened to her. The man is a total prat.' And then he beckoned to the boy on the grass. 'Come on.'

'What about me?' said Joe.

Jake thought for a second and then said, 'You'd better come along as well. Go with David and stop him from getting Cass hurt, will you?'

'Who shall I say I am?' said Joe, falling into step beside them.

Jake shrugged. 'David is so up himself he probably won't care.'

'So,' said Daisy, warming to Antashinia's story, 'this man you love – have you managed to find each other since you both escaped? Did he escape here too? Have you seen him again?'

The au pair nodded and smiled coyly, reddening as she did so. 'Oh yes, I have seen him a little, but we have to be so very careful. My family have found him somewhere safe to stay till we can be together, but I have to keep very quiet about the things that I know, you understand? He may have escaped, but many people are still looking for him. If they find him . . .' She pulled a face. 'You know.'

'They'd kill him?' whispered Daisy.

'No, no, I don't think so,' said Antashinia. 'No, I am thinking that they will throw him in prison for a very long time – and perhaps me too, for helping him. But I think it will break his heart to be locked up. And we will be apart again. I couldn't bear it.'

'Oh God, that is just so romantic,' said Daisy enthusiastically. 'So where is he?' she asked, creeping closer.

Barney sighed. 'Look, Daisy, I don't think you should be asking, and I'm damned certain that if I was Antashinia I wouldn't tell you.'

Daisy wrinkled her nose. The au pair smiled enigmatically, while under the table Snoops twitched and barked in his sleep, dreaming of long walks on the beach and being at home sitting at the feet of his master.

In the abandoned Portakabin by the railway line Mr Marshall was busy making Cass a cup of tea.

'Look,' he said, 'I do appreciate that this is all a bit irregular, but I would be very grateful if you could tell us what you know about James Devlin. Or . . .' he paused. 'The thing is, one of my men suggested that I really ought to tie you up – play act, you know – but I thought you're the kind of woman who would see sense without all that nonsense. And please, I don't want you to think that I'm threatening you, Mrs Hammond – because I'm not, truly. But the man I'm currently working for is – well, he's not what I'd call subtle. Violent, nasty piece of work. I'm worried that if I don't get the information I want from you, he might . . . Well, to be perfectly honest, I don't know what he might do.'

'That sounds like a threat to me,' said Cass grimly.

Mr Marshall looked almost embarrassed as he handed her a mug of Tetley's finest.

Cass stared at him. The terror she had felt on the playing field had been replaced by a peculiar numbness and an odd sense of distance which she found almost as unnerving. It felt as if she was watching a film and all this was happening to someone else. Cass's hand trembled as she closed her fingers around the mug; she struggled to make it stop and then said, 'I keep telling you, I really don't know where he is.'

Mr Marshall shook his head. 'Please don't say that. James Devlin's not worth it. Really he isn't.'

'No, I'm sure that you're right.' Cass stood her tea down on the window sill. 'I know you'll find this very hard to believe, but it wasn't James Devlin I met on the train. I met someone called Joe Bennett. And because this woman found James Devlin's mobile phone near the seat where he had been sitting, everyone assumed Joe was James. I know it's complicated, but the bottom line is I have absolutely no idea where James Devlin is. In fact, I have no idea *who* he is. I've never met him, ever. Do you understand? I wouldn't recognise him even if I saw him.'

Mr Marshall sighed heavily. 'I really would like to believe you, but we have the tapes.'

Cass stared at him. 'Tapes?'

He nodded. 'We tapped your phone. I know

who you were with, where you went – and who you met.' He pulled a fold of paper out of his pocket and held it out towards her. 'Please, Mrs Hammond, tell me where James Devlin is. It would be so much easier for all of us, especially you, if you told me now. God, this mask really itches.'

Cass looked down at the sheets of paper. 'This is illegal. How did you manage to get all this?'

Mr Marshall shifted his weight uncomfortably. 'It's the kind of work I'm in, Mrs Hammond. It goes with the territory.'

'Well you've got it wrong,' she said, exasperated. 'These calls were from Joe Bennett and those were from David, my husband.' She picked up her handbag, and across the room she saw Marshall flinch. 'It's all right, I was just going to show you this –' She pulled out Joe's business card and handed it to him along with the tape transcript. 'Take a look: the numbers are the same,' she said.

Reluctantly Marshall did as he was told. 'Right,' he said. He sighed miserably.

'I don't know James Devlin. I've never met him. There's been a misunderstanding. You've got the wrong person.'

'Right,' said Marshall again. Behind him the door to the office opened.

'Can I have a quick word, guv?' said a thickset man in a ski mask.

Mr Marshall stepped out into the hallway,

pondering what he had just been told. How had he got it so wrong? And what would Gordie Mann say when he found out? If he found out . . . An idea was beginning to form.

'Well?' he said. 'What is it?'

Eddy shifted from foot to foot. 'Well, you know that bloke who punched you – the biker?'

Mr Marshall nodded. One of the reasons he had put the balaclava back on was to try and hide a glorious black eye and some very nasty bruising across the bridge of his nose.

'Well, Bob nipped outside for a fag and he saw a bunch of bikers down by the gate at the far end of the lane.'

'Bikers?' Mr Marshall repeated.

The masked man nodded. 'Yeah, like the bloke who punched –'

'All right, all right,' said Mr Marshall. 'Bugger. How many are there?'

The man shrugged. 'Fuck knows – it's getting dark out there, but Bob reckons there's at least a half a dozen. Apparently one of them was on the phone and it sounded like they were either calling up reinforcements or fetching the Old Bill.'

'So what do you suggest we do now?' said Mr Marshall miserably.

Eddy shrugged. 'Not my job to plan strategy. I'm strictly a grunt, guv.'

'I'm not asking you to take responsibility for it, I'm asking you for an idea, man, your thoughts.'

Eddy shrugged again.

Mr Marshall mulled it over for a few moments. 'Where does this track lead to?'

'Down to the river eventually.'

'So does that mean the only way out of here is back down towards the bikers?'

'No, about half a mile down that way the track crosses the railway lines, and then you can double back and end up in Mill End Bank, a little village a couple of miles off the A10.'

Mr Marshall nodded. 'Right, in that case I think discretion is the better part of valour. Get the lads together and bring the Land Rover round the back.'

He hesitated, wondering what he should do about Mrs Hammond, but decided that actually he didn't need to do anything. She wasn't tied up, she had a cup of tea, and the cavalry was already on its way.

8

David Hammond was standing in the driveway of Cass's cottage, backlit by the security light, when Joe and Jake and the biker boy showed up. As they approached, David squared his shoulders and nodded an acknowledgment. 'Right-oh, chaps. Now, what I suggest we do is take a drive down there, see what's going on – reconnoitre the situation, and see if we can't sort this thing out. OK?'

Joe stared at him in amazement; it sounded like something Biggles might come up with. David's clipped received pronunciation made it sound like a plan; common sense suggested the man was an idiot.

'Do you know what you're saying?' said Joe. 'This isn't the kind of thing you sort out on your own. Have you rung the police and let them know what's happening?'

David sighed. 'Look, this is all very straightforward; I think we can handle it. These guys are complete idiots.'

Jake and Joe looked at each other, while the spotty boy sniffed and lit up another fag.

'And you can put that out,' snapped David, clapping his hands together. 'No smoking in my Jeep, we need to be going. Come on.'

'I'll ring the police again as soon as you're gone,' said Jake, in an undertone to Joe, as David marched off towards his 4x4 with the biker boy at his heels. 'For God's sake, go with him and stop him getting Cass hurt, will you?'

Joe nodded, wondering if he was up to the job, and then hurried after David. The last thing he wanted was to be left behind. As Joe clambered up into the back seat, David turned and looked him over. 'And you are . . . ?'

'Joe Bennett,' said Joe, extending a hand. David's handshake was less than perfunctory, barely more than the briefest pressure. This was the moment when tact was called for. Joe braced himself for whatever question was coming next, but David just nodded and slid the key into the ignition, so Joe added, 'I was meeting Cass this evening. At the Chequers.'

'Oh right. I saw her sorting through her portfolio earlier. Some sort of artist, are you? Or are you the one who's putting on an exhibition of some of her scribbles?'

'I'm an architect, actually.'

'Right,' said David, obviously not at all interested. 'OK.' And then, turning to the boy, he said, 'Well, let's get this show on the road, shall we?'

And with that the three of them set off into the darkness.

In the back seat Joe watched the Norfolk countryside unroll, silver-edged under a heavy summer moon, hoping that Jake had had the good sense to get on the phone the instant they left the cottage. As he settled back into his seat, Joe could feel the outline of Cass's sandal, still in his jacket pocket, pressing into his hip and prayed that she was all right.

A few miles outside the village, the Jeep slowed and pulled off a narrow unlit country road on to a single unmade track that ran alongside the railway line. A hundred yards from the entrance was a metal five-barred gate pushed back into a hedge and there, picked out in the headlights, Joe could see a motley collection of bikers. They were having a smoke and chewing the fat, standing around amongst scrubby dust-dredged bushes, piles of brick rubble and building debris that were heaped along the verges. As they drew level, David killed his lights and jumped out, followed by Joe and their guide.

'So what's going on then?' David asked the biggest of the bikers.

'You the Old Bill?'

David was about to say something when Joe said, 'No, but they're on their way.'

David glared at him.

'Good,' said the boy. 'We've been keeping an eye on what's been going on.'

David peered into the gloom. 'And what exactly *has* been going on?'

The biker considered for a few seconds and then said, 'They brought her down here. They're all in some sort of shed a bit further down on the left. You can just make it out –' he pointed into the silver-grey gloom. 'We thought we'd stop them getting out, or follow them if they tried to make a break for it. We heard them driving around a while ago. Probably checking that they were safe or stowing the vehicles out of sight – you know.'

A little further along the track, Joe could see a flicker of light.

'Right-oh. Let's go and take a closer look,' said David, briskly rubbing his hands together. 'See what they're up to. I've got a score to settle.'

'Shouldn't we wait for the police to get here?' asked one of the bikers anxiously. He shifted his weight. 'It's not like we don't enjoy a bit of a fracas, but kidnapping and all that is way out of our league. We thought this was one for the Old Bill.'

Joe couldn't help but agree with him, but David sighed. 'Look, these guys are rank amateurs. Trust me – one big bang and they'd all fall down. And besides, I'm only suggesting we take a look-see, check out what's going on, and then work from there.' And with that David pulled a heavy-duty torch out of the Jeep, which at least he had the good sense to keep switched off, and headed up the track into the darkness, Joe following close behind.

As they walked David said, 'This is bloody typical. I don't know how well you know her, but Cass is a total liability. She needs someone to look after her – she's always getting herself into some sort of a muddle. She's really not safe out on her own.'

Joe stared at him in astonishment. 'Getting kidnapped is hardly something that happens every day of the week. You can hardly blame her for being grabbed off the street by thugs.'

David sighed. 'It's always the same with her: likes to be in the spotlight, does Cass. Centre of attention. I suppose she's told you about me?'

Joe took a breath; he didn't like to say that actually Cass hadn't mentioned him at all, but David was way ahead of him. 'The thing is – and this is something that I've already talked to Cass about – we are all entitled to make a few mistakes in life. We're grown-ups, it happens. Let's face it, none of us are perfect, and although she hasn't actually said anything, I think she realises that a lot of what's happened recently is her fault. I mean, not entirely her fault – we're all human – but maybe she'll have learned her lesson. And here we are, look –' he snorted – 'me bailing her out again. It's always the same. The woman really is a total liability.'

Joe decided there was nothing he wanted to add. From a stack of rubbish, brick rubble and building waste by the lane, David pulled out a length of timber and handed a second to Joe. 'Just in case,' he murmured. 'Morons, these guys, but you can never be too careful. Come on, it can't be that much further now.'

Ahead of them, a dense but paler shape was picked out against a purple-black sky. It was a large Portakabin set on a rough oval of concrete, a single light burning in one of the smaller windows. There was an odd sense of desolation about the place. Away in the distance an owl hooted grimly, while everywhere around David and Joe was still and wreathed in deep, velvet black darkness. There wasn't a vehicle in sight, not a breath of wind, no noise, no voices nor any other sign of life.

Moments ticked by. As they watched and waited, Joe felt the hair on the back of his neck prickle and then stand. The heavy stillness was uncanny. The owl hooted again. Joe swallowed hard. Something in the undergrowth rustled. Too small to be a man, it scuttered past them in the dark. There was another, and then another, busy in the gloom.

'Christ, rats!' said David thickly.

'Rats?'

'Bloody things.' David shifted his weight from foot to foot. 'I hate rats.'

'So what do we do now?' hissed Joe after a few seconds. He glanced across at David, who was as white as whey in the moonlight.

'I don't know – Christ, there's another one,' David stammered, hopping now, his earlier bravado evaporating fast. 'Where the hell are they?' Anxiously he glanced left and right. 'Can you see anybody?' He skulked nervously, his unease contagious. 'Christ, I think one just ran over my foot,' he mewled miserably.

Around them the darkness was increasingly busy with all sorts of scuttling sounds. Joe looked round, wondering if the kidnappers had heard them coming up the lane. Maybe they had heard David pulling the wood out of the stack, and were even now creeping up behind the two of them in the darkness.

'Maybe we ought to go back to the gate, wait for the police?' Joe suggested for the umpteenth time.

But before David could reply they heard the sound of footsteps inside the cabin, then a door handle creaking and, as they watched through the gloom, very, very slowly the Portakabin door began to open.

Alongside him, Joe heard David gasp and then squeak, 'Come on, we've seen enough. Let's get out of here, go back and wait for the police. Quick, quick, before they see us. Come on, we don't want any trouble.' And with that he turned tail and fled, throwing the makeshift club down as he ran.

But Joe, instead of backing up, found to his horror that he was rooted to the spot, his hands tight around the lump of timber in a two-handed batter's grip. He took a deep breath and braced himself for whatever might be coming. Over one shoulder he could hear David scurrying away behind the pile of brick rubble to one side of the track, his bravery suddenly tissue thin, while Joe, heart beating like a snare drum, held his ground and waited.

Light arced across the uneven grass and broken concrete pad, cutting an illuminated slice into the night. Still Joe held fast, trembling, adrenaline coursing through his body as hot and heady as malt whisky. He swallowed hard, adjusted his grip so he was braced and ready, bent his knees. The door was almost fully open. Any second now . . . any second . . . He took another deep, steadying breath and pulled the club back. A shadow appeared and spread across the concrete like an ink stain. Here it comes, thought Joe. Here it comes.

'Hello?' said a tiny, uncertain, but familiar voice from inside the cabin. 'Hello?' Slightly stronger now. 'Is anybody there?'

'Cass?' said Joe in total astonishment. 'Is that you?'

Seconds later, Cass Hammond stepped out into the darkness and looked around nervously. Joe's heart leapt; she looked gorgeous and frightened and so fragile that it was all he could do not to run over and throw his arms around her.

'Joe?' She sounded incredulous, her voice crackling with tears. 'Is that you? Oh my God,

I'm so pleased you're here. How on earth did you find –'

But before she could finish the sentence, David snapped, 'So there you are,' stepping out from his hiding place behind the building rubble. 'What the hell is going on here?'

Cass looked from face to face. 'David?'

He made a move towards her. 'Come on, Cassandra; I really think that we should be getting home now. The police will be here soon. Presumably they'll want to interview you. Come on.' He sounded very brusque and businesslike. And with this he moved forward and made as if to catch hold of her arm. Instead, Cass swung round and looked at Joe, eyes wide.

'Joe,' she said, as if David hadn't spoken. 'Oh, Joe, you've no idea how pleased I am to see you.'

David gasped. 'What?'

Joe smiled. 'You know, if you didn't want to have a drink with me you only had to say, there was no need to go to all this trouble on my account.'

David stared at them. 'What is going on here?' he growled. 'Do you realise that this woman is my wife? We should be getting back –' and then, even more incredulously, 'Cass, can you explain to me the exact nature of your relationship with this man?'

Caught in the light from the open doorway and completely unperturbed, Joe pulled the sandal from his pocket and held it out towards her.

Smiling, Cass lifted her skirt to reveal bare feet and then pulled the other shoe out of her handbag. 'Is this my Cinderella moment? I always knew that I'd have one eventually,' she said, smiling softly.

And then there was a warm silence as their eyes met. Joe dropped the makeshift wooden club to the ground and took her hand, and she stepped into first one shoe and then the other, letting Joe take her weight. And all at once Cass's control crumbled and she stepped into Joe's arms and burst into tears. He held her close against his chest. 'Sssssh,' he said, smoothing her hair. 'It's all right, it's all right. I've got you now.'

'God, I was so scared,' she whispered between sobs. 'It felt like I was in a bad dream. I thought to begin with that they might kill me —'

'It's OK, I've got you,' Joe said.

David was almost purple with rage. 'What the fuck is going on here?' he snarled. Neither Joe nor Cass replied.

The police were waiting for them when they got back to the entrance to the lane. It took most of the night for Cass to explain what had happened and that Joe wasn't James Devlin and all about the mistaken mobile phone pick-up that had led her to believe Joe was James, and how that was a mistake and whoever kidnapped her still thought Joe was James, and that her phone was tapped, and all the other bits in between.

It took so long and was so complicated that her

head hurt and she was almost sick with tiredness by the time it was all over and done with. Meanwhile the police checked Joe out, rang Jake, and gave David a warning about not reporting the earlier abduction, then they went off, presumably to search for the kidnappers. In the small hours of the morning a police car finally dropped Cass and Joe back at her cottage. It was so late it was early, the dawn creeping up sneakily over the far horizon.

'Do you want to come in for some coffee?' Cass said, standing on the doorstep, shivering.

Joe smiled, stroking the hair back off her face. She looked pale and heavy-eyed, pashmina pulled tight around her narrow shoulders to cut out the early-morning chill.

'I'd love to, but I really ought to go and collect my car from the pub and get home. You look shattered. I thought that you'd want to come home and go to bed.'

Cass looked up at him, punch drunk with tiredness and stress, and smiled sleepily. 'I do. Is that an offer?' she said.

He laughed. 'Could be. Might be. Are you serious?'

Cass snuggled up against him. 'Could be, might be. It's too early for you to drive home now, let's go to bed and find out,' she said in a husky whisper. 'I've got a spare toothbrush. To be perfectly honest, I'm not actually promising wild rampant sex; what I'd really like to do is cuddle up and be snuggled.' As she pressed herself against him, Joe could feel her body moulding to his and sighed. She looked up at him again. 'By the way, I think you ought to know that I'm married.'

'Uhuh, funnily enough, I noticed. Is he likely to show up here again tonight?'

'I wouldn't have thought so. He ran off with our cleaner, you know. Did I tell you that?'

'No, Jake did. The man is a complete idiot.'

Cass smiled. 'I know, but as Jake will also tell you, I've got the most dreadful taste in men.'

'I'll bear that in mind,' Joe said and kissed her tenderly.

At a tad after four, at around the same time as Cass and Joe crept up to bed past Jake, who was snoring in the spare room, and Danny who was curled up on the bottom bunk in his, in Brighton Daisy was very carefully – with all the overblown caution of someone a little too drunk for comfort – lifting the pots of bright red geraniums on Barney's steps. Gingerly she moved them one by one, looking for the spare front-door key. She knew it was there somewhere, it had to be; Barney always managed to let himself in however pissed he was. Daisy hadn't got the money for a taxi home and Barney wouldn't mind her sleeping on the couch.

She lifted another pot – eureka! Glued to the pot and the key were lots of very sleepy snails and a big grey stripey slug, – oh yeuk. Daisy closed her eyes and, wincing, picked the key out from between them. It occurred to her as she lurched down the steps that Cass was still away. Maybe she could sleep on her bed or Danny's. Good plan, save her from wrestling for sofa room with Barney's menagerie.

Carefully, Daisy unlocked the front door, slipped off her high heels and tip-toed across the flagstones, creeping past the sleeping dog, down through the kitchen to Danny's bedroom. Behind her, unnoticed, the front door swung idly to and fro on the early-morning breeze.

In the tiny back bedroom Antashinia and Snoops both dreamt of being curled up in bed with the man they loved. In the dream Snoops thought he could smell home. He opened one rheumy eye and sniffed again. He could smell freedom.

When Cass woke up there was a moment when she wondered what was going on. There was someone in her bed. Definitely. Yep, there it was again, that little sigh and snuffle, a jiffle of movement, the sounds of someone breathing. Had the last few months all been a terrible dream? Had David never left? Worse still, had she given in and taken him back? Someone close by snorted in their sleep and wriggled closer.

There was an arm draped across her waist. It felt heavy. Cass could sense another curled above her head, fingertips brushing her hair. Spoons –

she was spooning with . . . with . . . her brain, thank God, was rapidly clearing. And she sighed. Joe. It was Joe Bennett, not David. The tension ebbed away.

Beautiful Joe Bennett. It was all right after all. The breath on her shoulder, still sleep-deep and even, was not David's but Joe's. Joe who brought gifts of fruit and made great pasta; Joe who had been there at the Portakabin; Joe who she had propositioned and dragged into bed. Well, OK, maybe not dragged . . .

She moved, he moved, and then he moaned softly as he curled tighter still, pulling her closer. Cass shut her eyes, revelling in the contact. Joe was warm and smelt nice and it felt so very good to be cuddled, a frisson of desire shimmering through her as she sensed him slowly waking up.

'Umm,' Joe purred, still more asleep than awake as he pressed his lips into her neck and hair. 'God, you feel lovely,' he murmured, tracing the curve of her hip and belly, his fingers gentle and persuasive. Cass closed her eyes, it felt so wonderful. She could feel her whole body responding to him. It had been a long time since she had felt like this. It would be so very easy to let go, to melt into him. Or at least it would have been if Danny hadn't coughed furiously and then rolled over in the room next door. Who needed a conscience when you'd got a six year old?

Their current situation might be difficult to explain to anyone, let alone Danny. Very carefully,

Cass slipped out from under Joe's arm, pulled her dressing gown on and went down to make tea. Joe's shoes and coat and her sandals were in a heap at the bottom of the stairs. She picked them up and, without thinking, buried her face in his jacket, breathing in the smell of him. When Cass looked up she noticed Jake was sitting at the kitchen table watching her.

'So . . .' he said, sliding a mug her way and pushing out a chair with his foot. 'Why don't you sit down and tell me all about it?'

In his flat Mr Marshall was busy packing. He'd thought about it very carefully over the last few hours. Three things were making him think that leaving town was a good idea. One, the police were no doubt even now swabbing, fingerprinting and photographing the Portakabin where they had taken David and Cass Hammond. Surely it wouldn't be long before something brought them hotfoot to his door. Two, it had been a long time since he had had a holiday. And three – well, three was perhaps the most compelling of all. It was going to be very, very hard to explain the current state of play to Gordie Mann. So, discretion being the best part of valour, he hadn't rung Mr Mann; in fact he hadn't talked to him at all. About anything.

If Mrs Hammond had been telling the truth about James Devlin – and he strongly suspected that she was – then they were back to square one.

And if she hadn't been telling the truth, then the next stage involved something altogether more physical. Neither prospect filled Mr Marshall with delight.

He folded another pair of boxer shorts into the holdall. He was much more at home with messy divorces and lost relations than this sort of strong-arm stuff. It had been an error of judgement to take the job with Gordie Mann in the first place. It wasn't his bag really. In fact, whichever way you cut it, Mr Marshall didn't want to be involved, but he couldn't see an easy way out. He closed the suitcase and set it down on the floor. He had a sister in Canberra. He'd been meaning to go and visit her for years.

It was barely eight o'clock. In Brighton Antashinia was hysterical. Barney sighed, it looked like Cass might have been right, after all. Maybe he should have asked for references, maybe he shouldn't have taken the first person that rang. In the kitchen, Antashinia was gabbling wildly at him and frantically waving her hands in the air.

Feeling slightly trapped, Barney stared at her puffy eyes as she sobbed furiously and decided on balance he was no judge of character. Given all the cheery acquiescence and superb cooking of the previous day, it probably had been too good to last. Although, even in Barney's experience, pretending to be sane and normal usually lasted more than twenty-four hours.

'Don't worry. It's all right,' he said, patting her on top of the head, despite it obviously not being all right at all. 'Why don't you tell me again, more slowly this time, what is the matter. I didn't quite catch what you said.'

She snorted and wiped her nose on the back of her hand.

Barney had been woken from a deep and dreamless sleep by the sounds of Antashinia first rummaging and then rampaging through the flat, yelling and sobbing, looking under tables, throwing open cupboard doors, rushing from room to room, finally running out into the road, shrieking incoherently, wringing her hands, tears streaming down her great red moon of a face. Barney had quickly pulled on a dressing gown and followed her outside. He decided that she was most probably on some kind of medication, or possibly needed to be.

It had taken him quite a while to persuade Antashinia to come back indoors. People had come out to stare at her and point. It was hard enough to make out what she was saying when calm, but now, edging towards total hysteria, it was like trying to pick words from a raging thunderstorm.

'Heeeeeezzzzzzz gone,' she sobbed at the top of her voice. 'Gone. The front door, it was open. He go, he leave, he run away. He go to find, to find – to find heeeeeem.' The au pair swallowed hard and then, throwing back her head, began to wail like an elk with toothache. 'Whatever will he say?

Whatever will I do? It is too horrible. What if Snoops gets runned under a car? He loves Snoops. Oh my Gooooood,' she bellowed. 'Snoops he is not here,' she said, exhausted now.

Ah, the dog. Now it was beginning to make sense. Barney opened the pantry, took a glass from the draining board and poured a large shot of brandy into it. In his experience, alcohol always helped to soothe frayed and ragged nerves. Antashinia looked up at him as he drank it down in one.

'No, so you said. Shame about that.' He refilled the glass. 'But there's really no need to upset yourself. Maybe Daisy took him out for a walk,' Barney continued brightly. The second glass went down even more easily.

The girl shook her head. 'No, I don't think so. She is asleep in Danny's room. I looked there in case Snoops is trapped.'

Barney sighed, wondering how the hell Daisy could sleep through all the wailing and gnashing of teeth. 'Ah, OK. Well, in that case, I'm sure he hasn't gone very far. Probably sniffing round the bins somewhere on the square. I mean, where would he go?'

Antashinia sobbed. 'They will find him and they will drag him off to prison, my lovely, lovely one.'

It had to have lost something in translation. 'It's all right, my dear. They don't put dogs in prison in this country,' said Barney, patting her arm.

* * *

Gordie Mann looked at the extraordinary collection of things Margaret had assembled in the dining
room of the house she had shared with James. It
was still early in the morning. She had a little dab
of dust on the end of her nose and was unchar-
acteristically unkempt, a look that made her seem
small and vulnerable, and made him feel horny as
hell. Finally the prim façade was crumbling. Gordie
sighed. God, what a woman. What a waste. What
a terrible fool James Devlin was.

There were a pair of antique china dogs, two
silver candelabra, various shepherdesses and their
sheep, a few other ornaments and trinkets of above
average pedigree, several pieces of jewellery that
James had bought Margaret to appease his
conscience over the years, a couple of dozen paintings, a pair of matching onyx table lamps, and
some small pieces of furniture. It looked like the
beginnings of a half-decent village auction.

Hot and tired from her exertions, Margaret
pushed a strand of hair back off her face, trying
to ignore the glint in Gordie's eye. Margaret had
been up since six, fetching and carrying things
downstairs.

'As far as I know, none of these things are listed
anywhere or insured separately on the household
contents,' she said, setting a hollow bronze statue
of a Greek nymph down amongst the rest of the
things. 'They're not pawned, stolen, borrowed
against or itemised. And there are several other
bits and pieces. I have –'

Gordie's expression stopped her dead in her tracks. 'Margaret, it doesn't have to come to this, you know,' he said, picking up a porcelain figurine of a dancer from amongst the items arranged on the dining table. 'Of course I'm more than happy to try and sell this for you, but we could come to some kind of arrangement. You don't have to sell your precious things, my dear.'

'They're not my precious things,' said Margaret briskly. 'And let's be honest, Gordie, they're only collecting dust. If the bailiffs come in I'll get next to nothing for most of this stuff, and if I sell up I won't be able to take it with me. It needs to be in a country house – and I need the money, Gordie.' She tried very hard to tread the fine line between sounding needy and desperate.

Gordie Mann shook his head. 'Maggie, Maggie, Maggie, you deserve so much better than this, my sweet. If they were to find James's body –'

Margaret swung round and glared at him. 'Do you really think he's dead?'

Gordie pulled a face.

'No, me neither. That bastard is far too selfish to have killed himself. No, you and I both know he's holed up somewhere waiting for all the fuss to die down. He's probably left the country, dyed his hair, had plastic surgery – who knows, anything is possible. One thing I'd stake my life on is that James is not dead. The police are still hoping that a –'

'Is that why you're keeping company with Henry

Turner?' said Gordie with studied casualness, setting the figurine down, cutting across her words before she could finish her sentence. 'I don't blame you really. In my experience it always pays to have a man on the inside.'

Margaret decided not to pass comment. 'Whatever has happened to James, the fact remains, Gordie, that I need money and I need it now. None of these things are on the insurance inventory. And there's lots more around the place. I thought I could sort out –'

'Margaret, please stop this,' he said, catching hold of her hand. 'Surely you know me better than this. How many years have we known each other? You know that I wouldn't see you in a muddle, lass. If I can help in any way. I mean, this is ridiculous. There can't be more than a few hundred quid's worth here, if that. There has to be another way. An easier way.'

Gently extricating her hand from his, Margaret made a point of not meeting his eye. She could hear the tone of his voice. Any other way that Gordie could come up with was not something she wanted to contemplate. In the hall the phone rang. It stopped for a second and then rang again. She hesitated.

'Why don't you go and get that, hen?' suggested Gordie. 'I'll take a look through this lot,' he said, his attention apparently moving on to the stack of paintings propped up by the fireplace.

Margaret picked up the handset and listened

intently, then took a piece of paper and a pen from the bureau and scribbled down an address and phone number, before thanking the caller.

'Something important?' asked Gordie, without looking up.

Margaret paused, trying to work out what it meant. 'I'm not sure. I've got to go down to Brighton,' she said briskly.

Gordie stared at her, his expression fixed and stony. 'Brighton?' he repeated.

She nodded. 'Yes. Look, Gordie, please take this stuff and see if you can sell it. I wouldn't ask, but I am absolutely desperate.'

'It's James, isn't it?'

Margaret paled. 'What?'

'In Brighton? Was that him? Is he ringing you now? Are you holding out on me? I thought better of you, Margaret.'

Margaret stared at him in astonishment. 'Don't be silly, he wouldn't dare ring here. First of all, James would assume that the lines were tapped and secondly, even if he didn't, what is he going to say to me? *"Sorry, I've made a terrible mistake – can I come home?"* For God's sake, Gordie, credit me with a little more sense. The man has embezzled two million pounds, is wanted by the police, has left me and the children destitute and up to our necks in debt. I'm almost certain that the very first chance he gets he's going to ring here, looking for a way to creep back.'

Gordie waved the backwash of industrial-strength sarcasm away. 'Knowing James the way I do, I'd say almost anything is possible.' He stared at her. 'Margaret, I have to ask you this – and you can tell me to mind my own business if you like, but I need to know. Do you still love James?'

'Oh, Gordie,' said Margaret, feeling her eyes fill up with tears. 'How can I? How on earth could I still love him after everything he's done? I loved him for years. I kept thinking that if I loved him enough it would all come right in the end, but it never has. How can I love a man who made me feel so bad about myself, so very worthless? No, I don't love him any more. I'm tired of him, tired of never knowing where he is or who he's with, what time he's going to come home, or if he'll be home at all. I'm just tired. Gordie.'

Gordie's face softened. 'So you don't want him back then?'

She shook her head. 'No. No, I don't. Not ever.'

'In that case, don't defend him, Margaret, don't protect him. He's left you in the lurch, whatever he says.'

'It wasn't him on the phone,' she snapped emphatically. 'It wasn't even about James, it was about his bloody dog. Apparently the damn thing was wandering along the seafront in Brighton and someone handed him in at the local police station. He's microchipped, so the dog warden rang here.'

Gordie nodded. 'That's very odd. How did the

dog end up down there, do you think? Have you got any contacts in Brighton – family? Friends?'

Margaret shook her head. 'No, why?'

'It's a strange coincidence, because that's where Mrs Hammond has ended up as well.'

Margaret stared at him. 'No? The woman James was seeing?'

Gordie nodded. 'The very same. I was rather hoping Mr Marshall would have some news of the pair of them. Maybe I should ring, see what he's turned up.'

Margaret hesitated as the possibilities dawned. 'Oh my God, you think he's down there too? You think they're down there together?'

'Seems like a fair bet to me. Did James take the dog with him when he left?'

'No,' Margaret said. 'I think it disappeared when the au pair went, but to be honest it's all been a bit of a blur. I really can't be sure.'

'Well, whatever the explanation, I think it would be worth our while to go see what's going on. It seems too much of a coincidence that the dog and Cass Hammond have ended up in the same town. Do you want me to drive you? I've got the Jag outside; we could be there in a couple of hours.'

Margaret hesitated. She wasn't sure she liked Gordie thinking of him and her in terms of 'we', but her options were limited. The bottom line was that her credit cards were up to the hilt, there was no petrol in any of the cars, and the account at the local garage had been frozen.

'I don't want to put you to any trouble,' she began.

'It'll be no trouble,' said Gordie. 'No trouble at all.'

'In that case, I need to get cleaned up and properly dressed,' she said briskly. 'Get myself organised.'

Gordie smiled. 'Of course you do, hen. And I've a couple of phone calls that I need to make. How about you go and get yourself ready. I'll wait for you down here.'

At Cass's cottage she was busy making more tea.

'I don't think you should be on your own,' said Jake thoughtfully, while stirring an unhealthy amount of sugar into his mug. Danny was playing with his cars on the sitting-room floor. Cass was far too nervous to let him go outside.

'The police have told me that they'll keep Danny and me under surveillance until this is cleared up.'

Jake sniffed. 'Right you are then. That's just what we need. Are we still going back to Brighton today?'

'I think I ought to. I told Barney I would.'

'I'm sure he'd understand if you didn't want to go,' said Joe, who was busy feeding the toaster.

'I know,' Cass paused, horribly aware of the tremor in her voice. 'The thing is, *the problem is* that I don't feel safe here any more.' She looked across at the pair of them, her lip trembling in spite of her efforts to keep it under control. 'I know this sounds pathetic, but I'm really scared, and I'm worried about Danny. First of all Mrs Devlin turned up here and now . . .' She stopped, struggling with tears. 'I'm afraid that they might come back. What if Danny was here? What if I was alone? And the guy who did all the talking, the one in charge, he said he was working for someone else, someone he was frightened of. I don't want to be on my own at the moment.' Bright-eyed and anxious, Cass looked from face to face. 'It sounds so pathetic.'

'It doesn't sound pathetic at all,' said Joe gently. 'Look, how about I come down to Brighton for a few days with the pair of you? I'm about due a holiday anyway, and for some unfathomable reason I feel as if this is all my fault.'

'That's silly. And I couldn't possibly ask you to –' she began, although every bone in her body wanted him to.

'You're not asking me,' he said. 'I'm volunteering. And besides,' he grinned, 'I really liked sleeping with you.'

Across the table Jake sniffed and pulled a face. 'Oh please, do you mind?' he said. 'Too much information. I've only just had my breakfast.'

Cass laughed in spite of herself. 'So does this mean that we're all going to Brighton?'

Joe nodded. 'Certainly looks like it from where I'm standing. I need to go home and sort a few things out. Pack, make some calls.'

On cue, Jake got to his feet too. 'In that case

I should go and get ready as well. Presumably you have to ring the federales to let them know what you're up to?'

Cass stared at them as realisation dawned and then she said in a tiny voice, 'You're both going to go?'

'To Brighton, yeah, sure, why not?' asked Jake. 'I don't see that Barney'll mind. He invited me to come down anyway, and presumably lover boy here is going to bunk down with you, so that'll save on laundry. Anyway, it seems a sensible idea, safety in numbers and all that. I'll leave the cats a big bowl of crunchies.'

'No, not to Brighton. I meant now,' murmured Cass, and with that she promptly burst into tears. 'Oh God, this is nuts. I'm so sorry, but I don't want to be here on my own.' The two men stared at her as she struggled to regain her composure. 'What a wuss I turned out to be,' she murmured thickly, sniffing back the tears.

'Tell you what, why don't you and Danny come and sit with me round at my place until Joe gets back?' said Jake, handing her the kitchen roll. 'And then . . .' he paused, obviously working it out on the hoof. 'And then we can head off to the seaside together. Are we driving down in convoy?'

Joe nodded.

'There we are then – you, Danny and me in the Bentley, and lover boy here bringing up the rear with the law in front. We'll look like royalty. I'm sure I've got a peaked cap somewhere. And I know I've got a cravat – paisley, gold and green. I'll wear that and my navy sailing club blazer. What d'ya reckon?'

9

In Brighton, Barney, Daisy and Antashinia had scoured the streets and back alleys around Sussex Square for what seemed like hours. Actually, it probably was hours. They had looked high and low, whistling and calling until they were all dry and hoarse and horribly fraught. It was no good; Snoops was nowhere to be found.

'We can't stop now,' said Antashinia anxiously.

Hanging on a set of iron railings, sounding for all the world as if he was about to part company with what remained of his lungs, Barney peered at her between coughing fits.

'He's not here.' The morning air really didn't agree with Barney. This was not his preferred way to start the day. Having walked God knows how far and peered into basements, bins and heaven knows what else besides, Barney had decided that enough was most definitely enough, however forlorn and anxious the au pair looked. He needed more brandy to help coax the blood through his poor tired old veins.

'I really think we ought to go back inside. This is getting us nowhere. He would come if he could hear or see you.'

By the kerb, Antashinia started to whimper.

'Now look, stop that. He is a beautiful dog, someone is bound to have found him and handed him in,' said Barney gently. 'I'm sure he will be fine. Let's go back inside before I have a seizure. We'll get the kettle on, and then I suggest that you phone the police.'

The girl rounded on him, all white-faced and anxious, her fingers clenched into fists below her chins in a cartoon gesture of terror. 'Oh no, no, not the police! No, you don't understand, Meester Barnneeeee, we cannot ring the police. They – they will take him away. They will take him to prison and I will never see heeeeeeeem again. Truly, I don't lie. For ever – I know this.' The more upset she became, the more impenetrable her meaning.

Daisy patted her gently on the shoulder. 'Now, don't be silly. Of course they won't take him away. They won't, really,' she said as Antashinia looked even more anxious. 'The police in this country aren't like that. They love dogs. Snoops will be fine. Would you like me to ring for you and explain?'

The girl shook her head and began a miserable high-pitched keening. 'No, no. I know you are trying to be kind and to help me, but you are wrong.

They will take him away and I will never ever see him again, not ever.' She started to rock backwards and forwards, surely not a good sign.

Daisy and Barney exchanged glances. 'All right, that's enough,' said Daisy briskly. 'Come on, this isn't helping, now, is it? Tell you what, let's go back inside. Maybe he will come home on his own. And if he doesn't, then we can go and have another look later on.'

It was Barney's turn to moan. Daisy glared at him.

Slumped on the kerbside, head in her hands, Antashinia wailed, 'But what am I going to do now? What am I going to say? The dog, Snoops, he love him, he was his most treasured possession.'

'Really?' said Daisy.

The girl nodded. 'He belonged to the man that I love. Snoops is all I have left to remind me of him, all I have until we can be together – and who knows when that will be?' She sobbed, her misery punctuated by incomprehensible phrases in her mother tongue.

Daisy handed the girl another tissue. 'Come on, let's go home and I'll make everyone a cup of tea.'

As they passed Barney, who was still clinging to the railings, she mouthed, 'I'll ring the police on the mobile.' And Barney nodded.

'We did about this sort of thing in history – oppressive regimes, people being thrown into prison without trial, torture, human rights violations,'

Daisy said conversationally, helping Antashinia to her feet and guiding her back towards the flat. 'Where did you say you came from again?'

Sitting in his Jag, Gordie Mann flicked the tab end of his cigar out of the window, tapped Mr Marshall's number into his mobile and waited. He wasn't best pleased to get Marshall's voice mail. He rang again and then again. Finally, on the third or fourth attempt, Marshall answered. He sounded breathless.

'Where the fuck have you been?' Gordie snarled. 'I thought you were going to keep in touch?'

Mr Marshall cleared his throat nervously. 'So sorry I've not been back to you. I've . . . I've been following several very promising leads. Ummm . . .'

'And?'

'And, er, well, it's still early days yet, but I think we've cleared away a lot of the dead wood. It's as important in an investigation of this nature to work out what not to follow up as it is to decide –'

'I don't need a lesson in surveillance techniques,' snapped Gordie Mann. 'What I need are results. Soon. Do I make myself clear?'

Mr Marshall said nothing.

Gordie regretted taking him on. It had seemed like a good idea at the time having Devlin tracked down at a remove by a professional, but on reflection it wasn't Gordie's style really. He much preferred direct action.

'What about the Hammond woman – have you had any luck with her?' He was almost certain he heard Mr Marshall whimper at the other end of the line. 'Are you all right, man?'

'Yes, yes, I am fine, thank you,' Mr Marshall answered in a bizarre falsetto.

'So what about Mrs Hammond?'

'Er, yes, well, she is one of the leads we are still actively pursuing. Obviously. And I hope to have something for you soon, very soon. I'm on it even as we speak.'

Gordie sniffed. 'My patience is not endless. Anyway what I want now is for you to get your arse in gear and get your boys down to Brighton for me . . . chop-chop, *tout suite, capiche*? Margaret has just had a call to say that James's dog has been picked up by the Old Bill down there.'

'His dog?' Mr Marshall repeated. 'Really?'

'That's what I said, didn't I?' growled Gordie. 'His bloody dog.'

'How on earth did it get down there? Seems a bit odd to me.'

Gordie groaned; the man was a complete fool. 'Have you considered the possibility that it might have something to do with the Hammond woman?' he said, heavy on the sarcasm. 'We know the dog was important to him. She could easily have brought it down with her. I want you to rally your men. S'too much of a coincidence for my liking.'

'Righty-oh,' said Mr Marshall, sounding affronted by the slur on his professionalism. 'I'll get my chaps sorted, get the tap set up to let me know what Mrs Hammond is up to, and then I'll ring you back.'

'Good man,' said Gordie. 'I'll give you the address of the animal welfare place.' He unfolded the piece of paper Margaret had given him. 'I'll hold fire till you get yourself down there and into position, and then we need to work out what we're going to do. Maybe we could use the dog as bait. If we let Mrs Hammond know we've got him, then presumably there's a good chance she'll let Devlin know – and we've got her wired. Or if we took it back to where it was found and let it go, the dog might lead us straight to wherever it's been holed up with Devlin. Seems like a reasonable bet to me.'

At the far end of the line Mr Marshall looked thoughtfully at his hand luggage and suitcase standing ready by the back door. How the hell had James Devlin's dog ended up down in Brighton?

And then something made his heart lurch. Maybe Mrs Hammond had been lying to him after all. Of course. He could kick himself. Obviously she had learned her stuff from Devlin. So she *was* seeing him. They were in it together.

He shook his head, partly in disbelief and partly in admiration. The lying cow. God, she was good. Mr Marshall picked up the phone. He didn't like violence, but he didn't like to be outsmarted either.

He decided to leave it to Eddy – Eddy would sort it out.

Through the windscreen Gordie watched as Margaret Devlin teetered towards the Jag in her high heels, having requested a moment to freshen up at a service station. Gordie felt his heart flutter as she smiled at him. He smiled back. There were a lot of people who would find it hard to believe that Gordie Mann still had a heart after all these years.

'Got to be worth a shot,' said Gordie into his mobile.

'Yes, well, obviously,' said Mr Marshall.

'Ring me when you're down there and all set,' said Gordie. 'I'm planning to take me time, have a spot of lunch so's to give your lads a bit of leeway.'

'Right you are,' said Mr Marshall.

Margaret opened the car door as Gordie hung up. 'All set?' he said, watching her fold herself into the deep leather seat. She was so tiny, so fragile.

She nodded. 'Yes, thank you.'

Gordie smiled to himself. God, the woman had fantastic legs.

Parked on a strip of grass by the exit to the Welcome Break and apparently engaged in an animated conversation with his partner, a youngish-looking man, actually a detective sergeant, called in to control.

'Mrs Devlin and Mr Mann are just pulling out of the service station back on to the M11 heading south.'

In the control car DI Turner said, 'Does Mrs Devlin look as if she is under any duress, Sergeant?'

The DS looked at his companion, a female constable, who pulled a face and shook her head. With a sigh, he said, 'It doesn't look like it from here, guv, but it's not easy to tell from where we're sitting. Anything could be going on in that car. You know what Gordie's like.'

'Indeed I do,' growled DI Turner, feeling his dander rise. 'Indeed I do. Stick with them, Sergeant. I don't want to lose them.'

'We won't, sir.'

'Good job,' said DI Turner. 'Keep me in the loop.'

In the unmarked police car, caught up in a flurry of traffic, DI Turner looked thoughtfully out of the window. He too was on his way down to Brighton at a discreet distance from Margaret and Gordie. His partner coughed in a way that indicated he wanted to talk.

'What is it?' said Turner.

'I don't like to mention this, sir, but are you letting your feelings for Mrs Devlin get in the way of . . . well, you know . . .'

Turner stared at him. 'No, not at all. The dog is the best lead we've had since Devlin vanished. East Sussex CID have been very co-operative, everyone is up to speed on this. Everyone who knows Devlin said he absolutely doted on the animal. It vanished at around the same time as he did, and now it shows up in Brighton. We can't let this slip by. There has to be a link. And if he risked taking the dog with him, then presumably he'll want to get it back.'

'Strange that Cassandra Hammond washed up in Brighton too. She seemed very credible when we took her statement. If she's a liar, then she's a bloody good one.'

'And then there's Gordie Mann, he has to be tied up in this somewhere,' said Turner. 'All the pieces are here on the table, we just need to sort through them. Mind you, if Gordie gets to James Devlin first, we might not have anything left to arrest.'

'You don't buy the suicide theory then?'

Turner snorted and shook his head. 'No. Which is a great shame from Margaret's point of view. It would be a damned sight easier for her and the kids if Devlin were dead and buried. You can't help but feel sorry for the woman, dragged down by that scum.'

'James Devlin?'

'James Devlin, Gordie Mann – nothing but trash the pair of them. A good woman like that needs to be taken care of, nurtured, protected.'

His driver nodded, his expression giving nothing away. 'She seems to have got in with a bad lot,' he said noncommittally.

Turner sighed. 'We all make mistakes.

Apparently she worked for Mann when she first left school. And as for James Devlin, well, he was a charmer, she was young – sort of thing that happens all the time.' He looked wistfully out of the window at the summer morning. If he had his way it would never happen again.

While Daisy made a pot of tea and cut everyone a slice of Victoria sponge, Antashinia made up her mind. She had to ring and tell him that Snoops was lost. He would know what to do, he always knew what to do. Antashinia trusted him.

Somebody saluted Jake on the M25.

'For God's sake, take that bloody cap off, will you,' Cass hissed as they drew up alongside a minibus full of Japanese tourists.

'Oh, will you please stop whining. I'm not doing any harm and look, they love every minute of it,' said Jake, ventriloquist fashion between almost closed lips. As he spoke, he waved and nodded regally. Alongside the Bentley a fusillade of camera flashbulbs went off while happy faces pressed themselves to the bus windows, gesticulating and pointing and grinning wildly. Cass tried very hard to ignore them. It wasn't easy.

Joe was driving ahead of them in his sexy silver Golf. She could see him checking his rear-view mirror periodically to make sure she was still there, or maybe just to look at her. Cass grinned. When they pulled up at a junction she could see his eyes, all crinkly and smiling. This was ridiculous; she grinned, trying to make herself concentrate on the road ahead.

Behind the Bentley, were two rather jaded-looking policemen in an unmarked navy blue Vectra. Travelling at bang on fifty, patently in a convoy, the three vehicles stuck out like a wart and whiskers on a beauty queen.

Strapped into his booster seat in the back, Danny, apparently oblivious to the goings-on around him, was playing with his *Gameboy*, listening to a story on his headphones and occasionally glancing up to watch the world go by. He was behaving himself; unlike Jake, who kept fidgeting about and wriggling and moaning.

'Are we nearly there yet?' said Jake, sorting his way through the bag of sweeties Cass had given them to share.

Danny looked up. 'If you say that she shouts.'

'No, I don't,' growled Cass.

She caught the two of them in the rear-view mirror exchanging world-weary glances in a man-to-man sort of way.

'I need a wee,' whined Jake.

'You should have gone before we went,' said Danny, pressing the buttons on his game.

'Exactly,' said Cass, 'instead of spending the last ten minutes adjusting your cravat and running around looking for a monocle.'

'That's it, that's women all over. No patience. I know I've got one somewhere, I only wanted to go upstairs and look in the dressing-table drawer before we left.'

'For the tenth time.'

'Don't be ridiculous. It was five at the very most; maybe seven. I'm certain it was in there somewhere. I probably missed it the first few times – easily done when you're being rushed and harassed and bullied.' He lingered lovingly over the word 'bullied'. If Cass could have reached him, she would have given him a clout round the ear.

Gordie and Margaret had a rather nice pub lunch in a hostelry Gordie knew before they went to reclaim the dog. After all, Gordie needed to let Mr Marshall and his men get into position, and it was an opportunity to show Margaret the kind of man he was. Surf and turf, a bottle of decent wine. He knew how to treat a lady.

Margaret glanced into the back seat of Gordie's Jag, wishing to God that she had brought a blanket or at least some newspaper or kitchen roll with her. She remembered with a shudder the last time they had taken the damned dog out. It had been during the school holidays, when other families jetted off to Barbados or the Seychelles; James had had the bright idea of taking the children and the bloody dog down to the beach for the day. A proper family day out, was what he said, with a picnic and rugs and a game of boules on the sand. Not Margaret's kind of thing at all. The dog had started throwing up all over the back seats before they had even got out of the drive.

James said it was probably nervous or excited, or both. Margaret thought that there was a bloody good chance it was attention seeking. The children made a real fuss of it once the nanny had scraped the mess up, while all the while the dog was whimpering and whining and rubbing up against James like he was some sort of god.

The inside of Gordie's Jaguar smelt of good cigars and well-polished leather. There was no place here for damp dog, warm sick and paw prints. God alone knew what the damned thing had been eating, or how long it had been roaming the streets since it left Little Lamport. It had always had a penchant for dustbins, rubbish bags and dead things rather than the expensive designer-dogfood the vet recommended. Margaret felt her stomach lurch with revulsion. Oh no, she most definitely did not want it throwing up all over Gordie's Jag. Maybe she should have a word with the dog people in Brighton about having it rehoused or put down.

In his flat, James Devlin listened to Antashinia on his new mobile. She was hysterical. It was hard enough to understand her when she wasn't. He waited for her to run out of steam, and then said in a very measured, reasonable tone, 'Look, don't panic. I understand, calm down.'

'But Snoops,' she stammered, 'he's gone. Gone.'

'I know, I know. What I want you to do when

you get off the phone is find the number for the local police and then ring them. Do you understand? They'll put you in contact with the dog warden. Just make sure that you speak very slowly and clearly.'

'Yes, Daisy and Mr Barney have said that too. But – but –' she began, gathering speed.

'But nothing,' said James gently. 'If they've got him, they'll tell you. Then you can arrange to go and pick him up. It's very simple. All you have to do is tell them that you worked for Mrs Devlin –'

Antashinia gasped. 'No, I couldn't. Because I'm not –'

'Wait, wait. Of course you can. Tell them that you are Mrs Devlin's nanny and you have come to pick up Snoopy because she is too busy. Can you honestly see Margaret coming all this way to collect him? She hates him, she'll probably say she doesn't want him back and let him be rehomed. Do you want that?'

There was a panicky cry at the far end of the phone.

'Exactly, so you ring them now. You'll be fine. Give me a minute and I'll find the chip details. I've got them in my wallet. OK – have you got a pen? Right, you remember the address and the postcode for the house in Lamport?' He paused; he could hear the panic in her uneven breaths. 'Antashinia, relax. Snoops loves you. One look at him wagging and woofing and you'll have him out of there in no time.'

'But I can't, I can't,' the girl whimpered. 'What if she is there? Mrs Devlin.'

'Calm down. Everything will be all right,' James reassured her, his mind working overtime. The likelihood was that, even if they rang Margaret, she wouldn't drive down and pick the dog up. She hated Snoops almost as much as she hated James. There was, however, a slim possibility that she might wonder how the dog had got to Brighton. A dozen scenarios skittered through his head.

'Look, if she is there, you can say that you took the dog –' At the far end of the line the girl whimpered loudly. 'No, no don't fret,' said James sharply. 'Listen, you've got to pull yourself together. Let me think, let me think . . . If Margaret's there, say you thought she had got more than enough on her plate with the children and me disappearing and everything, and say that you love Snoops and you're sorry. Very sorry. She'll be angry and she'll shout – you know what she's like. But the good thing is, Margaret hates Snoops. Chances are she'll let you keep him.'

'And what about the police, if they ask?'

'Tell them that I gave you the dog as a leaving present.'

The girl gasped. 'But that's a lie.'

'I know, but we need some sort of an explanation as to why Snoops is down here. Besides, who's to know I didn't give him to you?'

Bloody girl. It struck him there was a fair chance

that the dog, realising he was close by, had come to find him. He smiled. Snoops adored him.

'When did he go missing?'

'This morning.'

'OK. Ring the police station and then ring me back and let me know if they've got him.'

'Now?'

'Yes, now.'

'OK.' And with that the line went dead.

James Devlin crossed to the window and looked out. From his second-floor flat he could see the dark grey waters of the English Channel, a sliver between the rooftops.

If he opened the window, beyond the noise of the traffic it was possible to hear the soporific sounds of the water as it meandered back and forth, rolling the stones tirelessly along the fore-shore.

James sighed, it was barely lunchtime and already the day was oppressively warm and heavy, with the promise of thunder later. Brighton wasn't London, but it still had the anonymity that he needed. When the time was right and interest had died down, he planned to go abroad and find a way to take Snoops along too. He wondered how much Snoops going missing would change the game plan.

In the window, James caught sight of his reflection. Gone was the neatly trimmed executive hairstyle, a little long at the back to add a touch of panache and boyishness. Instead he'd shaved his head, pierced one ear and was wearing a white collarless cheesecloth shirt and jeans that he'd bought from the market. A little designer stubble complemented the new look. James turned to admire himself in the mirror above the fireplace, full face, then one side, and then the other.

Over the past couple of weeks he'd lost weight, which added an almost chiselled quality to his whole face and accentuated his cheekbones. He tried out a wolfish smile on his reflection. James Devlin's new look was a million miles away from Armani suits and hand-finished leather brogues. He looked like an artist, or perhaps a blues guitarist or a drug dealer. Maybe he should get himself a necklace and a few of those leather thong-and-bead bracelets to finish the look off. In Brighton it was a style that wouldn't get him a second glance, possibly not even a first. James looked at his watch. And then the mobile rang again.

'They hev him,' Antashinia sobbed tearfully. 'They hev Snoops.'

'It's going to be all right,' James said, posing for the mirror. He should start using a sunbed again. 'Now go and pick him up, just like I told you.'

'I can't, I can't,' she howled.

'You can, of course you can. Then, once you've got him, I want you to take him to the flat.'

'To the flat.'

'Yes.'

'Bring Snoops back to the flat.'

'That's right. Ring me when you've got him. Antashinia. . .?'

'Yes,' she said thickly.

'It'll be OK. You'll do fine, I know you will.'

She sniffed. 'Thank you. I miss you so much. I love you so –'

James sighed. 'I know, I know, but it won't be long now, I promise.'

As he spoke, he took another look in the mirror and tried out a sullen, moody rockstar expression. The look really suited him; he imagined himself at the bar in a club, waving the barman closer, ordering a designer beer or a JD on the rocks. God, girls would love him. Not that he had ever had any problem in that department, oh no; women instinctively recognised an alpha male when they saw one. James squared his shoulders.

It would be good to get back to normal. Spending your waking life with one eye over your shoulder was awful; listening at night for every noise, every sound, straining to make out whether those were footsteps on the stairs, wondering if the sirens that roared up and down the main road were the ones that were coming for him. Living on edge did not suit James one bit. And as the days passed, far from getting easier it was getting worse. His new thin, slightly haunted look had been hard earned.

There was a part of him that thought he should try and go it alone. Maybe get a passage to South America. Good-looking Englishman with a cute dog and enough money salted away to live well – it should be a breeze. There were several people he could talk to. But popping your head up over the battlements could be a dodgy business, particularly owing the kind of money he owed to the kind of people he owed it to. One false move and the only ticket he might get was one-way – into the foundations of a flyover.

'I ring my father, get him to hurry things along,' Antashinia was saying. 'He will understand that this thing with Snoops makes things go bad.'

James was about to speak but wasn't sure what to say. 'Not if you do what I told you,' he said after a few seconds.

When things had gone from bad to impossible, Antashinia had offered to help James get out of the country. He had said yes because he couldn't see any other way. Antashinia's family had found him the flat, taken his car and all his gear down to some beach somewhere and left them to be discovered, along with a note he had written. But afterwards, in the still of the night, it struck him that maybe it hadn't been such a good idea after all. As far as James could work out, Antashinia's father was something dodgy in Eastern Europe; the price for their help might be more than he could afford.

Taking her to bed had been a totally stupid move, but how was he to know the silly cow would fall in love with him? When the shit hit the fan with the business and the money and everything, she had seemed so very keen to help. But now he was in it up to his neck, every instinct told him that Antashinia's family weren't the kind of people you messed around with.

It was the first flush of afternoon when Cass drew up in the Bentley outside Barney's flat. She wondered if he had been waiting for her to arrive because no sooner had she switched off the engine than he was up the steps and haring across to the car looking worried, or maybe it was cross.

'There you are! Thank God you're back. I was about to give you a call. We need you to take Antashinia to Lewes – now. Bit of a disaster,' he said, flapping his arm around dramatically. In his wake trailed Daisy, looking all whey-faced and exhausted and probably hung-over, pulling on a cigarette like her life depended on it. Behind her scurried a large round-faced girl with lank shoulder-length hair who had quite obviously been crying. A lot.

'Well, nice to see you, too,' growled Jake. 'You think you've got problems,' he moaned, wriggling across the seat and easing himself out of the car. 'My bloody leg's gone to sleep and I'm dying for a wee. She wouldn't stop, you know. Nearly three hours we've been on the road. Three hours without a stop. She must have a bladder like a horse.'

Cass glanced in her rear-view mirror. Joe had managed to find a space a few cars back; another Vectra, silver this time, had pulled in ahead of her and was trying to reverse into a space more suited to a Fiat Uno.

Not to be outdone, Barney continued talking to Cass, apparently totally undaunted by Jake hurtling past him, clutching his crotch and heading down into the flat. 'You would not believe the morning we've had here. It's been complete and utter fucking chaos. You've no idea the palaver that's been going on while you've been away,' Barney said, managing to make it sound like an accusation.

Cass stared at him, wondering if he had any idea at all how it felt to be kidnapped by a man in a balaclava and then questioned for most of the night by the police.

It was the girl who answered. 'You are Mrs Hammond, yes?'

Cass nodded.

The girl smiled and held out a huge damp paw that totally engulfed Cass's hand. 'My name is Antashinia. I am so very happy to meet you. I found your number where I work before, and ring to talk with you because I couldn't stay in my job any more and I thought as you knew him you might be able to help, and then he give me another job.' The words came out in a great torrent and then the girl looked up, all dewy eyed and adoring, at Barney. 'And I am so very, very unhappy now.'

Cass nodded, trying to ignore the fact that Barney still looked livid and the girl's expression didn't fit with what she said; maybe it had lost something in translation.

'Right, OK. Barney told me he'd found someone. So what's the problem? Isn't it working out? I mean, you can't have been here more than –'

'No, no, it's not that at all. I am very happy with the job. But I hev lost the dog,' she said.

Daisy held up her hands in surrender. 'OK, let's not rub it in, shall we? Before anyone points the finger, I own up: it was me. OK? It was my fault. I left the front door open. Again. And yes, I do know that burglars could have come in, and that we could have all been murdered in our beds, but it was an accident. All right? He got out. Me –' She pointed at herself with both hands. '*Mea Culpa*.'

'I'm not with you. Who got out, Barney's dog?'

Daisy shook her head. 'Good God, no. Kipper is even lazier than Barney; he's way too lazy to bother running away. It's Antashinia's dog – or rather her boyfriend's. We've hunted high and low all morning, all over the place. Then we rang the police. Anyway, the thing is, someone's found him. So he's OK. The dog warden's picked him up. We just need to go and collect him.'

The red-eyed girl started to whimper miserably.

'Please,' said Barney angrily, 'will you stop that. The damned dog is fine. Now, if everyone will stop flapping, we'll get this sorted out. The man who rang explained that the dog is OK. Normally they get taken to the police kennels – some secret

334

location in the middle of Sussex, apparently – but because we rang and had the chip details and all that, we just need to go to some animal welfare woman in Lewes and pick him up . . .' Barney paused. 'Probably some mad old man-hater with fourteen cats and an ageing mother, but there we are.'

Cass looked at him and then past him. Upstairs, Barney's ageing mother was waving at them joyously. She was peering through a pair of binoculars whilst wearing her favourite red hat, and appeared to be smoking a pipe, or possibly it was a hookah.

Daisy yawned. 'Can we go now? I've got stuff I need to do.'

Barney glared at her. 'If it wasn't for you, we'd all be doing stuff. I've got important stuff to do, stuff that keeps you and your mother in bloody shoes and Cream Label. I'm not accustomed to starting the day playing hare and hounds round the back streets of Brighton, you know.'

'Yes, but that's only because most days you're not back till lunchtime after playing hare and hounds round some woman,' growled Daisy.

'You're just like your mother,' countered Barney.

'You mean neglected and betrayed?'

Joe ambled over, hands in his pockets, grinning. 'So what's going on here then?' he said.

Cass wished that he hadn't asked and then smiled as their eyes met. God, it was nice to have someone that laid-back and good-looking on your side. Her stomach did that shivery excited thing again. It was getting to be a habit. She had this terrible warm fuzzy desire to touch him, and from the way he was looking at her she suspected the feeling was mutual.

'You OK?' he said to no one else but her.

Before she could reply, Barney snapped, 'Oh, for goodness' sake – as if we need any more trouble. Who the hell are you?'

Cass sighed. 'Barney, don't be so bloody rude. Joe, I'd like you to meet Grumpy, Sleepy, and –'

The fat girl started to sob.

'Snotty,' suggested Danny, letting himself out of his booster seat and climbing from the Bentley, he handed Antashinia his box of emergency tissues.

Hidden away in a back street in Lewes, two unmarked police cars were already in position, observing the comings and goings at a slightly run-down red-brick cottage. They were waiting for someone to come and pick up James Devlin's dog.

Meanwhile Snoops was holed up in the front room on a beanbag, having made himself at home within about ten minutes of being let out of the dog warden's van. Rose Cottage had been chosen for several reasons – not least because it was easy to watch, with limited access but enough buildings around to disguise the watching police officers. Moreover, the animal welfare officer who lived there was an ex-policewoman, a stalwart with a spotless service record, a sharp eye, and a reputation for remaining steady under pressure. She was as solid as the Isle of Wight and about the same size.

Gordie Mann took another quick look at the map while Margaret popped into a newsagent. He smiled; she was worried that the dog might make a mess, worried that it would be too much trouble, worried that she was taking up too much of his time. Bless.

Margaret's surge of panic made him feel all big and strong and generous. Shouldn't take them much longer to get there now. Not that he had been rushing unduly. Even if he couldn't find a way to get to James Devlin through the dog, at the very least Gordie was earning extra brownie points with Margaret, getting the family pet back, rescuing her in her hour of need. She must miss having the wee thing about the place, wagging its tail, happy to see her, keeping her company.

He turned as she clambered back into the car with a carrier bag. 'Are you all right, hen?'

Margaret, who seemed more than a little preoccupied nodded. It had to be the stress of it all, it couldn't be easy for her.

'Oh, by the way, while you were in there I arranged for one of the lads to nip round and collect all that stuff in your dining room. I've got this chap I use. I'll see what can be done – although I meant what I said earlier about there being other ways we could sort this out. You know that I've always enjoyed your company. We used to have a few jaunts out like this in the good old days, remember? Days out in Yarmouth, racing at Newmarket . . .'

Margaret preferred not to remember: Gordie trying to get her drunk on brandy and Babycham, all Glaswegian charm, her resisting. They hadn't so much had a friendship over the years as a long drawn-out battle of wits. 'How long do you think before your chap can come up with a price?' she said.

Gordie caught her glance and shrugged. 'If you're determined to go that route, Margaret, perhaps I ought to bring him over and let him do a valuation of the rest of the house contents, sift the wheat from the chaff . . .' Gordie paused and then patted Margaret on the thigh. She looked terribly pale and tense.

'Don't you worry yourself. Won't be long now before we get the wee dog back. I'm sure he'll be fine. We'll pick him up and be home in time for tea. Unless of course you fancy staying a wee bit longer?' He watched her, trying to gauge her reaction. 'Get a bit of sea air, relax. It can't have been easy for you the last couple of weeks. We could book into a hotel, take our time. Enjoy a bit of luxury.'

'I have to get back for the children. With the nanny gone, my mother offered to help – but I said I wouldn't be long. I can't impose on her too much,' Margaret replied, quick as a flash.

Gordie sighed. Poor girl. She looked uneasy, a bit sad really, her mouth set into a tight unhappy line. Probably holding back the tears, thought Gordie, turning his attention back to the traffic. God, if he ever got his hands on James Devlin he would make the bastard pay in spades.

'If you could just tell me where we're supposed to be going,' said Cass to Joe, who was map reading in the passenger seat. The East Sussex countryside was beautiful, the summer green trees and leafy hedges picked out under a spotlight of sunshine in the unbroken blue sky. Such a shame they had company, Cass thought. As if he could read her mind, Joe looked up and grinned. Cass shivered.

Daisy let out a groan, while Antashinia sat in the back, oblivious, staring anxiously out of the windows, chewing her nails and picking at the sleeve of her cardigan. 'What if they don't let me have him?' she whimpered. 'What if they keep him? What am I going to do? What am I going to dooooooooo?'

Cass sighed. Everyone had run out of things to say to placate her. The girl had been whittling and worrying since she got into the car. She seemed, Cass thought, to be thoroughly enjoying herself. Maybe she was one of those people who revelled in a bit of misery and high drama.

'You know that police car that was following us?' said Joe in an undertone.

'Uhuh?'

'Well, it's just vanished.'

'What do you mean, vanished,' said Cass, glancing into the rear-view mirror.

'Gone. They turned off at the last junction.'

'That's not vanishing, that's turning off and going somewhere else,' said Cass, glancing at Joe. 'They kept changing cars on the motorway. And it's all right,' she said. 'I'm feeling fine now. I feel a lot better since we left the cottage. They probably think it's low risk down here. Now, if we can just find where we're supposed to be going.'

'You need to take the next left,' said Joe.

'Here?' Cass asked, practically standing on the brakes, indicating and pulling into a farmyard.

'Actually, I meant down there,' Joe said, pointing to the next junction. 'And besides, that was a right,' he added helpfully.

Cass looked at him and pulled a face. 'Really?'

Joe nodded. 'Tell you what, how about if I just point?'

In the control car, in a car park close to the place where Snoops was currently holed up with a slice of ham and a leather chewy, DI Turner was watching and waiting. Waiting was always the worst.

Margaret Devlin sighed; she couldn't think of any way out of it, she would have to take the dog home whether she wanted to or not. She glanced down at her suit and matching navy shoes; she'd only had them three weeks. If the dog threw up or crapped on them, she would be livid.

Mr Marshall's men were already in position in a car about fifty yards from the animal welfare woman's cottage. They were making a concerted effort to look inconspicuous. Watch, wait, follow, and report back – they had their orders. Waiting was always the worst.

Joe pointed out the turning for the street where the animal welfare lady lived. 'You know, I don't think I've had quite this much excitement since I was a kid,' he said as they got out of the car.

In the back Daisy groaned again. 'Where on earth did you find this one?'

'On a train. Joe, we're going to go and pick up a stray dog,' said Cass wearily, locking the car and following Antashinia and Daisy up the path towards the cottage.

Antashinia, clutching a sheet of paper with the dog's microchip details on it, rang the bell. Moments later a large woman threw open the door and looked from face to face. She was broad, with iron-grey hair clipped into a severe military style. She was wearing a sweatshirt with a cartoon beagle on it and navy stay-press slacks covered in a patina of dog hair. Antashinia shrank back as the woman eyed them up and down.

Cass was about to speak when Daisy piped up.

'Hi, we rang you earlier. We've come to pick her spaniel up,' she pointed at the au pair.

The woman nodded. 'Jolly good. If you'd like to come in, he's through here. Lovely animal, settled in a treat. Terribly affectionate.'

She glanced at Cass and Joe. Nothing warmed the expression above her chin and certainly nothing encouraged Cass to believe that the dog woman would be happy to welcome an extended rescue party.

Cass smiled. 'I think we'll go and wait in the car,' she said.

The woman nodded curtly. 'As you like. Shouldn't take very long.'

As they turned, Joe said, 'Whoa, friendly or what?'

Cass waved the words away. 'Let them sort it out. Daisy's her father's daughter, and besides, I'm not sure I can cope with listening to Antashinia wailing much more.'

'I'm surprised Barney didn't want to come along for the ride.'

Cass grinned. 'I think all that raw female emotion was getting to him. In any case, it looked as though he and Jake had other plans.' She mimed tipping a glass. 'And Danny was really pleased to see Hermione again. The pair of them get on really well. I think the plan was a few hands of five-card stud and then a little blackjack.'

Cass settled back in the Bentley and stared at the front door of the cottage. The afternoon was warm and she felt sleepy. It was nice to finally stop – it had been a long couple of days.

'Penny for them?' Joe said, as he pulled his rucksack up on to his knees. 'Do you fancy something to eat? How about a banana?'

Cass laughed. 'You're nuts. What is it with you and fruit? Actually, I was thinking how nice it was to be still and quiet.' She wanted to add 'and alone', but couldn't quite bring herself to. 'You know this has been the weirdest time of my life. Last ten years nothing – and then – wham.'

'Wham?'

'Uhuh, one minute I'm poodling along in a nice cosy rut, and then next thing it's all gone. It happened so fast. I thought I was going to be married to David for ever, maybe have another baby, paint, teach . . . And then, just when I thought I'd got everything worked out, it all imploded. I hadn't realised how miserable I was or how bad it had got. Once David left, I could see clearly for the first time in years. I knew that I needed a fresh start, but this wasn't exactly what I had in mind. I was thinking more in terms of getting a proper job and buying a car, rather than fancying a criminal, being bugged, kidnapped, and heading off to Brighton.'

He grinned. 'So you really do fancy me? You weren't just saying that yesterday?'

Cass blushed scarlet. 'Me and my mouth.'

'What about you and your mouth?' said Joe, leaning forward. Cass shivered, but before he could kiss her something across the road glinting in the afternoon sun caught her eye. As she looked more closely, Cass realised it was a man in a car with a pair of binoculars.

'There's a guy over there – I'm sure he's watching us,' she whispered, pulling away from Joe as if there was some chance that the man might be able to overhear them.

Joe swung round. 'Where? Are you sure? It's probably just the law, keeping an eye on you.'

Cass shook her head. 'I wouldn't have thought so, unless the police are driving clapped-out Montegos.'

Gordie Mann reversed into a parking space a couple of streets away from Rose Cottage. It was a tight squeeze. 'Do you want me to come in with you?' he said.

Margaret sighed. 'No, I think I can manage, thank you.'

Aware of being under scrutiny, Joe and Cass settled well back in their seats and broke out the bananas, Joe making a great show of not looking at the man watching them. 'Maybe we should give them something to look at?' he said mischievously. Before Cass could reply and before they could come to any real conclusions about who their mystery observer might be, Daisy threw open the back door of the car.

'Well, that's a bloody relief,' she said, throwing

herself into the back seat. 'We've got him. All done and dusted. Do you think you can drop me off in town?'

Cass stared at her in surprise. 'Are you finished? That was quick, I thought you'd be in there ages.'

Antashinia arrived a split second behind her carrying an excited wagging, yapping, wriggling springer spaniel held tight against her capacious bosom. The dog was licking her and whining, obviously delighted to be reunited.

As they were all strapping themselves in, Cass looked up and saw to her complete amazement Margaret Devlin heading down the road towards Rose Cottage. It was obvious that Antashinia and the spaniel had spotted her too, because Cass heard a gasp and a whimper from the back seat.

Cass swung round and stared at the au pair as comprehension dawned. 'Oh my God – that's Snoops, isn't it?' she hissed in an undertone.

Antashinia nodded. 'Yes, you know him?'

Cass faced forward and slowly turned the key in the ignition. 'No,' she said, 'but I met the woman who owns him. Now are you going to tell me what the hell is going on, or shall I just let you out here?'

The girl whimpered. 'I will tell you, but please, not here. Mrs Devlin hates Snoops, and she hates me even more.'

Not for the first time that day Cass wished that she was driving something less conspicuous. As she pulled level with Rose Cottage, Margaret

Devlin, who was waiting on the doorstep, momentarily turned and it seemed to Cass that for an instant their eyes met. A fraction of a second later, the cottage door opened and Margaret Devlin stepped inside.

When Cass looked round Antashinia had slithered down into the footwell and was clutching the dog against her like a baby. 'She hates Snoops. Mr Devlin told me to say that he give me Snoops as a present so that she would not hurt him – you understand?'

Cass nodded. As they pulled away, she saw the man in the Montego start the engine. She hoped that somewhere close by the police were still keeping an eye on her.

Gordie Mann's mobile vibrated wildly in his jacket pocket. He was watching over his shoulder, waiting for Margaret to come back with the dog. He glanced down at the screen. It was Mr Marshall. Gordie hesitated for a moment, then decided to ring him back when Margaret returned with the dog. Even before the thought had passed through his head, Margaret came running back towards the car looking terribly upset and white-faced.

Gordie opened the door for her. 'What on earth is the matter, m'dear?' he said anxiously.

Margaret was beside herself. 'He's not there. She hasn't got him. Someone had already been by and picked him up,' she snarled. 'They were here only a few minutes ago. I don't know how we didn't see them.' She paused, eyes narrowing down to slits. 'And I think I know exactly who it was.'

'I'm not with you,' said Gordie.

Margaret sniffed. 'It was the nanny – she adored that bloody dog. I wouldn't put it past her to have stolen him, the little bitch. I knew she was trouble from the first minute I clapped eyes on her.'

Gordie stared at Margaret.

'In which case there might not be any connection with James,' he said.

Margaret glared at him. 'How on earth would I know? She rang the police to say the dog was lost and told the animal welfare woman that James had given her the dog as a going-away present and she hadn't had time to change the microchip address over. As she had all the details from the chip – the serial number and everything – the woman had no reason not to believe her.'

'Oh God, I'm so sorry. You must think I'm terribly heartless. Fancy losing the wee dog, on top of everything else.' Gordie stared at her and then a thought formed. 'Wait a minute. Did you give her the dog's details? How come she had the microchip serial number?'

Margaret shook her head. 'I don't know. She didn't get it from me – I never had it. I never wanted the damn thing in the first place – getting a dog was James's idea. I'm glad it's gone.' Margaret sniffed miserably and looked as if she might burst into tears, then all of a sudden she paused. From the expression on her face, Gordie could see a whole bagful of pennies dropping. 'Oh my God,' she murmured. 'Wait, wait – James gave the chip number to her. It had to have been him.'

Gordie nodded triumphantly. 'That's right. I think we've been following the wrong person.' Pulling out his mobile, he punched in Mr Marshall's number. While he waited for Marshall to answer, he asked Margaret, 'What do you know about the au pair? What's her name?'

Margaret stared blankly at him. Gordie sighed. Poor wee thing, this must be so hard for her. 'I can't remember,' she said thickly.

'Tell you what,' said Gordie. 'We'll stop and have a drink once I've put this call through. A brandy –'

Margaret didn't say a word but it certainly looked like she could do with one.

10

Gordie Mann got out of the car and walked down to the end of the road, telling Margaret he needed to find a spot to get a better signal. Pressing the phone to his ear, he said, 'So what have you got for me?'

'Nothing at the moment. But don't worry, the A team are already in situ,' said Mr Marshall. It was by far the most positive he'd sounded since Gordie met him. 'I'm not on site yet – traffic's a bit heavy. Let me give you the number of my man on the ground, the guy heading up the surveillance. You can talk to him directly, probably makes more sense.'

Gordie could hear traffic sounds on Marshall's mobile. 'You on your way down here?'

'I'm about six miles from Gatwick at the moment,' said Mr Marshall. 'Do you want me to text you his number? I just need to let him know you're going to make contact.'

Gordie glanced back towards the Jag. Margaret

was in the front seat, wringing her hands, looking overwrought and stressed. He had been hoping to make things better for her, not bloody worse. The text notification pipped.

Once he got through, Gordie listened to Marshall's man and tried very hard to get his head around what he was being told.

'So you're saying that the Hammond woman came to pick the dog up?'

'Yeah, that's right,' said the voice at the far end of the line. 'In a bloody great Bentley. You could only have missed them by a matter of minutes.'

'You're sure it was her?'

'Absolutely certain. Stake me life on it,' said the man.

'And she went in to get the dog –'

'Nah, she didn't go in at all. It was two girls – a great big one and a skinny little number with a skirt halfway up her arse.'

'And what did Mrs Hammond do?'

The man grunted. 'I think they were going to go in, but then they changed their minds.'

'They?' snapped Gordie. 'What do you mean, *they*?'

'She was with some bloke. The pair of them sat in the car and waited while the girls went in and got the dog. They didn't seem that keen to be seen. Sort of sat right down, you know what I mean?'

'As if they were hiding?' Gordie said slowly. Some bloke? His mind sifted through the possibilities. 'What did he look like?'

The man puffed thoughtfully. 'Slim, quite tall – six foot two or three – medium build, blondish, smart, good looking, bit of a tan . . .'

Gordie grinned without a shred of humour. 'James Devlin,' he murmured under his breath. 'The cocky bastard. Did you see any sign of the Old Bill?'

'Well, we didn't see anyone, but if they linked Devlin with the dog, chances are the bloody pick-up was being watched. They'd be nuts if it wasn't.'

'Umm, right you are. I want you to keep with Mrs Hammond.'

'We're already on it. Just changing cars now,' the man said.

'Good. Keep me informed of what's going on.'

'And what shall we do about Devlin?'

Gordie paused for a few moments. 'Nothing – yet. I want to get my hands on him, but I need to sort things out this end first. Just keep tabs on the pair of them, let me know where they are and what they're up to.'

'And if we get the chance to grab him?'

Gordie sucked his lip. 'Take it. I want to talk to that bastard face to face.'

Cass glanced into her rear-view mirror in time to see the red Montego turning off the main road towards Hastings. She sighed; maybe she had been mistaken after all. Behind them now were four or five vehicles, mostly cars and a Land Rover that had just turned out of a farmyard. She hoped one of those vehicles was an unmarked police car.

'Can you explain how come you ended up in Brighton at Barney's house?' Cass asked Antashinia.

The girl blushed. 'Mr Barney, he offered me the job.'

'Yes, I know that,' said Cass. 'What I meant was, how did you know about Barney and the job?'

'I didn't. I found your number at Mrs Devlin's house. She say that you know James, that you and James . . .' she hesitated. 'You know.'

'Yes, I know what she thought I was doing,' said Cass grimly.

'I didn't believe that,' said Antashinia. 'But I thought perhaps you were his friend, so I ring to talk with you, because I couldn't stay with her any more and I thought, as you know James, you might help me. And when I ring, Barney give me another job.'

'Ah, right,' said Cass. 'So you rang up to talk to me?'

'Yes.' The girl smiled. 'And I started to explain and then Barney give me another job. Which is very nice.'

'And what about the dog?'

'James tell me I can have Snoops.' She pulled a piece of paper out of her pocket. 'See – I have the number for his microchip and everything. He said so.'

Cass nodded.

So that was it. How come something so simple could end up so very, very complicated? All that had happened, everything from finding the phone on the train, the link with James Devlin, being bugged, being grabbed, being terrified, finding Joe – all of it was an accident, a chain of bizarre co-incidences – aided and abetted by Barney. And now Cass, Snoops and Antashinia had finally all washed up together. She only hoped that Margaret Devlin would see it that way if they ran into her again.

DI Turner pulled a face and stroked his moustache. There were moments when he really missed smoking. The East Sussex police had loaned them a room. Sadly it wasn't a room with a view, but it did have a couple of tables, a pinboard and some chairs.

'Right,' said Turner, after a moment or two's deliberation. 'Let me get this straight: Mrs Hammond drove to Lewes to pick up the dog?'

His sergeant nodded.

'Not Margaret Devlin?'

'Bloody strange.'

Turner's sergeant nodded again. 'Only Mrs Hammond didn't go in and get the dog herself. She sent a couple of girls in – one of them is her employer's daughter . . .' The sergeant consulted his notebook. 'Daisy Hesquith etc etc. And the other one, according to the animal welfare woman, was "heavily built, appeared to be very distressed about losing the dog, and spoke English with a strong Eastern European accent" –'

DI Turner held up a hand. 'Whoa. Just run that by me again, will you?'

'The other girl was foreign, sir. She told the animal welfare woman that Devlin had given her the dog as a leaving present.'

DI Turner smiled wolfishly. 'Bingo! That's it. We've got him. Margaret Devlin's nanny.'

'Sorry, sir?'

'That's who the other girl is – that's the link.' Turner could feel it in his bones. 'I was there at Devlin's house when the girl brought the dog in. Great big lass, hands like shovels, barely able to understand a word she said. Devlin's here, I know it – I can smell the bastard. Now, all we need to do is watch and wait and see what happens next.'

The sergeant stared at him. 'Are you sure, sir? The animal woman said the girl was no oil painting. And the dog was a leaving present –'

Turner nodded. 'Oh yes, but you're missing the point. The dog was still there well after Devlin left. So when did he give it to her? Certainly not before he went, so it has to have been after. In which case, at the very least she's seen him since he left Lamport – and at best she knows where he is now.'

The detective sergeant's expression didn't change. 'But why is he running around with an ugly au pair?'

Turner sighed. 'Because it's not the girl Devlin

loves, it's the bloody dog. Call it a hunch, but every cell in my body tells me that James Devlin is around here somewhere. Right now we need to talk to the local mob, bring them up to speed. Keep a tail on Mrs Hammond and Margaret Devlin and Gordie Mann, and let's see what we can find out about the au pair.'

'Right you are, guv.'

DI Turner grinned. They were close now, very close, he was certain of it.

'Can you drop me off up there on the right,' said Daisy, as she, Cass, Joe and Antashinia got back into Brighton.

'But I thought you were supposed to be working in the shop this afternoon,' said Cass.

'Oh, be a sport. I've been working my arse off all morning,' Daisy moaned. 'Barney asked my mum to come in and cover for a bit till we all got back. She'll be fine. Can't you get him to ring her and break the news that I'm not coming in? Barney won't mind – it'll confirm his worst suspicions about me being a wastrel, and it'll give her something else to whine at him about. "You always take her part, you take me for granted, you bastard. I'm always there for you, I always help you out when you get in a muddle . . ."' Daisy broke off and smiled. 'She loves it really. Besides, I've been wailed at and dragged round the streets since God knows what time. I'm totally knackered and I'm hardly dressed for retail, now, am I?'

'If you want Barney to ring your mum, you have to ask him.'

'Oh, come off it, Cass. Tell you what, how about you cover for me?'

'No. I've got to go back and rescue Danny from your grandmother before she wins all his pocket money, stop your dad and Jake from drinking themselves to death, unpack my artwork from the boot, and explain to Barney why I want to move . . .' Cass paused, looking across at a grinning Joe, wondering what best to call him, '. . . in for a few days,' was all she could manage.

Daisy wasn't impressed. 'Oh, please, Cass. Barney won't mind. Besides,' she said pointedly, looking at Joe, 'we operate a strictly-no-strays policy. Nothing that's not pre-booked, pre-discussed, paid for in full and parasite-free is allowed over the threshold since dad rolled up in a taxi one night with six flea-ridden kittens, a billy-goat called Albert and a bottle-blonde with a bad attitude.'

Joe grinned at her some more. Cass pulled a disapproving face. 'I wasn't thinking of adopting him. And he can sleep on the sofa. Can't you?' All of them knew she was lying.

But before he could reply, Daisy added, 'Then again, if you don't fancy sharing with the resident zoo, there's always the bottom bunk in Danny's room. It's really comfortable. Or maybe Grandma would let him sleep up there. Only, watch your-self – I'm sure she's got this thing about younger blokes. I sometimes think Charlie is taking his life in his hands, working for her.' Daisy pulled out a cigarette from her handbag and lit up. 'So tell me again: why exactly is he here?'

Cass considered for a few seconds. Because she was afraid and because Joe had rescued her and because he was nice and gentle and made her stomach do that thing and because he had offered. She smiled at him.

'Because he's very cute and kind and is riding shotgun to make sure that no one kidnaps me,' Cass said.

'Yeah, right,' Daisy said. 'I'm going to try that one on Barney next time I pick up some hunk and drag him home.'

Joe's grin broadened. 'Cute and a hunk, huh?' he said, preening.

'Don't take it personally,' growled Daisy. 'I didn't mean you specifically, I just meant generally. OK, well, if I've got to go and be a wage slave, then you'd better let me out on the corner here by the lights.'

Sitting alongside her on the back seat, Antashinia had gone very quiet. She was calm and happy now, cooing softly in her native tongue, stroking Snoops into a wagging, ecstatic state. Cass didn't like to think what would happen to her; she seemed so vulnerable in many ways and Cass had a terrible feeling that, even if James really had given her the dog, it wasn't all over yet.

'See you all later,' said Daisy cheerily, slipping out of the car at the next junction.

'Will you?' said Cass, surprised.

Daisy nodded. 'Oh God, yes. I want to be there when we draw lots to see what we're going to have for supper.'

'What?'

Daisy grinned. 'Antashinia will explain to you on the way home, and then you can get Barney to translate. I may never go home to eat again,' she said gleefully. 'It's like the national lottery with food. See you later, Antashinia. I'm so glad you've got the dog back.' And with that she was gone, slamming the car door behind her.

The au pair looked up and smiled coyly, blissed out now she had Snoops safely in her arms.

Back at the flat Barney and Jake were well over halfway down a bottle of brandy when Cass and Joe came in. Antashinia scuttled off to her room with the dog, looking relieved and exhausted.

'So you got it all sorted out and brought the car back in one piece?' said Barney, topping up his glass. 'Not bad, not bad at all.'

'No thanks to you,' Cass said. With Joe's help she slid her luggage and the portfolios down on to the kitchen floor, and then began ticking the items off on her fingers. 'I got my dog, her dog –' she indicated Antashinia. 'My paintings, my son, your friend, your au pair, your daughter –'

'And your new lover?' said Barney, looking pointedly at Joe.

Speechless, Cass reddened furiously.

Joe put a box of Cass's prints down on the

counter, pulled out a chair, sat down at the table, and said, 'Actually, no, not yet. But I've heard you're a bit of a ladies man, Barney. I was wondering if you could maybe give me a few tips. Cass said you could charm the knickers off a nun. By the way, how *did* you get on with that American woman?'

Barney pulled a face and then handed him a glass. 'I see my reputation goes before me. Better pour yourself a drink, lad, and settle down. Trust me, it's not a tale for the faint hearted.'

'Wait,' said Cass. 'Before anybody tells anybody anything, I think we need to talk about your wonderful new au pair.'

'Oh, here we go,' said Barney, looking all hard done by. 'If I needed a lecture, I would have stayed married.'

Cass waved the words away. 'Jake, you need to hear this too.'

'Why? That's not fair,' complained Jake. 'I didn't hire her.'

Cass pressed on regardless. 'No, I know, and neither should you have done, Barney. Antashinia was James Devlin's au pair. And that dog we've just been to rescue is Snoops.' Jake's jaw dropped. Cass turned her full attention to Barney. 'She rang up to talk to me – she wasn't applying for the job at all. She thought, because of what Mrs Devlin told her, that I knew James and might be able to help her.'

'Right.' Barney nodded. 'So,' he said.

'So? What do you mean, so?' said Cass.

'*So do you know where he is*?' hissed Barney.

'Of course I don't bloody know, but I think having Antashinia here is asking for trouble. We don't know what's going on. Oh, and we saw Margaret Devlin in Lewes –'

'What? Why?' asked Jake.

'I didn't stop to ask, but I think she had probably come to pick the dog up.'

Jake grimaced. 'That woman is mad. What if she turns up here?' Alcohol was playing havoc with his paranoia.

'I don't see how she could,' said Cass. 'She doesn't know where Barney lives, and I wouldn't have thought the dog warden woman would be allowed to give out those kind of details.'

'Unless Antashinia left a forwarding address . . .' said Jake helpfully.

Cass stared at him. 'But she hated her.'

Barney pulled a face. 'Sorry, I missed that; who hated who?'

'They both hate each other,' said Joe, helping to bring him up to speed.

'Typical women,' said Barney, topping up Joe's glass. 'Take my advice, lad, never let them have a joint bank account, a front-door key, or buy your underpants – best to retain some vestige of power and an air of mystery. Now, when it comes to Americans . . .'

Cass looked at them. 'Do you think we should tell the police? What should I do?'

'Pour yourself a brandy.'

Cass glared at Barney, who shrugged. 'Calms the nerves a treat. Oh, and I should warn you, Antashinia is terrified of the police. Why don't you talk to her, see what's going on, and then decide.'

Exasperated, Cass shook her head, excused herself and went upstairs to get Danny. Having missed out on all the action, Mrs H wanted to know what was going on. Cass gave her the edited highlights, concentrating on heroic happy-ever-after dog retrieval rather than kidnapping, police surveillance, or crooks on the run. As they spoke, Danny kept one eye on the TV, but he didn't fool Cass for a second: he was hanging on every word.

'Come on, honey,' she said after a few minutes. 'Get your things together.'

Danny looked up 'Ohhhh, Mummmmm, can't I stay for a bit longer? I was telling Mrs H about when we went to the Science Museum and she said we could get Barney's microscope out and look at ear wax and nose bogies and stuff.'

Which was followed by an interesting little silence.

'There's been a lot of comings and goings today,' said Mrs H brightly, trying for a magician's distracting sleight of hand by pouring herself a large gin and tonic. 'Would you care to join me? Sun's over the yard arm in . . . in . . .' she pulled a face. 'Well, in somewhere or other.'

Cass shook her head. 'No thanks, I'm exhausted already; one drink and I think I'd be asleep.'

'In that case, why don't you leave Danny here

and go and take a nap? He's perfectly all right, and I enjoy the company.'

'I feel as if I am imposing.'

Mrs H smiled. 'Don't be silly. I'll get Charlie to bring him down in a couple of hours. Children's programmes are on and without Danny here as cover it looks like senility has set in.'

'If you're sure you don't mind . . .'

'Not at all. Now are you going to tell me all about your new young man? The one I saw you with earlier. Good-looking chap with the VW – very nice,' she purred appreciatively. 'You must bring him up and introduce him.' As Cass was about to reply, Mrs H said, 'Actually, there are a lot of new cars on the square today. It's been like Piccadilly Circus since you showed up, as if the parking isn't bad enough already.'

Cass smiled indulgently and, following Mrs H's gaze, glanced out of the big sitting-room window and instantly froze. Parked directly opposite the flat was a red Montego and inside was a large man in a trilby cradling a pair of binoculars.

'How long has he been there?' Cass whispered.

Mrs H shrugged. 'I'm not sure, dear. Not long – maybe half an hour. Arrived just before you got back. There was a Land Rover parked there before that. Every so often, one of the chaps gets out and walks around a bit, has a cigarette. The man in the hat came past about ten minutes ago.'

Cass felt a chill trickle down her spine like iced water. What the hell was going on? She looked past the Montego at the other cars parked on the side of the road. Presumably one of them had to be the police. But which one, and where? Cass stared out of the window, wishing that she and Danny were back safely downstairs with Joe and the others.

Mrs H looked at her. 'Are you all right, my dear? You've gone very pale. Are you sure you don't want a drink?'

'No, I'm fine, just a bit tired, that's all,' she blustered. 'I was wondering if I could borrow Charlie for a minute or two? I've got a little job for him.' She didn't want to worry Mrs H, but she didn't want to go back out into the street alone either. 'And the man in the Montego – and the Land Rover, if it comes back – can you keep an eye on them? It might be nothing . . .'

Mrs H nodded and tapped the side of her nose conspiratorially. 'Certainly. Just like the old days in St Petersburg. Pass me the phone, Danny, so I can ring Mummy if the Bolsheviks show up.'

When Cass got back downstairs with Charlie in tow the men had adjourned to the sitting room. Joe looked up as she came in. 'You OK? You look awful.'

Cass sighed. 'Thanks for that. And thanks, Charlie.'

Charlie looked bemused. 'I'm not with you – I thought you wanted some help with something.'

'I just didn't want to come back on my own. I had a bit of a problem yesterday . . .' she paused, her voice cracking.

'What sort of problem?'

Joe came over and helped her move the portfolios up on to the kitchen table. 'Some guys following her. The police know all about it, but –' Joe looked at Cass, obviously trying to work out how much to tell him.

'It's left me a bit jumpy,' Cass said, trying hard to paint on a firmer smile. 'I think it's making me a bit paranoid.'

Charlie held up his hands. 'No sweat. Whatever you need. You'll be OK now?'

Joe nodded. 'Sure, she'll be fine, but keep an eye out and watch Danny, will you? Don't let him go anywhere on his own.'

'OK.' Charlie looked from face to face. 'This is serious, right?'

Cass nodded. 'They thought I was involved with a criminal in Norfolk – some guy who stole a lot of money – and they grabbed me.'

'Shit,' whispered Charlie. 'You need any help, just say the word.'

'Thank you,' said Cass, finding it hard to know what to say next. Charlie nodded. 'It's OK. I'll bring Danny back down myself.'

Full of tears and fears and little tremors that made her feel sick, Cass picked up a couple of paintings and headed for her room.

Joe followed close behind. 'Are you sure you're OK?' he said as they stepped out of sight of Jake and Barney.

Cass stopped and shook her head. 'You know

the Montego we saw earlier when we were in Lewes? Well, I think it's parked out in the square. It's the same guys – they're watching the house.'

Joe stared at her. 'Are you sure?'

'Well, I'm as sure as I can be without going over there and asking them,' she whispered. 'I've got Mrs H keeping an eye on them.'

'OK, OK, I'm sorry. What about the police? They said they'd keep an eye on you. Maybe it's them – I mean, they could be undercover.'

Cass looked up at him. 'I suppose they could be. The problem is, I don't know what's going on, Joe.'

He took the paintings she was carrying, set them down and put his arms around her. It felt really good. 'I'm scared,' she whispered, snuggling close.

'So would I be, if I was working for Barney,' he said, holding her tight against him.

She laughed. 'Thank you for coming down here with me.'

For a moment their eyes met. 'It'll certainly teach me never to offer strange women fruit on trains again. You know, Barney gave me a blow-by-blow description of how he goes about seducing women.'

'And?'

'And I'm amazed he's never been arrested.'

'Oh, he has. Mum had to hock her jewellery to raise the bail money,' said Daisy, swinging in through the kitchen. 'And no snogging in public thoroughfares, please. Old people furkling around brings me out in a rash and makes me feel nauseous.'

'I thought you said you were supposed to be working in the shop this afternoon?' said Cass.

Daisy took an apple from the bowl of fruit on the counter and smirked, then lapsed into a round-shouldered, weary, hangdog, heavy-eyed expression of misery and malaise. 'I was, but Mum said I looked dreadful and told me to go home and get some sleep. So I said I'd grab a couple of hours here, as I've been invited over to tea.' She took a big bite out of the apple, recovering miraculously as she did so.

'You invited yourself,' said Cass.

'Uhuh. Your point being?'

Joe picked up Cass's paintings. 'In that case, if you're staying you can make yourself useful and help us take these down to Cass's room.'

'Bugger off,' said Daisy, pulling a face. 'I'm going to go hang around in the sitting room and listen to Barney and Jake incriminating themselves with tales of raucous exploits, loose women and chemical excess, ancient and modern. Blackmail is one of the few ways I've got of supplementing the spending money for my trip round the world.'

Joe laughed. 'OK, well, in that case, far be it from me to stand in the way of private enterprise. I'm going to go and get the rest of the stuff out of the car. Won't be long –'

Cass had just started to stow the canvases when Antashinia came and knocked on her door.

'I want to thank you for helping me today,' she said, trying hard to enunciate each word clearly. 'I am thinking I would like to stay here very much, but I am not being able to stay for long. I have rung my father and he thinks it is better if I go soon. Also I have to arrange for Snoops to go home . . .' she paused, stooping to scratch the ever-faithful hound behind the ears. 'Thank you.'

Cass stared at her. 'But I don't understand. You can't go, you've only just got here. They love you. I thought you liked working for Barney.'

The girl smiled coyly. 'I do, and I wish I come here sooner, but I can't be here, not stay – the law, it's not good for us.'

'Are you here illegally?' said Cass, seeing a whole new raft of problems emerging from the depths.

The girl giggled. 'No, not at all. I have the right papers. But my father thinks it is better for my family and for him if I leave soon and am going home. He is worried about what will happen with me and the police and the dog. Also me and my family are having to make many plans and arrangements for getting married.' She smiled nervously. 'I am not sure when, but my father and my mother is very happy.'

'You're getting married? Oh, OK – I didn't realise. Well, congratulations.'

The girl beamed, suddenly transformed from an ox into an angel by a beatific smile. 'And there is going to be a baby.'

'Oh,' said Cass, trying to hide her amazement.

'Well, that's wonderful. I hope you and – and your husband will be very happy.'

The girl blushed poppy red. 'It was not meant to happen, but these things, you know. It has, so it is best if I go home and be with my family.'

Cass nodded. 'I do understand. It's a real shame that you can't stay. Barney told me that you were wonderful.' She paused, wondering how to bring up the subject of James Devlin. It seemed almost cruel, particularly when the girl was obviously off to make a bright new future for herself without the Devlins' interference. Working for Margaret Devlin can't have been easy. 'Well, I hope it all goes well for you,' was all she could come up with.

The girl giggled. 'Thank you. Now I have to go and get tidied up before supper.'

Cass nodded. 'Looks like they could do with some food to soak up the brandy.'

Antashinia laughed. 'Mr Barney, he say I am his Darling Delia. But then he is very . . .' she struggled, pulling a face, searching for a word.

'Drunk?' suggested Cass.

The girl's smile broadened. 'As a monkey,' she said with glee.

DI Turner glanced up from the file on the desk and smiled. 'So this Antashinia is the daughter of Ivan Benoti, who used to be a big noise in the Balkans and now has an import–export business, trading all over the EC.'

'Legit?'

DI Turner pulled a face. 'From the look of this, nothing proven. He started out in the building trade and then went into shipping materials in – timber, steel, all sorts of building supplies. He's a very wealthy man, and not someone you mess with. He's got four sons; Antashinia is his only daughter. His baby.'

'How did she get mixed up with James Devlin?' said his sergeant.

Turner sighed. 'From what I can gather, it's totally coincidental. I've talked to the agency about the Devlins. The woman there said they'd had some trouble before, but she was very non-specific. I think the gist of it is that Devlin's roving eye got the better of him – no surprises there. Mrs Devlin handpicked Antashinia: plain, practical, and as reliable as a tea towel.'

'So, no hanky-panky?' asked Turner's sergeant.

'None that we know of, but it seems that James Devlin did treat her well, and she adored the dog.'

'Do you still think Devlin's here, sir?'

DI Turner nodded. 'I do – I most definitely do. He adores the dog, and he needs an ally. To find an ally with contacts like Miss Benoti must be a real bonus.'

'Or a mixed blessing,' said the sergeant.

Mr Marshall had booked a window seat on the plane. He liked a nice view. As they flew over the South Coast he tried to see if he could make out Brighton below them. He had Gordie's down payment in cash squirrelled away in his hand luggage, along with all his savings and various bits and bobs he could lay his hands on at short notice. It was a long way short of two million, but not bad under the circumstances. His instinct to run came as quite a revelation. Mr Marshall didn't see himself as a bolter, but then again the more he thought about it, the more he realised that he didn't want to be involved with Gordie's plans to find James Devlin, and he was more or less certain that Gordie wasn't the kind of man who would take a week's notice and treat him to a leaving lunch.

'Margaret, as far as I can work out, we're within spitting distance of finding James. Now, would you like me to drive you home or . . .' Gordie practised the speech under his breath as he carried back a tray of tea and cakes from the café counter.

'Or can I persuade you to stay – no strings, obviously. Separate rooms, if that's what you prefer. We could find a nice hotel, or maybe a rent a cottage for a couple of days. Think about it. We can ring your mother and explain about James – I'm sure she would understand.'

As he drew level with their table in the gardens of the Olde Cosy Tea Roome, his phone rang. He looked apologetically at Margaret, who smiled, shrugged and set about sorting the tea out.

'They're all holed up together at the house in Sussex Square,' said the man at the end of the phone. 'Your man, Mrs Hammond – the whole shooting match.'

Gordie smiled thinly. 'Good work.'

'So what would you like us to do?'

'Good question. Best-case scenario would still be to pick up Mr Devlin for a wee chat. I presume you've got a quiet spot where we can see what he has to say?'

'Certainly have.' There was a brief pause. 'By the way, is the boss with you?'

Gordie glanced over his shoulder. Margaret was sitting at the table, setting out side plates and cups. It gave him a warm feeling inside; he'd see her right. 'Son, I am the boss,' he said. He didn't know where Marshall was and he realised that he didn't care. This was much more how he liked to play. In control and hands on.

In Sussex Square they were having sausage and cream-and-mustard mash with onion gravy for supper; Joe having won the chance to draw for the main course after a viciously contested best of three tiddlywinks marathon on the sitting-room floor.

Watching drunks, the elderly, and a small boy (Mrs H, Charlie and Danny had come down to join in) in a needle match over food was an interesting way to pass what remained of the afternoon. Danny had suggested a few hands of five-card stud, but as he had cleaned Mrs H out while Cass was in Lewes she warned everyone off.

Dessert was supposed to be decided by a knock-out competition of paper, rock and scissors, but Cass called a halt after the first round in case someone lost an eye. It was decided, after much sulking and complaining and whining by Barney and Jake, that Danny should pull a ticket out of the dish. He pulled out the ticket for crêpes and ice cream with warm black cherries in thick sharp syrup, which helped cheer them up no end.

'Is it always like this?' asked Joe, as he opened another bottle of wine. The cork eased out with a pleasing thunk.

Cass, holding out her glass towards him, shrugged. 'I don't know. From my experience so far, it's never been the same long enough to spot a pattern.' Catching his gaze, she felt warm and fizzy. God it was wonderful to fancy someone again.

Joe smiled back. He lifted his wine in a toast. 'Here's to comfort food, rescued dogs and well-oiled old drunks.'

'A little less of the old, if you please,' snarled Barney from behind a huge pile of fluffy white mash, sausages sticking out Desperate Dan fashion, like cow horns. 'Pass the gravy.'

'Please,' said Danny.

Mrs H smiled and patted his hand. 'Such a nice boy,' she purred.

'Yes, but then that's because he's got a nice mother,' growled Barney, taking the gravy jug from Antashinia.

'Do you fancy a walk?' said Joe quietly, once

the plates had been cleared away, the pudding eaten and the coffee finished.

Cass nodded. 'Umm, sounds like a great idea, but I'm not sure. What about . . . ?' she paused and looked towards the door, thinking about the men in the car watching and waiting outside.

'It'll be all right,' said Joe. Cass smiled; it would be nice to walk down to the sea, hand in hand. Have a little while to themselves.

'I'll go and get a cardigan,' she said.

'Why?' said Jake. 'Are you cold?'

'No, we were just thinking about popping out,' said Joe casually.

Cass groaned and shook her head.

'Great idea, we could all do with some air,' said Jake, getting to his feet.

'Help the digestion. I'll get my hat,' said Barney.

'Where are we going?' asked Mrs H.

'For a walk,' said Danny.

Cass looked at Joe, who shrugged, and then round at the table full of faces and laughed. 'So that's everyone then?'

'Oh yes,' said Barney. 'Dogs, kids, old women – do us all good. Besides, there is safety in numbers.'

'Can I go and pack the dishwasher?' said Antashinia.

'I'll give you a hand,' said Cass.

Joe got to his feet. 'OK, in that case I'll nip and get my jacket out of the car and then we'll go.' And with that he loped off up the steps into the first shadows of the early evening.

Cass helped scrape the plates, wondering where all this might lead the two of them. Living in the cottage in Norfolk with David seemed like a million years ago. Joe was lovely; she let the idea of having some sort of a future with him trickle through her mind as she wiped the table down. Maybe it would be all right after all.

A few minutes later Antashinia helped zip Danny into his fleece, while Jake looked around for his other shoe and Barney slapped his fedora into shape. The dogs pranced and danced and yapped with anticipation. Cass dropped the cloth into the sink. Joe was taking his time. But then again maybe he needed a minute or two to catch his breath; after all, it had been pretty crazy since they'd met up for the walk in Wells.

'Right. All set?' said Barney, briskly pulling on a heavy cream linen jacket and adjusting his hat.

'I'm not sure that I want to go,' said Daisy.

'Well, don't go then,' snapped Barney. 'We don't want you coming along if you're going to whine and spoil it for the rest of us.'

'Since when did you like walking anyway?' rounded Daisy.

Mrs H, who had been adjusting her hat, glared at the two of them. 'Play nicely,' she barked.

'So, what's the hold up?' said Charlie, coming back from retrieving Mrs H's wheelchair from the utility room. He would have to take it up on to the road and then come back for her.

'We're waiting for her fancy man to come back

and then we're off,' said Jake, waving in Cass's direction. 'Where did you say he was?'

Cass glared at him, hoping Danny hadn't heard. 'He won't be a minute; he's gone to fetch his jacket from the car.'

'In that case,' said Barney, 'let's go. We can meet him up there. We're not going very far, are we? And Daisy, you have to come. If Kipper makes a break for it, I'm far too bloody drunk to catch him.'

Taking hold of the dog's lead, Daisy sighed theatrically. 'You do know this is going to cost you a fortune in therapy when I'm older, don't you?'

Caught up in the bustle of getting ready, Cass kept glancing towards the door. Surely Joe ought to be back by now?

'Come on, come on, we haven't got all day,' said Barney.

Having snapped the lead on Milo, Cass found herself swept out of the flat on a tide of other people's enthusiasm. She looked over towards the Golf. There was no sign of Joe, which was odd. She looked around again in case he was bending into the boot or taking a look at something. She looked up the road and down, her brain refusing to register the obvious. He had gone. He wasn't there. There was no sign of Joe anywhere in the street. And there was no sign of the Montego or the Land Rover either.

'Which way shall we go?' Daisy was saying. Kipper was whimpering and tugging to be gone.

Milo pulled at the lead, anxious to catch up. Snoops had practically twisted his lead into a knot. Danny was skipping ahead when Cass, as if in slow motion, grabbed his hand and looked round, trying hard to catch her breath, while the pulse raced double-time in her ears.

'What's the matter?' said Charlie, who had just come up from the basement with Mrs H.

'Look after Danny,' she said, and then ran back towards the Golf to see if there was some sign of Joe, some shadow, a remnant. And there was. In the gutter by the rear wheel was a set of car keys. Cass picked them up gingerly, as if they might bite or break, and then pointed them at the car. At first there was nothing, and then she pressed the button and the sidelights flashed. Joe hadn't dropped the keys and gone off on a wild-goose chase in search of them. He had already unlocked the car when whatever it was happened. In her head, she could picture it: the men in the Montego or the Land Rover had grabbed him.

Cass stared down at the keys in her hand, trying to work out why. Realistically, there could be only one reason, and it had nothing to do with him being Joe Bennett. It had to be because someone had put two and two together and come up with seven. Whoever had taken him thought Joe was James Devlin. She looked around the square and could see no one. Wasn't she meant to be under police surveillance? Where the hell were they?

'What's the matter?' said Jake, more loudly this time. 'Where's Joe got to?'

Cass's expression sobered him up in a millisecond.

'What is it?'

'I think they've taken him, Jake,' said Cass, her voice tight as piano wire.

Jake's jaw dropped and then he said quickly, 'Maybe he's – maybe – Oh my God,' and then he stopped and, looking left and right, swung round to the others, arms outstretched as if he was herding ducks. 'I think that we should all go back inside,' he said loudly. 'Maybe a walk isn't such a good idea. Looks like it's going to rain. Come on, quickly, everyone – back inside.' And he made as if to shepherd them all back towards the steps.

Cass held out her hand. 'Jake, can I borrow your mobile?'

He nodded. Everyone else looked at them as if they were mad. Cass took the card the police had given her and punched the number into the keypad, walking away a little so she wouldn't be over-heard.

When she got through to the police station, they asked her to hold while they patched the call through to someone called DI Turner. Apparently he was the officer in charge of the Devlin case.

'I think they've taken Joe,' she said, once she was connected. 'I thought you were supposed to be watching me, watching my family – keeping us safe.'

'Take a deep breath, Mrs Hammond, stay calm,' said the man at the end of the phone. 'Now, tell me again more slowly: what's going on? First of all, are you talking on your own phone?'

'No,' Cass snapped. 'I've borrowed someone else's.'

'OK, that's good. Now then, tell me what's going on.'

Cass explained about the trip to Lewes, Snoops, Antashinia, and then at the end of the sentence said, 'They've taken Joe – they must think he's James Devlin.'

'You know this for a fact, do you, Mrs Hammond?' the man said in a slightly patronising tone.

Cass wanted to punch him. 'No, of course I don't know it for a fact, but I can't imagine that anyone would snatch an architect off the streets of Brighton for the sheer hell of it, can you? What are they going to do? Hold him till he draws up plans for a loft conversion? For Christ's sake, it has to be something to do with James Devlin.'

'Mrs Hammond, please calm down. There's no need for you to worry, there are officers watching you –'

'Never mind me,' roared Cass, suddenly livid. 'What about Joe? Why didn't your precious officers protect him if they're so –' She stopped as a thought formed.

There was an odd pause at the far end of the line and in the silence Cass caught a glimpse of the big picture. 'You saw them take Joe, didn't you?' DI Turner said nothing, so she continued: 'You did, didn't you? Tell me that I'm wrong. You did – I know you did.'

Finally DI Turner said gently but firmly, 'Mrs Hammond, I'm sure you understand that currently this is a very delicate situation. We don't want to compromise an ongoing investigation –'

'What the fuck does that mean?' said Cass, furious now.

'What it means,' said DI Turner more firmly, 'is that you are being watched by us and also by people we suspect of being involved with James Devlin. We had to make a decision.'

Cass felt the world lurch. 'You let them take Joe?'

'On both of the previous occasions the perpetrators of these abductions have let the victim go when they realised that they had the wrong man.'

Cass struggled to breathe. 'So you let them take Joe?'

'He and the kidnappers are being followed, Mrs Hammond. Closely. We have the situation under control. Now, where are you going?'

Cass looked round in surprise. '*What do you mean, where am I going?*'

'Apparently you and your son, employer, neighbour, and various other people and dogs who I'd be happy to name if required, are all milling around outside the flat in Sussex Square.'

Cass looked round, wondering where the police

surveillance team were, very aware now that she was being watched. She shivered. 'OK, so you've proved your point. We were going for a walk. What do you suggest we do?' said Cass, trying hard not to let the hysteria strangle her into silence.

'I suggest that is exactly what you should do, Mrs Hammond – go for a walk and leave the policework to us. When you've finished your walk, go back to the flat. We will keep you informed of any further developments.'

'You were hoping this would happen, weren't you?' said Cass. 'You followed me hoping they would try again, didn't you?'

DI Turner was as silent as the grave, which convinced Cass she was right.

'Go for your walk and then go home, Mrs Hammond,' he repeated after a moment or two. 'As I said, we've got the situation under control, and I will make sure you are kept abreast of any developments. Would you like me to arrange for a female officer to come round and stay with you?'

'No,' said Cass. 'No, I wouldn't. What I want is for things to get back to normal, for Joe to be safe, and for all this to be over and done with.'

'It will be,' said DI Turner. Cass hoped to God that he was right.

'Well?' said Jake, when she turned back.

Cass bit her lip. 'They've got Joe.' Her voice broke. Just when she had been thinking about the two of them having a future. If anything happened to him, she would never forgive herself. He was quite the nicest thing that had happened to her in years. Cass struggled with a great wave of anxiety.

'Fuck,' said Jake. 'What are we supposed to do now?'

'Go for a walk, apparently,' said Cass. 'So let's walk.'

'Good idea,' said Mrs H. 'A turn around the block will do us all good.'

'Are we being used as bait?' asked Jake in an undertone as they headed back towards the others.

Cass shook her head. 'I've no idea,' she lied.

As Joe had been about to lock up, he'd heard the approach of a diesel engine, the sound of brakes, and looked up in time to see two men in ski masks jump out, but too late to do very much about it. Before he could react, Joe sensed someone behind him. There was the sensation of something over his face, a strange smell, and an instant later someone turned the lights out.

Margaret Devlin stared out across the great grey expanse of the English Channel from the picture windows of the luxurious penthouse suite in the Grand. The night was closing in fast.

Gordie handed her a glass of champagne. 'Margaret, I can't tell you how much I have longed for this moment,' he said. 'Or how often I've thought about it over the years.'

She looked up at him. Over the years she had thought about it too. But not in quite the same way. Then again, what else was there for her now? Poverty, bankruptcy? At least selling her soul to Gordie Mann might buy her a little time. She smiled grimly and tapped her glass gently with his. Who was she kidding? A huge part of her attraction where Gordie was concerned was her unavailability; now she was the wrong side of forty it might be her only attraction. He moved closer, she shut her eyes and braced herself.

At which point his mobile rang. There was a moment when Margaret thought that he would ignore it, but then Gordie pulled back, took the phone out of his pocket and flipped it open. She didn't need to be told what was said; she heard it for herself.

'We've picked up your package, Mr Mann,' said a voice at the far end of the line.

Gordie Mann's smile broadened to a wolfish leer. 'Good man,' he said. 'I do hope it's not too damaged.'

'Not at all, everything's in full working order at the moment.'

'Tell me where you are.' Gordie listened and then nodded. 'Right you are. See you in about half an hour.'

Margaret looked up at him. 'James?'

Gordie nodded and knocked the champagne back in one. 'I'm going to go and sort this out once and for all, Margaret. And maybe . . .' He looked at the empty glass. 'Maybe when I get back we'll really have something to celebrate.' He smiled. 'I won't be long.'

Gordie paused at the door and looked back over his shoulder. 'It'll be all right, hen. Don't you worry.'

Margaret smiled and sipped her champagne. She wasn't worried, nor did she linger for more than an instant on any thoughts about what 'sorting it out' meant. Instead, she decided to try to look on the bright side, which was what both the family solicitor and the doctor had suggested. She had her health and two beautiful children and her whole life ahead, they'd said. Why did that seem like small compensation?

Margaret topped up her glass and then reached for the phone to order room service. She was hungry. A few more hours and she would either be Gordie Mann's mistress or a grieving widow, or very possibly both . . . with a large insurance payout, if Gordie did things right.

DI Turner listened in on the surveillance. Apparently Mrs Hammond's one-time tail had taken Joe Bennett to a shed in a run of disused farm buildings a few miles inland on the South Downs. The team had been told to hold off until DI Turner arrived and to have a hostage negotiation team on standby in case it all went horribly wrong.

'Are we away then, guv?' asked his sergeant.

Turner looked out of the window at the car park as he pulled on his jacket. 'Certainly are. Trouble with this one is that it won't get us any nearer Devlin,' he said. 'Mrs Hammond's right: these clowns think Bennett is Devlin, that's why they picked him up. It would be handy if we knew who they're working for. And why they want Devlin.'

'We've still got the surveillance on Mrs Hammond and the au pair in place, sir.'

Turner nodded, his mind thinking longingly of Margaret Devlin in her negligee.

'With respect, sir, there's no reason to think that anyone is going to make a move tonight,' said the sergeant as they headed out into the gloom of the evening. 'Let's face it, Devlin could be holed up anywhere. Her having the dog might be a smoke-screen, or he might really have given it to her.'

'I know, but they're all here, all on the spot. It seems inconceivable that it won't kick off some-time soon.'

In the unmarked car, Turner picked up the next piece in the jigsaw on the radio. Apparently Gordie Mann was on his way to join the lads in the shed. So, there it was, all neatly packaged.

Cass felt sick. Worse than sick. All she could see when she closed her eyes was Joe's smiling face, offering her a peach; all she could feel were his arms around her at the Portakabin, warm and reassuring, and his breath soft on her shoulder as they cuddled up together in her bed. God, let him be all right, please. She tried hard not to panic and scream. It wasn't easy when she could sense that everyone else was desperate to find out what was going on.

'Jake, we've got to keep a lid on this. I don't want to upset Danny, Daisy or Mrs H,' she said in an undertone as they walked back to the group from Joe's car.

Jake lifted an eyebrow. 'Right. So Joe disappears and we pretend nothing is going on?' he said darkly. 'Like that's going to work.'

Cass looked back at the rest of the gang. All eyes were on her. 'Bugger,' she hissed.

'So,' said Barney as she drew level, 'would anyone care to tell me what the fuck is going on?'

There was a pause while Cass hunted around for something plausible and then Jake shrugged. 'What can I tell you? Bit of a domestic, that's all. Joe's gone off in a huff – I warned you that Cass had got lousy taste in men. Come on – once round the block and then I think we should break out the emergency booze and have a friendly game of shove ha'penny.'

'I thought we might go clubbing,' said Barney.

'As you like, but no strippers tonight. I think I'm getting one of my heads,' said Jake.

Barney chuckled. 'Can you remember . . .' and an instant later launched into a story of derring-do, feathers, G-strings and sequins that Cass felt would help Daisy no end with her travelling fund and she hoped would go right over Danny's head.

They didn't go far. Cass kept scanning the cars, the faces, unable to think of anything but Joe. Jake looked back and gave her the thumbs up. She shook her head.

'Let's go home,' she said when they had been walking for barely ten minutes.

'Thank God for that,' said Daisy. 'These shoes are killing me.'

Gordie Mann pulled up under the lee of a row of old stables and smiled to himself. Finally he was within a cat's whisker of having if not his money back then some small recompense for the devil's dance that James Devlin had led him over the years. Not that it was just about the money – oh no, James Devlin had pipped him at the post over lots of things since they first met. He had always been quicker thinking, better looking and altogether more respectable with his clipped middle-class accent and his nicely chiselled features.

And then of course there was Margaret, the one thing Gordie had always wanted, the one thing that had always eluded him no matter how hard he tried.

When he had first introduced Margaret to James at Newmarket Races all those years ago it had never occurred to him that James would win her from him. In his own mind Gordie was crystal clear about Devlin's true motives. James knew that Gordie couldn't get Margaret into bed and so he had to – and not just get her there, but keep her. Rub Gordie's nose in it.

Gordie winced; the pain was as raw now as it

had been then. Had he not been in love with Margaret, there was no way James would have pursued her so passionately. In his heart of hearts, Gordie felt that it was almost entirely his fault that Margaret found herself in her current predicament. Were it not for him, James Devlin probably wouldn't have given Margaret a second glance. For that alone he felt he had to make amends.

Outside, the night sky over the South Downs was Persian blue, stars like silver sequins stitched in the heavens. Tonight Gordie Mann would have his revenge for a lifetime of slights and insults, and then he would drive back to Brighton and have Margaret Devlin. And this time he wouldn't let her go.

Antashinia's mobile rang just as Cass, Jake and the rest of them got back to the flat. She talked for a few moments in her own language as she unhooked Snoops's lead, hands moving in concert with the conversation. Then she stopped, her body language subtly altering, till she was hunched and protective, sheltering the words with her body. Cass didn't mean to listen, her thoughts were elsewhere, but her senses, raw and exposed as live electrical flex, meant that everything sounded as sharp and clear as glass breaking. And she could have sworn that she heard Antashinia say 'James' at least twice.

When she caught Cass looking at her, Antashinia smiled shyly. 'This was my father. He worries, you know – about me, about everything. Would you like me to feed the dogs? It will be better when I am back at my home.'

Cass stared at her for a second and knew without a shadow of a doubt that the girl was lying. Cass bit her lip; maybe she was wrong, maybe the thing with Joe was making her paranoid, maybe she was just being over sensitive. But she didn't believe from the way Antashinia had responded to the phone call that it had been a casual call to enquire about the state of her health.

Cass stared at her, wondering what she knew about James Devlin and if she knew where he was. The moment passed and she didn't say it out loud. Even if she asked, what good would it do Joe? Meanwhile, Antashinia set the dog bowls out on the counter top and began to scoop out dog meal, humming under her breath.

Time dragged. Cass couldn't settle. Once Danny was in bed it was even worse, because she didn't have to hide her anxiety. She sat and then she walked and then she sat and then she tidied and then sat some more, and then paced and sat and fiddled and –

'For fuck's sake,' snapped Barney. 'What is the matter with you? The dog was less trouble when it had fleas. Oh, I know, don't tell me, lover boy hasn't called to say he's sorry.' And with that, right on cue, the phone rang.

Cass wished now that she had told him the truth.

'Mrs Hammond?' said a crisp authoritative voice on the end of the phone.

'Speaking,' said Cass, shaking.

'This is Sergeant Langbourne. I'm a police officer.'

'Yes,' said Cass, every molecule stretched tight. 'What is it?'

'There's been a break-in.'

'What?' said Cass before she could stop herself.

'We have arrested a man breaking into your house this evening.'

Cass felt the breath caught in her throat. 'Oh my God. I was told that the phone had been tapped,' she began. 'Maybe it's one of –'

'This perpetrator claims to be your husband.'

Cass tried to make sense of what she was hearing. 'My husband? David? Are you sure? I don't understand – I'm separated. And . . .' She struggled to think it through: did he still have a key? Had she had the locks changed? Surely David didn't need to break in?

'I'm almost certain that my ex-husband has got a key and anyway, he knows where I hide the spare. You know about . . .' she paused, wondering how best to describe the muddle her life was in. 'All the other stuff that's going on at the moment.'

The policeman was ahead of her. 'Yes, ma'am, we are aware of your current situation, which is why we've been keeping an eye on your residence; it was how we picked this chap up in the first place. He was interrupted whilst forcing a rear downstairs window with a tyre lever.'

'What?' Cass said. She swallowed hard; thank God they had all come down to Brighton. What if she had been at home on her own with Danny? What if – her mind raced off, scaring her half to death with as many alarming possibilities as it could find at short notice.

'I don't understand – why was he trying to break in?' said Cass, thinking aloud.

'He said that he had nowhere else to go. He is asking to speak to you.'

Cass hesitated. 'OK.'

She could hear muffled voices and then: 'Cassandra?' David sounded absolutely livid, his tone tight and sparse as he tried to hold on to his temper. 'Will you please explain to this *gentleman* that I am your husband?'

Cass hesitated for a few seconds. 'Cassandra,' snapped David again. 'Are you still there?'

'Yes, of course I'm here. Would you like to tell me what you were doing breaking into my house in the first place?' she asked.

'Oh, for God's sake. It was nothing. I don't really want to go into that now. If you could just expl –'

'I don't want to explain, David. And I don't want you breaking into my house. In fact I don't want you in my house at all,' she said coldly. 'Is that clear?'

'What? Yes, but –'

'But nothing. And it's not *nothing*. I don't want you back, David, not now, not ever. And if you don't agree to stay away then I'll tell the police that I've no idea who you are. Am I making myself perfectly clear?'

David practically choked. 'You bitch,' he hissed. 'For God's sake, Cass –'

'I'm under a lot of stress at the moment; it would be such an easy mistake to make . . .' she paused. 'Do we have a deal?'

'You wouldn't dare.'

'Want to try me?' she said. She could almost see David deflating.

'All right – it's just that, one way and another, I've had a very bad day.'

Cass smiled without humour; that made two of them. 'Would you please pass me back to the police officer?'

'Mrs Hammond?' said Sergeant Langbourne.

Cass took a deep breath. 'The man you have there is my husband; we're in the middle of getting divorced. He has a flat somewhere in town. I'm not sure what he thought he was up to, but I've explained to him that he can't stay at the cottage.'

'Do you want to press charges, ma'am?'

'No, I just don't want him in my house.'

'Right you are. The problem is, he has no documents on him, nothing. He told the arresting officer that he had gone back to the flat he's been sharing with a friend and discovered all his possessions had been vandalised. The flat had been turned over, and while he was upstairs someone broke into his car. Sounds to me like he's really upset someone.'

Cass sighed. 'He has a talent for it.'

'I'm sure he'll be all right. But don't worry, he has somewhere to go – your daughter's just arrived to pick him up and take him back to her place.'

'My daughter? But I haven't got a daughter.'

The policeman coughed uncomfortably. 'Sorry, my mistake. I believe I recognise the young lady – she works in a café in the supermarket in town.'

Every sense was alive as Gordie Mann strode briskly across the apparently deserted yard towards the tumble of old sheds and barns. All around, shadows formed complex inky pools on the sunbaked mud, the abandoned farm buildings drained to monochrome in the moonlight. He turned up his collar as a stiff breeze rolled in over the Downs, whipping stray dust into the night air, filling his nostrils with the scent of old musty straw and cows long dead.

Gordie squared his shoulders, set his jaw. Not long now.

'Mr Mann?' said a voice from the darkness.

'Aye,' said Gordie.

A small man with broad shoulders, wearing a ski mask and camo gear, stepped out from the shadows as Gordie got within a yard or two of the entrance. The eye and mouth holes were an uncanny and unnerving white against the black dense puddle of the mask.

'If you'd like to come with this way, Mr Mann, we've been expecting you,' said the man in much the same restrained tone that the maître d' of Gordie's favourite restaurant used to lead him to a reserved table. Ex-military, he had to be, thought Gordie appreciatively, falling into step behind his guide. No one else could manage that fine line between deference and complete intimidation like someone from the services.

He felt the adrenaline begin to rise; he was so close now, so very, very close.

'Mind your step,' said his companion. They made their way in through the main farm complex, between a jumble of fallen beams and old sacks, not a light anywhere. The yard created a vortex, wind curling and circling, trapped inside the court-yard. The air was heavier and thicker here, making Gordie's lungs complain and his throat dry as chaff.

'First left, Mr Mann,' said the man. Gordie ducked in under a lintel, through a small anteroom into a larger space lit by a single bulb dangling from a flex. In the centre of the room, tied to a chair, was a hooded man. It took Gordie all his strength not to punch the bastard, but he wanted to see his face, wanted James Devlin to know who it was who had finally outsmarted him. Two men in ski masks flanked the bound prisoner, arms crossed over their not inconsiderable chests. These were the kind of men Gordie preferred to deal with – not Marshall with his faffing and flustering and principles, but real men who understood action.

Gordie nodded to the two men, rubbing his hands together in anticipation of what was to follow. 'Take his hood off,' said Gordie, miming the action for emphasis. 'James and I need to talk.'

'I have to go soon,' Antashinia said. She had been strangely silent since the phone call.

Cass, still waiting for news of Joe, stared at her. 'Sorry?'

'I am heving to take the dog soon.'

'But we already took them out.'

The girl nodded. 'I know, but I have to take him to the flat.' She pulled out her mobile and started to text, eyes bright. 'My father he will come tonight to pick up me and my boyfriend. I have to go and meet him.'

'I think you should really talk to Barney,' said Cass. 'He was really hoping you would stay.'

'I know, but I say to Barney about the baby and those things and he understands.'

Cass looked at Barney; she doubted that he had understood any of it. He was currently sleeping off a day's brandy consumption, flaked out on the sofa, with a trail of drool drying nicely on his chin. Jake was stretched out alongside him, with his feet up on the coffee table. They looked like some terrible parody of an old married couple, both drunk, snoring and scratching and farting, even though it was barely ten o'clock. On the other side of the fireplace Daisy was watching TV, curled up in one of the big red armchairs, eating some of Antashinia's homemade biscuits, the dogs sitting in barely disguised anticipation at her feet.

'When did you tell Barney that you were leaving?'

'When we were out walking. I say to him that I have to go and he said, yes, yes just make sure dinner is all cleared away and that the dog is fed. And that we are almost out of milk.'

'I don't think he realised that you meant you were leaving for good, Antashinia.'

The girl looked bemused. 'I don't understand. What is "for good"?'

'For ever. I don't think Barney understood that you weren't coming back.'

The girl frowned. 'But my father – and the baby – and the dog.' She bent down and swooped Snoops up in her huge arms and held him tight to her bosom.

'Yes, yes, I know about all that,' sighed Cass. 'Oh, look, it'll be all right. Don't worry, I'll explain to Barney once he's sobered up.'

Perhaps letting Antashinia go was the easiest way to get life back to normal. After all, she was the last tangible link to James Devlin.

Alone in the hotel suite, Margaret Devlin dropped the catch on the door so that she wouldn't be disturbed, picked up Gordie's briefcase, set it down on the bed and, taking a paper clip from one of the brochures on the dressing table, set to work picking the lock. It didn't take very long. Obviously

Gordie's wife wasn't nosey or he would have bought something a little more secure.

Very carefully, with a skill honed from years of practice, she sorted through the contents. There was a cheque book, three pens, a couple of hundred pounds in cash in a manila envelope, various oddments of paperwork, an address book, and a couple of quotes for what looked like legitimate building jobs.

Margaret sighed; it was hardly worth the effort. And then she opened a notebook and flipped through, scanning each page with the eye of a woman often betrayed. On the last page was a brief list of details about Cass Hammond, including her address in Brighton.

Margaret Devlin smiled and then poured herself another glass of champagne. That Hammond bitch really did have a bloody nerve. Maybe it was time to pay her another visit, let her know that James wouldn't be coming back to whisk her away to God knows where with a fortune in other people's investments. More likely – if Gordie had his way – he'd be found in bits under a bridge after a nasty accident.

Margaret sipped from her glass and called down to reception to organise a taxi. If she played it right, Gordie wouldn't even know she'd been out.

11

In the farm building on the edge of the South
Downs, Gordie hung back in the shadows and
held his breath. One of the men in ski masks
stepped into the pool of light created by the single
bulb and slipped the pillowcase off the bound
man's head. Instantly the man sat up, surprised,
scared. He blinked once, twice, trying to let his
eyes adjust to the change; and as they did, he peered
into the gloom, apprehensive, every part of him
tense, braced for whatever was to follow.

Gordie could pick out the pulse in the man's throat
as he tried to fix on their faces, his words stifled by
a strip of gaffer tape over his mouth. There was an
instant of elation, then a moment's silence as deep
as the ocean, as still as space. And then Gordie
shook his head and turned away in frustration.

'What?' asked one of the masked men. 'What
is it?'

'Take him off somewhere quiet and turn him
loose.'

'Loose?'

'Aye, you heard me.'

'Are you serious?' asked the masked man incredulously.

'He's not our man.'

The masked man hesitated for an instant and then nodded. Gordie was pleased with his reaction; not a flicker of emotion or frustration. That showed discipline – no point arguing with the client, or the truth. Gordie wondered if these guys worked exclusively for Marshall or whether they ever freelanced.

'You heard the man,' said the ski-mask guy, shaking the impromptu hood out. An instant later the man on the chair was plunged back into darkness.

Walking out into the deep shadows of the farmyard, Gordie pulled the mobile out of his coat pocket and tapped in Margaret's number. He wasn't sure how he was going to break it to her that James had eluded them again.

'You sure you want to just sit here, love?' said the cab driver, catching Margaret's eye in his rear-view mirror. 'Meter's running, you know.'

'I'm well aware of that,' she snapped icily. In her handbag Margaret had the two hundred pounds that she had taken out of Gordie's briefcase to cover emergencies.

'I just want to get my bearings,' she said, peeling twenty quid off the roll and slipping it to him. 'I want you to keep the engine running and don't go anywhere.'

'Right you are.' The man nodded, folding the note into his jacket pocket, while Margaret got out of the car and walked very slowly down the road, her eyes fixed firmly on the goings-on in the various basements she passed. She felt a need to get her eye in. Unfortunately the blinds were drawn when she got to Cass's flat.

Margaret hesitated at the top of the steps, not sure what to do for the best. Should she go down and knock, or should she wait a while longer? Maybe she should go back to the hotel and wait for Gordie to show up. The devil that drove her was calmer now, icier, more thoughtful – but not necessarily in a good way. She wanted revenge, she wanted to know what was going on. But more than anything, Margaret wanted to make sure that she won.

Meanwhile, downstairs in the basement flat, Cass's mobile rang. 'Hello?' she said, trying to pick out the words, moving away from the sounds of the TV to try to find a better signal.

'Hello,' said a voice, and as she recognised it her heart leapt.

'Joe?' Cass whispered, trying hard to hold back tears of relief. 'Oh my God, Joe, I'm so pleased to hear your voice. Are you all right? Where are you? I'm so sorry –' Despite her best efforts, her voice cracked and then broke. 'I thought they might hurt you. This is all my fault. Oh, Joe –'

'Shsssh, stop. It's all right,' he said gently. 'It's OK, I'm fine. Once they found out I wasn't James Devlin, they let me go.'

'Thank goodness. I – I couldn't bear – I –' Cass stopped short, not knowing what to say next. How did you tell someone you hardly knew how much their being safe meant to you? That you truly cared, that given enough time you might easily love them? 'Oh, Joe,' she said in a tiny voice. 'I am so sorry.'

'It's all right,' he said again. 'I'm fine. Really. Is there any chance you could come and pick me up?'

'Of course. Where are you?'

He laughed, the sound making her shiver with relief. 'God only knows . . . Hang on – I don't think I can be that far away from Brighton . . . It's very rural, though – looks like I'm probably somewhere on the Downs.'

'Where are you now?'

'They dumped me in a field, but at the moment I'm heading for what looks like a road.'

'And are you all right?' Cass asked hesitantly.

'I'm fine, I just want to get back – and – and . . .' He laughed. Cass could hear the tension in his voice.

'What?' she almost whispered.

'See you. Put my arms around you, carry on where we left off the other morning. Cass, I . . . I . . .' he stopped, and she knew then that he was thinking all the same things she was. 'I want to

400

get this sorted out so that it's all done and dusted and we're all safe again, and we can get on with being together and seeing if we can maybe make this work. This is crazy. I'm an architect, not Rambo.'

Cass's eyes prickled with tears. 'I'll get in the car and head in the general direction of the Downs. Ring me as soon as you know exactly where you are.'

She thought for a moment that Joe might stop her, tell her to wait, to be more sensible and hang around at the flat until he had the exact location, but instead he said, 'Good – I can't wait to see you.'

'See you soon,' Cass said softly, aware of all manner of complex thoughts and feelings tied up in those few words.

As she ended the call and went into the hallway to get her jacket, Daisy looked across from her seat in front of the TV. 'Who was that?'

'Joe.' Cass couldn't keep the sense of relief or delight out of her voice.

Daisy's face brightened. 'Oh, good. Got over his little strop, has he?'

Cass hesitated and then realised that Daisy had no idea what was going on.

'Yes, yes he has,' she said quickly. 'He sounds fine; I need to go and pick him up.'

Antashinia, who was busy knitting, looked up. 'This is good. Do you think I can come too – you can give me a lift, yes?'

Cass stared at her. Although Antashinia didn't know what was going on either, she felt slightly wary about taking the au pair with her. Also, if she was honest, the last thing Cass really wanted was someone else there when she picked Joe up. But then again she was nervous of going out on her own.

'I'm not sure where I'm going yet,' Cass said.

Antashinia looked all hard done by and hangdog. 'Oh well, I suppose I could always get a taxi. But it doesn't matter so much to me where you are going. You could maybe drop me off on the way to where you go, or on the way back, I don't mind. It will be fine, whatever you want to do.'

Cass considered for a few seconds. The idea of driving alone at night didn't fill her with great confidence and Antashinia was a big girl.

'OK,' she said. 'How long before you'd be ready to go?'

The girl got to her feet. 'I will be some minutes maybe, but not many. I need to take with me my things and to get Snoops, that's all.'

Cass nodded, and then she looked back at the sleeping drunks on the sofa. She could hardly leave Danny alone with them. She would have to go upstairs and talk to Charlie and Mrs H. As if reading her mind, Daisy said, 'Don't worry, I'll keep an eye out for the kid, if you like.' She paused to light another cigarette. 'But don't go thinking that I'm going soft. You owe me. Big time.'

Cass laughed. 'OK.'

While Antashinia collected her things together and snapped the lead on the dog, Cass picked up her jacket and the keys to the Bentley.

'Let me give you a hand,' she said, picking up one of the au pair's boxes.

The girl blushed. 'You are kind.'

Cass shook her head. 'Not really, I just want to get going and fetch Joe. I want him back here so I know he's all right.'

The girl beamed. 'He is a nice man, your Joe. It is love, I know this very much,' she said. 'I see it in your face and his.'

Cass blushed. If only she was so certain. Between them they manhandled Antashinia's things out into the street and then loaded the car, Snoops dancing attendance behind them all the while.

Margaret Devlin, now seated back in the taxi trying to decide what to do next, couldn't believe what she was seeing. Not more than a hundred yards away Cass Hammond and What's-her-name, the au pair, and the bloody dog, all as bold as brass, were heading towards a Bentley carrying various boxes and bags.

What the hell was going on here? Margaret reached forward to let herself out of the cab and then thought better of it. When, an instant later, her mobile rang she was almost relieved to hear Gordie's voice.

'It wasn't James,' Gordie said flatly, before

Margaret could say more than hello. 'The man they picked up – it wasn't him.' She could hear the bitter sense of dejection and disappointment in his voice.

Across the road Cass Hammond and the au pair were busy stacking things into the boot.

'We've lost him again – if we ever had him, that is. I was so bloody certain he was in Brighton,' Gordie sighed. 'Looks like it's back to square one. I'll call Marshall and see what he's come up with.'

'Actually, I don't think that will be necessary,' said Margaret softly.

'What?' said Gordie, sounding surprised. 'Why not?'

Margaret covered the phone and then tapped the taxi driver on the shoulder. 'I want you to follow that Bentley,' she said. 'And try not to be seen.'

The man turned round. 'You're joking, right?' and then, as their eyes met, he said, 'Are you serious, Mrs?'

'Never more so,' said Margaret. Then she sat back in her seat and very quietly explained to Gordie exactly where she was and what she was doing and what she could see. She was careful, however, to avoid any mention of why she was there and how she had managed to get her hands on Cass Hammond's Brighton address in the first place.

When she'd finished, Margaret heard Gordie laugh softly. 'Well, damn me – I always knew you were a canny woman, Maggie,' he said. 'Keep talking. I'm already on my way back into town.'

There was a car with its lights off parked up opposite the farm gateway that Joe stumbled through on his way back to the main road. Stroke of luck, he thought wryly, turning his collar up against the night chill. Presumably the occupants would know where they were.

Joe breathed in the smell of the summer air, relieved to be free, relieved to be alive and safe. He had never been more scared in his life, or so certain that he wanted to live, or so sure he wanted to see Cass again and hold her in his arms. The last few hours seemed like a bad dream. His ribs ached, his body felt bruised and sore.

Although the gang of goons hadn't beaten him up, they hadn't exactly treated him with kid gloves either. Joe was walking faster now, aware that more than anything he wanted to be with people, back with the rest of humanity. The grin held as he got level with the car; he just hoped he wasn't going to disturb anything too important. To his bemusement, a man got out and said. 'Mr Bennett?' in a level, authoritative voice that suggested, even in the dark, that he was a policeman.

Joe, eyes already adjusted to the gloom, stared at him in astonishment. 'How the hell did you know I'd be here?' he said.

The officer handed him a blanket. 'We've been keeping an eye on you since you got picked up in

Sussex Square, sir. Now, are you all right? Would you like me to call you an ambulance?'

Joe didn't know whether to thank him or punch him. 'No, I'm fine,' he said. 'No thanks to you. Why the hell didn't you prevent my being kidnapped? I could have been killed.' He started to shake with a mixture of fury and shock. 'What did you think you were playing at?'

'Gently now, sir,' said the man. 'We were watching you every step of the way. Armed response and hostage negotiation teams were on standby . . .'

Joe looked at him. 'But you still let them take me?'

The policeman shifted his weight. Even in the gloom, Joe could tell the man was uncomfortable.

'What were you hoping for? Something that would help you find Devlin?' he snapped.

The officer coughed. 'I'm not privy to –'

But Joe was ahead of him. 'What about Cass? Are you watching her too? Is she safe?'

'Mrs Hammond is still in Brighton, as far as we know,' said the officer. 'Now, if you'd care to get into the car, sir, then we can get out of here.' He indicated the unmarked police car.

Before he got in, Joe pulled the mobile out of his jacket. 'I need to call Cass and let her know what's going on,' he said. 'I've just arranged for her to come and pick me up.'

The policeman appeared to be about to say something, but then he nodded. 'Right you are, sir. But make it quick.'

Joe punched Cass's number in. She seemed to answer before it had had a chance to ring.

'Did you find out where you are? Are you OK?' she said.

He couldn't help smiling, both at the sound of her voice and also her very obvious concern. In the background he could hear sounds of the car, and a dog barking somewhere close by. 'It's OK, I'm fine,' he said. 'I just wanted to let you know that the police have picked me up.' He glanced over his shoulder at the policeman. 'Apparently they know what's going on and have been watching.'

Cass seemed to hesitate before she replied. 'They told me that, too. The trouble is I can't help feeling like we're being used.' He heard the catch in her voice. 'I'm so glad that you're all right.'

'I am – I'm fine. I'm not sure how long it will be before I'm back at the flat. I'm assuming that they'll want to question me.' A dog yapped again. 'Where are you now?'

She laughed. 'In the Bentley. I was just on my way to rescue you.'

'That's reassuring – thank you. Have you got Milo with you?'

'No, Antashinia wanted a lift to her boyfriend's flat. I was going to drop her off on the way back.'

'Back?' he said.

Cass giggled. 'I thought coming to get you was more important.'

*   *   *

Gordie Mann, listening on the hands-free, followed Margaret Devlin's directions as she tailed the Hammond woman and her ex-au pair and the bloody dog towards God knows where. Surely between the two of them they knew something about James Devlin's whereabouts? He needed to get his hands on them – and fast. Gordie had almost run out of patience.

'They've just done a U-turn,' said Margaret in surprise.

'What? Do you think they saw you?' snapped Gordie.

'No, no, I don't think so. It looks like she doesn't know where she's going.'

'Margaret, I've got GPS so as soon as you know where they are heading – the street name – let me have it. I'm going to ring off for a few minutes. I want to arrange some back-up.'

Without waiting for an answer, Gordie rang the man in the ski mask who had done such sterling work. It was always handy to have an extra pair of hands.

DI Turner and his crew followed on behind, unmarked police cars on standby to pick up the main players as and when necessary so that the tails wouldn't be spotted. Turner smiled thinly. It couldn't be long now.

'Whereabouts is this place again?' said Cass, peering into the darkness. She hardly knew Brighton, but this part was totally unfamiliar to her. She was certain they had been past the station at least twice and doubled back through terraces of townhouses and distinctive white-painted villas long converted into flats and apartments. They were now heading out towards one of the more modern housing estates that ringed the eastern fringes. On her right the sea, slate-grey in the moonlight, rolled in and out over the shingle beach, making a sound like someone breathing heavily in the night air.

'Up here. Not far now. Over there –' said Antashinia, pointing. 'There, there. If you could stop by that streetlight, it will be good.'

Cass pulled up outside a rundown modern block. In the back of the Bentley, Snoops barked and began to dance around, yapping and wagging furiously. It seemed that he knew that they were nearly there.

'Are you going to be all right?' asked Cass. After the day they had had, she wondered for a moment how vulnerable Antashinia would be on her own.

The girl nodded. 'Oh yes, I will be fine. My boyfriend he is here. I just need to take my things up.'

Cass nodded. 'Would you like me to give you a hand?'

The big girl smiled back at her. 'No, it's fine. But would you for just a little while wait and keep the things here till I go and find him? My boyfriend, he will come down and help me.'

Cass nodded. Antashinia caught hold of Snoops's lead and headed off into the darkened alley that divided the house from its neighbour.

Seconds passed. Cass waited, peering out into the street, up and down. A few cars down, a white Transit van pulled up. The driver switched off the lights but didn't get out. It gave Cass an odd feeling and after a few seconds she locked the doors, her paranoia getting the better of her.

Cass started to fidget; how much longer would Antashinia be? She looked idly out of the window, very tempted to phone Joe back. Further along the road a cab slowed and then drove by, then a Jag. God, this was boring. How much longer would she be?

The minutes tick-tick-ticked past. Finally Cass saw a flicker of movement in the alley and perked up as Antashinia stepped out into the lamplight. She hadn't got the dog with her, and she was looking upset. Cass opened the door without thinking. 'Are you OK?'

The girl sniffed, wiping the back of her hand across her face. 'I will be fine. He's not so pleased that I bring the dog here. But he said, he told me, once I pick Snoops up to bring him to the flat. But it is not right. I did not understand him. He didn't mean us to come here. He meant Mr Barney's flat. He would have come for me, he said. He is worried that the police will come after Snoops.'

Umm, Cass looked round. It wasn't a very salubrious-looking area. Maybe Antashinia's boyfriend wasn't the kind of person who welcomed police interest. Cass could understand why he might not want the dog – Snoops was lovely, but a total nuisance with his constant yapping and barking.

'So, is he coming down to give you a hand with your things?'

Before the girl had time to answer, a man climbed out of the Transit van and headed along the road towards them. He was tall with a heavy, thickset body and a face that looked as if it had been chipped out of a concrete block, badly. Cass was about to warn the girl to jump back into the car and lock the doors when Antashinia's face cracked into a huge smile.

'Papa,' she said. 'You are early.'

The man, who at first glance looked as if he hadn't got a smile in him, grinned from ear to ear, and said something that even Cass understood to mean he was very, very pleased to see Antashinia and that he loved her very much. The girl giggled and threw her arms around him. It was a bit like trying to hug a truck.

'He always thinks that I am still his little girl,' she said to Cass, then turning back to her father: 'This is my friend, Cassandra. Cassandra this is my papa, Ivan.'

Cass extended a hand, which vanished without trace into Ivan's.

'Cass, she work for Mr Barney too. She looks after all his things.'

The man smiled and nodded. Antashinia said

the same thing over again in her own language and the man beamed and pumped Cass's hand even harder. The girl said, 'It's all right, he is very pleased. At first he think you might be the other one – Mrs Devlin.'

Cass smiled, not breaking eye contact with the giant Ivan. 'I'm very glad you explained. Are we taking your things up to the flat now?' She glanced across at the shadowy building.

'No,' said Antashinia. 'Papa said he will take them all now, put them in the van – it will save moving them again. We are leaving tomorrow morning.' And with that, Cass opened the boot and handed the first of the boxes to Antashinia's father.

'What about your boyfriend, I thought he was coming to help too?'

The girl nodded. 'He is, but I think he is a little nervous.'

Cass looked at the retreating form of her father, shoulders as wide as a telephone box. Who could blame the boyfriend? God alone knows what Ivan had threatened when he discovered his precious little girl was pregnant.

As Cass lifted out the last box, another figure appeared in the alleyway: a tall rakish man with a shaved head, earring and designer stubble, who strode over to the car as if he owned it. He was older than Cass had been expecting; possibly early to mid forties, maybe as old as Antashinia's father.

'What's the hold-up? I thought we were going

to take this stuff upstairs,' he said, looking left and right. Cass stared at him. He had a voice that totally belied his appearance and, even in the lamplight, Cass could see that his shaved head was a few shades paler than his face. He had a public school accent, clipped and tight and smooth as glass. And as their eyes met, Cass had a revelation, a revelation that made her gasp.

'My father is here,' said Antashinia brightly to the newcomer, pointing towards the Transit van.

A flutter of something like fear passed across the man's face. Cass couldn't take her eyes off him. She knew without a shadow of a doubt who he was; every bone in her body told her that this was James Devlin. An instant later, Cass had the confirmation she needed.

'What is the matter, James?' Antashinia said, looking up at him, her great moon face full of concern, reddening as she said his name.

Cass's heart ached. Antashinia truly loved him.

'Nothing,' he said briskly, picking up the last of her things and heading for the van. 'Nothing at all. I'm worried about leaving Snoops alone in the flat, that's all.'

Antashinia smiled coyly at Cass. 'We are going to be married,' she said in a tiny whisper. 'As soon as we can.'

Cass stared at her, wishing there was some way it could come out right in the end, but knowing that it was impossible.

'Antashinia . . .' she began, wondering whether

now was really the moment. But someone had to say something before it was too late. Then again, surely the girl must already know, after all, she had worked for Devlin and his wife. 'You do realise that James is already married, don't you?' Cass said, as gently as she could.

'Exactly,' said Margaret Devlin from the shadows. 'Thank you. You took the words right out of my mouth.'

Cass swung round. The last person she had been expecting to see was Margaret Devlin, large as life – well, all five foot of her, fully wound up and ready to kill.

'Where is he?' she growled, fists clenched. 'The bastard.'

'James, how nice to see you,' said a big male voice with a soft Scots brogue.

Cass looked to see where the other voice was coming from, and as she did glimpsed the look of terror on James Devlin's face. She had no idea who the newcomer was, but it certainly didn't look like James was particularly pleased to see him.

Devlin glared at Antashinia, his eyes ablaze. 'Sweet Jesus,' he said thickly. 'Is there anyone you haven't brought with you?'

The girl looked bemused. 'I don't understand, James. What is the matter? Who is this man?'

'They'll kill me,' James muttered miserably. 'Your father, Gordie – take your pick.'

Margaret Devlin smiled wolfishly. 'Oh, you don't want to worry about either of them, James,' she said in a voice that could cut through sheet steel. 'Compared to what I've got in mind, a trip with either of these two would be a walk in the park.'

Devlin's face paled so rapidly that Cass thought for a moment he might faint.

'So,' said Gordie, tugging at his cuffs. 'Let's have a wee talk about my investment, shall we, James. Where is my money?' He paused for an instant. 'Well, what have you got to say for yourself?'

As he spoke, two well-built men in army sweaters and camo gear joined Gordie from the shadows. Seconds later, from the back of the Transit van, two strapping great lads jumped down. They had to be Antashinia's brothers; those faces were surely carved from the same block of concrete as their old man's.

Cass looked from face to face as she felt the tension rack up a notch or two. It was obvious even without subtitles that Ivan, his features a mask, shoulders set square, had no intention of letting Gordie – or, come to that, Margaret – run off with Antashinia's prospective bridegroom.

Just as it seemed that all hell was going to break loose, from the corner of her eye Cass saw an interior light flash on, and in that split second a voice from the far side of the road said, 'Well, well, well, fancy seeing you here, Mr Devlin. How the devil are you, man?'

James Devlin's expression changed. It looked for all the world as if he had just spotted Santa Claus.

415

There was a flurry of activity in the shadows and Cass suddenly realised that they were surrounded by police officers.

'Gordie, would you and your helpers mind staying exactly where you are,' said DI Turner. 'And keep your hands where we can see them. You too, Ivan,' he continued calmly. There was a ripple of resistance and resentment from Antashinia's brothers, but Ivan said something and the boys' machismo deflated like a punctured lilo.

DI Turner, dapper in his sports jacket and neatly trimmed moustache, walked into the jaundiced spotlight of the streetlight and smiled. 'Relax, boys. It's all over. We've got more law round here than there are stray cats, so don't anybody try anything. Nice and easy does it.'

James Devlin held up his hands in surrender. Cass thought he looked relieved.

'Whoever thought we would turn out to be the cavalry, eh, James?' said DI Turner as another officer patted Devlin down. 'You should see your face. Rock and a hard place, eh? Mixing with nasty rough boys both sides of the Channel, James? Let's be honest, you're really not in their league, son. I think we ought to go for a ride down to the station, don't you?' he said, indicating the way to the police cars.

Cass spotted Joe sitting in one of the cars parked across the road and, breaking away from the rest of the troupe, she ran towards him, although Joe was out of the car long before she was even halfway across the road.

DI Turner turned and watched her as uniformed men and detectives rounded up Gordie, Ivan and their cohorts.

Cass looked up into Joe's eyes, relief washing over her. 'Oh my God, I was so worried,' she whispered, hardly daring to touch him.

Turner followed along behind her, looking pleased with himself. 'Why don't you pair bugger off home. We can interview you tomorrow. We're going to be busy with this lot for an hour or two.'

'I'm sure that that was the guy at the farm,' Joe said, glancing towards Gordie. 'He had a Scottish accent. Very soft voice, like a snake.'

DI Turner snorted. 'That's our friend Gordie, all right.'

From somewhere close by came the sounds of frantic animated barking. Cass looked up; at the second-floor window Snoops was yapping like a maniac, pawing at the glass, desperate to be let out.

DI Turner smiled at Margaret. 'Would you like me to send an officer upstairs to get the dog for you?'

Margaret stared at him. Cass waited. And waited. And then Margaret said in a tiny voice. 'Oh, Henry, it's been terrible. Thank God you're here. I've been so frightened.' And promptly burst into tears.

Cass looked at DI Turner, wondering if he would be so gullible.

'It's all right,' he said, in the kind of voice normally reserved for the very scared and the very young. 'I'm here now.'

Apparently he was.

As he put his arm around her, Margaret looked over his shoulder at Cass and smiled, cat-like. 'I don't think I can bear to have Snoops back, not after all this. Every time I look at him, I only see James,' she said, looking all damp-eyed and tragic in the direction of her husband, who was being handcuffed and guided into a police car.

Cass couldn't believe what she was hearing. Joe caught hold of her arm. 'Let's get out of here,' he said. 'Before they change their minds and want us back.'

Cass grinned. 'Or someone asks us for a lift.'

He pulled her close and kissed her hard. 'Have you any idea how much I have wanted to do that?' he said. As her body melted into his, she nodded. 'Oh yes,' she purred. 'Almost as much as I have.'

12

Barney eased the cork out of another bottle of champagne and topped up Cass's glass. The shop was packed with people who had been invited to the private view of her Brighton exhibition. Several of the frames already bore a red spot to announce they had been sold.

'Good turn-out,' said Barney, lifting one of the canapés from a tray being touted round by a very obviously pregnant Antashinia. 'It's been a fucking nightmare to organise. I wish you'd just give in, move down here and take the PA job on permanently. It would save me so much bloody aggravation. Caterers, invitations, the press – it made me feel positively ill.'

Cass laughed. 'Barney, you know I'm working with Joe now. We think we've got the green light to do up the palazzo in Rome. It's the most amazing building . . .' She paused. 'And besides, you don't need me now, you've got Antashinia.'

'Have you any idea what a bully that bloody

girl is?' said Barney. 'Christ, since her English has improved there's no living with her. "Do this, do that. Do it now." It's like living with a regimental sergeant major.'

Cass took a sip of champagne. 'I'm glad they didn't charge her.'

Barney sniffed. 'Poor cow, it's obvious she was under duress. I don't think she'd got a clue what she had landed herself in.'

'And you spoke up for her?'

He reddened. 'Come on, I'm not going to let someone who can make lemon meringue pie slip through my fingers without a fight. And her father is a fantastic builder –'

Cass stared at him. 'Really?'

Barney nodded. 'I know – amazing, isn't it? He and the boys had come over here to work on building a complex of new luxury apartments.'

'I thought they were heavy-duty thugs?'

'So did the police, but apparently not. Kosher time-served builders, with certificates to prove it. Made a lovely job of tiling my bathroom, and Ivan is going to convert part of the basement into a proper self-contained annex for Antashinia and the baby.'

Jake came across looking pleased as punch. 'Selling like hotcakes.'

Cass lifted her glass and tapped hers to his.

'Where's his nibs?' said Jake, scanning the crowd.

'Don't know. Last time I saw him he was trying to find somewhere to park.'

An instant later Danny burst through the crowd carrying a plate of party food, pushing aside the invited guests. He was followed more slowly by Joe, who was carrying a bunch of pink roses.

She smiled as their gaze met, still feeling that odd flippity, nippity thing in the bottom of her stomach. 'What, no fruit?' she said, as he gave her the flowers and kissed her.

'I would hate to disappoint you,' said Joe, and handed her a small box tied up with a pink ribbon. 'Happy private view.'

Cass opened the box. Inside was a charm bracelet, with a tiny silver slipper and miniature silver pumpkin. She laughed. 'It's beautiful.'

'I thought you ought to have something to remember your Cinderella moment,' he said, eyes alight as he fastened it on to her wrist. 'I was going to put a banana on there as well, but it didn't quite fit the theme.'

'Maybe next time.'

'I just wanted to say that I love you,' he said. 'I thought maybe we could spend the rest of our lives collecting charms – a house, a baby . . . What do you think?'

Before Cass could reply, Barney stepped between them. 'I was going to ask: are you pair shacked up together yet?' he said, taking a bite out of a seafood vol au vent.

'No,' said Joe, taking his arm. 'She's still living in her cottage and I'm stuck over in Wells. But

I'm working on it. I was hoping while I was here you might give me a few tips and pointers.'

'Well, personally, I've always found drink helps,' said Barney. 'That and looking a little hangdog and vulnerable.'

Joe looked over his shoulder at Cass, grinning from ear to ear.

Jake glanced down at the bracelet, as Joe and Barney vanished off together into the crowd. 'Romantic bastard. You know, you really have got the most bloody awful taste in men,' he said.

Cass lifted her glass and grinned. 'I'll drink to that.'

Hot Pursuit

Gemma Fox

The heat is on . . . but can Maggie stand the pace?

Maggie Morgan has been longing to find Mr Right all her life but even she didn't expect him to be delivered to her door, giftwrapped in a skimpy towel, one sunny summer morning.

Sexy Nick Lucas seems almost too good to be true – and maybe he is. Arriving out of nowhere, he seems to have no history: things just didn't add up. But then again he's not the first man Maggie's been out with to have led a double life.

As Nick's past starts to catch up with him, Maggie becomes embroiled in an exciting cat-and-mouse chase across the country. Temperatures rise and passion sizzles but although Maggie has the hots for Nick, can she take the heat?

ISBN 0 00 718302 X